LOST TRIBE

CORSAC FOX

BOOK 5

BLAZE WARD

KNOTTED ROAD PRESS

Lost Tribe
Corsac Fox, Book 5
Blaze Ward
Copyright © 2025 Blaze Ward
All rights reserved
Published by Knotted Road Press
www.KnottedRoadPress.com

ISBN:
Paper: 978-1-64470-433-2
Hardback: 978-1-64470-440-0

Cover art:
Jay O'Connell https://www.jayoconnell.com/
Illustration 108050035 © Raffaele1 | Dreamstime.com
Illustration 22850687 © Seamartini | Dreamstime.com

Cover and interior design copyright © 2025 Knotted Road Press

Reviews
It's true. Reviews help. Even a short one, such as, "Loved it!" So please consider reviewing this book (and all of the ones you've read) on your favorite retailer site.

Never miss a release!
If you'd like to be notified of new releases, sign up for my newsletter.

http://www.blazeward.com/newsletter/

Buy More!
Did you know that you can buy directly from the Knotted Road Press website?

https://www.knottedroadpress.com/shop/

ALSO BY BLAZE WARD

The Science Officer Series

Start with: The Science Officer

The Jessica Keller Chronicles

Start with: Auberon

CS-405 (Command Centurion Kosnett, part of Jessica)

Start with: Queen Anne's Revenge

First Centurion Kosnett (sequel to Jessica)

Start with: Encounter at Vilahana

Additional Alexandria Station Stories

Alexandria Station Collection

Handsome Rob (Alexandria Station Universe)

Start with: Can't Shoot Straight Gang

=====================

Corsac Fox

Start with: Flight of the Corsac Fox

Operation Marrakesh

Start with: Trial by Leviathan

Captain Daring

Start with: Revoked

The Hunter Bureau

Start with: Mirrors

Fairchild

Start with: Fairchild

Last Stand

Start with: Lost Dreams

The Lazarus Alliance

Start with: Escape

Shadow of the Dominion

Start with: Longshot Hypothesis

Star Dragon

Start with: Birth of the Star Dragon

Kincaide's War

Start with: The Eden Package

Star Tribes

Start with: Winterstar

Blaze also writes Action-Adventure Here

CONTENTS

For Esko

PART ONE
NUBIA

ONE

"All hands to action stations," the call came over the speaker.

Vanguard Ulysses Fortier—Uly—was at his station, listening to his own words come out of the speakers and contemplating all of the *everything* that was about to unspool in front of him.

He glanced over at Dan, seated between Suka Kuri and Nasrin Monfared to one side. As usual. Smiled at her, because she brightened any day.

Focused back into what was about to happen. Opposite Dan and the Combat Team, Aibek Sulaymanov watched. It was his first visit back to Bastion since he'd nearly gotten himself killed attempting a reasonably polite pirate raid on the place. Uly could see a hint of nerves around his eyes and under his silver-gray skin, but he was handling himself well. Helped that his family was along, currently aft in their quarters.

Bastion might be a safe moorage, but Uly wasn't about to cut corners. He'd gotten sloppy when dealing with Isann and made his new friends pay a terrible price. He would do this by the books.

"Drew, what's our status?" Uly asked, after folks got that last reminder.

They should have already been on station and ready, but sometimes things came up at the last moment, and folks aft had just run out of time.

"Thirty seconds to drop, Uly," Drew replied over his shoulder.

Nubia was arranged far differently than any other ship Uly had ever sailed on. Four workstations side by side in front of him, everyone facing forward to screens and that enormous overhead transsteel window that let them see open space.

Because the Yarikh who had built the ship had been sailors first, explorers second, and warriors only third. However, *Nubia* was still a dangerous warship. He hoped to find one of their longsailor craft someday, just to see what other art those folks had committed in steel with it.

Next to Drew, Del—Lt. Delbert Blakeslee—handled Sensors. Then the Khet, Yaqub Zobo on Guns, though it wasn't really his forte and Uly knew he needed to train or recruit a full-time Gunner at some point. Lastly, Haydar Ramezani handled Communications. And Data. And First Officer duties if pressed into a corner and forced to admit it against his will.

Haydar had finally told Uly how many years he had spent as a pirate in his wilder youth. And possibly a few of the less crazy things he'd done, if they were to be believed. Except that, knowing Haydar, he'd toned his stories down and taken out the bits nobody would actually believe.

The Variable Pulse Spatial Generator shut down and they fell out of that other space marked by swirls of blues and pinks that described FTL travel. With Uly's overhead view, he'd probably watched it more in the last few weeks than all of his time sailing prior, but that served to accentuate how different his future would be.

Then his boards began to fill with data. The planet Bastion in the distance, with the *Watchtower* in orbit. A variety of ships close by, as well as at various distances.

"I have *Batyr* in close orbit of the station," Haydar announced. "And Sterling on Channel Three. You need to hear this, Uly."

Uly located the button and activated it.

"...threats to the station and the moorage," Sterling was saying. "Repeat: Hostile squadron has landed nearby and have been issuing threats to the station and the moorage."

"Sterling, it's Uly," he said simply. "I'm here."

Slight lag while that got transmitted. On his screen, Uly watched Haydar do his data magic so three vessels were outlined in red, off to one side where all the other cargo vessels were giving them a wide berth.

And, on closer examination, friendly vessels were inside the area where the station's guns could protect them, and the three newcomers were outside it. Not by much, so they understood the range of a 12dm wavebolt, but enough.

Then the scans took on sharper resonance. Sterling, no doubt, having aimed every sensor he had at them.

"Haydar, am I reading this correctly?" Uly asked. "One Heavy Interceptor maybe comparable to *Batyr*, and a pair of lighter ones? Wolfpack triad, basically?"

"That's my read, Uly," Haydar nodded with half of his tentacles. "A threat to shipping, but only because they can stand off Sterling, as long as they stay outside of the station's range."

"Drew, light the navigation displacers," Uly ordered. "Take us in closer. Haydar, hail them. Yaqub, stand by with your teams. They might wish to start trouble today."

Nods. He'd pulled a chunk of crew off *Batyr* to help fly *Nubia*, then recruited a number of sailors at Isann to backfill gaps on both vessels and start training more to expand his fleet.

Again.

Uly had a moment of wry levity that his life seemed to involve stealing any variety of alien ships, each bigger than the last, then having to find crews for them. *King Hewitt II. Iron Wasp. Wren. Nubia.*

Then *Nubia* began to move.

TWO

Sterling was still getting used to permanently sitting in the big chair. Those Commander's stripes on his arms felt like they weighed a ton today, but honestly, this was the thing he'd dreamed of since he first saw a ship flying through space.

Mostly, he was just pissed that *Fire Diamond* had already sailed for home. He could have used Lukyan and a little extra firepower today.

At least until Uly had arrived.

He turned to his new First Officer.

"Lt. Kovalchuk," he ordered. "Let me know when *Nubia* starts after our party crashers."

Yuriy blinked for a moment, then nodded. Still getting used to how Uly thought. *Nubia* would be aggressive. Bastion was their home port and nobody got to threaten that. Not even these Samuur punks, though they had been mostly bluster up until now.

"Lt. Havrylyuk, confirm your weapon systems," Sterling continued.

"Everything green, Conductor," Vitali replied. "Standing by to engage."

"Excellent news," Sterling reminded him, thinking back to all the ways Uly would handle these situations and making sure he followed suit.

"Lt. Temitope, assume that we'll need to slide in on a forward escorting flank when *Nubia* confronts our friends," Sterling ordered his Pilot. "Plot your course and stand by to engage."

"Aye, sir," Bello said. "Already set. Four options calculated, depending how feisty Drew's feeling today."

All those hours watching training videos. Sterling had gone through them, then filtered and edited a few based on what Uly had wanted transmitted to new officers and crew. This was the start of what Suka Kuri was calling the Starfare School. And she expected him to teach Gunnery as an expert.

Twenty felt like fifty, but he had a lot of ex-pirates sailing with him, and they knew how to fight. And when to.

Sterling still wasn't sure who the Samuur were. All communications had been text. And weird grammatically, like they didn't speak Spacer, but he was getting to be conversational in Yarikh now, after learning Isann to talk to some of his new people.

How many descendant tongues existed in this region? The space Uly called the Spinward Reaches and the *Auga* marked on all their maps as Imperial Sector Fourteen.

Several dialects, it seemed.

"I have movement from *Nubia*," Yuriy spoke up. "Bello, on your two screen."

"Got it," Bello replied. "Engines coming up. Vitali, we'll be a little low so all your systems will range and cover."

Sterling leaned back and nodded.

Well-trained crew. Excellent ship. Three intruders who had sat well outside of weapon range from the station, where they issued demands that he'd ignored.

Apparently, they'd been expecting to find another corner bodega and a bunch of civilians here. Bastion, *Watchtower*, and *Batyr* had kept them honest.

And now Uly was home.

THREE

Uly watched the three enemy vessels shift around to face *Nubia* instead of Sterling and the station. Bow-on, they looked almost flatly triangular. Or maybe arrowheads.

Three of them. A squadron leader and two escorts. Dangerous. Still a bit primitive from the scan logs he was reading, but in line with what Uly had come to expect for this region of space, which had been entirely a backwater a year ago when he started construction of his new base, fortress, and homeworld.

And, apparently, he had new neighbors.

Hopefully, they'd talk instead of opening fire right now. If they chose to misbehave, they'd discover that his ship mounted 15dm weapons bigger than anything Uly had ever seen. Better range. Better thump.

And he was going to be within range to engage them before they understood that, at least the first time.

"Haydar, any response to hail?" he asked.

"Text only," Haydar said. "Bluster and bullshit for the most part. Claims that the Samuur own this system and demand tribute. Silly buggers certainly waited far too long to press that notion. Might have been a threat before the station was complete. Empty bravado now."

Uly nodded and opened a channel.

"*Batyr*. Huff."

"Obviously, we're going to go chat with our new friends, Sterling," Uly said. "Stand by."

"Already in motion and prepped, sir," Sterling replied. "They've been here two days and not done much, but I presume that they understand the range of 12s."

"Won't do them much good," Uly said. "You maintain the defensive sphere for now. I want to see how serious they are."

"We've got your flank, Vanguard."

Uly nodded and cut the line. Sterling would be there.

"Haydar, I need make a statement to our friends."

"Channel eleven, Uly," he replied.

Uly considered his words. His options.

"Attention Samuur squadron, this is the Corsac Fox," he began. "I have claimed this system. Ships coming to trade are welcome. Pirates will be hunted down and destroyed. Neighbors willing to be friendly can stay. You will choose how I deal with you and your people going forward right now. How will this resolve?"

He played it back, nodded, and transmitted it.

All three vessels had their bows pointed at him right now. Shortly, they would be inside the range of *Nubia*'s Spatial Generators, and would be stuck here until they backed away.

"Enemy flagship just fired," Haydar barked sharply. "One 5dm bolt. Looks like a single forward mount."

"One bolt only?" Uly asked, a bit confused.

That was like waving a red flag in front of a bull. From the scans, those three vessels were all reasonably heavily armed. A 5 up front and twin 3s aft for the big ship. A single 3 fore and aft for the other two.

And they had fired one bolt?

"Sterling, stand down," Uly called on the squadron line, coming to a certain conclusion.

"Sir?" Sterling asked.

"That 5dm will only barely be a threat when it arrives, Sterling," Uly said. "We'll handle it here. Yaqub, defensive fire only."

A pair of 2dm bolts launched with a dull thump and raced down to intercept the incoming bolt, impacting and rupturing it into a harmless ball of plasma.

"Del, anything else from the squadron?" Uly confirmed.

"Negative, sir," Del replied. "One bolt. They could have at least made it interesting."

Uly nodded.

Then smiled. Haydar's tentacles were the only thing pointed his direction to see it. Except Dan. She matched his smile.

"Yaqub, one 15dm in response," Uly ordered. "Target *Virta*, that squadron lead. Do not do anything else except defensive fire as needed, am I clear?"

"Affirmative, Uly," Yaqub said. "One bolt. Hold the line."

Whatever measuring system the Yarikh had used, it translated into modern as a 14.7dm weapon, so everyone just called them 15s. A frightening number in any context.

One raced down onto *Virta* now. The squadron leader fired a pair of 3s from the rear turret, then needed his neutron omnipulsars and finally his 5 again to keep it from slamming into his shields with anything more than a pretty light show.

Still a flash of light visible to the naked eye for a moment when he looked up.

Uly waited.

"We're being hailed again," Haydar said. "Full A/V this time."

"Main screen," Uly said. "Let's see what they have to say."

Cat. Lynx maybe, with big, fluffy ears and a thick, light tan beard like he's also seen on a miniature schnauzer one time. Big green eyes with vertical slits. Felt like a short snout.

The ears were rotated forward, but one moved sideways as if listening, then back. Almost like Mazhin tentacles that way, so Uly figured he'd learn how to read that language at some point, too.

"Greetings, Corsac Fox," the man(?) said brightly, as though greeting an old friend. "I am Commander Kalev Karjalainen. We have come to challenge your rights to this system, and honor has been satisfied."

Uly glanced over at Aibek and got a slight shrug, so the Isann were unfamiliar with the species. Not that Uly was surprised, as the Isann had only recently really explored more than a few nearby solar systems from their home.

And the Spinward Reaches were huge. At least when seen on a map. Nobody knew how many of the stars he could map were actually occupied.

And the Samuur, it appeared, were militant, though not entirely aggressive.

Honor? Satisfied?

Had they been waiting for Sterling to walk out and challenge them? Certainly, they had thrown one punch and waited for Uly to respond. And now they were all friends?

Weird, but he'd also come to understand capitalism, as stupid as that system was. There were obviously more and better ways to structure your civilization.

"Greetings, Commander Karjalainen," Uly replied. "As your honor has been satisfied, would you care to come aboard my vessel and talk in deeper details about what it means that we have met thus?"

Uly waited. Watched ears twitch and whiskers flicker. He'd missed those, earlier. Camera pickup was focused just wrong. Or not that sharp in resolution.

Then the screen froze, so he was probably having a quick argument with his senior officers or squadron commanders about what to do next.

Uly did the same, turning to Dan.

"I'm guessing that honor might demand it," he said. "The behavior fits, if I understand the phrasing and body language correctly. We'll invite all three conductors and host them for a dinner, if they'll come. Or just a diplomatic argument across the table before they head home."

"I'll be ready," she said simply.

Uly smiled. She would be. He could hand it to her and mark it off his list, because she could handle it.

How had he ever gotten so lucky?

The screen came live again, so Uly flipped the same switch here.

"Corsac Fox, we will come," Karjalainen said simply.

"Excellent," Uly pointed. "This is Commander Dan Chastain, my Chief of Staff. She will work with your people to sort out all the details. I look forward to meeting you in the flesh."

Dan flipped a switch on her console and the main screen went dark as she started talking locally with the Samuur.

Uly turned to Haydar.

"You know the species?" he asked.

"I wouldn't have known how to spell it, save that they sent text first, Uly," Haydar shrugged with most of his upper body.

"You take charge here, then," he said. "I need to learn more."

FOUR

Suka Kuri had been sitting next to Dan on the bridge, but Uly had silently asked her to accompany him, so she had followed, kneeling on a pad she kept in his office because none of the chairs ever felt right for her greater size and she hadn't felt like commissioning something she could carry with her everywhere.

Yet.

"Your thoughts on the Samuur?" Uly asked her as they settled.

"Not a species I know, Uly," she replied. "I will need to meditate for a bit and see if they jar any memories. I will remind you, however, that I was born almost as many light-years away from here as you. Just in a different direction is all."

He smiled. It was a calm, relaxed smile.

"Yes, but you've had a much more sophisticated, urbane life than I have," he said, causing her to laugh.

"Why did they act as they did, just now?" she pressed.

"Sterling said that they had been here for two days, threatening but not actually attacking," Uly said. "Waiting, it seemed. Possibly for me. Possibly for Sterling to sail into range, though I'm not sure that they wouldn't have all fallen on him at once in that case. Better that we were coming and could handle it. One shot from them suggested single combat, Suka Kuri. Trial by champion, as it were, like some of the more primitive civilizations might do it. We replied with one shot. And that seemed to be the formula they needed."

She shook her head and smiled.

"What?" he asked.

"I pause and wonder how many conductors I've ever encountered that might have handled this situation thus, Uly," she answered. "Most would have been like Sterling, sitting back in safety. Others would have immediately attacked to annihilate the Samuur squadron. And I am aware of how dangerous this ship is. Would those three have stood any chance against you?"

"Not really," he shrugged, further cementing his legend in her mind. "That they fired first, and fired exactly once, knowing that they had to have scanned us, meant that it had become something formal. At least that was my best guess. Seems to have worked."

"That, it has," she nodded. "Another new species to add to your trade network?"

"Something," he said. "Won't really know until we have a chance to talk to them. Can you identify their language, at least?"

"I'd say at first blush that it was another derivative of Yarikh, from the accent," Suka Kuri nodded. "Like Isann, but gone a different direction. Written, I suspect that there might be a great deal of overlap, like some of your older Human tongues."

"Dan's going to impress them with the Combat Team," he said, changing directions. "The Congress itself. I'd like you to be the scholar and diplomat, like you did with Aibek and his people. If the Samuur are aggressive and dangerous, we might need to delay our trip to the Ononguli Sphere to handle it. I won't know for a bit, either."

"And the weddings?" Suka Kuri pressed. "Or wedding, I suppose, since Chief of Chiefs Kadyr seems intent on handling it as a singular thing?”

“Part of me is concerned that it might look to an outsider like I am accumulating a harem of beautiful women, like some grand potentate from primitive history, where they usually did so as a show of power and ostentatious wealth,” he replied.

Suka Kuri, noting the hard lines that appeared around his eyes and mouth as he contemplated such a thing.

“Dan is probably correct to assign most of the guilt for all this to me,” she offered. “I originally instructed her to collect at least one female member of every species she encountered for her Combat Team. However, even looking back, it was not clear to either of us then that this might be the logical next step.”

“And it is logical, when she brought it up and told me that I was going to do this,” he nodded, relaxing some. “I’d have never even considered it otherwise, but it creates a thing. The Congress of Wives. Each of them can *Speak* for their species at the highest level of the government I’m trying to create at Bastion. And it means that this form of government that succeeds me, whenever I need to step down, and hopefully cannot fall into a model like the Auga. Or the Khet. Or the Ononguli.”

“Because every species will be represented,” Suka Kuri nodded back, seeing the shape of the thing. “And all are equals as Wives of the supreme ruler, as well as being as his closest advisors.”

“At least until a woman takes that position,” he smiled. “But even then, it’s likely always going to be as much political as anything. Let those sexist societies who base all of their laws on gender and biology have to come to grips with love that is not limited to one shape or type of pairing.”

Suka Kuri wondered how many Khet or Ononguli might grasp that without her rubbing their noses in it. Possibly a great many, because non-heterosexual expression appeared to be something around ten or maybe fifteen percent in both cases. Useful for genetics for long-term species survival, but not an iron-clad rule.

"And your successor will marry them all?" she asked, mostly to clarify things.

Every decision Uly and Dan made today would need to be communicated to Moss School at the very minimum. Probably Sabre as well. And everyone else.

Her task, as always, would be to educate the galaxy. Fortunately, she had a lifetime of experience at it already.

"It stabilizes things," he replied, turning stern. "These are, at the end of the day, political marriages. They cannot produce children, with one exception. I expect that some of the women will seek alternate means to have children later. All of those children will be welcome. All will be mine, regardless."

Suka Kuri didn't bother pointing out how rare that attitude might be among most species and civilizations. Uly was special, and everyone who encountered him quickly came to understand that.

"Do you not expect to be intimate with all of them?" she asked.

The women had all spoken on the topic among themselves. And asked her. There had been certain assumptions, but even Dan hadn't known with certainty how Uly would act with any of the others. Several were extremely young, for all they were adults. Others were well outside their comfort zone.

"They will tell me," he said bluntly. "I will accommodate them. As long as everyone understands what we're trying to accomplish here."

She doubted that Uly understood the effects of his charisma on those women. She could speak to that, even if he was far too young for her.

Were she seventy years younger, though...

"But you do not have any doubts about the wedding plans?" she confirmed.

He shrugged, as a groom probably should, though she'd never

bothered getting serious or formal with anyone in her time. Too busy learning and traveling. And having fun. It had gotten her here, and that said everything she needed.

"Dan's handling that, as well," he said. "Says that doing it this way will establish a layer of precedence that will be important later, though I haven't pressed."

"Oh," she offered. "You might need to."

"Oh?"

"You will marry Dan first," Suka Kuri explained carefully. "Then Nasrin, in order that you met each woman as you progress through the Combat Team. Anari and Sterling appear to be moving towards a much closer relationship, so you'll only have one Emro wife for now."

"For now?" he interrupted.

"Moss School," she smiled primly. "We might yet need a Sabre School wife for you at some point. I haven't decided yet."

His eyes got a little big, but he kept his lips pressed together and nodded.

"When the ceremony is complete, you will have gotten formally married to Dan, Nasrin, and Yanouk. Katya will possibly align you with Zehlennko as well, but they don't know yet so we're not assuming. Then Ciah, Yeong-Suk, and finally Zamira Ismailov, who joined us at Isann and is busy teaching everyone Karmap these days, while she learns our forms."

He nodded.

"What's interesting is where the Samuur might fit in there," she pondered aloud, smiling because Uly had gone all serious again. "But I'll sort that out as we get to know them better. It might be necessary to invite them to join us at Rayzian."

He muttered something, causing her to perk up sharply.

"What was that?" she pressed.

"Conversation with Dan while we were still at Isann," he said.

"Comparing you two, I still think she's the more dangerous, but I'm beginning to think it's closer."

Suka Kuri laughed. Not that she would deny it, but Uly was allowed to see through her guise as a fussy old woman scholar.

After all, she could have gone Sabre in her time. Moss was just so much easier on the knees.

"Let us prepare for new guests," she said, rising. "And new friends."

FIVE

Dan had talked extensively with Commander Karjalainen, as well as Commanders Nyman and Lehtinen from the other two ships, the former being female. That cheered Dan. Gave her confidence that these Samuur might not be a problem.

She still had armed everyone and was ready for trouble. Her group included Zamira, who had joined them a month ago and was already fitting in. She knew what was coming and had accepted her part in the politics of the thing, but Dan suspected that Ainura and especially Elder Gulnaz Isakov had taken the young woman aside and explained things.

Helped that Zamira was extremely mature for her age. And intensely focused on learning martial combat forms from all nations and species. And she wasn't an innocent in personal things, like some of the others were. Had, in fact, questioned her sharply in private about Uly and both of their thoughts on a harem for the man.

Anybody but Uly, and it might turn into such a thing.

But this was Dan's project. Her Congress. Idly, she had wondered if the Congress might eventually include a husband at some point, a species that worked their biology or culture so radically different.

When that moment arrived, she would figure out how it needed to work. And tell Uly what he was going to do. He trusted her, implicitly and explicitly, knowing that she had his best interests in mind, even if he didn't understand what she was up to some of the time.

For now, the Combat Team was turning slowly into the Congress. Stepping up. Ascending to that higher place that it needed to be, in order to become one of the anchors upon which Uly's government at Bastion would be founded.

If she could pull it off.

Today, the first real test would be the Samuur.

Dan had the hatch as their shuttle docked. Listened as things thunked and beeped. Waited for it to open. Scanners had shown a pilot and three passengers, as everyone had agreed to, but Dan still wanted to impress upon them that she could make them behave if she had to.

They understood honor, but hadn't really explored the edges of what that meant. She wanted to make sure that there wouldn't be violence, by appearing ready to deal with it.

Commander Karjalainen was there first in the airlock hatch.

She'd seen their uniforms on the screen, but it hadn't conveyed the vivacity of the colors. Bright orange. Top buttoned up the front. Pants fairly baggy, which she presumed was to keep from rubbing a bald spot in the fur. The indigo trim on the orange heightened the effect, conveying a wild energy as well as a feeling of wealth and power.

At least, assuming Samuur saw colors the same way. Never a safe assumption with true aliens, but it did make them impressive.

"Commander Chastain," Karjalainen nodded as he came to rest. "My squadron mates, Commander Ursula Nyman and Commander Matti Lehtinen."

"My Ground Combat Team," Dan replied, introducing everyone, including Suka Kuri who had insisted on being here.

Three Emro women made an especially large impact, over and above the number of species present.

"All female?" Commander Nyman inquired carefully.

"Indeed," Dan confirmed. "Each species that have become the Corsac Fox's allies have contributed a member. We are also among Uly's closest advisors."

"And you are his Chief of Staff," Nyman noted. "Interesting."

Then they both turned back to Karjalainen.

He looked up at Anari. Way up. Samuur were about Human size, but broader in the body. Muscles under that fine, tan fur.

"I imagine that you could tie me in square knots if I got in too close," he nodded, then turned to Ciah, still the shortest person in the room. "And possibly you, as well, yes."

Ciah had her game face scowl on. Karjalainen grinned, which was interesting to see on a catlike face. He turned back to Dan.

"Indeed impressive, Commander," he said. "I look forward to meeting such a man as the Corsac Fox, who has gathered such a formidable force together. Shall we?"

Dan shrugged, but only on the inside. Weird cultural resonances she picked up from all three of them.

Proud warriors, but friendly about it. Almost like professional athletes competing regularly against one another, rather than the Ononguli pirates who were always at pains to tell you how tough they were. No threat. Just an assessment, like folks in a dojo preparing to spar friendly.

Interesting.

"This way," she nodded, turning and leading the others.

Her ladies would fall in, but Suka Kuri joined her at the front and walked at a sedate pace that the Samuur matched easily.

She looked forward to their reaction to Uly. He wasn't all that impressive physically. Tall and skinny. Weighed about the same as she did. Not all that handsome, either.

Until he turned the charm on. The Mazhin who had been around long enough believed that he was Mazhin in a Human body and had adopted him as such.

What would the Samuur do?

SIX

Uly had taken a spot a little off center of the long table, then sat Dan next to him and scattered the others around. The Samuur had blanched a little at the informality of the thing, but it had felt right, after talking to Dan.

Commander Karjalainen ended up not quite across from him. The female commander was down on his right. The male was closer to his boss.

Suka Kuri made tea.

It was not a process. It was an Event, handled by a Living Legend. Everyone fell to silence and watched her move, as delicate and precise as wielding a sword.

Rather than play complicated games, she merely served the table counter-clockwise, honoring Ciah who happened to be first on her right.

They sipped, after the Samuur trio sniffed carefully and watched the others go first. Community pot was a fantastic way to protect against being poisoned, assuming that the ingredients were safe to all the species present.

Uly smiled at his guests. Watched them relax. Read the flickers of ears and whiskers as they spoke silently amongst themselves. Not as good as Mazhin, and Nasrin was probably reading them closer, but he could see the nervous edges melting off.

As intended.

"I am Ulysses Fortier," he told them after a bit. "Vanguard by rank and commander of this vessel. I am also the Corsac Fox and intend to build up a trade nation in this corner of space. On your right is Aibek Sulaymanov. He is Isann, and potentially a neighbor, depending on the coordinates of your homeworld. Others of us come from much farther away, but I welcome all who wish to trade and live amiably and honorably."

Uly smiled at each of the three in turn as they digested that. Loaded language. Intentionally.

Spikes driven into minds to possibly break them down into a new kind of thinking. He was getting pretty good at that.

"We are Samuur, Corsac Fox," Karjalainen replied. "These systems have long been empty, but traders brought us news of new neighbors come to claim them. We sought to test their—your—mettle to hold them."

"Had you come a few months earlier, you might have gotten to meet other neighbors," Uly said. "The Ononguli Sphere is a major power a bit distant and their *Vatazhko* had come to consult with me as we plan a greater war against the *Auga*."

"*Auga*?" Karjalainen asked.

"Suka Kuri, could you explain the *Auga Empire* to our new friends?" Uly asked her. "You would do it the best justice."

"Actually, I think Yanouk would do an excellent job," Suka Kuri smiled. "She has taken to studying them in greater detail recently."

Uly turned to the young woman and caught her faint blush. Moss School, for all she had learned combat. The woman was still a scholar, dating back to before he had ever met her.

He nodded, then settled back as she began a history lesson in the style of a mesmerist casting a spell on the entire table.

She certainly had everyone in the palm of her hand when she was done.

"And from there, Uly withdrew his forces, negotiated a treaty with the Ononguli, and began building the *Watchtower* at Bastion to form the nucleus of this new nation," she concluded. "We have met the Isann previously, and now the Samuur."

Time seemed to start up again with a jolt. Everyone had finished their tea, so more got poured as an excuse to recover.

She really was amazing. Uly thought back to the quiet woman he'd met all those years ago, another prisoner of Adrian Sobol's piracy. She had blossomed almost as much as Nasrin the Wildrose.

Karjalainen locked eyes with Uly as he sipped his tea.

"And you're going to stop them?" he asked calmly.

"Yes," Uly replied. "The *Auga* are bullies. I don't like bullies. I find their behavior dishonorable, because they have all that strength, and use it to oppress the weak instead of protecting them. One might even consider them evil. At least as a culture. I'm certain individual *Auga* might turn out to be somewhat mundane."

Again, the glances back and forth between the three. Subtle, but he'd lived for years among Mazhin. *Spoke* for them, even. Uly was used to entire conversations conducted around him by smell.

"And the Ononguli are your allies in this thing?" he asked, pointing to Katya, then Ciah. "And the Khet?"

"And the Isann," Zamira interjected from down the table.

She didn't speak that often, possibly feeling young around this group, but not that much younger. About in the middle of Dan's team, comparable to overall expected lifespan.

And he'd seen her move on the dojo floor.

"How soon will the *Auga* arrive at your doorstep?" Ursula Nyman asked from her spot on the end.

She was similar in size and coloration to Karjalainen. Maybe a bit bigger physically. Perhaps that one's height. And outweighed him.

Obviously smart.

"Assuming the normal pattern of expansion they have expressed over the last five centuries, they should reach this area of what they call Imperial Sector Fourteen in roughly four hundred years," Uly told her, watching her eyes blank for a moment.

"Then they are not a threat to you," she countered.

"They are a threat to everyone," Suka Kuri overrode her. "Are you familiar with the fable of the ant and the grasshopper?"

It took Nyman a moment.

"The one builds?" Nyman replied. "The other panics?"

Suka Kuri nodded.

"Uly builds," she intoned serenely. "Will the Samuur panic?"

Had Uly set off a sudden round of literal fireworks in the middle of the table—bangs, flashes, and smoke—he probably wouldn't have gotten as big a reaction from the three newcomers.

It honestly wasn't fair for anyone to attempt to compete with that woman, but Uly suspected that his new friends really didn't appreciate what an *Exemplar of the Arts* truly implied.

Yet.

For all the silence, it took them several seconds to recover. Uly waited patiently.

These were not Ononguli, full of piss and vinegar. Nor were they the Khet of Z'Gosza, calculating every way they might earn an extra basis point of profit on any action or nonaction they took. Not even the Isann, living in the shadows of the *Karaŋgılıkka*'s demands that they *Sail into Darkness* to see what was on the other side.

Who were the Samuur?

"We were sent to investigate strangers," Karjalainen finally said. "You are beyond the realm the Paramount claims, but represented a potential threat. What will you build, Corsac Fox?"

"A realm that will outlive me," Uly replied. "One that can keep the *Auga* at bay, if I am unable to stop them in my lifetime. One that will guarantee the freedom and equality to anyone who wishes to abide by one set of laws for all. The *Auga* rule, with all other species entirely subordinate. I am Human, as is Dan, but there are few of us at present, so I find it necessary to recruit others. Khet. Ononguli. Mazhin. Emro. Thogin. Isann. Anyone willing to fight injustice."

"I cannot speak for the Paramount," Karjalainen finally said. "Will you come to Saari, that he might learn these things?"

Uly considered his options. And the behavior of the Samuur.

"Is Bastion safe while I am elsewhere?" he countered.

Karjalainen looked at him blankly for a moment. Nyman rescued her squadron commander.

"Honor has been served, Corsac Fox," she said. "Bastion will be safe from the Samuur."

Karjalainen nodded, as did Lehtinen.

"Then I will travel to Saari," Uly said. "And meet with your Paramount. Perhaps recruit the Samuur to the greater cause of protecting the galaxy from bullies."

That puffed them all up.

"Now," Uly said. "Let us have a meal together. Here, that is a sign of peaceful intent and friendship, and I hope to include the Samuur in such a thing from this day forth."

"From this day forth," Karjalainen nodded as they all rose.

The Spatula already had something good cooking nearby.

Uly always needed more allies.

PART TWO
FIRE DIAMOND

SEVEN

Maks had originally intended to travel home aboard *Treta Envoy*, the luxury liner that he was now a part owner of with Anna. The one that had housed all the construction crews while they had built the *Watchtower* for Uly, before Maks ended up as Acting Governor while Uly had gone off and done the impossible.

Yet again.

It was Uly. Betting against that man was a dumb way to lose all your money. Lukyan had said it first. Maks had learned quickly.

However, Anna had put her foot down and ordered him to transfer command of *Treta Envoy* to Eugen so that Maks could travel aboard *Fire Diamond* with her.

How the hell had he ended up a major advisor to the *Vatazhko*? The literal Lord of the Endless Plains herself?

Shit.

Worse, Chervonya had accompanied her aunt. And had looked at him askance a time or two too many for Maks's comfort.

Like today, as he'd been pleasantly minding his business in a corner of the wardroom with lunch. Well, lunch was done and he was comparing some local pastries to what Vahid would have made on *Nubia*. Not really a comparison. Serviceable. Bland.

Maks understood how truly spoiled he'd gotten.

Then Chervonya had walked in, spied him in the corner, and speared him with a look that had his ass nailed to the seat while she went through the line and brought a tray to sit directly across from him.

He didn't warn her about the rolls. Sipped some tea instead and calculated escape routes from the room, including the overhead duct if he got really desperate.

She ate. Daintily. Carefully, because lunch was meat and vegetables in a blue sauce today and really easy to end up wearing if you weren't sharp.

Beautiful woman. Dangerous smart. Politically as connected as they got, since the *Vatazhko* was her aunt and had relied on Chervonya to watch over Maks and the construction for the last year.

Maks stretched the sweetroll out as long as he could, wishing he could savor it instead of merely consuming it.

She got about done and speared him again.

"You haven't said a word," she noted.

"Your look did not invite conversation," he countered carefully.

Always carefully. This woman could break him off at the horns if she wanted. Or have Anna do it, which was the same thing.

And for all the light teasing over the last however long, he'd never gone beyond that, even when she might have been inviting it.

He'd have had to ask and didn't want to step into that bear trap, either.

"You're not the governor anymore, Maks," she noted.

"I am currently not anything, Chervonya," he replied. "Not Conductor of *Treta Envoy*. Not Ambassador to the Barbarians like you. Generally a nobody minding his business in the corner of the wardroom until someone important has something for me to do."

A bit rude. But also the truth. Anna's decision, and Maks

couldn't figure out if he'd pissed that woman off, or merely been brought along for when she got around to him.

"You're not a nobody, Maks," she said bluntly. "Anna relies on you for counsel."

He shrugged. The *Vatazhko* hadn't asked him anything in more than a week.

"What are you going to do when we get home?" she shifted when he remained silent.

Maks paused to consider what he might tell her, knowing that Anna would hear it shortly.

"I don't know," he offered honestly. "Not entirely a free agent here. Anna might order me to do any of a number of things. And she might not. Do you have any clues?"

"I can't imagine she ignores you," Chervonya replied.

He shrugged again.

She paused and studied him. Maks finished the damned roll and missed Vahid's cooking.

"What does Maks want?" she finally asked.

"To contribute," he replied, leaving it at that. "I presume that I will when she has a need. Until then, I'm hanging out."

More pause. More watching. More deep thoughts from a dangerously smart woman.

"Do you like me, Maks?" she asked.

And that, my dear friends, is what a bear trap looks like, when you stumble on one in the woods.

"Yes," he replied evenly, not going anywhere past that.

"You haven't given hardly any sign of it," she pressed.

"You are the niece of the *Vatazhko*, Chervonya," he explained. "And Ambassador to the Barbarians. I was the guy hired to build Uly's station. Then I was the one Uly made Acting Governor in his stead."

He left off the rest. She was bright enough to fill in the subtext.

Or not.

He had to remember that he was almost a decade older than the woman. That she really was only barely an adult, for all she was smart, beautiful, and connected.

He'd been out in the galaxy and seen some shit in his time.

"You're not any of that now, Maks," she reminded him.

He nodded. She was correct.

Had Anna set him up? Or both of them?

Oh, what the hell?

"And you've given no hints of any significant interest in me, Chervonya Borisov," he tossed it back into her lap, mostly to watch her sputter, catch herself, review all her files, and conclude that he was right.

The frightening part was how fast she got there. An eyeblink he almost missed.

Then she watched him again.

"You're right," she said. "We've both been boxed in by circumstances that prevented this conversation. I do like you, Maks. You are entirely different from any other male I've known."

"Blame Uly and Dan," he nodded.

She nodded back.

"You and Lukyan are almost Human that way," she continued.

"That good or bad?" he asked.

"Good, I think," she said. "Different in good ways. Calm. Logical. Professional. Interesting. All the things that most Ononguli conductors are not. Too many of them are like your cousin Adrian. Or want to be."

"Adrian is a fool," Maks said.

And he could say that, since he'd just spent a year with many folks from Adrian's old crew. And hearing their stories.

"Probably," she agreed. "But I wanted to know more about Maks Sobol."

"You've talked with me just about daily for more than a year," he reminded her. "Do I have any secrets left?"

"Probably," she smiled impishly. "I guess I'll just have to work harder at finding the rest."

With that, she rose, carrying her tray off and bussing it, leaving him sitting there confused.

Which was about normal with the woman.

Maks already figured he was doomed. Hopefully, he'd enjoy it along the way.

EIGHT

Anna Shevchenko had established a good pattern on the flight home. Coffee in the morning with Lukyan to pick his brain or get updates. Tea after lunch with Chervonya to discuss in deeper detail all the things she'd done, seen, or considered in her year-long mission to the Spinward Reaches.

She'd easily be elected to the council in another decade or two, assuming she wanted it.

For now, Anna watched Chervonya sip and noted that the young woman appeared off-center today. More than once, she opened her mouth as though about to say something, then shut it again.

Intrigued, Anna let her dangle. Chervonya had been on her own for a year and done an excellent job. What was troubling her?

"Maks thinks you've forgotten him," she finally managed, which was not where Anna expected her niece to roam.

"Hardly," Anna countered. "Though if he thinks so, then perhaps he's finally recovered from all the stress of Bastion."

"Recovered?"

"Building the base for Uly," Anna nodded. "Managing the construction project and doing a damned good job of it. Then having to step in and be governor in Uly's absence. I'm certain that it took a lot out of him. Dealing with you probably didn't help?"

"Me?" Chervonya gasped.

"I've watched the way he watches you," Anna said.

"Really?" she asked. "Because I more or less confronted him at lunch on that very topic."

It was Anna's turn to be surprised.

"And what did he say?" Anna asked.

"That I intimidated the hell out of him," Chervonya replied. "Except that he didn't say it that way. Merely that he was keeping a low profile and then asked if I was interested in him, like he didn't know."

"Had you ever told him?" Anna pressed.

"Not before today, upon reflection," Chervonya chuckled quietly. "Too busy expecting him to turn back into an Ononguli on me."

"I don't think you need to worry about that," Anna laughed with her. "Him or Lukyan. Uly has infected both of them, like he did so much of Adrian's crew. Turned them into something else. Maybe Human. Maybe something new."

"Something the Horde needs?" Chervonya asked. "Or needs to avoid? Why haven't you involved Maks more in your planning? Why is he moldering as we sail home?"

Anna considered her words carefully. Chervonya was revealing more than she probably realized, though you had to have known her as long as Anna had to see it. From a kit, really.

"Partly, as I noted, to give him time to recover," Anna finally explained. "And partly because I'm not sure where he's going to go next."

"Next?" Chervonya seemed surprised.

"Uly and Dan and the others are coming for the wedding that will see the Corsac Fox linked with the Bondarenko and their allies,"

Anna reminded her. "It will be the event of this generation, at least until the *Auga* start their next war."

"Yes."

"After that, I expect Uly to largely return to his Spinward Reaches," Anna continued. "Especially as they want to locate the Yarikh. Or find what happened to them. Uly cannot be in two places at once, so he will have to rely on people he trusts to represent him in various places while he is absent."

"Like Rayzian, and thus he might dragoon Maks into being his Governor again?" Chervonya asked sharply.

"Assuming he doesn't realize that Maks's mom is far more dangerous and he ends up enlisting Lyra instead," Anna nodded.

"Will Maks do it?" Chervonya asked.

"You tell me," Anna countered. "You know him better."

"Duty," Chervonya nodded to herself now. "Uly will appeal to duty and Maks would. Or convince his mother, who is about to be Uly's aunt by marriage. Whatever Uly asks, Maks is likely to respond, assuming that you haven't already tasked him with something more important."

"And thus, I have let Maks have as much space as I can on the sail home, because he might find himself thrust right back into the middle of the action when we get there," Anna replied. "Where his wishes and his duty conflict directly. And we both know which way Maks will step if that were to happen."

"So you haven't forgotten him?" Chervonya asked.

"Not in the least," Anna smiled. "But if you were intending to do something, you might want to move soon. Maks might only have his personal freedom until Uly arrives, if you wanted to drag him off into a corner and have a serious talk with the man."

Chervonya fell silent, but Anna knew her well enough to see the machinations in her eyes. Maks was probably doomed, but in a good way. At least she hoped so. Anna wasn't sure how she could reward him for all the things he had done for the Horde over the last several years.

If he liked Chervonya, she'd happily give her blessing there.

Not like she and Lyra hadn't had a few serious conversations on the topic along the way.

"What about you and Lukyan?" Chervonya suddenly asked.

Anna felt the gravity generators hiccup or something as she blinked.

"What?" she asked.

Chervonya grinned.

"I've watched how he watches you, Anna," the scamp said. "Has he ever...?"

"He came close once on the flight out," Anna admitted after a long thought. "Was a little drunk and almost made a pass at me. I do not believe that he has had a drink of anything since."

"Same problem Maks has," her niece nodded sagely. "Powerful woman who has rank on the man. Most Ononguli men couldn't handle it. Maks can. Lukyan seems to."

Anna paused and considered it.

At first, she'd been a bit surprised that he hadn't ever even walked up to that line save the once. Then a little put out that he seemed to be avoiding her after that.

Except that his behavior had changed after that night. He treated her like a male in charge, doing his damnedest to ignore her gender as much as he could.

She'd seem him slip a time or three. Maybe encouraged it.

But he'd stayed back at a careful distance.

Because she was the *Vatazhko*. The Lord of the Endless Plains.

"He does handle it well," she admitted.

"So Lukyan has exactly the opposite problem that Maks does, doesn't he?" Chervonya asked.

"How so?"

"Maks couldn't say or do anything while he was in charge and I was across the table from him, but that's gone now," Chervonya described. "Lukyan is your transport, so as long as you're on his ship, he is trapped. You need to get home and get off his ship, then see if he's interested. Or rather, how interested. I know he can subordinate himself to you. I've watched it. Maks does the same to me, which still surprises the shit out of me."

"Me, as well," Anna said. "Both men."

"We shouldn't let them get away, should we?" Chervonya asked. "Maks will be a rich, famous player when he gets home. People looking for a connection to Uly will have to go through the Bondarenko and the Sobol. That boils down to Maks, because I presume that Halyna Bondarenko travels home with her new husband, plus all the folks that I expect to return to Bastion."

"Return?" Anna pressed, setting the other aside for a moment.

"Probably half of *Treta Envoy*'s crew, if I had to guess," Chervonya answered. "Plus their families. Plus folks looking to ally with Uly directly. You might be able to load that ship right back up when you get home and immediately turn it around to haul folks to Bastion for a profit."

"The Horde will not appreciate that," Anna reminded her. "I expect the firebreathers to raise a stink."

"Send some of them out to see for themselves," Chervonya laughed. "If nothing else, it gets them out of your horns for a while."

Anna nodded. It might be worth doing.

"And you should probably trap Lukyan in a corner somewhere and nail him down," Chervonya turned serious. "Assuming you intend to. I understand that you never had kids because most men are dipshits about that sort of thing during peacetime, but Lukyan is probably the exception. Him and Maks."

"Him and Maks," Anna agreed. "What does it say that the two most interesting pirates we know have both been infected with civilization by Uly?"

"That Uly is the most dangerous person in the galaxy," Chervonya stated simply, nodding. "Maybe the *Auga* Emperor is up there with him. Maybe not. Not even you, Anna, if I can say that without pissing you off."

"A year ago, you would have," Anna agreed. "That was before I saw all the things Uly could do with just that amount of time and those little resources. That is exactly why the Sphere needs him. Maybe the entire galaxy."

She let silence cover them at that.

She needed Uly, if the Ononguli Sphere was to survive.

NINE

Lukyan saw the look on Maks's face when his friend came in, then checked the calendar in his head.

Not Tuesday. That was good. Always a worry. Maybe a superstition at this point. Hard to say.

"Sit," Lukyan said, gesturing to the chair.

He was in his office, doing paperwork. Mostly goofing off. Nothing serious, because his crew had learned not to engage in any grab-ass shenanigans the first time Anna had been walking by and tore a kilo of ass off a few of them.

There were days when he was sorry she'd depart and leave the goofballs to get out of line again.

"You look like hell," Lukyan offered.

"I love you, too," Maks snarked back.

But he sat. Eyes came back into focus.

"Who's grinding your horns?" Lukyan asked.

"Honestly?" Maks asked.

Lukyan nodded.

"Chervonya finally cornered me," Maks said.

"Warned you," Lukyan smirked.

"Glad I didn't take the bet," Maks said. "Who won the pool?"

"Have to check," Lukyan replied. "What'd she ask?"

"If I was serious enough to maybe court her," Maks said. "Not like that, but those were the implications."

"And?"

"Part of me is all in," Maks answered. "One hell of a woman. Everything and then some."

"But?"

"But she's another Anna Shevchenko," Maks said. "Power player at the top level of the game. She gonna be interested in a two-bit pirate conductor like me?"

"Pretty sure you're worth more than that these days, Maks," Lukyan laughed. "Investor and all that. And your dad's made me some serious profit in places I never imagined."

"Same," Maks shrugged. "We both went off to be big, bad pirates. Not exactly how it was supposed to turn out, eh?"

Lukyan laughed again.

"It never does, and I've been at this twice as long as you," he said. "My advice?"

He waited for this best friend and former First Officer to nod.

"Jump on it," Lukyan said. "Both horns. If she's as good as I think, she'll do the same, and most of the time you won't be bashing against her, but some other jackass who got in your way. Or hers. Don't let this woman get away, unless she wants to."

"Voice of experience?"

"Maybe," Lukyan shrugged. "My teenage years were filled with dumbshit moves on my part. Like most of us. I had to get that far away from home to discover I wasn't in love with my brother's wife. Took long enough. Happy now."

"Gonna get serious with Anna?" Maks asked.

More shrugs.

"I'm like you, Maks," he said. "Small-time player treading water nervously in the deep end of the pool. No idea if she's interested or would toss my ass out of her office and ground me for suggesting it. Only reason we're even here is because we happened to be in harbor when Uly showed up and the whole galaxy went sideways. Same as you. Anna needed people who knew Uly to advise her in things. Dunno what happens when we get home."

"A wedding to end all weddings," Maks laughed harshly. "The Horde will have a shit-fit over this. And then, hopefully, get over themselves."

"You going back out to Bastion?"

"Not sure I have any free will here," Maks replied. "Like when Chervonya was giving me orders, only it's Anna next."

"I don't think she's going to burn you, Maks," Lukyan offered. "If anything, she probably needs you twice as much when we get home. You should seriously step sideways into business for yourself as a Trade Factor like you threatened that one time."

"You think?"

"Bondarenko and Sobol are both going to need an expert on Humans and Uly," Lukyan reminded him. "Since I work for Anna directly these days, that's pretty much you for now."

"It was a joke, Lukyan," Maks snapped. "What the hell do I know about being a Trade Factor?"

"What did you know about being a governor, Maks? How did that turn out?"

Lukyan watched his best friend kind of slump. Settle. Think.

"Shit," Maks finally said. "I know how to do it."

"Good," Lukyan replied. "How?"

"I need to talk to someone," Maks said, rising and walking out without looking back once.

Lukyan shrugged. At least he had some solid investments with Maks's dad. Probably end up sliding those over to whatever the hell Maks built. It smelled like a lot of money.

And it wasn't like Anna was likely to ever let him go back to being a pirate, was it?

TEN

Rabiu Khadijan looked up when the hatch opened and Maks Sobol stood there. Ethir looked at the Ononguli closely as well.

"You look like hell," Ethir offered in his high-pitched voice. "Who do we need to beat up for you?"

Rabiu winced, but all four of the Thogin cousins had come on this mission. Ethir as part of the Legal Department. Waltin, Ralphye, and Hobse because Ethir didn't trust them without adult supervision.

Nobody would, knowing those three. And the four of them could take an adult Ononguli down before the fool knew what had happened to him.

Rabiu gestured the forlorn man into their office and the spare chair. He and Ethir had only been staring at the walls and wasting oxygen anyway.

"Nobody to beat up," Maks said. "Yet, anyway. Got a different problem."

"Talk to us," Rabiu ordered.

Occasionally, he thought back to the overweight pudgeball he'd been turning into. Back when he'd been Khet. Well, he was still Khet, but he didn't ever want to go back to Z'Gosza again, except to maybe show off at some reunion or something.

He was half the size he used to be and folks might think he'd been sick or something. Instead of running off and becoming a pirate. Or a Privateer.

Or part of Uly's Legal Department.

"I am in over my head," Maks began. "And then I realized that I had the perfect folks to call on to help."

He smiled at both of them and even Ethir got a little askance.

"Oh?" Rabiu asked dubiously.

"Skipping over all the preliminaries, I desire to create a thing that has never, to the best of my knowledge, existed in the Ononguli Sphere," Maks explained. "Then turn myself into it and succeed. That's where I need expert assistance."

Yup, seriously askance. Boy was up to no good. Good thing he liked Maks.

"What, exactly, can the Legal Department help you with, bucko?" Ethir asked, pausing to crack his knuckles outward and cackle a little.

About normal for him. Rabiu smiled.

"The Horde is all about piracy," Maks said. "Any time peace with the *Auga* breaks out, we're immediately off preying on other folks. Like *Compass Rose* and all that."

"With you so far," Rabiu nodded.

"What they do not have is anything like a Trade Factor," Maks said. "Bitrus or Bukra, back on Z'Gosza. A person running a public joint-stock company engaged in trade speculation for the sake of pure profit. Never worked around here because of pirates hitting ships too often, then turning around and selling stolen goods under the table."

"That's going to change with Uly," Rabiu reminded him. "Has, in fact."

"Exactly," Maks smiled. "So I need to charter an institution dedicated to trade. To financing hulls and crews. To cornering various markets on goods traveling between at least three major capitals at Z'Gosza, Rayzian, and Bastion. Do you two do freelance business consulting?"

Rabiu glanced over at the mad cackling emerging from his partner, but he really couldn't fault Ethir. That was like dangling raw meat in front of a predator and expecting it to eat a salad instead.

Finally, Ethir wound down and breathed.

"Better?" Rabiu asked.

"Oh, bubba, you got no idea," Ethir replied with a wicked grin.

"Ethir, I'm Khet," he said, as if that said everything. And it might. "I was born for this sort of thing. The most important decision at the moment is where we wish to charter it. Z'Gosza offers certain benefits, but I think ends up being too far away to adjudicate conflicts. Similarly, Rayzian will be central to Ononguli trade, but I suspect, Maks, that you're already far beyond that. Perhaps looking at the Yarikh as a third spoke, for example?"

"That would suggest a Headquarters of Record at Bastion," Maks said, smiling, so Rabiu knew that the kid had been paying attention to all the ways that Uly had let Rabiu and the others build up a whole new thing.

Not a swindle. Not when it was fully legal.

Still...

"Indeed," Ethir agreed. "Good thing you have experts on Bastion commercial law handy, eh?"

"And I'll obviously need to offer sweat equity to potential partners in such a corporate entity," Maks continued.

"Careful," Ethir replied. "I might kiss you."

"I might be spoken for," Maks countered with a leer.

"Oh?" Rabiu perked right up.

That might change a lot of equations.

"Possibly the Ambassador," he said, so Rabiu nodded.

Safe hands then, rather than any wildcard. He liked Chervonya Borisov. She understood business.

Rabiu grabbed a clamshell computer from the drawer where he kept it and started typing.

"How, exactly, did you wish to proceed, Maks?" he asked, smiling.

Uly would more than approve binding Maks Sobol to Bastion as a Trade Factor. The Ononguli might complain, but they could get stuffed. Wasn't like they knew how to win a war with the *Auga*.

That was Uly's job.

Rabiu would make sure he had all the money and allies he needed on that day.

ELEVEN

Lukyan really did look forward to his morning coffee with Anna, grumbling and general tetchiness notwithstanding. She was easy to talk to when she wasn't in a horn-breaking mood. Easy on the eyes, too.

Today, he figured fifty/fifty she'd bop him one. Couldn't be helped. He knew things that hadn't gotten out yet, and figured that she needed as much warning as she could get.

Wasn't like she could really stop it. Maybe not even control it.

At least set up her own contingencies.

"I'm not sure I trust that smile on your face," she began as soon as his butt hit the chair.

Lukyan shrugged. She wasn't wrong.

"On the one hand, it's kinda a secret," he said. "On the other, it's only kinda a secret and won't be for long."

"What have you two pirates done now?" she asked.

Smart woman. Immediately assumed him and Maks were up to no good.

Also not wrong.

"I suppose I get some of the blame for being present and encouraging such behavior," Lukyan admitted. "Mostly, it was Maks's idea both times."

"Uh huh."

Not fooled. Smart woman. *Vatazhko* wasn't a beauty contest, though she probably would have done well there, even at her age. Like a fine cheese, that way.

"By the time we get to Rayzian, I'm reasonably confident that Maks will have chartered a new corporate entity dedicated to trade on a much bigger scale than even he's ever imagined," Lukyan offered. "Let alone you."

"Oh?"

Yup, perked right up. Then she saw implications. Lots of them.

"How big?" she asked, skipping all the silly preliminaries in a single bound.

"Pretty damned huge, Anna," he said. "Wide ranging, too."

"How wide?"

"Rayzian to Bastion to Z'Gosza, for a start," Lukyan nodded. "Got cultural experts on all three handy. Hell, Maks knows all three at least as well as any one person. You'd need a team of folks to top him. And he's in the process of hiring them as we speak."

"As we speak?" she asked, confused. "And you know this, how?"

"Because I was offered a five percent stake based on sweat equity and cash investments as soon as I can liquidate certain things and arrange bank transfers at Rayzian," Lukyan smiled.

"And you took it," she mused darkly.

"One, it's Maks," he said. "Known the boy for a decade now. Former First Officer. Still best friend. And he's onto something big. I'd like to get filthy, stinking rich, Anna. Wealthier than you, maybe."

"He's soliciting investors?" She got cagey now.

"Uh huh," Lukyan smiled. "A limited number of slots for early investors at nice returns. Something about a dual-class stock structure that the Legal Department came up with. It's a Khet thing so I trust the design."

"And the Legal Department is involved?" she pressed. "Was it their idea?"

"No, this was entirely Maks," he replied. "And the time he and I were a little drunk."

"You don't drink anymore," she noted.

He paused, watching her. Of course she would notice things like that.

Would she understand why?

"I do not," Lukyan agreed at a slower pitch. "Realized I was getting a little too indulgent and needed to take sharper control of myself. Not a bad drunk. Not like some. Still."

"Still," she said, seemingly letting it slide. "You are now a business partner with Maks?"

"Directly, yes," he confirmed. "His dad's been handling some of my newer investments recently and making me a nice return."

"Has he now?"

Lukyan nodded.

"Why don't you drink anymore, Lukyan?" she asked directly.

Probably to watch him squirm. At least he'd come to peace with having this conversation eventually.

"I got a little out of hand one night," he replied. "Said and did a few things that might not have been well received. Realized that the stress was making me drink. Decided to fix that."

"I remember the night," she stated.

Which meant that she'd been watching him make an ass out of himself and treat her like any other pretty, single woman in the Horde. Dumbass move on his part.

Water under the bridge.

"Not going to happen again," he promised her soberly.

Because he was. Stone-cold sober these days. Coffee, with or without caffeine. Nothing stronger.

Dumbass.

"Too bad," she mused, smiling slyly.

Lukyan wondered if the gravity system had just burped and needed maintenance. He blinked a few times as his brain caught up.

He made a sound. Probably interrogative. Possibly even coherent.

"I remember," she drawled. "For a long moment, I thought you were going to make a pass at me, Lukyan Chayka."

"Sorry about that," he apologized. "Won't happen again."

"As I said, too bad," she smiled again. "Looks like I'll have to do it, then."

Uhm, huh?

Blinks. Lots of them.

Shit, she'd talked to Chervonya. Those two had conspired.

More. Worse.

Something.

At least she was smiling.

Lukyan licked his lips once as his brain completed rebooting.

"I appear to be deeply confused," he offered, pretty sure he'd missed something important. "Could you clarify that previous statement?"

"I was talking to Chervonya," she answered. "About her and Maks. She asked about me and you. I wasn't sure, in spite of you coming that close to making a pass at me that one night. But she reminded me that I probably shouldn't overlook you, Lukyan. Or let you get away."

"Oh."

Not a lot to say to that.

Vatazhko.

THE Lord of the Endless Plains herself.

Trouble.

At least beautiful trouble.

"Feel like I'm doomed, but maybe in a good way?" he asked, way out on unsafe ice at this point, with no clue how he'd gotten there.

At least she smiled.

"In a good way, Lukyan," she nodded.

"But I'm a nobody," he countered, looking for the way out of some terrible practical joke.

"You are the one who recruited the Corsac Fox," she countered right back at him. "Who immediately understood the importance of him commanding Adrian's former crew. Of commanding their loyalty in spite of Horde politics. Who got him to come to Rayzian to treat with the Council. To bridge the ugly, species divide that considers the Ononguli the highest form and everyone else secondary. Who has supported Uly as much as he has me, and made it clear where he thought the best future for the Sphere waited. You don't give yourself enough credit, Lukyan Chayka."

He wanted to argue with the woman. Wanted to correct her fallacies of logic.

Except that she was right. In those terms, she was absolutely right.

"There are days I don't feel Ononguli," he said, trying to deflect her.

"A new kind of Ononguli, perhaps," she nodded. "Better. More grown-up, maybe."

Him, a grown-up? What was the galaxy coming to? Had a Tuesday snuck up on him when he wasn't looking?

Still, she was the *Vatazhko*. She commanded. He obeyed.

Or got his ass grounded. Or thrown out, though he knew Uly and Dan would always take him in, assuming Anna didn't make it a point of honor between nations.

She was the hardest woman he'd ever known. No, hardest Ononguli woman. Dan and her Combat Team still outdid Anna, though he'd NEVER tell her that.

"So, what does this entail, Anna?" he asked, trudging his way to the gallows.

"For now, nothing," she said. "We're on your ship in flight. Later, when we're home, you and I can have a more meaningful conversation, assuming you're still interested?"

"Yes," he said. "Very interested. Very scared. Very confused. But very interested."

Shit. All that *and* brains? *And* money? **And** everything else?

What fool wouldn't be?

Except that he knew things.

She didn't intimidate most people. Most people were intimidated all by themselves.

Different thing.

Anna Shevchenko didn't aim it at him very often.

Today, she smiled.

"So, you spend some time thinking about it, Lukyan," she said with a nod. "Figure out what you're comfortable with. I've already done some of that thinking. When we get to Rayzian, we'll have a quiet dinner, just the two of us, and talk."

"I'd like that, I think," he said.

Might as well be honest with her.

"I would, too," she said. "And I think that's probably enough conversation for today."

Lukyan agreed. Bounced his ass right up out of the chair, careful not to wear his coffee. Nodded to the woman.

Fled.

But hey, she really was all that. And apparently liked him.

Would wonders never cease?

TWELVE

Anna watched Maks come into her office and noted how different he looked, even from the last time she'd seen him this closely. Had it been a week ago? Felt like years.

Maks Sobol had transformed into something else. Someone else. Who?

"You wanted to see me, Anna?" he asked simply.

She noted that he didn't feel wary today. Not like he usually did, walking on eggshells around her even when he seemed calm.

There was always something there in the back of his eyes. Or had been.

She could recognize it by its absence, whatever that meant.

"Sit, Maks," she said gently, gesturing.

He did, watching her with a new equanimity. And calmness.

Was this what Maks looked like when he grew up? If so, Chervonya would have a bundle on her hands. And enjoy it.

"Lukyan tell you what I've been up to?" he asked, even as she opened her mouth.

"He mentioned something, but we didn't go deep into details,"

Anna deflected, mostly to see where this new Maks Sobol would take things.

She'd always known he had it in him. Anna had known Lyra since before he was born, though not spent much time around the woman since she'd given up the pirate life to have a quieter retirement with Voldomir.

"Partly his fault," Maks nodded calmly. "Partly Uly's. Partly yours. Mostly mine, though I intend to blame Mom for everything."

"Oh?" Anna asked, still finding out who this new man was. And what Lyra had done.

"Something the Ononguli Sphere has never done. Never had," he said. "We've always been pirates during peace, then hunters during the regular wars with the *Auga*. Piracy's ending, so there will be a new Ononguli Sphere born pretty soon."

"And what will Maks Sobol be doing then?" Anna pressed.

"Getting rich," he smiled. "Khet scales of wealth. Gonna turn myself into the first Ononguli Trade Factor."

Anna was familiar with the term from the various contracts that had gone back and forth linking Z'Gosza and the Horde along what Uly called his Galactic Silk Road. Major trade organizations, highly formalized, dedicated to wealth acquisition.

Anna started to say something, but the smile she only saw in his eyes stopped her.

New Maks Sobol.

Calm. Deliberate. Dangerous.

Chervonya was in for a treat, assuming she didn't back out when the scope of what Maks was doing became obvious.

"I would ask if it would work, but obviously you've given it a lot of thought and recruited some interesting players," she said. "What motivated you to do it now?"

"Uly is going to *break* the Spinward Reaches," he smiled calmly. "Like he did Lacium and a few other places, en route to forcing a civilization-level change on the Khet of Z'Gosza. When he does that, there will be an utterly huge space where piracy is met by a big, fucking hammer in his hands. That means that pirates need to move on. Somewhere else, or to find some other lifestyle. I figure that a few armed merchant caravans running like spokes from Bastion to the major players will be both impossibly profitable, and will work to extend Uly's trade empire in all directions. Lots of money to be made. Eventually, when the *Auga* get off their asses, Uly will need a lot of ships and crews to go fight them. Might as well have ships, and more importantly, shipyards capable of helping him."

"Shipyards?" Anna asked, intrigued.

"Miners are never the ones that get rich, Anna," he noted. "Something Rabiu and Haydar both have mentioned. The folks that get wealthy are the ones selling shovels to miners, metaphorically. The support services that aren't sexy but are utterly necessary. Buying and selling parts and supplies. Building and repairing ships. Plus, Uly is going to want to rely on folks he knows for building his warships and warfleets. Again, I intend to be in place and working smoothly when that day comes. After chatting with the Legal Department, they are undertaking a few studies for me as freelance work to estimate the scale of what needs to be accomplished in three-, five-, and ten-year windows, so we can determine how much investment we need, and what sorts of returns we can offer investors later."

Anna blinked, trying to square the man in front of her with the guy who had first welcomed her aboard *Scavenger Angel* that day. Same body. New person had taken over.

"You recruited the Legal Department?" she asked, understanding that to be Rabiu Khadijan and Ethir Ewen. Haydar Ramezani and Piruz Kossari had remained with Uly, but would be following along aboard *Nubia* soon.

Maks nodded.

"Sweat equity and other valuable considerations, for a five-percent ownership-level share, shared evenly between them and Dan's Combat Team," he said. "Additionally, a ten-percent ownership-level share reserved for Uly, to both engage him and to make sure he's cash-flow positive when he needs to be, as well as having deep financial reserves he can draw on in the form of a major galactic bank."

More blinks.

"You sound Khet," she finally said.

Maks grinned.

"Rabiu has been a bad influence," he replied with a nod. "And Piruz. Ethir's sneaky, but doesn't really have a strong business background. He's better on the legal side, having spent so much time dancing around the edges of the *Auga Empire* and their bullshit. And remember, *Compass Rose* worked in the Khet sphere for a decade. Lukyan knows how they think, same as I."

"And Lukyan is a partner," she said.

"I do have a few other slots reserved," he offered slyly.

Anna felt a tremor of nervousness slither up her spine. Where had Maks gotten this sudden smooth suaveness?

Was this was freedom looked like?

Maybe. He'd been worried initially about going broke, like most pirates did. Then had managed to serve her well and make nice money on the side, both with *Scavenger Angel* as well as *Treta Envoy.*

But he was proposing stepping up to the top level here.

"Oh?" she asked, when he paused and let it linger.

"I think that offering the Horde a similar five percent would connect them nicely later. At the same time that they'll be able to show a profit as we go," Maks nodded. "Something that the Lords of the Endless Plains would administer on your side, meaning you as long as you were *Vatazhko*, Anna. Similarly, the Bondarenko will get a share, to further cement their willingness to work with Uly later when it matters."

"When it matters?" she asked, still intrigued.

This wasn't even the Maks she'd sent to Bastion. This was an older man, hardened by fire and political maneuvering. This was *Governor* Maks Sobol.

She heartily approved.

"As you have noted, Anna," he said, already treating her like an equal instead of a boss. A partner. "At some point, the marriage is likely to send a tremor of discontent through the entire Sphere. The Sobol are still a little pissed publicly that Adrian remains a prisoner, but you'd be amazed how little ambition there is in clan politics to actually get him back. The Bondarenko will also have their hard-headed specists who can't imagine that Uly is worth their time. However, if they own a bank and a shipyard, they'll turn their horns back and keep the grumbling to a minimum. At least, that is my calculation. Need Mom and Dad to weigh in with their expertise, but I'm confident it will work."

"When I sent you to Bastion, I had no idea you'd turn out like this," she noted.

"Thank you for sending Chervonya," he replied. "Having her handling ambassadorial tasks let me focus on project management at a very deep and detailed level. And to follow the money, both the politics of it as well as the velocity. And having the Legal Department handy taught me many things first hand, or I would have never attempted something like this."

"What holes do you have in this plan?" she asked, impressed at what he'd accomplished.

"I'm sure there are a bunch that I haven't come across yet," he said. "If I could get you to set aside the *Vatazhko* at some point and look over the corporate documents as a potential investor, you'll probably find some things that Rabiu and Ethir missed, as well as me and Lukyan. You've been doing this for a long time."

Anna nodded. Getting Lukyan settled had done something to take a weight off her horns. Now it felt like Maks was stepping up to help her invent the future, by creating an image and drawing the rest of the Horde in to follow.

They'd understand shipping and commerce. Maybe not how Maks likely envisioned it, but enough to head them in the right direction, while she tried to turn the entire Ononguli Sphere herself.

"I'd love to help, Maks," she decided. "Let's set up a double-date sort of thing. Off-hours. No titles. Dinner and drinks and business, without the politics of being an Ononguli in it."

"Double date?" he asked.

Anna realized that Lukyan hadn't told him anything yet. Probably still digesting.

"Yes, Maks," she smiled. "A double date. Of sorts. Especially if we're all likely to be business partners at some point in the near future. Seems like maybe we should work on the social side and get to know each other better as people, and not just titles."

He paused and studied her, looking for something before he finally nodded.

"I'd like that, Anna," he said.

"So would I, Maks."

Because he'd just brought the entire future of the galaxy into her office and offered her a slice.

How did she take advantage of it?

PART THREE
BASTION

THIRTEEN

Uly had been looking forward to this. To something. It was all an adventure, waiting to be discovered and he didn't think that much would change.

At least not initially. It would take time for everyone to adjust to a new way of living and thinking. Helped that Dan had plotted and planned it out, at least subconsciously, and the Mazhin had supplied the model upon which she was building everything today.

Uly didn't think that anyone had ever given Dan enough credit for the amount of brains she normally kept hidden behind those curls. He knew. Couldn't do any of this without her.

So he smiled when she entered his quarters. Kissed her once to say hello. Then a second time to relish her. Revel in her.

How'd he get so lucky?

"You ready?" she finally asked.

Uly glanced down to check his uniform one last time. The good one that Omid had sewn for him by hand, because that was how Omid expressed love.

He liked to think of it as his Warlord Costume. A rich medium blue he'd heard called *royal*, trimmed in scarlet and mint. Slightly baggy pants that he was still getting used to. T-shirt tucked in and covered over with a button-up jacket with all sorts of pockets, straps, and accouterments.

A welcome change from the maroon that had defined him for years.

Dan wore green. Pants and jacket in a dark emerald that nonetheless seemed to fluoresce as he watched. Her, making a statement as a civilian, because that's what she was creating. A civilian power structure separate and distinct from the military one that his blue represented.

"Yes," Uly said. "I am. Shall we?"

He took her arm and they exited the hatch, heading aft to one of the big training gyms that was frequently the dojo where Dan and her Combat Team trained in.

Today, it was packed. As with Sterling's promotions, the major players had been invited, then a lottery held for other slots, excluding lottery winners from the first round.

Full. And many people smiling.

Commander Karjalainen and his two associates had a front-row spot next to Suka Kuri, who appeared to be providing a running commentary for the newcomers.

Chief of Chiefs Kadyr Usupov held Court in the center, surrounded by the Combat Team on one side, with Sterling, Haydar, Solomon, and Kolya on the other. Nearby, all of the Humans and Mazhin from *King Hewitt II*, because they'd been there from the beginning.

Uly had quietly vetoed holding major festivities, knowing that they were establishing a pattern here that would need to be repeated each time a new species chose to join his...whatever the hell he was creating.

It felt rude to call it an empire, because he had no intentions. Nor was it really a republic like *Batyr*, though it shared many characteristics.

He leaned over to Dan and caught her eye as they walked slowly towards the center.

"Not a Convocation," he whispered simply. "But a Conclave. Let's call it that."

"Yes," she replied. "I like it. I like it a lot."

He nodded and they came to rest in front of Kadyr, with Aibek standing right behind him and both of their wives and Aibek's two kids at hand as witnesses.

Many witnesses.

A new thing was being born. Hopefully, a newer, better future for the wider galaxy, if he could manage it.

Uly nodded Kadyr close and whispered in his ear, catching a nod and a pleased grin. The Isann had met Uly and heard the siren call of the *Karaŋgılıkka*. It spoke to them on a cultural level that few others were prepared to understand, but Uly had seen it.

Perhaps taken advantage of it, but only to draw his new friends out into the wider galaxy and make them valuable contributors to it.

It was good.

"My many friends from many lands, we have gathered today to celebrate a beginning," Kadyr called, his voice dropping a bit and growing mighty with power as the chamber fell silent. "All beginnings are endings, but the endings are things that should remain in the past. We should look forward to the adventure at hand. At *Sailing into Darkness* with open eyes and a welcoming heart."

He paused and rotated in place, seemingly binding everyone in the room with the force of his personality.

There had been a specific reason Uly had asked Kadyr to officiate. Just as there had been that spark that had made him Chief of Chiefs of the Isann.

He completed his circle and smiled even wider.

"The Corsac Fox founds a new thing," Kadyr said. "A new Conclave of the Many Species, where all are welcome and all may join us in peace, trade, and bringing the gifts of the future to the dark corners as yet unknowing of the wider moonlight. Or the Endless Plains. Those who will join as a people will bind themselves to the Corsac Fox in marriage. To bring their voices to the table of elders who will decide the fate of nations. Others will also have a place to speak, but the Congress of Wives will be supreme. Ulysses Fortier will *Speak* for the entire Conclave, just as Sheridan Chastain will *Speak* for its Congress."

Again the pause. Uly heard Suka Kuri's quiet voice only because everyone else had fallen to a silence that almost felt painful.

Uly and Dan had separated by a decimeter or so. Close, but no longer touching. At hand, if there was trouble, which was how it should be.

"You are here at the Founding," Kadyr intoned resonantly. "You will carry these words and deeds to all corners. All peoples. All civilizations. Let them know moonlight even on the darkest nights. Corsac Fox, you will take the hand of Sheridan Chastain. You will turn to one another and smile."

Uly couldn't help the grin. She was as nervous as he was, but it was all going according to plan and practice.

He could do this. It only felt like the weight of the entire *Auga Empire* on his shoulders, but he had Dan to share it. And many others soon.

"Marriage is a solemn oath," Kadyr said. "A sincere and sober duty greater than the individual, especially as it pertains to the nations. You must enter it with a serious mind. A serious heart. At the same time, it must not always be a serious task, as you are taking one another as friends, companions, and partners. And a lifetime to explore what such things mean. It will bind nations as much as it binds hearts. It is a duty, but it is also a beginning, into which much joy and adventure can be had. Corsac Fox, will you take Sheridan Chastain as your spouse? As your Speaker for the Congress? As your partner in all things?"

"In all things," he said.

It helped that she was crying too, because he felt a vast energy rise up from the room and engulf him. The love of a hundred friends.

It gave him strength.

"Sheridan Chastain, you will bind yourself to the Conclave of the Many Species with your actions. Will you take Ulysses Fortier as your spouse? As your Speaker? As your partner in all things?"

"In all things," she replied.

He pulled her close and kissed her.

The crowd sighed. Uly sighed. Dan still had tears running down her face.

It was good.

"Corsac Fox, Speaker Chastain, you are bound," Kadyr called. "Let all know these things and carry my words to the outer darkness. It has begun. You will be its Heralds to those as yet in ignorance, that they might know moonlight. My friends, I present to you the wedded couple."

Uly and Dan turned slowly in place as everyone applauded, whistled, stomped, and otherwise carried on. Kadyr let it go for a time, then raised both hands.

Silence fell.

"Speaker Chastain, you will take your place at his left," Kadyr ordered.

Uly let go of her hand and felt her slide around behind him, coming to rest in the space opened when Sterling shifted the men out a meter.

"Nasrin Monfared, you will join us," Kadyr ordered.

Nasrin took a step to her left, into the space Dan had vacated. The rest of the Combat Team—most of them, anyway—stepped a meter to their left as well, in the order that he had first met them, excepting only Anari Supasei.

Uly hadn't gotten all of the story. And wasn't sure he ever wanted it. Apparently Dan and Suka Kuri had taken the young Sabre

School Seeker aside and asked her hard questions in the privacy of Dan's office.

Then taken Sterling aside as well, once Anari had spoken.

Neither were ready to publicly commit at that level, but Uly supposed that the two were now engaged in an extended betrothal, one that would turn serious later when they were ready.

And only when they were ready.

He reached out and took Narsin's hand, watching her tentacles quiver with suppressed energy that wasn't saying anything. Or perhaps everything. He smiled and felt her relax.

"Corsac Fox, many species have come, in order to bind themselves to your Conclave by one of the oldest sacraments," Kadyr announced. "The Mazhin would join you as a people, and Nasrin Monfared as a spouse, a partner, and a friend. Will you bind yourself to this woman? Will you take her as a companion? As a spouse? As a partner in all things?"

"In all things," he said simply, still smiling.

This was, at the end of the day, probably the easiest part. Having an entire Congress of Wives would take a lot of effort and care. All of them were making it up as they went. But doing so for a much greater cause than merely themselves.

"Nasrin Monfared, you will bind yourself to the Conclave of the Many Species with your actions. Will you take Ulysses Fortier as your spouse? As your Speaker? As your partner in all things?"

"In all things," she replied, using words as well as tentacles. He'd learned enough to follow much of her semaphore, even if he lacked the olfactory capability to follow parts.

As with Dan, he pulled her close. More carefully. Delicately, even.

They shared a kiss that was all the more interesting because he was suddenly in the center of all her tentacles, like a swimmer in seagrass as they caressed his skin and tasted his hair. She wasn't crying like Dan had been, but he could taste her nervousness.

For all her years with Dan and the Combat Team, she was among the youngest in terms of overall life span, barely an adult when they met and barely older now, however much more mature she'd grown.

Those asshole *Danumash* lords had expected her and Omid to service all the male Mazhin as *Socials*. Because they had no idea that women might actually be people.

None of the men had ever touched her. Ever kissed her, even, seeing the youngster as a sister or niece to be protected instead of a woman to be ravished.

He would take his time. At the same time, that described most of the women behind her.

After a time, they broke the kiss. The Mazhin smiled, both the old-timers and the newcomers who were learning about a galaxy beyond a simple Mazhin trade ship with brown gumbo. More celebrating as they were presented.

Quickly, Nasrin took her place on his left next to Dan and on her outside flank because Dan had the title of First Wife, among other things.

Primacy, because certain cultures did practice various forms of polygamy and accorded the First Wife greatest rights in the household.

Uly could only imagine what life might have been like, had he had a second mother as a child. She'd have had to be utterly amazing to survive and hold her own around Anselm Fortier and Tamsin Simon. He'd worry about that another time.

Yanouk stepped up. Smiled nervously down at him from her immense height. Took his hand.

He remembered the first time he saw her, Suka Kuri, and Hiko Seiichai aboard the then-*Iron Wasp*, when they were all prisoners of Adrian Sobol. She'd grown into a woman since then, there was no other way to describe it. A most interesting woman, studying dance, combat, art, history, and all the many other things that Suka Kuri,

Dan, and everyone else had to teach her, on her way to becoming an Exemplar herself, someday.

He could see it in her today.

In all things.

One by one, each woman from the Combat Team stepped up and bonded with Uly. Became part of Dan's new thing that she was creating, the Congress of Wives. Became part of Uly's life in ways that would be worked out at each woman's pace, because Nasrin and Yanouk were the youngest.

Katya Zehlennko was next, nervous because she would have precedence on another—more important—Ononguli wife soon. A more prominent one from a powerful family.

In all things.

Ciah Dambe, the troublesome warrior child grown beyond learning to be an accountant and becoming something far grander, even as she occasionally turned her head to the business side of things that all Khet learned as quickly as they learned to walk.

In all things.

Yeong-Suk Kang. Like the Thogin cousins, part of a band of petty criminals that he had rescued. She had stepped up and claimed a space with Dan and the Combat Team when she came to understand what that meant. If her small group were the only Guezal anyone around here had ever seen, she still represented them and smiled at him nervously.

In all things.

Zamira Ismailov. Newest of his friends, joining Dan only after the Isann had been culturally conquered by Uly and *Nubia*. And still stepping far outside of the bounds that she had originally expected, but Dan had selected her team with great care, turning away others that didn't fit her ideal.

Either for her Combat Team, or the greater thing she had been quietly thinking about because Uly had asked her to create the future.

In all things.

All seven women stepped up now and surrounded him, each with a hand on him as Kadyr called the room to order.

"My friends, it is begun." His words echoed off the bulkheads. "The Conclave of the Many Species has come into being. The Corsac Fox will *Speak* for it. Dan will *Speak* for the Congress of Wives. You are all bound to this greater thing, so you will carry this moonlight to all corners and all listeners. I command you thus. Go in peace and strength."

He stepped back and Haydar and Sterling both slipped in for hugs, which surprised Uly because neither man was particularly tactile generally.

Still, it was a day for beginnings.

Others stepped close to speak, or touch someone in passing for luck, or simply to smile, before most filed out to where a reception would be held in the next chamber, as soon as Vahid and Omid could take over again and approve final preparations.

And then the future.

He pulled Dan close and watched the triumph in her eyes.

"We did it," he said. "It is begun."

"It is begun," she agreed. "Now, let us step into that future."

FOURTEEN

Suka Kuri had kept a low, running commentary for the Samuur visitors. Already, she could see the machinations flowing, and Uly had pointed out how much they spoke with ears and whiskers.

Trust Uly to see that, but he was already at least partly Mazhin. The Samuur had picked up on the whole concept and events quickly as well.

They were at once gobsmacked and delightedly intrigued by such a thing. And the implications that they might eventually tie themselves to Uly's new Conclave by such an act.

Suka Kuri found it interesting, pondering who the Samuur might locate that would meet Dan's high bars for admission. Commander Ursula Nyman was a most interesting person, but she was already mated and had cubs at home, or she might have said more.

As it was, they conspired in noisy whispers, at least as far as Suka Kuri was concerned, watching those semaphores flow around her. Once it was done, she shepherded them into the next chamber and got them installed at Uly's table where Dan would sit, while each of the other women would anchor one of the other tables.

Showing the flag, she thought she had heard it called, but she wasn't sure.

Kalev Karjalainen contained his nerves well, but not entirely.

"And all will be welcome?" he asked, indicating the ceremony, the new wives who were Uly's representatives, and *everything*.

"All who will pledge themselves to the Conclave," she stated, already smitten with the term.

It suggested a meeting of equals, which really was a new thing in the galaxy. Suka Kuri could say that, as widely as she had traveled.

Most places were generally dominated by a single species. Socially. Economically. Politically. The Khet of Z'Gosza. The Ononguli Sphere. The *Auga Empire*. Even the two Human realms of *Batyr* and *Danumash*, from what she had learned.

And Uly had upended all of that to create a land of equality. Of laws that would apply to everyone, rather than laws that only constrained some species, leaving the others free reign.

"What are the implications to the Samuur?" Ursula Nyman asked.

"We do not, as far as I know, even have the coordinates of your capital," she reminded them. "Merely a rough direction that places you well off Uly's Silk Road in the general direction of the back flanks of the Ononguli Sphere. Not that close, or you would have met one another ere now, but not that close to Bastion or Isann, either. Do the Samuur remain in their dark corner, or emerge?"

More semaphore. Quiet whispers in a quieter room, but she let them have their privacy generally, smiling at Ursula and ignoring the two men.

"Will the Corsac Fox visit?" Ursula asked.

"You are, I think, close enough to the route he would take to Rayzian," Suka Kuri answered. "And, I think, he would like to speak with your Paramount, in order to better understand your kind. We will all be neighbors, after all."

"And the *Auga*?" Ursula pressed. "Uly calls them galactic bullies."

Suka Kuri noted the way the two men quietly bristled at the term. How Uly had been able to immediately understand that about these people, she still marveled at, but it was Uly. Not all that impressive physically, being long and skinny for his kind. Dark skin and a beak of a nose, compared to the others. Handsome enough in a rugged way, perhaps, but not truly beautiful.

But he understood people. Instantly. Instinctively.

"They would conquer the entire galaxy under their rule," Suka Kuri explained. "Where the *Auga* rule and all other species are subject to their laws, without any voice. Such behavior offends Uly's sense of rightness, so he intends to fix them."

"He is one Human," Ursula replied. "With two ships, a station, and a planet with hardly any population."

"And a dream that calls to the many nations," Suka Kuri smiled, extending it to the other two. "The Isann have known Uly for only a number of months, and yet they have joined him. The Khet and the Ononguli are partners. Friends. There are many others out there, waiting to be found."

"Like the Yarikh?" Kalev asked. "I have heard other others talk as if there was a lost Human nation, somewhere beyond Isann."

Suka Kuri nodded. Aibek and Kadyr had already started making plans for others to go, based on things Sterling and Anari had found.

"Just so," she replied. "More friends that we might discover."

She watched the third commander stir. Matti Lehtinen hardly ever spoke. Quiet, conscientious, competent, but not all that talkative.

"Should we go find them for Uly?" he asked simply.

Suka Kuri noted that in only a little more than a week, the Samuur already called him Uly, just as everyone else did. The Corsac Fox was the terrible legend.

Uly was the man.

She turned to study Matti closer. A touch smaller than Kalev. Much smaller than Ursula.

Intent. Focused.

"Are you not supposed to return to Saari with Kalev and Ursula?" she asked, glancing at the other two and noting their surprise.

"One ship could handle that task," he waved a paw negligently. "Another could wait here and protect the system from marauders such as have begun to be a local plague. That leaves a third free to seek. Would Uly accept such a thing?"

"I believe he would," Suka Kuri said, marveling at how Uly did it.

How he motivated people to stand up and step beyond themselves.

Just look at this old woman turned terrible sage and oracle by extraordinary circumstances.

She kept her chuckles to herself.

The other two were surprised, but generally favorable, reading their ears.

"Who would go?" she asked Matti.

"*Virta* should escort *Nubia* to Saari," Matti nodded crisply. "And these might be Dan's people, rather than Uly's?"

"Both are Human," Suka Kuri said. "They come in a wide range of skin tones. But yes, we think that they look most like Dan."

"Then Ursula and *Niemi* should handle that task," Matti continued. "That leaves *Koski* to protect the Bastion."

"Would you submit to Sterling Huff's authority?" she pressed.

"He brought a single ship out to challenge all of us by himself," Matti smiled. "Even if he didn't and we didn't understand that Uly was coming. That was an act of bravery and honor, because he had to protect the merchants from the marauders he thought us to be. I would be proud to serve him."

She nodded. The Samuur were all about honor, first and foremost. Understanding that made most of their behavior fairly predictable.

Identify the honorable action and watch the Samuur embrace it. She could work with that.

Looking up, she caught Dan's eye, then noted that the troughs of food were beginning to be delivered.

"Come, my new friends," she said, rising. "Let us join the line for food and conversation. We have much to learn from one another."

And a whole new set of surprises for Uly and Dan, except that she didn't think they would come as much of a surprise.

Uly had a way with people.

FIFTEEN

Dan listened to the explanation and tried to keep her jaw from falling open. Suka Kuri saw that and just smiled as she kept talking.

Uly was a bit in shock from his day, but following intently.

They had retired to his office after dinner. She supposed that the wedding couple should have taken something of a honeymoon, but duty never slacked. And Uly had more than a handful of new wives.

And any one of them would be a handful.

But Suka Kuri had topped herself. Again.

"And we can rely on them?" Dan asked.

"I believe so," Suka Kuri replied. "Uly used highly loaded language, once he came to understand the Samuur. They responded. Friendly, and intense. I propose that we make use of that energy to draw them deeper. Already, it will present the Paramount with the makings of a treaty of friendship, if nothing else."

"What do we know about Paramount Kallio?" Dan asked.

"Leader by acclamation," Uly said. "Election by and from a class of elders and conductors that represent the peak of power and wealth among their kind. Rather like old Vikings from legend. Terrible warriors, but honorable people, as long as you understand their definition of honor."

Dan nodded. Not a people she'd studied all that much, with them being at the other end of the spectrum from a dark-skinned woman like her, but Uly would know. He had been trained to be an officer, once upon a forever ago.

"Is his rule stable?" Dan asked.

Uly turned to Suka Kuri.

"Acclamation generally means that he must fuck up terribly before someone challenges him," she said with a wry grin. "Otherwise, yes, he is stable. Assuming that the Corsac Fox is a positive outcome."

"I think them voluntarily splitting their squadron into three tasks shows positive thinking," Uly said. "We need to make sure we keep things good when we get there."

"Do we invite them to Rayzian?" Suka Kuri asked.

"Absolutely," Dan interjected. "If we would make allies of them, we need to show them the power of our other allies. Plus, they can attend the next wedding ceremony and participate as friends of the Corsac Fox."

Dan caught Uly's nod. He still didn't understand everything she was doing. Or some of the longer term implications, but he absolutely trusted her to handle it. To organize it.

To pull it off.

Absolutely.

In all things.

"Okay, then do we take them up on the offer?" Suka Kuri asked.

"We'll need to bring Sterling in," Uly said. "He'll be responsible for two-thirds, so he needs to be prepared. But if I didn't think he could handle it, I wouldn't have put him in charge."

Dan paused as an idea struck her. The other two noted and fell silent.

"I have a thought," she said.

Both nodded.

"If we're sending Ursula Nyman and *Niemi* to look, we need to send some folks from our side with them," Dan said. "I think that Anari is probably best suited, since she's gone the furthest on their language and culture from the *Karaŋgılıkka*. But we also need to send a Human along, just to let them know we're here."

Uly pursed his lips.

"Thin there," he offered. "I need you. Kolya, as much as I love him, is not a people person. Nor is Del. Drew flies. Sterling stays at Bastion. Solomon has a job in security, as do Emil and Gennady. Same with Quinton and Blair in Operations. Marlowe is exactly the wrong person to send. That means we're down to Cleve, Leon, and Kit. Thoughts?"

Dan could see how pinched that was. Certain folks had important duties on *Nubia* and would wish to resist, at least until Uly ordered it. Or she did.

She flashed back to butts and elbows, that first day when she'd boarded *King Hewitt II*, Marlowe trying to fix things with the help of three extremely junior engineers that were hardly more than teenage trainees: two civilians that Hylda Hobbs had hired and one assigned by the *Danumash* Navy.

All had grown up with the help of their former Mazhin slaves, and forged a full Engineering Department that ran smoothly, so she was down to personalities.

"Kit," she said. "He's the most adventurous of the three. Leon is a bit of a stickler for rules. Clive is a bit of a homebody when left alone. Should I approach him or will you?"

"Actually, Dan, that's my job," Suka Kuri interjected. "This is mostly my idea, so I should bring him in. And I agree. Kit Simonson is probably your best bet of the three. And he'll take orders well from Anari when Uly makes her his ambassador."

"I will?" he asked. "Okay. Done."

Dan smiled. Every time he opened his mouth, she had another

chance to compare him to an ever-more-distant punk named Lieutenant Michel Dupuis, hopefully lost forever and rotting in whatever hell their old ship *Marshall Castillon* had turned into.

If she or Suka Kuri needed him to do something, he did it. Just like that.

In all things.

"You got it handled?" Uly asked them both.

Dan shared a quick glance with Suka Kuri that conveyed volumes.

They'd handle it.

And find Uly more friends.

The *Auga* were coming, after all.

SIXTEEN

Kit Simonson looked up nervously when the Elder approached. Not that he didn't trust her. She was probably the smartest person on the ship. It was the smile on her face as she got closer. The way she smiled at him.

He went ahead and put his torque back in the toolbox and wiped his hands on his jumpsuit as he tried to stand up straighter. Most of Engineering had fallen pretty quiet, turning to watch when they noticed her. Mostly just hums and burps from various machines.

Lots of faces looking at things.

Kit wondered what he'd fucked up so badly that the Elder herself was coming for him. Nothing immediately jumped out. Still felt like Mom had just walked into the kitchen and seen him with his hand in the cookie jar.

"Ma'am?" he asked as she slipped close.

Helped that Sadeq was wandering over, tentacles asking a whole raft of questions. Kit didn't grok the language all that well, but he could follow the emotional flow after this many years around Mazhin.

The Elder turned to the Chief Engineer and smiled at him. Sadeq felt it, too. Stopped dead and let his tentacles taste things.

"I need to ask Kit a few questions, Sadeq," she told the Chief. "Can you spare him for a time?"

Sadeq caught Kit's nervousness and nodded.

"You're off duty for now," the Chief ordered. "I'll have someone else finish this. Let me know when you're back."

Kit nodded back automatically. Shrugged in general. Turned to the Elder.

"Ma'am?" he repeated, maybe a little more twitchy than before.

"Let's go sit somewhere," she offered, then led him to the aft wardroom and let him fix some coffee before she sat across the table and smiled.

Smiles. Uh huh.

"I have a project," she finally began. "Your name came up as the best candidate, based on circumstances."

Kit nodded again, wondering what fresh hell he was about to step into. And how he'd get it off his boot.

"How would you feel about an extended mission that detached you from your usual duties aboard *Nubia*, Kit?" she asked.

"You picked my name out of the hat?" he asked back.

"Specifically, I needed one of the Human crew as a representative," she replied soberly. "The list came down to Cleve, Leon, and you. The mission involves temporarily transferring to one of the Samuur ships to travel with them on a scouting mission for Uly."

Kit scowled, trying to wrap his head around that. Sounded like fun, as long as you didn't mind being surrounded by tigers that smiled. Big folks, both physically and emotionally. Kinda loud, but in a jolly way instead of angry.

"Where?" he asked.

"The Samuur squadron has offered to put one of their ships at Uly's disposal," she told him. "Well, Sterling's, and it will go look for the Yarikh. I intend to send Anari Supasei as an Ambassador, but they will be meeting what we think are lost Humans, so I want someone who can speak to them on that level. To show them that they have cousins or at least kin nearby where they might expand back out again."

"Out?" Kit was kinda lost. Not unusual. He preferred machines. They broke in predictable ways.

"*Nubia* was a Yarikh vessel," the Elder nodded. "We think that they largely retired to one world several thousand years ago and turned their backs on the wider galaxy. Having found *Nubia*, we would like to invite them to join us again."

"Oh," he managed.

Yeah, that did sound kinda fun. And sure, Cleve and Leon were probably almost as bad as Marlowe or Kolya, if you were about to land in someone's central square and say hi.

"Samuur vessel?" he asked, suddenly pondering if they'd let him tinker in their engine room.

Isann gear was even more primitive than that crap *Danumash* stuff Hilda had hired him to maintain, back in the day. Back before he'd known how big the galaxy really was.

And what assholes the *Seven Crowns* really were.

Before Uly and Dan.

"*Niemi*," she replied. "Under Commander Ursula Nyman, with Anari along."

"That the woman conductor?" he asked.

"Correct," the Elder said. "Dan and the Samuur both thought that she would be best suited for this mission. I need you, Kit."

Huh. Wow. Him? Sure. Logical. Crazy. Logical. Sound.

And new toys to learn. Maybe help the Samuur lady get better power and control out of her gear, since he already knew where they could take it, after maybe a couple of days of quick study. Isann-level stuff, he was guessing.

The Elder was apparently reading his mind, from the way she smiled.

Mom had been the same way with cookies.

"Okay, I'm in," he told her, mostly to make it formal. "How soon?"

"You'll go off duty now and pack personal gear for a long mission in the field on another vessel," she instructed him. "I'll square things with Sadeq. Then you will meet Ursula and get her blessing before departing. Let Omid know what you think you might need that you don't have with you currently, okay?"

Gonna go find new Humans that didn't involve returning to *Danumash* or ending up in a *Batyr* POW camp? Awesome.

"Yes, ma'am," Kit nodded.

One adventure, coming up.

SEVENTEEN

Anari wondered which fork in the road of her life had caused it to turn completely insane, but after a moment of contemplation, it probably turned out to be all of them.

Mostly the night she stepped up and *demanded* that Dan and Uly kidnap her at gunpoint and carry her off when they stole *Iron Wasp* from the *Auga*. Maybe the dumbest thing she'd ever done.

Maybe the smartest.

Maybe both.

The Exemplar wasn't giving anything away but a smile as they headed to an aft conference room close to the flight bay.

Sterling was seated there when they stepped in. Anari felt the warmth of his smile lift a weight off her shoulders, but blushed and hid it. He did the same. One of the Samuur was sitting there as well, so they all got settled.

Turned out to be the female conductor. Larger than the males by a bit. Smiling, so that was good.

The Exemplar spoke first, addressing all of them.

"I have spoken with Kit Simonson," she announced, referring to one of the Humans from Engineering. "He is preparing to go. Anari,

I don't believe that you have been formally introduced to Commander Nyman. This is Ursula. Ursula, Anari Supasei, Seeker of the Sabre School and Moss School."

Anari nodded. She and Yanouk approached it from different sides, but still studied both in equal parts.

The Commander nodded back.

"Sterling, I have spoken with our three Samuur friends," The Exemplar continued. "Kalev is going to return home with *Nubia*. Matti intends to remain in harbor under your orders as a guardian until someone comes to relieve him. Ursula has volunteered to lead a mission to the various sets of coordinates that you have calculated might be the last refuge of the Yarikh. Anari will go as a formal Ambassador from the Corsac Fox. Kit will be our Human representative, if and when they are successful."

Anari felt a jolt of surprise run through her. Ambassador? Her? Except that Suka Kuri spoke with perfect calm when saying those words.

And she'd already been hardening her soul to a long separation from Sterling, going to Rayzian with the Team. Maybe not so long? Sterling had digested and synthesized five radically different sets of navigational data into a singular whole that was probably the most detailed and sophisticated map of Imperial Sector Fourteen in existence.

And it would get better as they explored and convinced the Samuur to add their details.

Sterling smiled up at her, like he was having the same thoughts. Yay.

Anari turned her attention to the Samuur woman. Bigger than the males, who tended to be bigger than the Humans she knew, not counting Solomon who was a big man according to Dan.

Everyone was shorter than her. Smaller.

"Ursula?" Anari asked, confirming.

"Anari," she replied.

"Is your ship prepared for an Emro?" Anari asked, gesturing to her immense height.

She was used to ships built for smaller species. *Auga* tended to make things big enough vertically because they had many Emro worlds, but the Ononguli and Yarikh did not.

Lots of hunching when she walked.

"It is not," Ursula nodded, pained. "At least no more than this vessel is. Is that adequate?"

"I will need to have a bed transferred over and installed in a room where I can fit to sleep," Anari said. "Among other, similar equipment."

After all, it appeared to be a done deal. Suka Kuri was working out the travel details at this point, not negotiating the mission.

"I have a list from the Exemplar," Ursula replied brightly. "And we're clearing out a room for four crew members for you to have as Ambassador."

The woman paused and turned to Suka Kuri.

"The Human, this Kit Simonson, he will be fine bunking with Samuur engineers?" Ursula asked. "It is highly irregular."

"Only because you have a monospecies crew, Ursula," Suka Kuri replied. "Engineering on *Nubia* includes Human, Mazhin, Ononguli, Khet, Thogin, and others, all bunking together. Assuming that your crew does not object to his presence, he suggested to me that he might try to see if he can improve your systems."

"Improve?" Ursula asked.

"Kit has trained on a variety of systems that are generally more advanced than the Samuur have, based on what I've seen and heard," Suka Kuri described. "He thinks that you are between Ononguli and Isann, technologically, so could be updated significantly."

"Interesting," Ursula managed. "And he intends to?"

"Assuming you allow it, yes," Suka Kuri said. "Some things will probably require new ships, once your people at home have a chance to update your industrial base to turn out the necessary systems. Again, this is something that the Corsac Fox would make available to you."

Anari caught the hint of bribery and swindling contained in those words. The Samuur could also slip off somewhere and buy the things they needed, possibly from Khet or Zuath systems they could find easily enough if they went looking.

However, Uly would offer much better terms. And not turn around and sell information about primitive worlds to folks with state-of-the-art ships who could attack and loot the place.

"I will speak with my people before they leave," Ursula said, confused and possibly in a bit of disbelief to Anari's ears. "From there, it is a question of how quickly we could depart."

"I can supply you with my maps," Sterling said. "And I'll talk with Matti about his new duties now that Uly is making me Governor for a time. We can resupply you from station stores as soon as you're ready."

"Do you always move so quickly?" Ursula asked, eyes darting to all three of them.

Anari and Sterling turned to Suka Kuri.

"It is part of Uly's secret," she smiled. "He identifies an issue or an opening, locates the people best suited to handle it, then quickly adapts to changing circumstances and pursues it. I know that Sterling planned to ask the Isann to explore, but this is a better resolution, as *Niemi* appears to be a faster ship. And one better suited to long-term exploration."

"We have often spent many months abroad," Ursula replied.

Anari stirred, watching the others turn to look at her.

"Should we ask the Isann to resupply us at their homeworld as we transit?" she asked. "And perhaps include an Ambassador as well, since they are likely to be closer neighbors when we are successful? And possibly include a cargo vessel that could meet us somewhere to resupply forward?"

"That is an excellent idea," Sterling replied. "I'll talk to Aibek and Kadyr before they go. And it solves multiple issues nicely. Thank you."

Anari blushed under his words, but reveled in them. They made a nice team. And Uly had established a pattern that Dan intended to expand and enforce.

Maybe they'd be ready when she got back. And *Governor Huff* had done his thing.

Something to look forward to. There was an adventure coming.

EIGHTEEN

Uly studied the bridge of *Nubia* as everyone settled. Sterling was on the main screen, finishing up his last report before Uly left and the young man was in charge for several months. It would have been nice to have Maks there, but Sterling would grow into it, and it would be rude to dragoon Maks a second time. Unless he moved back out here someday and offered.

Then Uly might take him up on it.

"From there, I'll be splitting my time between the station and *Batyr*," Sterling concluded. "Matti is planning to run a close patrol to all the nearby stars to confirm that nobody has set up any new operations, then will maintain a presence here. There will be some squadron training in a week or so when he gets back, but most of my schedule will be driven by *Niemi* and how quickly they can complete their mission."

"Excellent, Governor Huff," Uly replied, reminding the man that he was in charge now. "I look forward to what you'll be able to accomplish in the near future, and hopefully we'll bring news from Rayzian that will make this all even easier."

"Good luck, Corsac Fox," Sterling nodded. "And safe travels."

He cut the line and Uly quick-scanned the bridge. Aibek was traveling with him while Kadyr returned to Isann to find Anari an Ambassador and prep those folks for the possibility that the Yarikh themselves would return, fulfilling one of the final promises from the *Karaŋgılıkka* so many centuries ago.

"Haydar, connect me with Karjalainen, please," Uly said.

"Channel two," his First Officer replied without looking back.

Uly swapped them over and saw the smiles on Commander Karjalainen and his crew.

"All set?" Uly asked.

"Just awaiting the word, Uly," Kalev replied.

"You've got your course," Uly said. "We'll trail some initially, but will still arrive first at the next rendezvous and meet you there, Kalev. See you in two days."

The man nodded and disappeared as *Virta* dropped into warp and vanished.

"Drew, take us out," Uly commanded.

He missed having Sterling on Guns, but Bastion would be in good hands. And Sterling had trained everyone here as part of the new Starfare School of the Emro. Even Drew had gone through the classes and passed with flying colors, though not without some eyerolling.

Man was a civilian and liked to remind people of that. Even Uly hadn't been able to convince him to join a formal navy. Still the best pilot Uly had ever met, so Drew could do that.

And then they were gone. The stars vanished and *Nubia* was on its first big diplomatic mission, headed to Saari and the Samuur, en route to Rayzian and the Ononguli.

And Halyna Bondarenko, who would soon be another of Uly's wives, assuming that the new structure didn't end up offending Anna and the Ononguli Sphere to the point that they broke the engagement.

He'd deal with that if it came. At the same time, he would bring newer allies than even the Isann. Important, because the Sphere would have to expand that direction if the *Auga* continued to push them back from their current Sphere.

Assuming Uly failed somewhere.

He didn't need wars between his allies over diminishing real estate.

Uly waited ten minutes for things to settle before standing.

"Drew, you have command," he called. "Everyone else rotate to your normal watch schedule in warp. We'll arrive before they will, so I intend to have first team on duty when we drop, in case we need to scout."

And with that, he headed aft, trailed by Dan, Suka Kuri, and Nasrin. They followed him to his main office and settled as he waited.

"Rayzian," Nasrin spoke first. "What will Anna say?"

"She'll probably start grumpy, then get over herself," Suka Kuri offered. "We can always claim that we stole the idea from them after she presented it. The timing, at least, is not a lie, even if Dan and I had been working towards something at least similar long before this."

Uly nodded. He knew that those two had started with the concept of the Combat Team, with one representative of each species. Plus both Moss and Sabre Schools.

A thought struck him. Dan perked up.

"Yes?" she asked, seeing him blink in surprise.

"Moss and Sabre," he said, motioning to Suka Kuri. "The expressions of Emro culture writ large, though only ten percent of them ever pursue one or the other seriously?"

"Your numbers are essentially correct, Uly," Suka Kuri replied. "Each world is different, of course, but they tend to average out."

He grinned. Nasrin's tentacles locked on.

"Oh," she barked sharply. "Yes, you're right."

He supposed that it might look like mind-reading, at least to species with practically no olfactory sense to speak of, which was everybody but the Mazhin.

Everyone turned to the Wildrose.

"You have two Emro on your Combat Team," Nasrin stated. "Moss and Sabre. Except that we have caused a third school to come into being, however small and quietly it has begun. And the fact that for an Emro School, it has no Emro students as yet."

The other two women took a moment to see it.

"Where would we look?" Dan asked first, an intuitive leap across a vast chasm, in order to recruit a woman that could handle Sabre School as well as Starfare.

She had to exist. He had one Exemplar and two potentials on his hands.

Suka Kuri got serious.

"We'll need the Mazhin network," she pronounced solemnly. "Already, we have a note to find a Thogin woman to speak inside the Congress, though they are rare on this side of the *Auga* and the Ononguli. Now we will need to expand that to a specific subset of Emro women. I will put together instructions that can be transmitted, but the Mazhin should probably carry it with their clanships."

"Will they?" Dan asked, causing everyone to pause. "Will Uly having a Mazhin wife cause the Convocation to become involved? To demand that you present yourself and explain?"

"They can try," Uly smiled. "Just as the Ononguli. They can ask nicely, or they can get stuffed. Alternatively, they can perhaps petition the Congress to have Nasrin represent them."

"Me?" his tentacled wife asked.

"You," Suka Kuri pronounced. "You are their representative to the Conclave. Let them deal with that, first. It will teach some old women a touch of humility."

Uly didn't quite catch what Nasrin muttered, but suspected it bore a striking resemblance to flying pigs. He smiled. Her tentacles blushed when she glanced at him. He'd ask later.

"Let them," Dan said. "If we present larger than we really are today, that is only today. Tomorrow, we will have more allies on our side. Eventually, they will have to pick us—all of us everywhere—or the *Auga*. Let them face that as well."

Nasrin shrugged, then turned to the Exemplar.

"Sabre School initially, I'm guessing," she said. "Moss might work, too. Or will she be a regular Emro woman who heard the siren call of space instead of the dojo or the library?"

"Are there Emro pirates out there?" Uly asked, watching all three woman semi-collapse into confusion.

"There must be," Suka Kuri finally offered. "Piracy is a thing endemic to regions that have not felt the reach of the Corsac Fox. Emro make excellent ground troopers, so I would presume that a smart conductor would keep a few around, but not many. More and he risked them taking over."

"I think we look for an all-Emro pirate crew," Dan interjected. "We have already started making physical accommodations for Suka Kuri, Yanouk, Hiko, and Anari, so it is not much of a stretch. We can recruit her and her various sisters-in-arms to our side, resisting the *Auga*. Seduce them away from whatever piracy they have."

"Will she be their conductor?" Uly asked, wondering what kind of second Emro wife they might find for him. Or third, if they decided to also cover Sabre as well, with Anari more-or-less pledged to Sterling?

Nobody had ever promised that all of this would make sense, after all. And he doubted that he'd be back to Gralbo anytime soon.

Ever? Too hard to guess. It would have to be sneaking in, which would be functionally impossible, or at the head of a warfleet sufficient to convince the *Batyr* High Command to stand down and behave.

Somehow, though, he needed to eventually get a message home. Mom and Dad deserved that much. He'd sort it out later.

"No." Suka Kuri brought him back to the present tense. "Their conductor, if she is a woman, is likely to be wrong for a variety of reasons. But perhaps one or more of her officers will be suitable."

"Wrong?" Uly asked, intrigued.

"To claw her way to the top of such a command will establish certain patterns of behavior," Suka Kuri said. "The Emro tend to be generally egalitarian, seeing all gender expressions as valid, so less sexist than the Khet or *Auga*. Possibly less than the Ononguli. She will, however, have become her own person, and may be loath to give that up, in order to become a student of aliens in an entirely new thing to an Emro."

"You're wrong, I think," Dan said. "We will present the idea and let that be the siren song that will draw her in. It will draw others, as well, men and women alike, especially as there is an Exemplar of the Arts offering a new Emro school. I can filter down from there for the woman I want, knowing what Yanouk and Anari have turned into from when I first met both of them."

Uly nodded. Dan had very distinct and developed ideals for her Combat Team. And her Congress. And it required both a wide set of skills and a broadly curious mind.

A willingness to step up and outside of yourself, in ways that piracy didn't necessarily foster, Lukyan and Maks notwithstanding.

The other two women nodded at that.

"What about the Samuur?" he asked. "They have been infected in a manner similar to the Ononguli. We travel now to Saari, where we will meet their Paramount and perhaps he sends a ship with us to Rayzian. What do we want from them? Or who, to be more precise?"

"Samuur women have as much sexual dimorphism as Humans," Nasrin pointed out. "Just the other direction, being that much larger generally. She'll likely be big, unless we find another Ciah. Tiny, fast, and mean. I think we will have a smaller Anari, if you will. Kinda scary to think about, putting Anari's mind in Ursula's body, but that's your most likely candidate. I presume we're not moving quickly?"

"We are not," Dan agreed. "But, as Uly points out, they will be carrying home their own ideas from Bastion, and will tell the Paramount what he needs to do, presuming that we present favorably."

"We do," Suka Kuri confirmed. "I will have quiet conversations to start your filtering, Dan. I can do that with them."

Uly and Dan both nodded.

PART FOUR
NIEMI

NINETEEN

Anari liked the Isann Chief of Chiefs, even when Kadyr grumbled about missing the great trip to Rayzian.

But the Yarikh were a siren call that could not be ignored by his people. Not even for Uly.

They were over Isann now, trailing the main station by a bit and waiting for various messages Kadyr had sent to make their way around. Ursula's bridge was a bit cramped, but that was Anari's height more than anything. Kit had even managed to get pried away from the machines for a few hours to sit nearby and watch with bright eyes.

"Worse," the man said, looking up at her with a sad face, "I can't even go with you here, or I'd appoint myself Ambassador."

"There will be other days, Chief of Chiefs," she smiled at him. "It is my hope that you are their closest neighbor, and thus the first person they wish to trade with."

"Do we know if they will be friendly to visitors?" he asked. "It has been how long?"

"Millennia," she replied. "Based on my studies of both their history and other folks, I would presume an entirely new civilization has taken the place of the one that wrote the *Karaŋgılıkka*. Hopefully, one that remembers that tale and honors it. If they are hostile, then I hope that they end up having fallen so far that we represent a form of First Contact. That way, we can withdraw and leave them there."

"*Sailing into Darkness*," Kadyr quoted.

"How soon might you complete a translation into Samuur?" Ursula asked from her command station. "I have heard many of you repeat tales from it, but I would like to read them at some point. To savor such a thing. We did not have our own *Karaŋgılıkka*."

"I have started," Anari replied. "And will rely on you to help me with some of the idiomatic bits, because I remember how painful parts were to get into a modern standard that everyone could read. Suka Kuri will take some time synthesizing her definitive copy. Perhaps when she returns, but I will have something for you by the time you get to Saari."

Ursula nodded. The rest of her bridge crew smiled as well. Anari hadn't gotten to know everyone here in depth, but they were all friendly. Forthright, in ways that were at once refreshing and complicated, because they didn't shade things.

You got unvarnished Samuur opinions on things. Suka Kuri had reminded her to occasionally count to three in her head before replying, simply to file off any sharp edges that they might provoke. Most of the time, they weren't looking for a fight. Or even an argument.

Merely stubborn.

Like that was a strange thing to her.

She smiled.

"Message from the station," Comms Officer Iikka Cemaletdin called from his station nearby. "They are set for docking, presuming that we have the correct hardware on our side, or a small transport."

Anari turned to the Commander. Ursula looked in turn to Kadyr.

"Your people consider themselves great sailors?" Ursula asked, with a subtle tease to her voice.

"Indeed," Kadyr teased back.

Ursula turned to the Pilot, Niina Savolainen.

"We'll dock," she ordered. "In and slow, then deploy magnets to brace us."

She rose and nodded, so Anari fell in beside her and Kadyr followed.

"Chief of Chiefs, let us stop to gather up your wife," Ursula said, turning down a side corridor.

Eventually, with Gulmira in tow, they ended up at the airlock. It banged a few times. Groaned once. Then fell silent.

"Commander, we're stable," Niina said over the intercom. "I show positive pressure on both sides."

"Open it up," Ursula replied.

Anari followed Kadyr through, remembering the first time she'd done this, following Dan and Ciah while ready for trouble.

She got a hug today instead. Didn't even know the man, but he stepped up after hugging Kadyr, so she hugged him back, then watched Ursula give everyone a bit of side-eye.

"You'll be fine," Anari told her, then watched the larger Samuur woman and a small Isann man delicately embrace before stepping back.

Kadyr was all business. He turned to Gulmira and some quick conversation passed silently.

"Yes," he said. "I suppose you are right. You usually are."

Gulmira laughed, then took Anari's hand and they followed Kadyr deeper into the station before splitting off. Ursula followed. Then ended up in a space that reminded Anari of nothing so much as a tea shop.

"What was that all about?" she asked Gulmira. "With Kadyr when we boarded."

Gulmira had that exact same grin she'd had on the day when Anari first met Zamira. Sneaky, but in a good way.

"I might have suggested a potential Ambassador to my husband," Gulmira grinned. "Based on the circumstances."

"Oh?" Anari asked, noting that Ursula leaned in close as well.

"My cousin," Gulmira nodded.

"Your *sixth-ranked dan in Karmap and Chief Instructor* cousin?" Anari pressed pointedly.

"The same," Gulmira grinned.

"Excuse me," Ursula said as a server appeared with a pot of tea and three mugs. "What is a dan?"

"A ranking system," Anari replied, turning to the woman. "First dan is a martial arts student who has mastered the basics of a style. Karmap is an Isann school. Her cousin, Gulnaz Isakov, happens to be the senior instructor of the form. Technically an elder, though not all that old. Certainly an expert. Will she go for it?"

That last to Gulmira, who nodded.

"Probably," Gulmira said. "I leaned on Kadyr that the two ambassadors were female, so a third made perfect sense. He doesn't have all that many women in senior positions of authority that he could enlist, but he does have a contact there. As do you."

"Because she's part of the family, more or less," Anari agreed.

Gulmira beamed.

"What about Kit?" Anari asked.

"He probably left the bridge as soon as we did, headed back to Engineering, where he is no doubt taking advantage of the shutdown to see about dismantling a few systems he wanted to explore. Hopefully, we'll be able to get them back together in time to leave."

"Kit will be fine," Anari said. "I remember him from the beginning, and he's always been a student of machines. Suka Kuri sent him because he is also personable, as you've noticed. But he is a gearhead at heart."

"As are the others," Ursula laughed. "He and my Mechanic,

Jasper Yanev, will be thick as thieves by the time we get where we are going. It will be good."

Anari breathed a sigh of relief inside. Kit had been the right pick. He'd nerded out with the technical crew and impressed them with his energy and enthusiasm, without taking them all that seriously most of the time.

Anari had been working on charming Kadyr and Ursula, so they had things covered.

"So, now what?" Ursula asked, sipping tea.

"We'll have a few days for resupply," Anari said, turning to Gulmira. "Perhaps a tour of the surface, like we did with Dan?"

"I think that would be an excellent idea," Gulmira replied. "Even if Gulnaz doesn't take the offer, Ursula can meet her and her students, and see the other half of Isann culture."

Anari nodded. It would be good.

She was an Ambassador now.

TWENTY

Ursula Nyman had seen many things in her time. Risen to command of one of the great warships of the Samuur fleet, though she had been utterly shocked that Uly and the others considered *Niemi* to be nothing more than a light escort.

Until she had seen *Nubia*, she would not have believed it. And the Ononguli and *Auga* had even bigger ships?

The Samuur had much to learn, if they were to take their place in the wider galaxy helping Uly. Thus, she was here meeting the Isann, on her way to the Yarikh who played such a legendary place in Isann culture.

And she was the center of attention, even walking next to Anari Supasei, who some of the vendors in the market greeted like an old friend.

Still, Ursula shopped. Haggled in broken tongues aided by the two women. Explained herself to strangers in ways that Anari had prepared her for, when Kalev had not. He probably hadn't imagined what form it would take to visit Isann, to say nothing of the Yarikh.

The Samuur had expected single combat, as one did. That Sterling had not engaged them had confused people. That Uly had done so delicately had been a welcome surprise.

Nubia could have crushed the squadron like so many cans of soup.

And the Isann embraced her as a long-lost cousin, in spite of size and fur. Strange, but honorable.

Always honorable. Welcoming. Friendly.

The Samuur had much to learn. And these strangers were, she had to admit privately, good teachers.

Eventually, they emerged from the far end. Went into a building and through to a courtyard.

Ursula recognized it from descriptions.

And recognized the inhabitants by uniform, if not face.

Furless, silver-gray faces still took some getting used to, but she was getting better at telling them apart. They showed gray hair with aging, as her kind did, but also in wrinkles around mouth and eyes.

Ursula supposed that she might develop the same, but it remained hidden behind fur as yet the rich taupe of youth.

"Commander Ursula Nyman, this is my cousin, Gulnaz Isakov," Gulmira introduced them. "Gulnaz, the commander of the Samuur vessel in orbit, Ursula Nyman. You remember Anari, who has been promoted to Ambassador in our journey to seek the Yarikh."

The Isann woman nodded. Bowed, even, so Ursula matched it.

"Welcome," she said simply. "My students."

Ursula knew she would fail to remember a dozen names, but worked at it.

They had tea, then a demonstration of the martial form known as Karmap. Interestingly, Anari joined the group and did not stand out badly.

But then, Dan had sharp standards for the women she would accept, and Suka Kuri had explained what it meant that she had two Emro students who might yet rise to the level of Exemplar of the Arts themselves someday.

Today, she finally began to understand what such a thing implied.

It also frightened her, just a shade. Sabre School made perfect sense. Starfare as a new School was an obvious extension that surprised Ursula for not already existing. At the same time, she supposed that Uly had caused it to come into being.

She probably needed to enroll at some point. There was much to learn from these new friends.

"Do the Samuur have something similar?" Gulnaz Isakov asked when the group finished.

Ursula felt her ears go flat sideways, rather like that one Ononguli woman's.

"Yes, I think," she finally replied. "I have not studied anything like that, save for certain basics of close combat that we learn in officer candidate school. But I seem to recall that it involves more leaping and grappling."

"A pounce?" Anari suggested. "Perhaps like this?"

And then she did a thing that Ursula had only seen in bad action vids back home, where everyone assumed special effects handled most of the work. A leap both forward and up, landing feet forward then collapsing hands inward from the shoulders.

Like pouncing on someone and riding them to the ground.

"Yes," Ursula agreed, a bit flabbergasted. "I am certain that Dan will be able to find such women when she visits Saari. Will they join fully?"

"The right one will," Gulnaz spoke up. "Zamira was not originally anticipating where Dan and Suka Kuri would go, but seems to have accepted the value of such a thing?"

"I believe so," Gulmira said. "It is a young concept, so they have not worked out entirely what it means, but Zamira seemed happy when we left. I think more students—more women—would improve her humor."

"Your husband contacted me as soon as your arrived," the elder stated, perhaps a bit of sourness evident from tone and facial movement. If Ursula was beginning to read alien faces better.

"I thought it a wonderful concept," Gulmira smiled.

"Yes," the woman nodded. "I saw your hand in things. Yours and Dan's."

"Mostly mine," Gulmira admitted. "Anari and Ursula needed someone. And the last commander of *Nubia* was an aunt of Dan."

It took Ursula a moment to parse that, but they meant metaphorically. The same skin and hair. The same bones. Perhaps a lost tribe of Humans, far distant from their other kin.

Would it matter that much to have three women representing the future?

And what did it say with these three? Maiden, Mother, and Crone?

Ursula couldn't help the chuckle. Everyone turned to look expectantly.

"Maiden, Mother, and Crone," she repeated carefully, hoping not to insult her new friends. "I have children at home. You are the great elder of wisdom. Anari brings youth. Is it not appropriate?"

Blank faces. Confusion, she thought, instead of anger.

Had she dishonored herself?

"Oh," Anari said. "A cultural idiom that does not translate into Isann well, I think."

Ursula spent a moment of puzzlement, then brightened.

"Ah, of course," she nodded, relieved. "Let me tell you the story of Koivula Karelius, the legendary heroine who was a slayer of dragons, a founder of nations, and mother to a line of demigods."

Ursula settled herself and reached back to her childhood. To tales that her mother's mother had taught her when she was barely old enough to understand them.

Her audience listened, captivated.

Yes, she was an Ambassador to the Isann, just as she and the others would be to the Yarikh.

She could do this.

TWENTY-ONE

Anari memorized the story as Ursula told it, knowing that Suka Kuri would demand that it be written down if it wasn't already. And translated. Collected.

Did the Samuur have a tome equivalent to the *Karaŋgılıkka*? Nobody had spoken of such a thing, but most cultures have some touchstone story. Or sets of them. Most simply didn't keep them in shape as a societal religion. Not like the Isann.

Still, it exposed new elements of their culture. And resonated with the Isann women around them, because the heroine was a demigoddess. Too many of the tales of the *Karaŋgılıkka* involved men rescuing helpless damsels.

Ursula came to silence, nervously looking around.

"Thank you," Anari said immediately. "That was lovely. I look forward to researching more of your tales and books when I get the chance."

That seemed to help. She relaxed. The others nodded and smiled.

Then, somehow and silently, everyone turned to Gulnaz. The elder had a wry grin on her face as she turned to Gulmira.

"Okay, fine," she said. "Tell your husband the blackmail worked. He won't know any better."

"What about us?" Nargiza, one of the senior students, asked when the laughter died down. "Do we travel with you?"

Anari looked around the group, seeing hopeful faces. At the same time, *Niemi* wasn't large enough for a dozen extra Isann women. Not comfortably, anyway.

"Perhaps you might travel to Bastion instead?" Anari interrupted. "Start a small school there and draw others in your wake? I expect many Isann to make that journey."

All eyes turned to her. Warily.

"Bastion?" Gulnaz asked.

"*Sailing into Darkness,*" Anari replied, watching that ripple through the women like an earthquake. A *rude* earthquake. "It will draw only the most adventurous—the most interesting—men, especially as Bastion becomes the center point for so many other things that will happen later."

A VERY rude earthquake.

Gulnaz narrowed her eyes at her cousin, but Gulmira shook her head, unwilling to accept any blame.

No, this was entirely Anari's fault. But it would advance that dream that Uly had first articulated, where all species were welcome as friends and equals.

Looking around, it seemed to be working its magic here.

As she knew it would.

TWENTY-TWO

Deep space. It had been a lovely week on Isann, in spite of smelling all wrong. Parts of her crew had even gotten to spend some time on the station and the ground, learning and being seen.

Ursula was happy to be back in space. Back where she belonged.

Niemi was loaded as full as she would allow. Nargiza and the others were making plans to pack up and move to Bastion at least temporarily, though Ursula had seen hints of a certain permanence in their eyes.

Would a similar group of Samuur do the same? She was absolutely certain they would. When? And how many?

Was Bastion about to turn into a kind of Samuur colony, at least by population? The Ononguli supposedly forbade all aliens as permanent dwellers on their worlds, accepting only itinerant merchants.

Uly welcomed everyone who could behave.

What would Bastion-raised Samuur be like?

Tomorrow's problem. They were in flight. Deep into the darkness, as Gulnaz might have said it. Anari had proven to be an impossibly deep reservoir of stories and interesting tidbits, once Ursula had gotten over herself and begun to share more of Samuur culture.

Everyone was gathered on the bridge today.

"Niina, how soon?" Ursula asked.

"Four minutes to drop, Commander," her Pilot replied.

Ursula turned to Sulevi Turunen.

"Status of weapons?" she asked.

"We're armed and ready, sir," he replied. "Defensive only but prepared to fight if we have to."

She nodded.

Nobody knew what they would find at Orwek.

Khorko had been a bust. Well, mostly a bust. Evidence of habitation at some point, but only ruins remained, mostly collapsed or grown over when spied from orbit. Road systems that led to what had obviously been cities.

And were just as obviously abandoned today. Long-since abandoned. Buried.

How did one decide to simply evacuate an entire planet?

Why?

Ursula had asked the other women and gotten no better answer. Nothing that made sense, save that perhaps some five thousand years ago, the Yarikh had begun to pull back. To retreat to some fortress in the wilderness and live out their days.

Even Zamir Aytiev, the Isann equivalent of Koivula Karelius in many ways, had only come much, much later, part of a subsequent civilizational collapse of the Isann, as they fell into a barbarism that had only been broken in the last century or so.

However, *Nubia* had survived. Selene Praxis had saved records for eternity. Ursula had watched a few samples to understand. The woman looked like Dan. Like a much darker version of Kit.

Human.

And utterly unknown.

She turned to Anari and they shared a smile.

"Counting down," Niina announced.

Ursula watched *Niemi* return to the real universe.

"Scan and status," she ordered sharply.

"Nothing immediate," Iikka replied. "Sensor wave outbound and not returning echoes."

Ursula nodded. Nobody immediately prepared to attack a strange vessel arriving, even if they had intentionally come out at a safe distance, as they had done at Bastion.

One world. Mostly blue with some grays and greens thrown in, visible below clouds. One medium-sized moon, so a gravitationally-stable series of places where things might survive for a long time.

They would calculate those and scan next. Ursula didn't think it would matter, though.

"Radio signals, Iikka?" she asked.

"Nothing on any channel, Commander," he replied. "Nor lights on the night side of the planet."

They'd come out over the darkness, exactly for that reason. Lights that powerful indicated technological civilization. As did radio broadcasts. As like Khorko, Orwek had none.

"Continue scanning," she ordered. "Report any anomalies immediately. Niina, prepare to insert us into orbit. Sulevi, lower your alert status one level, but keep your crews ready."

"Aye, sir," he replied.

She watched as *Niemi* came about, accelerating down and in.

For all the good it would do.

Anari caught her eye.

"We have a full list to explore," she reminded.

Ursula nodded, but remained silent.

What if the Yarikh really were gone?

TWENTY-THREE

Anari looked around the table. Kit was there, but tinkering with some gadget in his hands when she glanced over, looking up inquisitively when he felt her eyes, then going right back to whatever he was doing when she shook her head.

She turned to Ursula and Gulnaz instead.

"Nothing," Ursula said dejectedly.

Because that one had caught the same bug that had been driving Anari. Finding the Yarikh again, after all these centuries.

Not today.

"Not nothing," Anari reminded her. "A second world that appears to be fully habitable by a wide range of species. Filled with complete ecosystems of predator and prey, but yes, nobody intelligent that we've been able to find. Or, if they are there, operating at such a low level of technology that they don't even scar the surface of the planet in ways we can identify."

"Another Khorko?" Gulnaz asked.

"Presumably," Ursula replied. "Evidence that they were here later, if only from the way the cities are only mostly collapsed, instead of the anonymous mounds we found before."

"Then you're on the right track," Kit said.

Then stopped what he was doing and looked up nervously when he felt three sets of eyes on him.

"Logic and geography?" he offered hesitantly. "First place was longer dead. Second place less longer dead, or whatever the right word is. Means that they headed this direction. I mean, I know Huff is amazing at this shit, but it was still a shot in the dark, right?"

"Correct, Kit," Ursula said. "I have a series of coordinates to explore. And yes, you are correct that it would follow Sterling Huff's logic. Are we too late?"

"Do we hop clear to the end?" he countered. "Bracket them counting backwards, if the last place on the list is dead? Or do we pick the second to last place? Is there one that looks way more interesting, and we're being too methodical?"

Anari occasionally forgot how smart Kit was in things besides tinkering. Or as an outgrowth.

He looked nervous.

"No, that's an excellent idea," Gulnaz spoke up. "I vote in favor. Mostly because the waiting at each world is killing me."

Anari understood that concept. She felt the same.

It would, however, come down to Ursula. Commander Nyman of *Niemi.*

Ursula nodded, licking her lips.

"Kit, that gives me three options, second back," Ursula said, sliding a tablet around to where he could look at it.

Like she forgot about his brains occasionally, too.

Kit put aside his gadget and studied the page, his mouth screwed up to one side and his head down. Minutes passed, with him making no other motion than blinking.

"Number three," he said, tapping the screen to bring up a new readout. "Think that's the most solid bet."

Then he slid it back, picked up his doohickey, and looked down, hunched in like he was done talking.

Letting them handle it. He was like that, too, which was part of the reason Suka Kuri had picked the man.

They shared a glance, the three of them. And a nod.

Picking straws at random, certainly, but letting Kit's Human logic slip in. And they had supplies to visit several more worlds before they needed to turn back to Isann and rendezvous with a freighter Kadyr had promised would meet them partway.

Anari just didn't want to go home empty handed.

PART FIVE

SAARI

TWENTY-FOUR

Uly had grown to appreciate Kalev and his crew. They took it with a smile that *Nubia* could outrun them by a factor of almost a third faster through warp space, gamely sailing to each meeting point to find Uly already there, scanning the vicinity to update his maps for Sterling.

As it was, this was the last stop before they arrived tomorrow at Saari, so they had to invert everything from here.

He had Kalev on the big main screen.

"You could follow us in, Uly," the man said.

"I think it would be better if you gave them a few hours to process that I was coming," Uly pushed back politely. "Remember, *Nubia* will be the biggest thing anyone there has ever seen. I expect more than a few people to grow extremely nervous."

Kalev nodded and shrugged in one long, complicated motion involving chin, shoulders, head, whiskers, and ears. Then he smiled.

"And I might have a chance to be in the same room with the Paramount when you do," he said. "I'd rather like to see him gawk at you."

Uly laughed, echoed by others on the bridge. They'd come to like the Samuur. Excellent sailors. Warm and friendly people. Much louder than the Isann, but they'd fit in with many of the Humans Uly might have introduced them to.

One of these days.

"I'll give you six hours lead," Uly offered. "If you can't manage it in that time, the joke's on you."

Kalev laughed. Some of his crew in the background did as well, so Uly suspected that *Virta* would be pushing on this last leg to eke out any extra minutes to set up their practical joke.

Uly was still coming out hot and ready for combat, in case something went wrong in that stretch and he had to face a pack of rabid badgers trying to bring down a bear.

"See you on the far side, *Nubia*," Kalev said, then cut the line.

"*Virta* has gone to warp," Haydar announced blandly. "We got anything useful to do with twelve hours down time?"

"Sterling would probably appreciate a much deeper survey of worlds from here," Uly reminded the man. "Kalev and the others gave us a bare bones trail map, but I don't think they've expanded even this far, so there are places that might prove interesting. Or maybe places where pirates might decide to build bases later. Where would you construct?"

Rude, asking a semi-reformed pirate to access those memories, but Haydar had been a terror when he'd been Nasrin's age, to hear him talk; a Mazhin raider preying on other folks instead of following the more-common trade ship path.

Possibly a good way to gather up all the young, crazy males and send them off for a few years to bother someone else.

It had even worked, because he'd gone respectable later, only to fall into the hands of *Danumash* aristocratic barbarians and then be turned into a scientist slave for several years.

Haydar's tentacles took on a thoughtful pattern.

"We need to sit here to look?" he asked.

"Nope," Uly said, then stood up. "In fact, you have the bridge.

I'm going to go get some coffee and hope that nobody sounds any alerts in the next few hours."

"No promises," Haydar countered with a laugh as Uly got to the main hatch. "Drew, I need a course that runs across this arc…"

Uly let the pirates play. It would get it out of their system now, and he had a big warship if they accidentally surprised someone at any of the spots Haydar might pick out.

He found Yanouk trailing him so silently that he almost missed her, except that he had a second shadow when he turned a corner. Stopping, he looked up at the woman.

"My office?" he asked.

She felt nervous. Yanouk nodded.

He ended with coffee before doubling back. She stayed with him, then they settled. Alone.

"Hiya," he said, mostly to set a casual tone.

She smiled.

"What do we expect to find at Saari?" she asked, even though everyone had pooled things, including three Samuur commanders.

Yanouk was asking deeper questions. Moss School questions.

"Possibly one boundary of what becomes Bastion's sphere," he replied. "Whether we draw the line short of Samuur space or include them remains to be seen. Our three friends have all been friendly, but these were the explorers sent out to challenge for primacy. *Nubia* overwhelms any Samuur squadron, so they either welcome us or decide to bring their entire fleet to bear."

"If we include them, what happens to the Ononguli Sphere?" she pressed.

"They might expand this direction, but there is wide zone in between," he described. "Maybe eventually they start allowing others. Or turn the Sphere into something like I'm doing, where other species are welcome. That might not happen in my lifetime, but we're laying cornerstones here."

She nodded. Pensive. Indecisive.

"And you'll continue to accumulate wives?" she finally asked.

Ah.

"Dan will continue to accumulate women to whom I marry as part of **her** Congress," he countered carefully. "How far each of those relationships goes after that is entirely up to each woman, presuming only that she's loyal to what we're trying to build."

Silence wrapped arms around them.

"That includes you," he reminded her. "You will define the limits of things. I appreciate that you and Nasrin are both barely adults as your cultures count such things, so I haven't gone any further than that. What would make you happy, Yanouk?"

She jolted. Uly remembered being that age. Thirty would be here soon enough for him, having spent nearly six years vanished into the darkness and reported *Lost, Presumed Killed*, knowing how the *Batyr* Navy worked.

"I don't know," she said.

Uly leaned forward and held out a hand. Tentatively, she took it, squeezing lightly.

He studied her, seeing her as an exotic beauty, rather than a giant, green, alien woman. She was also that, but she was a woman first. And a pretty one.

She smiled back at him.

Uly rose and slipped around the desk, walking slowly and obviously until he was standing just a bit over her. Slowly, he leaned in, letting her decide if she stopped him, but she didn't.

As first real kisses went, rather simple and perfunctory, but a first, not counting the wedding itself. And possibly the first time she'd ever really been kissed, because Hiko was the only Emro male she'd known in years, and he was about as introverted as one could get. Fantastic artist. Might only speak ten words on any given day.

She held him when he started to lean back, so the kissing progressed for a time. Yanouk relaxed. Calmed even.

Eventually, he leaned back and smiled at her. She blushed.

"Better?" he asked.

"Yes," she whispered. "I'd wondered, but only Dan could have answered and I wasn't ready to ask her."

"She's far older than you," he agreed. "Yeong-Suk and Katya are the elders who might have more experience. And they'll tell me what they want and when, just as you will."

"And you'll have a whole Congress of Wives at some point," she said.

"I still have my own cabin," he said. "Dan sleeps across the hall from me, most nights."

"Most?" she perked up, possibly surprised.

But then, it wasn't a topic he really felt comfortable discussing with many people. He supposed that his half-dozen wives might need to be included, though, weird as that was to contemplate.

"Most," he repeated. "Not all. If one of my other wives decided that she wanted to spend a night, I presume that you'll need to work out some scheduling system among yourselves. In your case, I think your bed would be far more comfortable than mine. But I'm not making any assumptions. Simply explaining what I think all of you need to sort out and tell me what I need to know. At your own paces."

She nodded. Grinned even, as if that kiss had finally gotten her over some hump in her mind that had been blocking her until now.

"And a Samuur wife at some point?" she asked with a tease.

"At some point, they might decide to become allies, yes," he confirmed. "I doubt that even the Samuur would move that quickly, but I intend to invite the Paramount to send a ship with us to Rayz-ian. We'll see what they do."

Another nod. Eyes gone deep and pensive in ways where she suddenly looked remarkably like Suka Kuri. And he could see where she'd be in another fifty or seventy-five years.

Still beautiful, but fully grown into herself an Exemplar of the Arts.

"Past that," he continued, "you'll be senior if Dan and Suka Kuri do end up locating Sabre and Starfare School women to add to the Congress, so you will need to have a voice when they go looking. You'll be closer than either Dan or Suka Kuri."

"And I'll have ideas on what I think you need," she said calmly.

"Exactly," he nodded now. "You are all the Congress. I'm just the symbol Dan is using to bind each of you and your cultures to the thing we're building at Bastion. The thing that will outlive me, so eventually we'll need a way to identify my successor. Or the Governor of Bastion, first Maks and now Sterling, who will step up when I retire, one of these days."

"Exemplars don't retire, Uly," she laughed. "They merely grow more obscure and complicated."

He laughed with her. Suka Kuri liked playing that game on strangers, until they discovered that she could swear and drink with the best of his sailors. Not many wanted to be outdone by an old Emro woman, to their later regret.

"If I rise to Exemplar, that will be something we deal with then," he grew serious. "I have other things to do and accomplish first. Moss, Sabre, and Starfare are all facets of it, but not complete. Bastion is the complete expression."

"Zamir Aytiev," she nodded. "Legendary demigod upon which civilizations are founded."

"Whatever you folks do when I'm dead," he grinned.

"I'll make sure that you are Emro-sized when those legends are transmitted," she grinned back. "Maybe bigger. Certainly at least a demigod, so that your children inherit some of that."

"I may not have that many children," he started to say, but she shushed him.

"I will have children," she intoned severely. "And their father will be a demigod. At least on paper."

Then she grinned and he rolled his eyes at her. This was not the awkward teen he'd first met. She had grown into a woman. And led combat assaults under Dan's command.

A most interesting person, who also happened to be a beautiful woman.

He leaned in and kissed her again. It was more comfortable this time for both of them.

It would be pleasant, having a whole Congress of interesting people who all happened to be beautiful women helping him.

Because he still had to do the impossible and bring down the *Auga Empire*.

TWENTY-FIVE

Haydar had completed a lovely surveying arc, gone to bed late, gotten up early, and started digesting his notes. Looking around *Nubia*'s bridge, he wasn't entirely certain he'd share with anybody but Uly and Dan, but that covered most of his sins when you got right down to it.

For now, they were on final approach to Saari, with Drew, Del, and Yaqub locked in and ready. And Delbert would be prepared to handle the basic things when they landed, because Haydar had already warned him.

Whole new system to interview and digest. Haydar hoped that his tentacles didn't give him away, though Uly was grinning when he looked over.

It was Uly.

"Stand by to drop," Drew called.

Then they were at the edges of the Saari system.

Kalev had warned him, so Haydar knew what to expect. *Virta* was the second largest warship in scan range, with only the fleet flagship *Tiikeri* larger.

And even then, not much. They considered *Virta* to be a Striker, that thing that Uly might have called a Forward Cruiser, so maybe this new ship was a Battlecruiser or Heavy Striker. To Haydar, it was an Interceptor roughly equivalent in size to *Batyr*. Not even as dangerous, kilo for kilo, as *Fire Diamond*.

But he wasn't going to insult them by mentioning it. They were doing pretty well with the tech they had, so remote up in this dark corner that they hadn't realized what everyone else was building.

"We're being challenged by *Tiikeri*," Del announced in a tone maybe one notch more excited that Del normally got. About where most people lived their lives, because there was an illustration of Del in the dictionary next to the word *phlegmatic*. "Uly, on your number three screen. *Virta* is snugged up next to the main station in dock."

"Challenged, Mr. Blakeslee?" Uly replied.

"Affirmative, sir," Del said. "Similar to what we got at Bastion. They're sailing out now, solo."

"Mark him and let me know when he's approaching the outer range of a 15," Uly replied. "Yaqub, you'll give him one 15dm at that range, then hold back for him to respond. Haydar, do we know what they have for a forward turret?"

"Twin 5s forward, Uly," Haydar checked against his screen. "Twin 3s aft. Medium to Heavy Interceptor, regardless of local nomenclature."

"Understood," Uly said. "Yaqub, I'm not going to order you to kill the wavebolt in flight, so give them a fist and not a lance. If they can't kill it in time, we'll just have to deal with the social and political consequences afterwards."

"Aye, sir," Yaqub replied carefully.

Haydar understood. That ship might not be able to get a kill on a 15, even at that range, though four wavebolts defensively ought to do the trick. Might still be a punch in the snout.

But Samuur culture was all about honor, and presumably *Tiikeri* needed establish its primacy in front of everyone else in orbit.

Haydar still thought that drinking contests were a more fair method, even with Humans at the table.

"Target in range," Del called.

"Fire one, Mr. Zobo," Uly ordered.

Haydar tracked it with a few tentacles, letting everything else drink in every drop of data about the two dozen or so other Interceptors he could scan. And a roughly equal number of what his mind saw as transports.

Boxier affairs, because people put way more energy into designing cool-looking warships. Hell, he could still remember his teenage years.

Nobody else moved to support *Tiikeri*. Dumb, seen from the vantage of a former pirate punk like himself. Perfectly in line with honorable single combat between champions.

Even something this lopsided.

The wavebolt tracked fast and true. *Tiikeri* let loose with both 5s, showing that their commander had at least listened to Kalev.

Whether he had *believed* until this moment was a different thing entirely.

Then he followed with both 3s, because a pair of 5s at medium range wasn't enough. Haydar wasn't sure the 3s would be, until the second one impacted square and got enough disruption that his scanners dropped the probability of a kill below ten percent.

Omnipulsars a moment later reduced that, then impact, all pretty and grand, but not deadly lethal.

"Got his attention," Yaqub announced blandly.

He'd obviously been spending too much time around Del, even starting to sound like him, which might not be the worst thing in a bridge crew, come to think of it.

"*Tiikeri* closing again," Del called. "Presumably reloading."

"6s and 2s ready and holding," Yaqub replied.

"If he fires a single 5, give him 2s first," Uly replied.

Took him a moment, then Haydar saw the logic. Using a 6 defensively against a 5 was rude. A bit of overkill. Rubbing someone's nose in it, if you will.

Not necessarily the best way to start a relationship.

"One bolt tracking inbound," Del said in a voice describing the evening's specials for the fortieth time. "One bolt only."

"Mr. Zobo, engage it as you lie," Uly said.

Two smaller bolts raced out and went boom. And *Nubia* had better gunners, so the 5 largely evaporated instead of continuing.

Big boom. Pro gunners.

Dangerous folks.

Good thing they were the good guys.

"I'm getting a hail," Del said. "Commander Eskil Haldur, on the bridge of *Tiikeri*."

"Main screen," Uly replied.

Haydar looked up to see with eyes as well.

Medium-aged Samuur male. Felt bigger than Kalev, though not Ursula. Sharp eyes narrowing as he watched *Nubia*'s menagerie of folks work. No gray along the edges, so maybe young hotshot?

Kalev Karjalainen had said that *Tiikeri* was the flagship. The pride of the fleet. The one likely to come out and get in Uly's face.

At least they'd done it according to recognized patterns of behavior.

"Greetings, Corsac Fox," Haldur said with a sharp nod. "Honor has been served. Welcome to Saari."

"Greetings, Commander Haldur, and thank you," Uly replied. "We're flying in at Commander Karjalainen's invitation to meet with your Paramount, on our way across Samuur space to the Ononguli Sphere."

"We have been eagerly anticipating you, Vanguard Fortier," Haldur said. "Allow me to escort you into dock, though we are not presently certain that your ship will be able to do so."

"Understood, Commander," Uly said. "We felt the same, but will sort it out when we get close. Awaiting your course."

Haydar tuned the rest of the conversation out. Drew, mostly, with Del, establishing that they already knew Samuur flight protocols and could follow them. Kalev's notes had been detailed.

Haydar was looking at everything else. Everyone else. Accumulating. Collating. Synthesizing. He might have been humming under his breath. It was that kind of day.

Eventually, they got close. The station was probably enormous by Samuur standards. Significantly smaller than the *Watchtower* by overall volume. And armament, but he wouldn't mention that, either.

Let them decide to buy bigger guns, now that they knew what was possible.

Or not.

They were Samuur. Haydar had a much better understanding these days of what all that entailed.

Now, how friendly would they be when they had a Corsac Fox in their henhouse?

TWENTY-SIX

Dan had the ladies polished and tough-looking today, minus only Anari who had a way cooler mission anyway. Zamira was filling her space nicely, for all the lack of size.

That was only physical. The young Isann woman had the personality and attitude.

The shuttle was about to dock. She rose, gesturing the Team to their feet and glowering at Suka Kuri to remain seated. Advisor to Uly. Not a combat goon.

Regardless of what the woman might say otherwise.

Clunk. Thunk. Bang.

"I have positive pressure, Commander."

"Open us up," Dan said.

Arms were holstered or slung. Honor meant that you came armed, but you were not displaying them as a threat.

Not until a threat came at you.

Dan wondered if the Paramount had been warned just how much his three other commanders had explained to the strangers in preparation for this visit.

It was nice to look omniscient, when it was really just good planning.

And listening.

Three Samuur warriors greeted them when Dan emerged behind Ciah and Yanouk. Armed but slung. Also tough-looking, but not looking tough about it.

It was a fine line to walk, and they managed it nicely.

"Commander Sheridan Chastain," she said to the one in the middle. One woman bounded by two men. She liked them already. "Escort for the Corsac Fox."

"Yes, ma'am," the woman said with a sharp nod.

Dan looked around and cleared the room. Uly and Suka Kuri entered a moment later.

"This way," the guard leader called, immediately turning and leading the group through into a corridor and then to a largish conference room set with tables around a rectangle made of aluminum with a faux-marble top.

Kalev Karjalainen sat next to an older male, with Commander Eskil Haldur on the far side.

The three Samuur guards took up positions behind the Paramount, so Dan nodded her ladies to do the same, with Nasrin joining her at the table. As usual. Framing Uly and Suka Kuri.

The Paramount gawked, but only a little. One male in the center —Uly—not all that physically imposing. Three very distinct alien females protecting and advising him.

"Welcome, Corsac Fox," the fellow began. "I am Paramount Aarne Kallio, leader of the Samuur. You know Commander Karjalainen and have at least met Commander Haldur. Honor has been served. What brings you to Saari?"

Dan noted that Kalev was quietly grinning to himself, while Haldur was much more serious. Intense. Felt young, based on what Uly had said, so she presumed that he might be a Samuur equivalent to Uly. Young, brilliant, and lucky.

"Originally, our destination was merely Rayzian, the capital world of the Ononguli Sphere," Uly replied. "Having met *Virta* and its consorts, we decided to detour to Saari in order to better establish relations. Our goal is still beyond, but we can spare a few days here."

Dan nodded. House call, and not much more. Unless you folks wanted to turn it into something bigger. The Isann had jumped into that mud puddle with both feet and a great deal of laughter, once they realized how badly it could have gone for them.

And were all in today.

"Karjalainen tells me that you might welcome one of our vessels traveling with you?" Paramount Kallio pressed.

Ah, that's why Haldur is here. Local hero. Probably First Commander, with Kalev maybe second, depending on some of the more senior folks on staff duties these day.

"We would," Uly nodded. "The Samuur systems are roughly halfway between my new capital and the current border of Ononguli space, so you will meet each other eventually. I think it would be better if you came with us, as our visit will be a grand, celebratory thing."

"Adding a wife to your Congress?" Kallio noted. "Karjalainen has explained."

"And these are two of those women who represent the greater whole," Suka Kuri spoke. "All but one are aboard your station at the moment, with the other traveling aboard *Niemi* as a guest of Commander Nyman."

Dan watched that reminder jar the three men. Uly had already recruited two of Kalev's ships to help on his own missions. Would the Paramount accept that? Or would his honor take things a different direction?

"The local region, while dark, is bounded on all sides by neighbors, Paramount," Uly offered. "It is my hope to meet all of them and invite them to trade and visit. To become friends, and perhaps even allies in my greater war to save the galaxy from the *Auga*."

"Can you stop them?" Haldur asked now. "Kalev tells me that they have thousands of systems and enormous fleets of warships even larger than yours."

"I do not have to conquer the *Auga Empire*," Uly countered. "Merely make them respect a border and behave. If they push, we will have to push back, but the Empire is a lethargic creature. Sclerotic in its bureaucracy. Slow in all things, because they expect to spend millennia in the process. We can hold the line today and perhaps communicate with them. That is my purpose."

"And the Ononguli support you?" Haldur asked.

Obviously, he'd asked Kalev a *lot* of questions in the last few hours.

"They do," Uly nodded. "They helped me assemble my new base in half the time it might have taken. The *Vatazhko*—the Lord of the Endless Plains herself—traveled to Bastion to invite us on this current mission. Had *Virta* arrived a month earlier, they would have gotten a chance to meet her directly. She will welcome you at Rayzian."

Dan watched a quick conversation flow between the three men with ears and whiskers as much as looks. Not as good as three Mazhin, but she was already used to reading tentacles. Uly and Suka Kuri were probably following the conversation in real time.

Finally, they came to a consensus, but from the looks of things, most of it had already been laid out by Kalev.

The other two hadn't been listening.

Or simply hadn't believed him.

"I would be honored if you would accept the assistance of *Tiikeri* on your mission," Haldur broke the silence. "We can be loaded and ready to travel shortly. Kalev tells me that you might also buy supplies here and top things off?"

"We brought a variety of trade goods," Dan finally spoke up. This part was her job. "Kalev, Ursula, and Matti had lists of things that they thought would be valuable here at Saari."

And she was on a first-name basis with all three commanders. Uly could charm just about anybody.

Two of the three men were surprised.

Not listening or not believing. Dan smiled.

"If space could be cleared in a nearby warehouse, we could offload in two blocks," she continued. "One, a set of gifts for the Paramount and our new friends, the Samuur. The other, larger set has things that we would trade for supplies and possibly local currency and credit that could become the basis of a commercial trade bank."

Foreign words, but Rabiu and Ethir promised her that they had talismanic power with merchants. Any merchants. And those dorks would know. The three warriors were a little lost. Well, the Paramount seemed to be following her, but he was as much a political figure as military, so she would expect some level of bureaucratic knowledge.

"You expect that much trade?" Kallio asked after a blink.

"I hope it will foster such trade," Uly replied. "That it will draw the Samuur into the wider region, where they might see and meet others. And trade with them. The current state of technology available exceeds Saari's industrial base. We'd like to help fix that, both with trade to Bastion as well as establishing trade corridors into Ononguli space. And letting the great Mazhin merchant ships know you are here and open for commerce."

Silly, but capitalism was a religion to the Khet and something of a pastime for the Ononguli. It would work. Especially if it added a whole new chain of links in Uly's planned Silk Road.

Paramount Kallio turned to Kalev, as if acknowledging things said and not believed.

Not until now.

Dan smiled. Kalev grinned. The Paramount nodded.

"It begins," he said simply.

Dan approved. This was still only a beginning.

TWENTY-SEVEN

Haydar had needed an extra day to process it all, so he'd kept silent until Uly and the others got back from the station.

Oh, there'd be more things later. State Dinners and trade delegations, but that sort of thing could be delegated anyway.

"You won't believe what I found," he told Uly as they got settled.

Just the two of them in Uly's main office.

"Probably not," Uly nodded. "Unless you found another Lacium or Taeli that needs to be visited and given a stern talking to."

Haydar felt all of his tentacles go straight out sideways, then bounce in such that he might need fingers to detangle them.

"How do you do that?" he asked Uly.

But it was Uly.

"Found another pirate stronghold that needs to be stomped on?" Uly asked.

"Maybe," Haydar offered. "No direct signals or anything. But I was running a wider scan than normal, based on how Sterling likes to do it. Plus, we introduced enough parallax on things along the way to get a nice, stereoscopic view. I know how much that matters to species limited to eyesight."

Uly just laughed, but he understood how much richer Mazhin life was with tentacles.

"What did you find?"

"A system not that far outside of the Ononguli Sphere's most ambitious borders," Haydar nodded. "Located close. Off several trade routes that all run nearby, but not connected to any of them."

"And it jumped out at you because?"

"Uly, if I was drawing a random map intended to build my dream pirate stronghold somewhere, it would be almost a perfect duplicate of what we scanned," Haydar huffed. "It practically has a sign next to it saying *Beware of Criminals*. At least in my head."

"And you want to go visit?" Uly asked. "Before we enter Ononguli space?"

"I'm willing to bet that ninety-seven percent of the free citizens you might find roaming around will be Ononguli," Haydar replied, watching Uly bristle.

Free citizens.

His language was not accidental. Not with that man.

He and his close adopted kin had been **slaves** of the *Danumash* Humans for years. He knew exactly what he was saying to this terrible warlord. And why.

"Do we ask Aarne Kallio to send more than *Tiikeri* with us?" Uly asked in a low, lethal tone.

Haydar considered the Paramount. Honor defined the Samuur.

This wasn't an entirely honorable course of action. Not to sneak up on someone's moorage, intending to annihilate anything that moved if they fired a single shot.

Haydar understood that Uly would warn them. Give them a chance.

Most fool pirates would piss that opportunity away.

"We don't know who's there," Haydar countered. "I'm willing to bet one Mazhin Shilling that we'll find folks. And a second that they will be pirates. Past that, I don't think that Samuur ships are up to tangling with modern Ononguli craft. It would be like having Sterling and *Batyr* on your flank with *Tiikeri*, but not as good. No, I take that back. Eskil Haldur is supposedly the best they have as a commander, so I'll tentatively stack him against Sterling and Mr. Huff will likely still win on points, but it might be closer."

Because he'd seen how good young Sterling had turned out as a combat commander.

Uly nodded at that.

"Let me talk to Haldur," Uly said. "Maybe we ask them to send a few ships along to clean up whatever mess we make. Or, if you somehow guessed wrong, it potentially establishes a forward location where the Samuur can build their own base. Close to the Sphere and able to claim a portion of a new border, while also turning into a trade depot later."

Haydar smiled at that. Uly was always several steps ahead of everyone.

Already, he was helping the Samuur build themselves into a regional player, and he'd only met them a month ago.

But size equaled power, and Uly would need that when crunch time came.

"Anything else?" Uly asked.

"Warn Dan, in case she needs to bring along a small army of giant, tough furballs?" Haydar asked.

"Something," Uly agreed.

Haydar rose, message delivered. Uly stopped him at the hatch.

"Haydar?" he said.

Haydar turned to look with eyes.

"Thank you."

Haydar nodded.

Uly understood. That was all he really ever asked.

TWENTY-EIGHT

Uly had invited Commander Haldur to a small, quiet dinner. And let The Spatula get a little nuts with his notes on Samuur cuisine.

Showing off, but that was what Vahid did, any chance you gave him.

Just four of them tonight. He and Dan. Commander Haldur and his First Officer Hemmo Lindholm. Lindholm seemed almost Haldur's opposite in many ways. Calm. Deliberate. Logical. Rational. Hardly gave off any emotional signatures, while Haldur was a bundle of energy and fur intending to change the galaxy.

And charming in how he did it. Big, but friendly, like the cat he reminded Uly of. Emotional. Inquisitive. Constantly vibrating with energy.

"And from there, Haydar thinks that we might want to bring along perhaps a couple of other vessels, either to anchor the system when we depart, or help clean it up," Uly concluded. "Your thoughts, gentlemen?"

Haldur was all in. Not entirely surprising. Lindholm was more cautious. Again, as expected.

"How good are Ononguli warships, Vanguard Fortier?" Lindholm asked quietly when Haldur turned to him.

"Kalev gave you his scans of *Batyr*?" Uly asked, waiting for a nod. "Most pirate vessels will be less dangerous, one-on-one. *Batyr* was at the top end for pirates of that class when I first captured it. *Nubia* is small for a fast dreadnought, but far more heavily armed. We should be able to stand off anyone giving us trouble."

He'd already given them his abbreviated history, starting with *King Hewitt II*. Again, with more questions asked this time. Deeper ones. More cogent and focused.

"*Tiikeri* should be able to take one, then," Haldur noted. "Possibly two, but only two. If we bring other ships, they will be *Virta*'s equivalent. And we do not have that squadron, though they are off on more honorable missions."

"If we are looking at an Ononguli pirate outpost, *Virta* and a couple of loads of combat infantry might be all that is needed to hold the place," Uly replied. "*Nubia* can destroy them if I have to, but they are more likely to surrender before that happens. And I'd prefer fewer pirate bases operating in the region. Doubly so as Ononguli raiders will find out about the Samuur soon enough, and you are not equipped enough to stand them off yet."

"Yet," Haldur noted. "How soon can we fix that?"

"As soon as your yards can be upgraded to turn out Strikers," Uly said. "Double the size of *Tiikeri*, more or less, with more wavebolts in bigger diameters. Or buy them secondhand from others. I doubt that the Ononguli would part with many, but I can ask the *Vatazhko* for a favor here."

"You would do that for the Samuur?" Lindholm asked, ever logical.

"You are an honorable people," Uly speared him with a look.

A bit mean, but the man swelled with pride. Both of them did. And one old Light Striker wouldn't alter the balance of power in this region, but it would convince Ononguli pirates to stay away.

Or at least behave in port while trading.

"I will speak with the Paramount," Haldur announced. "Perhaps *Virta* and *Lehto* can both be spared, along with a transport. Do you really believe that we could hold such a place?"

"I am allied with the Ononguli," Uly turned stern. "And will place that system under my protection, so anyone causing you trouble is insulting my honor. That will not stand."

Nods. Sharp fellows.

He turned to Dan.

"How many troops would you need, if this turned out to be another Taeli?" he asked, mostly so she could show off in front of their new allies.

"If we don't have to storm it under fire, like we did Lacium, perhaps a few hundred," she nodded. "Assuming trained infantry prepared to accept orders from alien commanders. Lacium was a little iffy with a thousand troops, but not folks I had trained with long enough to fully trust. I've kept the best one hundred and fifty, and trained them up to where they meet my standards."

Then she turned a glare on Haldur.

"I'll need your elite infantry for this," she said simply.

He gulped a bit, but nodded.

"So I will convey," he said.

Nothing more. Nothing more needed.

The Samuur were an honorable people.

They would make terrible foes.

And fantastic allies.

Vahid opened the hatch as if he'd been listening and timing things. And he probably had.

"Now, my friends, I believe dessert is upon us," Uly said. "Let us celebrate a new beginning."

TWENTY-NINE

Drew didn't go in for all that military razz. Uniforms and polish and stuff.

He flew. Uly let him. And kept finding him more interesting ships to fly, though Drew wasn't sure if the man could top *Nubia*. Or what that would look like.

They were at the last drop before trouble, at least in his head. Swoop down and say hello to folks who might be dumb enough to shoot first.

Light Interceptor against Fast Dreadnought.

Easy way to get yourself splattered.

Drew reviewed his logs. Haydar's scans, supplementing everything Sterling had been able to create with several thousand years' worth of databases to synthesize.

The BEST way to fly, when you could predict where trouble might den itself. And Haydar was something of an expert there.

Drew locked things in and flipped a switch on his board.

"*Tiikeri* and *Virta*, this is Drew Roscoe, aboard *Nubia*," he announced. "Transmitting both of you a flight plan. You will not deviate from this until we land. Am I clear?"

"You are, *Nubia*," Commander Haldur replied evenly.

Just making sure.

"You'll be coming out on my forward port corner, *Tiikeri*," Drew continued. "*Virta* on my low starboard. Down one full flight level and we'll be out at a range that any station will not be able to engage us. Your immediate job will be defensive, but be prepared to drop into pursuit mode if anyone decides to run on us."

"Understood, Drew," the Samuur man said.

Drew turned back to Uly, ceding things back to him now that he had his choreography *just so*.

Always tricky, when mixing technology levels and unknown crews, but Uly had assured him that those folks would go junkyard dog on someone if they had to.

Drew nodded. Uly matched it.

"Samuur Squadron, engage and close," Uly ordered. "We'll be right behind you and drop simultaneously."

Drew ignored everything except his screens. Both ships vanished in a blip. Drew keyed his system and let the autopilot take over, just this once.

He could probably nail the timing perfect, but it would look better if all the ships appeared within a second and at close quarters. And it would make any pirates think that the Samuur ships were as modern as they were, which would go a long ways to shutting down any shenanigans before they got out of hand.

And...gone.

THIRTY

Yaqub would have liked to have been a full-time pilot, but his options had been to take over as Gunner on *Nubia* when Mister Huff got promoted, or follow the Human onto *Batyr*.

Better that Bello have that gig. *Nubia* was way more fun, and Yaqub had known that *Batyr* would see a lot less action in Uly's future.

Nubia would be at the center of things.

Like today.

They dropped out of warp and Yaqub could practically taste the unwashed masses of Ononguli over there. Not Khet. Wouldn't even understand a mister gate. Plus, Khet would have arranged things in a different pattern. Two or three medium-sized stations with craft around them, rather than the solitary larger one in the middle.

Not Taeli or Lacium, but still hefty. Badly designed, though. Looked like 6dm mounts on the sides he could see. Facing 15s? Only question at that point would be how many of you survived to surrender.

Because you sure as hell weren't hurting *Nubia* at this range.

"Yaqub, your screen two," Haydar muttered from next to him.

"Three ships that look dangerous enough to count. The rest are all transports with turrets welded on after-factory."

Yaqub had been trained by Sterling Huff. To Mister Huff's expected standards of someone daring to publicly call himself a *Gunner*. And Yaqub had gone through all the training videos Mister Huff had designed and recorded.

Three steps beyond anything he'd ever done in Khet service. Four steps beyond most Khet transports and pirates.

Mister Huff was very particular. And had managed to distill down his unconscious genius into a series of steps and patterns.

Yaqub had his Gunner Certification hanging proudly on the bulkhead in his cabin.

He locked onto the farthest target first. Then walked his targeting priorities backwards, assuming that even the 6dm defensive turrets could hit the closest folks, to say nothing of *Tiikeri* and *Virta* taking bites.

Then he waited.

"Uly, I have a navigational channel," Haydar said. "Civilian stuff. Standard sailing rules and movement lanes. System calls itself Daicia."

"Give me an override signal," Uly called.

Yaqub grinned. Every channel. Every radio. Everywhere, including your favorite bumpbash music station, was about to be broadcasting Uly's voice.

Hell of a way to say hello to some pirates.

"*Daicia Station*, this is the Corsac Fox," Uly announced. "I am taking control of this system in the name of *Vatazhko* Anna Shevchenko. You will strike your colors and stand down."

Yaqub wondered what it must look like to be on the short end of such silliness. Suddenly looking at two Interceptors and a Forward Striker, because they would see the size instead of the firepower.

Like it mattered today.

"I have a runner," Haydar announced. "Only one."

Yaqub was glad he hadn't bet the man. He'd have lost.

But then, scuttlebutt said that Haydar Ramezani had a lot of experience as a Mazhin pirate in his younger days.

Yaqub checked his boards. Number Three thought he could slip out the back and get away. Possibly could, if Uly felt like letting him, because it might require both Samuur ships to take him if he was that sharp and that frightened.

Run at first provocation, though? Got to be a lot of warrants involved.

"Yaqub, give him one wavebolt," Uly ordered.

Yaqub's movement was automatic. Sterling Huff demanded that.

Ka-CHUNK as a single 15dm MONSTER began tracking. Fool over there MIGHT be able to get out of range of it. Maybe.

Nobody else stepped up to engage that enormous wavebolt as it began slaloming through traffic. Wouldn't have even taken much. Couple of 2s or 3s would have ruptured it enough to do the job at the distance it had to cover.

Assuming you wanted that next 15 coming for you...

Yaqub figured that most of these folks already knew what a jail cell smelled like, and were just waiting their next arrest.

"Tracking true," Yaqub offered automatically. "Fifteen seconds to impact. Target has begun to engage with one neutron omnipulsar only. Looks like someone didn't have their wavebolt launchers online."

"Yaqub, can you wing him?" Uly asked.

Took him a second to translate that into Khet. Fin hit, not wings.

Human vernacular was *weird*.

Uhm...?

"Stand by," he offered, typing a couple of commands and hoping that he knew what he was doing.

Even at this range, a 15 was going to be a couple of wallops to the eyes and gills.

Still, maybe he could fin the fool.

Impact. Big and bright on the screens. Probably visible to the naked eye if you were looking the right direction.

Hopefully, he'd adjusted the warhead to go off just a wee bit premature. Wavebolt set to fist instead of plasma spike, because Uly hadn't ordered any different and Yaqub had figured a 15dm spike would be more like a blowtorch against a can of tomatoes.

Heh. Gotcha.

One Ononguli Probe, rolling over and starting to float to the top of the tank.

Didn't even look more than mildly scorched, which was a bonus. Spread the detonation across the entire shield facing by going off early, knocking everything down and blackening scales but not carving them all that bad.

"Daicia System moorage, you will surrender right now, or I will finish you off," Uly announced.

Yaqub gulped. With most conductors, that was more of a bluff than anything.

Uly was making folks an ugly, ugly promise that you better behave.

Or be cooked.

Except that these yahoos all looked Ononguli, so he was offering to crack their horns off.

And could do it.

Yaqub locked hard on the other two targets and turned the power on his targeting sensors up a notch. To the point that EVERYONE would see the scanner beams reflecting randomly off hulls.

Anyone feeling frisky? I got a gaff and a club here.

And the name Corsac Fox seemed to work its magic here as well, because nobody else wanted to play.

"Surrenders coming in on all channels, Uly," Haydar announced after a few seconds.

"Excellent. Yaqub?" Uly said, drawing one of his eyes back. "Nice shooting. Sterling will be proud of you when he hears."

Humans blushed. He'd learned that. Khet unconsciously telescoped their headcrest and fins. Meant the same thing. Autonomous response, but it brought a smile.

He'd done good.

THIRTY-ONE

Uly studied the collection of conductors Dan had assembled. As at Taeli, anyone wanting to come had been welcome to travel to the station to hear him in person. Ask him things in person.

Learn their fate in person.

All of them were Ononguli. About a quarter female across the thirty or so faces looking up at him as he stood on the stage. Mostly men.

Among the captive pirate conductors were Bohuslav Kovalenko, who had gotten the sharp end when *Vector Freelancer* got hit, and Iryna Bondarenko, whose *Kingfisher* supposedly only had two male crew members in forty from what Dan had mentioned.

Kovalenko had stayed in a back corner, presumably nursing his grievances. He remained silent now.

"And that's it?" Iryna Bondarenko called from the center below him. "Just like that, you're ousting us and installing a group of furry aliens to take over?"

Several other conductors grumbled restively around her, but Dan had the entire Combat Team up on the stage. Armed. And forty troopers around the edges of the auditorium, an even mix of Dan's people and Eskil's. They kept their sour silence at the provocation, but they'd been warned ahead of time that Uly intended to make this a point of his own honor. That way, that the Samuur didn't have to.

Uly locked hard on Bondarenko. He hadn't mentioned to her what was coming when he got to Rayzian. She might be far enough away from the Clan center to not know or care.

"I have claimed Daicia system," Uly stated. "It is outside of Ononguli space entirely, according to every map I have consulted. Additionally, I note that there is no planetside habitation, so this is not a colony. This a trading post in orbit. Nothing more. As to the Samuur, I hired them to assist me in surveying this sector and they will be establishing law and order as the Corsac Fox sees fit. I invite all of you to share your last year's trade records with the folks I will leave in charge here. I'm sure some of you are even legitimate businessfolk. The rest of you might be passably slandered as pirates, and by now most of you should have heard my opinion of piracy. Plus, I am literally leaving here to go directly to Rayzian, to meet with the *Vatazhko* herself and sign a new treaty. I'll be happy to transmit to her a list of all of your names and ships."

Uly watched them recoil at the vehemence in his voice.

"Alternatively, you can depart and go commit your piracy in Imperial Sectors Eight or Nine. Not in Fourteen, or I will hunt you down and annihilate you," he growled at the mob. "I am the Warlord of the Spinward Reaches, and that includes all of Fourteen up to the treaty boundaries of the Ononguli Sphere. That is my final word on the topic. If you have specific questions, you may get in touch with me directly tomorrow, but we are done here. The Samuur will be exercising authority until I or the *Vatazhko* appoint a permanent governor to replace the folks handling any technical duties now."

He didn't wait for any response or opinions, because he knew they would only anger him.

The *Vatazhko* could crack the whip on them and make them permanent outlaws if she chose. Uly would dump this mess in her lap, after suggesting that a permanent Samuur trade base linking to Bastion was his favored outcome.

The Ononguli in front of him weren't evil. Just undersocialized and lazy. Easier to be pirates than merchants. Easier to take than trade.

Easier, until a bigger hammer came along. He had a maul, and was willing to use it as a threat to get folks to behave.

Even *Vector Freelancer* hadn't suffered that much damage beyond needing a full reboot of all systems from a cold launch. Dan still had detailed Katya to watch Kovalenko personally, in case he got out of hand.

Then Uly was through a door and into a side corridor, where he moved to the command post that actually operated the station. Administrator Pavlenko waited nervously, obviously concerned that Uly intended to break his horns.

Instead, Uly moved to a long table and sat, gesturing the Ononguli man to join him. Dan and Suka Kuri did as well, with Eskil and Kalev needing a moment to do the same.

Calmer. Quieter. Everyone sitting around talking, instead of Uly issuing angry orders.

At least he was trying to keep from getting angry.

"And that's it?" Pavlenko asked into the abrupt silence.

Uly pointed to Kalev.

"Commander Karjalainen will speak in my name," Uly said. "I'm leaving all of the Samuur troops to handle station security, so you will send off all the people you currently employ. Or I'll haul them to Rayzian with me and tell the *Vatazhko* to find them new jobs."

It was a useful magic wand, being able to invoke Anna's authority. And she would do it. One less thorn in her side, especially where a new trade route was stirring to be born. And Uly more tightly bound to her cause, which was always protecting the Sphere from the inevitable *Auga* next attack, though it wasn't due for years, hopefully.

"And the Samuur will own this system?" Pavlenko asked.

"I honestly don't know," Uly offered. He could do that. "Anna might decide to extend her current boundaries this far, knowing that the Samuur can anchor and protect trade lines running back to Bastion. If she doesn't, then I intend to turn this into a free port, which means no pirates. No cargoes traded off the books. No Sphere or Corsac Fox laws being broken. And while I could do so, I also will not be subjecting all of your accounting books to a forensic analysis, prior to tomorrow. Expect that when I return, however, and remind anyone else coming in after this that they might be better suited to just keep flying. Am I clear on that point?"

"You are, Corsac Fox."

Uly hated being the *Big Bad Evil Guy*, but there were times when the Corsac Fox had to speak instead of Uly Fortier. When he had to make a statement that would get the attention of even hard-headed Ononguli.

Pavlenko turned to Eskil and Kalev now. Studied them as an entirely new species, which made sense. Until yesterday, Daicia had been facing the wrong direction. Looking back at the Ononguli Sphere instead of out *Into Darkness*.

They weren't, after all, Isann.

"*Virta* will remain as a guardian?" Pavlenko asked carefully.

"Honor demands that we protect you," Kalev answered in a deep, angry voice. "Uly has extended his writ to Daicia and asked the Samuur of Saari to help him make it safe for travelers."

It was useful, watching the man's entire career reset in a few seconds. From pirate innkeeper to merchant governor as he blinked a few times, then looked to Uly.

"My scans suggest that they are not up to current Horde technological standards?" he asked in a sideways kind of voice. Hopeful, but exceedingly nervous about what he was saying.

"They are not today, but will be soon," Uly agreed. "I intend to ask Anna to open such a trade with Saari, to help modernize them to galactic standards."

Pavlenko nodded, lips pursed as he considered something interesting from the way his face held perfectly frozen.

"Administrator?" Suka Kuri leaned in and smiled. "Have you considered asking Uly to write you letters of introduction for some of the conductors around here? Perhaps sending your friends on to Saari with their goods for sale? That would certainly save you the effort of inspecting and certifying some of those cargoes, after all."

Uly appreciated the way she finessed that whole idea. Tell the pirates to go to Saari to dispose of stolen goods, so that they didn't have to face Uly's wrath.

"I had explored that option in my head, yes," Pavlenko replied carefully. "Corsac Fox?"

"As long as you understand that their behavior will be on your head," Uly threatened him with a grim smile. "Perhaps you should suggest that a few of them sell armed vessels on as well. The Samuur could then disassemble those ships and learn how to build better, while you also began locating tools and machinery that their factories will need as they retool. I'm sure there is enormous lock-in profit in such a venture."

All words that Piruz and Rabiu had taught him. How to dangle carrots in front of capitalists.

Pavlenko pondered that. Turned to Kalev and Eskil querulously.

"I think that would be a grand idea," Eskil leaned in. "And I will also include letters of introduction, as will Commander Karjalainen. Trade through Daicia would be an excellent first step to introducing our commanders to the Ononguli Sphere."

Uly smiled. It was a start.

And he was just going to have to end up running that much later getting to Rayzian.

At the same time, Anna would appreciate the work he was doing.

PART SIX

TRAIFFE

THIRTY-TWO

Ursula had come to far better appreciate the Human Sterling Huff. She'd rarely had maps anywhere near as detailed, even close to Saari. Here, he had practically given her roadmaps with street names, for places nobody had visited in millennia.

At least metaphorically. System breakdowns with counts of planets and rough orbital periods. Habitability scores, apparently, based on some system he hadn't included, but had rated every single place he'd been able to locate and identify.

She could have sailed directly to Traiffe from Saari, were she of a mind, and done it in almost a least-time trip, just knowing where to sail to avoid slowing down.

And now they were here.

Kit's *Number Three*, when she'd tasked him with pulling a whisker out of a jar.

Traiffe.

Ursula glanced over at Anari and Gulnaz. Caught their glances. Their trepidation.

"Niina, how long?" she asked.

"Three minutes to drop, Commander," her Pilot replied without looking up from her boards.

But they'd flown together for long enough that her Commander's foibles were probably pretty predictable.

"Attention," she said, opening the ship-wide intercom. "We are about to arrive at our next destination. All hands stand by for whatever emergencies are likely to erupt at such an inopportune moment."

Ursula cut the line and focused on her breathing. Counting heartbeats as a way to measure those last light-minutes until arrival.

Was this the place? Kit had pulled it out of a random hash of data, using Human logic that was utterly opaque to Ursula. And he was the only Human present against which she could measure such things, beyond the memory of Uly and Dan.

In one corner, Gulnaz remained quiet. Almost invisible, but she had spoken of how this was Kit's mission and Anari's responsibility.

She glanced over and noted that Kit was sliding a set of parts and tools into a bag he'd brought with him. Ever fidgeting, but her life support systems were running eighteen percent more efficiently and everything smelled nicer than she could remember.

She'd keep the man, were he available, but understood that Kit wanted to return to his own kind. Or at least his tribe.

Home.

Was this the place where the Yarikh had gone? And were they Human?

Was this some fabled lost tribe, because Anari had mentioned that even *Danumash* and *Batyr* were merely modern incarnations, without a true record of where their original homeworld might be found?

Shortly, they would know more.

"Dropping," Niina announced, even as the stars returned and Ursula's boards began to fill with data.

Radio signals on several bands. Objects moving in orbit. Technological life.

"Commander, we're already being hailed."

THIRTY-THREE

Anari was on pins and needles, locking all of these memories so that she could repeat them to Yanouk and Suka Kuri when she saw them next. Her written reports would be detailed, but Anari understood that Moss School considered oral history to be the highest form of transmission, because you were required to translate yourself across cultures and idioms, frequently on the fly.

That you could do so was the mark of a true Scholar, though Anari wasn't there yet.

Yet.

"Commander, we're already being hailed," Comms Officer Iikka Cemaletdin spoke, his shock and disbelief evident.

Then she looked closer and saw several small vessels already detaching from the largest station and turning bow-on to *Niemi*.

Warships? Pirates? Yarikh?

"Anari?" Ursula asked.

"On main screen and broadcasting, please," Anari said, waiting for a long moment when the screen flickered. Then she switched to Yarikh, blessing all those hours spent reading and listening to logs. "Greetings. I am Anari Supasei of the Emro. We are multi-species emissaries of the Corsac Fox, tasked with locating the Yarikh, having discovered and recovered the ancient Yarikh Skyhawk once named *Invincible*. The records of Selene Praxis led us here. We come as friends."

Anari held her breath as that got transmitted. It was only a thin hope on her part that they still spoke the ancient tongue, this many lifetimes later. At the same time, technology tended to stockpile old language. New words might be added, but the core of things tended to remain essentially unchanged once you had a broad educational socialization.

And hope.

A face appeared finally and Anari smiled.

Human. Not a subtype she knew, but even with the few that Uly and Dan had rescued along the way, she could see that much.

Skin: Closer to Uly's reddish brown than Dan's ochre.

Hair: Black like Uly's. Curly like Dan's.

Face: Thin, with a prominent nose and chin, somewhat offset by a wide forehead.

Gender: First approximation Female, with elements about the eyes and jaw that suggested Dan rather than all the males.

Size: Felt Human. She'd lived on *Nubia* long enough to appreciate that every ship was different, and *Nubia* felt like it fit Kit and this strange woman watching her.

Age: Medium adult. She had a presence like Selene Praxis, who was a decade or so Dan's elder, but not much past their physical peak, which usually came in that decade after Dan's current age.

"Emro?" the woman asked in a rich, warm tone.

Anari unbuckled and rose, watching those eyes flicker as she watched a screen showing all of *Niemi*'s bridge.

"I am Emro," Anari nodded, then gestured. "Most of the crew is Samuur. Gulnaz Isakov is Isann. Kit Simonson is Human. We believe he is a close relative of yours. Kit?"

Anari looked over and saw the man finally manage to close his jaw and unbuckle, standing slowly. She knew he spoke some Yarikh, but was hardly fluent, to say nothing of conversational.

Still, he was one of the few Humans who could be spared for this mission, when Uly and Dan had so much more to do.

Kit held up a hand, palm out. That jarred the strange woman to do the same, her eyes growing larger and her mouth falling a little open.

"Kit Simonson, why did you come?" she demanded.

Kit turned to look at her and Anari realized that he didn't understand the woman.

Quickly she translated. Kit nodded, stepping down to center until he was close to Ursula, taking a moment to think, from the look on his face. Centered on the screen that woman was watching. He drew a breath, still nodding minutely, as if having some internal conversation.

"Because we thought we were alone," he replied.

THIRTY-FOUR

Kit could feel his heart hammering and his mind yammering like he was in a club somewhere with the music turned up to painful earthquake.

He heard Anari repeat his words to the woman, but didn't follow much more than the tone.

He was a mechanic, not a Moss or Sabre School badass like she was.

Still, the woman on the screen flinched. Almost recoiled like he'd slapped her.

She spoke. Gibberish and gobbledygook.

Anari repeated it in Spacer. Modern *Auga* that everyone else spoke.

"Where is your home, Kit?" he heard.

Kit laughed. He wasn't entirely sure where he was. Still, he'd studied Sterling's maps enough to understand. And a good mechanic always knows where he is in three-dimensional space.

So he turned his shoulders and found the spot in his head. Held up his right arm and pointed. Horizontal and down a little, but not too much.

"About thirteen thousand light-years that way," he said, turning back as Anari relayed it.

The woman flinched again.

"How did you find us?" she asked, turning a little more serious than merely deadly as her eyes narrowed.

"Selene Praxis parked her ship above a black hole," he said. "Marked by a pair of blue giants to show the path. The Isann found it three thousand years ago, but then fell into barbarism and couldn't recover it. The Corsac Fox and Anari here found the map in the *Karaŋgılıkka* and found the ship. It's intact, after all this time, so we sailed it home and read the logs. Past that, everyone fell into barbarism and is only now climbing out again. Including *Batyr* and *Danumash*."

He fell silent, listening to the tall woman relay all that with a lot of floweriness added in. Probably side channels of explanation, because he'd used some idioms. Couldn't be helped.

How the hell do you say hello to a group of cousins that didn't even know you existed five minutes ago?

More pause on their end.

"What happened to the Yarikh?" he pressed, aware that he'd just been elevated to *Speak* for the Corsac Fox.

Him. Silly, really, but Uly required it, and had smartly picked him out of the three of them.

Gotta make him look good.

Her eyes got scowly. Kit kept a smile welded on his. Innocence, because he honestly had no clue.

And had seen four ships moving out to frame them. All kinda small, but so were a pack of piranha circling.

"We departed from the wider galaxy," she said via Anari.

Kit was pretty sure he'd missed something. Or she had.

Then he thought about it for a long moment. Empty worlds, abandoned to entropy for dozens of centuries and falling in on themselves. Isann and Samuur only recently returning to the stars, possibly in the lifetimes of folks on the ground somewhere.

And the Yarikh had withdrawn.

He nodded to himself as it made sense.

"Can we come visit?" he asked, letting his backbrain find the concepts. "There are other Human worlds out there that didn't know about you. And neighbors stirring in your closer region, so I'm pretty sure that someone other than us would have stumbled into your orbit eventually. We want to talk and maybe trade, but mostly find answers to questions posed by historians and philosophers."

"What questions?" she asked sternly by tone.

"Whatever happened to the Yarikh, for one," he answered. "And are we all one people? I usually serve on a ship with a dozen different species working together. Human, Mazhin, Thogin, Emro, Khet, Ononguli, Zuath, Ugotha, Isann, and even Samuur."

He could stretch that far. Folks back in Engineering had turned out to be pretty normal dorks, once they got used to each other. Nerds.

Sailors.

"How many Humans are with you on this ship?" she asked.

"Just me," Kit replied. "Not a lot of us this far from home, and the Corsac Fox is busy trying to stop the *Auga* from conquering the galaxy. But he needed at least one, when the Emro and Samuur offered to look at old coordinates to see if they could find the Yarikh after all. If you come to Bastion, a dozen. Eventually, I know that the Corsac Fox wants to return to our worlds, but that's later. He's got to save the galaxy first."

"Save it from whom?" she practically growled.

Kit turned to Anari.

"This is the part where you bring them up to date, right?" he asked.

THIRTY-FIVE

Anari nodded to Kit's question. Moss School, of which she was still close enough, most days. And Suka Kuri had impressed upon both of them the words, understanding that Uly would need allies in the most obscure corners.

She turned to the conductor on the screen.

"Kit asks that I give you a brief history of the modern age," she said, waiting for the woman to nod. "He is a mechanic, rather than a diplomat by training, though he does have a way with words. Would it be acceptable for me to tell you the tale of the Corsac Fox?"

The woman seemed hard-locked on Kit, but she supposed that he was a most bizarre stranger. The rest of them were merely aliens, but Kit might be kin, long ways around.

Still, she nodded.

"Also, I am Anari Supasei," she said. "May I know by what name you would prefer to be addressed?"

There. She stirred. Possibly remembered her manners, with strangers calling.

"I am Smaragda Demetriou," she replied. "Director of this vessel."

Anari nodded deep enough to turn it into a half-bow.

"Ulysses Fortier and Dan Chastain set out with the aid of a few friends..." Anari began.

The tale took most of an hour, but that was Director Demetriou asking for occasional clarifications as she went. The tale was easily told, for all that it sounded like some grand legend a bard might invent to entertain a king for his supper.

She'd been there for most of it. Seen it with her own eyes. Tasted the truth of the tales.

She wound down finally. Studied the woman's face. Disbelief in place. Acceptance in others.

Resignation, perhaps.

After all, as far as Anari knew, the Yarikh had withdrawn from the galaxy, and now she was here, demanding answers, at a minimum. Rude, for a visitor, but probably still necessary.

She waited as the image suddenly froze, presumably so Director Demetriou could talk to someone off-screen.

"We're paused as well," Cemaletdin announced quietly.

Now, they waited.

THIRTY-SIX

Ursula watched texts flow on her screens. Typed occasional comments to Niina or Iikka so as to not speak aloud and disrupt Anari's tale. She didn't follow much of it, for all the woman had tried to teach her the ancient tongue, but it sounded impressive.

What is the status of the four vessels? she typed to Iikka.

Each generates several times more power than we do, despite their much smaller size, he typed back, sending her a display that caused her to stifle a gasp.

Indeed, each had far more power at their disposal than even *Batyr*, at less than two-thirds the displacement. Then she saw something that struck her as odd. The station itself was generating a warp field intended to keep vessels from getting too close, as most did.

No other vessels did the same save *Niemi*.

Are there no other warp generators active?

He looked at the question and began typing.

None, Commander.

What did that mean?

Ursula made a sound and Kit looked over. She pointed at the exchange and watched him blink in surprise.

"They withdrew," he muttered. "Maybe they don't mount a Variable Pulse Spatial Generator on their ships anymore?"

Insane, but it made a kind of sense. The Samuur a century ago had been limited to a single star system, before Zuath travelers showed them better technology. Saari maintained a little trade with distant Zuath worlds, but had never expanded much beyond their few colony worlds, content with what they had until tales had arrived of a terrible warlord building a new kingdom close enough to perhaps be a threat.

Uly had turned out to be an honorable friend instead.

Ideal, in fact, such that she was here.

"Wouldn't they be stuck here?" she whispered back.

"Not if they chose it," he replied, reminding her that he was smart, just introverted. "Then it fits their culture. Dunno if they want to know about the wider galaxy, but hopefully they're nice enough to throw us out instead of trying to destroy us."

"We're prepared to run," she reminded him. "Escape and evasion is not dishonorable, when confronted by overwhelming threat."

"Good," he muttered. "Kinda like to survive this."

She smiled. The furless tended to be weird, but he fit in well with her people. All had spoken well of the man.

Then the screen came live again, showing the other Human. The one that looked like a mix somewhere between Uly and Dan.

"Your arrival has sparked curiosity," the woman said. "Other ships are not welcome, being alien, but you come as a conglomeration of species that include the first Humans known in millennia."

"We share your curiosity and seek to assuage it," Anari said.

At least Ursula thought so. The tones were correct. Diplomatic and friendly.

"The Scholar invites the Human Simonson to visit," she continued. "You and one other may accompany him."

Ursula had gotten to know Anari well enough to see the pique in her stance at such demands, then watched her swallow it all and nod.

"It is well," Anari replied. "How shall we travel?"

"We will send a small craft alongside," Demetriou pronounced. "Three will travel to the surface to meet with the Scholars. We come shortly."

Then the line went blank.

Before Anari could do more than breathe, Ursula turned to Gulnaz, but the woman shook her head, eyes huge. She obviously wasn't prepared emotionally to actually visit the surface. Ursula nodded and turned to Anari.

"I'm your third," Ursula told the woman.

Anari inclined her head, understanding. There would be another time for the Isann woman.

Adventure shortly, so she began typing up orders for Niina, if something happened.

THIRTY-SEVEN

Kit had his messenger bag slung. He'd thrown in a change of clothes on top, but honestly he had no idea what happened next. And it wasn't like he was a warrior or anything. Not like the two women coming with him.

Both of them bigger than him, too. A lot bigger.

Still, he figured that the locals considered him the important one, from the way Anari had described it, so he put on his Ambassador face and went along, with Anari as his translator and Commander Nyman as a bodyguard or something.

Tough ladies. Good enough for him.

They were at the airlock when it opened. He walked first into a shuttle that looked almost like something *Danumash* might have built, but he got that. *Nubia* was a Human vessel, after he'd spent years on an Ononguli one. Or Khet-designed stations.

Everything fit here.

Hollow box with a hatch to his left for a flight deck, currently closed. Jumpseats pulled down, with two Humans who looked like armed goons keeping watch. In his mind, he called them Emil and Gennady, since both were male.

The female director stood there. Demetriou. He smiled at her and got one back.

Kit and Anari wore the blue uniforms that Uly and Omid had come up with. Commander Nyman was in orange.

The Yarikh wore a medium gray, with blue and black trimming and highlights. One-piece jumpsuit that zipped up the front, though it might have been shrink-wrapped onto the woman.

Kit was used to seeing alien women and having that moment of overcoming his *Danumash* heritage to see them as people. Even interesting and attractive people. Especially some of the women.

Director Demetriou was Human. And kind of a babe. Looked at him like something the cat had hacked up on the rug, but he understood that. Poor cousin suddenly knocks on your door out of the blue. With friends in tow.

He smiled at the galaxy and let her direct him to one of the jumpseats. Basic crossing harness, so he buckled himself in, with Anari kneeling nearby like he'd see Suka Kuri do when nothing fit.

Because nothing ever fit the Emro, until they made it fit.

Commander Nyman was on his other side, with Director Demetriou directly across, flanked by her two goons. She said something and they thunked clear of *Niemi* and were in space, moving. Presumably down to the surface, where he got to offer basic concepts and hoped that Anari could make him look good.

And he knew how smart she was.

The babe across from him said something that at least sounded friendly.

"She asks about your background, Kit," Anari said.

It dawned on him that he hadn't really ever talked much about it. Everything always kind of started with either stealing *Iron Wasp*, or maybe, if he was feeling friendly, the day Uly and Dan captured *King Hewitt II* and everybody spent a month keeping the damned thing from dying or exploding.

Marlowe got most of that credit. Him, Kolya, and Sadeq had

done almost all of the brain lifting, with him, Leon, and Cleve mostly muscle to fix things.

And now sounded like a good time to talk about *stuff*.

"The ship was named *King Hewitt II*," he said slowly, letting her translate on the fly. "I got hired as a trainee by Hilda Hobbs when she got a *Danumash* contract to haul cargo. Later, we found out that it was a live cargo, but I didn't know any better in those days, and the Mazhin didn't hold it against me because I was just an engine wiper."

Kit relaxed and talked about the training. About Hilda, who had been kind of another mother to him before she got killed. About Uly and Dan and all the shit they'd had to do to keep that old hulk from collapsing, exploding, or simply dying in deep space and taking the crew with them.

He didn't suppose that even Anari had heard a lot of this, because he had to talk about Sterling and Solomon and he caught her stutters as she absorbed it. But he knew she and Sterling were a thing. Or would be.

The Young Gentlemen, Captain Winter had called them, along with a few that hadn't survived, plus that asshole Thorley Eldridge who hadn't been able to keep his yap shut at his racism.

And specism. He'd have hated everyone involved, but Kit supposed that someone would have already killed that punk by now, somewhere along the way.

And he could say good riddance, because Eldridge had been a punk every day. Second son of baron on his way to high naval rank or something because of what he was.

Uly only cared about who you intended to be.

Kit wound down about the time that the atmospheric turbulence abated, so they must be low over their target. Box had no windows or screens to show anything outside, so Kit didn't know if they were over city, mountains, or ocean.

They'd land soon and he'd find out.

Hopefully, it would turn out all right.

THIRTY-EIGHT

Anari felt the shuttle touch down with a smooth grace she presumed indicated an autopilot. Drew might have landed that softly, but not most of the pilots she'd met as part of the *Auga*.

Demetriou rose, so Anari unfolded herself and stood, hunched against the low ceiling. The side hatch popped sideways, admitting an orange light.

Demetriou exited, along with her two troopers. Anari followed first, mostly to impress the locals with her size.

Sabre School occasionally meant that you won battles by intimidation. Convincing your opponent to seek other opportunities.

Outside, the sun was setting. Possibly rising, but the day was warm and it felt like late afternoon, with things fading to salmons and reds as twilight approached. The gravity was what she was used to from *Nubia*, so she automatically cataloged it as Human-standard.

Whatever that meant.

Ursula followed Kit, and Anari finally studied more than the immediate vicinity.

Concrete slab underfoot, but only a small one, with green grass

199

beyond. A building in the near distance, perhaps forty meters away, though it was hard to judge.

After a moment, she came to understand that the building was as much indoors as out, with columns and arcades designed to provide shade, while not being enclosed. It spoke to her of weather that never got particularly cold. Nor tropical hot, because there were several trees immediately in sight, and most of those looked deciduous. Possibly fruit trees, arranged in rows and clusters that spoke of a Moss School architect seeking to provide visual balance.

And succeeding.

"Come," Director Demetriou said simply, gesturing Kit to fall in beside her and walking towards the building.

Palace? Hall of Government? It felt official.

Anari fell in behind and walked with the slow, mincing strides she needed when walking around the medium-sized species.

Late afternoon. Warm but not hot. Gorgeous, with a few white clouds in a deeply blue sky.

Demetriou led them to a courtyard that was about half shaded by walls and vines growing on trellises. Grapes, which surprised her. She'd heard of such things, but never seen them in person and wasn't sure if they were safe for her kind.

Director Demetriou looked up.

"Given your size, I thought it better to meet outdoors, rather than subject you to many doors designed for my kind," she said with a nod and a smile.

Anari bowed.

"Thank you," she said. "I am used to making accommodations for small ships, but this is better."

No bench would fit her, so she waited until Kit picked one out, then knelt close where she could translate.

A few minutes passed in silence. Kit, studying everything with a sharp eye. Ursula absorbing what she could from someplace entirely alien.

Anari composed the next chapter of a long, oral poem and memorized it for Suka Kuri. Moss School required it.

A nearby hatch opened. Door, as they were called on the ground.

A procession appeared, led by six guards similar to the two watching, though the newcomers were dressed in more formal uniforms and bearing a mix of archaic polearms and pistols on hips.

It was the woman being escorted that drew the eye.

Older than Demetriou. Regal. Dark skin like Dan's. White-haired. Wearing the gray and cobalt of the others, but in robes that added red as well. Lines on her face spoke of worldly experience, but also smiles.

She was sober today, but it was not a harshness that Anari felt.

Curiosity, as Demetriou had said.

The woman was accompanied by several aides, also in robes that weren't as elaborate.

She came to rest and the six guards spread sideways while most of the aides stepped back.

"Greetings," Anari began. "I am Anari Supasei of the Emro. This is Ursula Nyman of the Samuur. Kit Simonson is Human, though he does not speak your language well. We come as diplomats from the Corsac Fox, who is also Human."

She left it at that. Watched the woman.

One of the male aides had stayed close and was translating into some third tongue. A near-relative descendant of the Yarikh of Selene Praxis, but subtly different. Accent, mostly. Softening of some syllables and hardening of others. Probably written the same, if they were reduced to such a thing, but obviously the one aide spoke the ancient language fluently.

She made eye contact with the man to acknowledge him as the woman spoke and he translated for her to translate for Ursula and Kit.

"Scholar Nomiki Marinos," he replied, nodding to the woman. "Leader of Traiffe. We have heard your tale, Anari Supasei, as well as that of Kit on the transport. The distances were originally thought impossible, but looking at him, he appears to be of the Yarikh."

"Such was our surprise," Anari replied. "Selene Praxis could be a close blood relative of Dan Chastain, one of our senior leaders, in color and bones. That was what led us to seek deeper."

Scholar Marinos asked something.

"Do you have a picture of Chastain?" he asked.

"I do," Anari said, reaching into her pocket to pull out a tablet that she activated and quickly flipped through. She turned it for the others to see. "This is Dan, Second-in-Command for the Corsac Fox. And this is Ulysses Fortier, commonly known as The Corsac Fox."

Gasps and muttering. About what she expected. Long-lost Humans, meeting up again?

Cultural earthquakes should be expected.

"And the *Auga* you spoke of?" Marinos asked.

Anari spoke as she located an encyclopedia entry.

"The *Auga*," she said. "Generally this tall. Dominant in the area that their Empire has conquered, and forever slowly expanding in their self-appointed mission to take and control the rest."

"And the Corsac Fox resists assimilation?" Marinos pressed through her translator.

"Uly believes that all people—all species—should be free to find their own happiness, as long as it does not endanger others," she replied. "He has made it his mission to stop the *Auga*. To make them behave. To let others know freedom as the *Auga* have themselves, but deny to lesser species."

And she could speak to that, having been originally trained to Sabre School, before those idiots who drafted her into their navy decided that she was too smart to be a warrior and made her an engineer instead. And not even Moss School. Merely a technician.

Uly and Dan had freed her to dream.

"Why are you here?" Marinos demanded.

Anari nodded. This was the meat of it.

"Partly, Uly located Selene Praxis's old ship and learned that Humans and Yarikh might be the same species," she said. "Or close enough. Curiosity thus drove him, just as it drives the rest of us. Partly, the Corsac Fox seeks allies that will help him hold back the *Auga*. The Ononguli and Khet are already friendly, as are the Isann as well as the Samuur, represented by Ursula Nyman."

"We have looked up Selene Praxis and *Invincible*," Anari was told. "The ship was marked lost and destroyed in records so ancient that only shards remain today. But Scholars esteem information, so we were able to find bits. How did the Corsac Fox locate the wreck?"

"It was not a wreck," she replied, watching the folks across the way all gasp when that tidbit was shared. "As to how he found it, I suppose that I must take some portion of the credit."

Anari paused to walk everything deeper than before. Starting with the *Karaŋgılıkka*, that vast cultural cornerstone of both the ancient and the modern Isann. Into the *Black Sword* hidden beneath the Black Moon, as recorded by Zamir Aytiev. The translation that had driven her to distraction, until Suka Kuri had seen the rightness of it and given her the key. Then working closely with Sterling to map it and find the trail.

Finally standing on the edge of that fabled lagoon, before walking those decks.

"From there, we reconditioned the ship," she concluded. "Several of us have learned both Isann and Yarikh, this tongue I am speaking, in order to translate the old logs and information so that Uly could take it home and make it his flagship. It also has vast cultural resonance to the Isann, represented by Gulnaz, who remained on the ship when only three visitors were allowed."

Rude, but she did want to remind them that others had come. Might have looked forward to it, though most Isann women didn't generally experience the religious aspects to the *Karaŋgılıkka* that the men did.

Marinos nodded, possibly ceding Anari the point that the Yarikh's diplomacy might be less than entirely hospitable.

Of course, if something went wrong down here, hopefully *Niemi* could escape and carry word home.

"You seek to draw us back out into the wider galaxy?" the woman asked.

Kit had mentioned that they had withdrawn, as though it also had religious overtones. She parsed her words carefully, understanding that everything would be translated at least once.

"Not if you have no interest in such a thing," she replied. "We sought to assuage curiosity first and foremost. To see if the Yarikh were Human, or vice versa. Kit and his kind had no knowledge of having kin in this direction, so you were a surprise that drove investigation. We could depart and leave you thus, with notes to future travelers to avoid Traiffe as an unwelcoming place. You must tell us what your modern culture venerates, because we have only the ancient things upon which to guess. The Isann have the *Karaŋgılıkka*, which allowed us to understand them so much better as a people. What legends do you have?"

She fell silent and watched body language. It had been friendly until now. Not exactly warm, but not hostile. Cool and polite, as befit strangers meeting.

Scholar Marinos muttered something, then stepped forward until she was ahead of her guards. Even the aide stayed behind as she moved to stand in front of Kit.

Anari watched her gesture him to stand. He did.

Anari noted that Kit had perhaps five centimeters height on the woman, but they might weigh the same because he had a slender build similar to Uly's. Marinos's eyes, even with Kit's nose.

Perhaps a meter separated them.

Kit stood still and watched. Anari was prepared to translate, but the Scholar did not speak.

Merely studied him from up close.

Kit smiled. He glanced at Anari.

"She seems friendly?" he asked.

"So far, yes, Kit," Anari replied.

He nodded. It was almost his default gesture, to note something agreeable, then agree with it.

Like it was all a grand adventure.

The woman spoke.

"The Scholar Nomiki Marinos asks if Kit Simonson is a technician," the aide said.

Anari translated.

Kit grinned, then slung the messenger bag around front and pulled out whatever device he had been tinkering with.

"Part of a coolant subsystem off *Niemi*," he said to Anari. "Think I can get another five percent efficiency out of it, but need to print or machine a couple of parts. Thought about it on the flight down. Obviously haven't had a chance to do anything yet."

He held it out as she spoke. Marinos took it in her hand and held it up, rotating it.

A conversation occurred in the other tongue. Anari got pieces of it, but not much. Other aides spoke as well, possibly offering engineering expertise, because Marinos turned to another dark woman aide with white hair, turning her back on Kit as those two spoke.

Emotions seemed calm. Technical questions and answers.

Finally, that third woman stepped up to stand next to Marinos. The male aide moved between them to translate.

"Which parts would you improve?" got translated three times, so Kit pulled out a sketchpad and quickly drew something.

"This routing has too much bend in it," he explained, pointing. "Creates internal friction that could be reduced by making it a pair of smooth forty-fives instead. Then widen the bore here and here. Might need to redesign it entirely, but these fixes can be done in place on the ship and tested. Plus they will fit in the available volume.

Really big changes probably mean we help them come up to modern tech, back on Saari or Bastion.”

More muttering. Anari watched the other group divide into two rough pieces, but not sides. Temperaments, perhaps.

Scholar Marinos turned to Anari now.

“We have scanned the vessel that drew you here,” she said. “It is primitive.”

“Indeed,” Anari replied, simultranslating. “The *Corsac Fox* is in the process of helping bring the Samuur up to a more modern civilization. *Invincible*, as we rescued it, is a shade more advanced than most of the rest of the galaxy at present, but I understand that to be where the Yarikh were as they pulled back and withdrew from the galaxy in ancient times. We did not know if you had fallen, or simply closed the door and remained in your study as scholars.”

They watched each other, even as others stirred and muttered, stilled when Marinos held up a single hand.

“We will speak more,” Marinos stated.

Then she withdrew, leaving only the male aide and the female Anari presumed was an engineer of some sort. Even Director Demetriou departed, along with her two troopers.

Anari rose to tower over the two remaining, though she kept her posture polite.

“And now?” she asked simply.

“The Scholar is intrigued, Anari Supasei,” the woman replied with a wry grin that reminded her of Kit in many ways. “I am Engineer Melpomeni Michelakos, and will be your host while you remain with us. This is Scholar Stefanos Iordanou, translator for the court.”

“It is a pleasure to meet you,” Anari said, translating for her friends. “How may we assist?”

“Be welcome, Scholar Supasei,” the woman said. “Curiosity has given way to fascination. It is a good thing.”

Anari nodded, then followed as they were led into the building itself.

Hopefully, there would be answers soon.

THIRTY-NINE

Kit played it cool and loose. Emulating Drew when that guy got to flying. Smile. Nod. Be friendly and open to new ideas.

As Hilda had once told him, all those years ago: '*Be teachable. You won't always be right.*'

It was a thing that had gotten him here. Walking on the surface of an alien world that might be a Human one. Really kinda awesome, when he thought about it.

And maybe this engineer babe might be able to help him with the coolant design. She'd looked at it and seen the same things he had.

Kit had never really been into older women, but she was as much a babe as the other two, regardless of her hair and wrinkles. Still hard-body. And smiles, which helped when his nerves wanted to remind him what he was doing.

Inside the place wasn't much different than outside. Marble floors with a rough polish for tread, rather than smooth that would turn to ice if you tracked any water on it. Art on the walls and in alcoves, mostly landscapes and small statuary, rather than portraits or busts.

A people that didn't venerate grand heroes? Or had they passed their age of heroic legend and settled into some sort of benign old age?

Words broke in on him. Engineer to translator to Anari.

"Engineer Michelakos asks what brings you such joy, looking at the smile on your face," Anari murmured in his ear.

Kit took a moment.

"Meeting neat people," he said, wondering how that got translated.

And what might get lost along the way.

Something good must have survived, because the woman nodded and smiled at him, then hooked her elbow in his and moved that much closer as they walked.

Hopefully, the food would be good. He'd hate to come this far and not be able to sit down to a good meal. Azad talked about his twin Vahid, and how many people The Spatula had conquered with a pot and an oven.

Eventually, they entered a courtyard. Two steps down, with a stream running diagonally along with plants and a tree he didn't recognize. Walkway all the way around like a balcony, with two or three doors on each side of the rectangle.

Felt quiet. Like the place you put visitors and left empty the rest of the time.

Peaceful.

Engineer babe led him to the middle door on the west side, since the sun was down and night falling. She opened it and walked him in, keeping up a running commentary. Like indoor plumbing might be magic.

He'd have said something, but *Danumash* still had corners like that.

Front room with chairs and a couch. Small dining area next to a restroom that was bigger than his cabin on *Nubia*. Bedroom in back, with windows covered with blinds against sunrise.

Lots of wood in the construction. Raw walls treated with some oil-based sealant but no color. Smell of fresh nature, which made him sneeze a few times, because you never had nature on a starship.

They circled back to the front room and she seated him, waiting for Anari and Commander Nyman to settle.

"This will be your room," the woman said. "Your friends will be on either side. It is late in the day. Have you eaten or will breakfast at dawn be sufficient?"

"Got snacks," he said, letting that flow across three people in his job as representative Human.

"Then we will leave you here for now," she told everyone. "There are watchers at the boundaries of the courtyard, mostly to keep curious seekers from bothering you. If you need something, locate one of them and they will get a message to us. I am not far."

He nodded. Shared a smile with her and wondered what she was thinking. Old enough to be his mom. If not older. Still in amazing shape. And pretty hot.

Or he'd been around alien women for too long and needed to reset his brain to deal with Humans again.

Something.

The two withdrew and he looked at his friends.

"That went well?" he offered.

"It did," Commander Nyman said. "Should one of us sleep here in the front room?"

Kit looked at her a little cross-eyed.

"No," Anari rescued him. "We'll treat this like a normal meeting. Kit, pound on a wall if you have an emergency."

"Yes, ma'am," he replied.

They both left and he found a simple deadbolt on the door that he shot. Moving the couch in front of the door sounded rude, though he thought about it.

Instead, he did another quick tour. Found a bookcase in a corner with some books on it. Weirdly, he could even sort of read it, but only because he'd been studying some.

Still, he found a chair and let the written word entertain him.

212

FORTY

Nomiki had gathered Melpomeni and Stefanos into her favorite study, summoning Elias Ioannidis as well. Outside, stars shined down on a perfect night. Perfect architecture. Perfect everything.

The turmoil was in her mind.

"Is he really Human?" she asked.

"The probe registers him so," Melpomeni answered. "To the limits of classification, which utterly astounded me. Could there really be a lost tribe of Yarikh out there?"

Nomiki scowled and turned to Elias, Historian to the Court.

"Who are they?" she asked bluntly. "How did we miss an entire tribe of Yarikh when we withdrew from the galaxy?"

"I have mapped the location that Simonson pointed," Elias replied with a serious face. "Even with a wide cone of uncertainty, they are some seventy percent out towards the recognized edge of the galaxy, and rather a ways around the curvature itself. If they have lost all knowledge of us, it is possible that we missed a colony somewhere."

"More likely?" Melpomeni interrupted, waiting for nods. "A ship decided that they didn't want to leave with us and snuck off. Possibly marked lost later. I will remind you that Traiffe is not our homeworld either, and I got the impression from the immense green woman that the Humans lack all knowledge of their founding, beyond primitive legend. Obviously, we could not probe deeper, and I doubt that Kit knows. If Anari Supasei does, it will be third or fourth hand at best."

"We need one of the Human leaders to explain," Nomiki said. "If they can."

"I got the impression that the Corsac Fox might be willing to come, but that he is immensely busy," Stefanos offered. "Forging treaties with powerful neighbors, even as he founds his own star nation. Obviously, the man has great charisma. And excellent advisors, if Chastain is creating that Congress of Wives as a way to bind people to the Corsac Fox and create a permanent, stable advisory council. A different model, but it has staying power. Do we need to become involved?"

"Can we even draw him here?" Elias asked. "Histo-sociographically, which is my expertise, we might fill the role of the magical shaman in the wilderness in a fairy tale. The young hero must go on a quest for some magical aid that will help them slay a dragon, however metaphorical. I would put to you that he has already done so. *Invincible*, which they renamed *Nubia*, presumably drawing on elements of Chastain's biological past."

"Skin tone," Stefanos noted. "The Corsac Fox is slightly lighter than ours. Kit Simonson almost albino. Chastain darker. Such difference could not have evolved that quickly. Is there another Yarikh culture out there beyond ours, from which they might have come instead?"

"Are you suggesting that the original homeworld might still be inhabited?" Nomiki asked dryly.

"No," Elias said. "We know it to be destroyed. However, perhaps some early colony in that direction did quietly survive, fifteen or twenty thousand years ago? Hid from us? Maybe Kit and his people descend from them instead. I will remind you that while we are

Human, we are also extensively modified from base stock like Kit Simonson. The probe shows that. He is essentially a throwback, but I believe that all of them are, based on Supasei's words."

Nomiki let that settle on her. Original Stock Humans. Direct descendants of Earth itself, without the medical and genetic advancements Traiffe had perfected?

Were her people indeed that magical shaman in the wilderness, powerful and immortal?

A thought niggled her and she turned to Elias and Melpomeni.

"If he is Baseline Human, how old is he?" she asked bluntly.

It took them a moment to process her question.

"Two decades, into his third," Melpomeni said. "They would grow up at the same rate we do. It is only after adulthood that we slow down so much. He might see you as merely being perhaps a well-preserved sixty, instead of the two hundred-plus you really are. I might appear to be fifty in his eyes, instead of one hundred and sixty-seven. He did look on me as a desirable older woman."

"That's because we are genetically perfect, Melpomeni," Stefanos reminded her. "Advanced Humans. They are Baseline stock."

"They are still cousins," Nomiki interrupted before those two got going again.

Some days, it was like dealing with children with those two.

"And they only know what Selene Praxis left them when she parked her warship in orbit of a black hole and departed," Elias reminded everyone. "They do not know anything of our intervening cultural developments. Or what we have become. Everyone else who has come has been willing to run for their lives when threatened. That or been destroyed to keep our secrets safe."

"And every one of them were aliens," Melpomeni offered. "Zuath and Ugotha, like Anari mentioned. A few others that maybe aren't as well known, living closer to the galactic center. Behind us, if you will, given that this Imperial Sector Fourteen is mostly rimward from the description given. Kit Simonson is Human. As are his leaders, with many aliens collected into some sort of matriarchal organization as equals. It was enough to inspire our curiosity. Now what?"

Nomiki nodded. She'd have ordered them all chased off, just like the rest, save for a Baseline Human had come with surprising truth of others out there.

The Yarikh had withdrawn. Selene Praxis had obviously lied about destroying her ship, but there was nothing anyone could do about it now, as long as the woman had been dead.

The present had intruded, while the Yarikh had dreamed of...

Nomiki blinked. Felt the others fall silent, watching her warily.

She turned to Melpomeni.

"What do the Yarikh dream of?" she asked her friend and advisor.

Melpomeni opened her mouth as if to say something probably tart, rude, and perhaps a shade vulgar, as was her wont, when she stopped as well.

Instead, she blinked and drew a breath.

"Do we dream?" she countered smartly after a moment. "Or is it a bland reverie of pleasantness that amounts to a form of singular indulgence leading to entropy?"

Elias bit his lip, so Nomiki turned to him expectantly.

"No, she's right," he said, apparently shivering with a cold that only existed inside. "We once dreamed. We perfected our culture, then perfected ourselves, just as the *Auga* appear to have done, though we are more in line with our ecological niche and thus perfectly stable."

"Utterly stable," Stefanos offered. "Entropy by default, because nothing changes."

He turned to Elias as Nomiki heard his tone change.

"How much have we lost, since the end of any so-called Age of Heroes?" Stefanos asked the Historian.

Everyone gasped, so Nomiki didn't feel so bad.

Elias's mouth fell open, catching flies were there any to be had.

"We have grown stodgy," Melpomeni pronounced with a nod.

"We thought that we were exploring the inner worlds of philosophical discourse. Was it merely mental masturbation instead?"

Yes, that was what had haunted Nomiki all day, since that primitive, little vessel appeared and thoroughly trashed her calm.

What did the Yarikh dream of?

Anything?

"We have advanced science," Nomiki offered. "Mastered biology. Taken the merely mechanical well beyond levels of Selene Praxis's flagship, which, I will remind you, is supposedly a notch beyond what the galaxy has risen back to, having fallen into raw entropy over the intervening era."

"Did we cause it?" Melpomeni asked, causing Nomiki to stumble intellectually.

"What?" she demanded of one of her oldest friends in the world.

"We withdrew," Melpomeni stated. "The Isann talk about their *Karaŋgılıkka*, their *Sailing into Darkness* that Uly Fortier used to emotionally capture their entire civilization. But Anari reminds us that Zamir Aytiev was on the descending part of that curve. A cultural, civilizational, and technological collapse that *Invincible* might have staved off. Others collapsed at the same time, but they use remarkably similar tools today, largely because physics is physics, and you only have to invent it once. Or rediscover something long lost, like *Invincible*. What Kit will see is not all that we know, because we live simpler lives today. But did we bring down the entire galaxy six thousand years ago when we decided to begin withdrawing back onto ourselves? Did we crash everyone else? And do we owe them assistance getting it back if we did?"

Nomiki paused to calm her heart and begin scrubbing some of the jolt of icy adrenaline that had coursed through her perfect being at those words.

To be Yarikh was to live long, fruitful lives filled with art and intellectual endeavors. But how rarely did anything really revolutionary happen? Traiffe itself was engineered for the ultimate in long-term stability. Births balanced against deaths, neither that common when two hundred and eighty years was a biological norm, offsetting unfortunate accidents by issuing permits for extra children as necessary.

What were they doing with such knowledge? Such lives?

Stefanos and Elias had fallen silent. Shock, rather than outrage.

It was a question she could not answer, and as Scholar to the Court, Nomiki Marinos was supposedly the best Yarikh equipped to do so.

How had she so utterly failed?

Nomiki hung her head.

"We have become lost, somewhere along the way," she offered. "Should I stand aside and another be elevated to deal with the newcomers?"

"None are better," Elias spoke first. "As Historian, I can make such pompous pronouncements without embarrassment."

He grinned, and Nomiki shared it. She occasionally teased him thus.

Melpomeni nodded.

"Elias is correct," she said. "We have a novel problem in a civilization that has dedicated itself to solving all intellectual issues."

"Intellectual," Stefanos noted. "Kit is physical. Emotional. Baseline, but he retains the vigor and fire of youth, and perhaps we have lost it? Have we turned into stodgy old farts when we weren't looking?"

"It is a terrible mirror he has accidentally held up to us, merely by arriving," Nomiki agreed. "And, as is our way, I will need to ponder it. Each of you meditate on such logic and join me here in the last hour before dawn, that we can compare notes before we meet our cousin and see what questions of his we can answer."

"Do we disrupt the wider galaxy with our technology?" Melpomeni asked.

"Not today," Nomiki replied. "The Corsac Fox is Baseline

Human. While young, he has perhaps a handful of decades before him. What can we do to thwart the *Auga* from eventually coming this far? And can we stop them today without elevating everyone beyond what their culture can immediately accept? As you asked, what do we owe the rest of the galaxy, if part of this really is our fault?"

"Uly broke the Khet," Stefanos reminded them all. "And is breaking the Ononguli as we speak. They may not see it that way, but that does not change anything. Can we use him to break everyone in the least painful, least dangerous way?"

"Answer me that tomorrow," Nomiki dismissed them.

She would need to meditate as well. And possibly simply do that all night instead of sleeping, not that she needed much sleep.

Tonight, it might be an entirely lost cause to even try.

FORTY-ONE

Anari had knelt and meditated in the front room all night, rather than even bothering to attempt a bed made for someone only two meters tall. Easier to rise every hour and do various forms for looseness, and she could sleep later.

It wasn't paranoia on her part, though she did admit to some level of apprehension. Still, she was Sabre School, and they did not do more than merely acknowledge fear as it passed. It did not bind them.

The walls had been solid enough that she didn't hear people moving about outside, so she'd checked through curtains a time or two.

No alarms. No knocks from Kit. Hopefully, he'd been able to sleep.

The first hints of impending dawn caused the courtyard to brighten from the dimness of a few lights set at ankle level. She gave up and moved outside, where she could do forms with proper space, nodding to the one guard who emerged from the shadows, then withdrew as she ignored the woman.

Forms for peace of mind. Tai Chi, done slowly. Weapon forms done open hand because she hadn't brought any. Terrible Gaff. Sunflower Fist. All the things that defined the Combat Team. They brought her calm.

As dawn broke, she finished and rapped on Kit's door. He answered immediately, so he must have been unable to sleep much, either. Ursula responded quickly as well.

"All well?" she asked.

"Slept on the couch," Kit admitted. "A little too wound up for my own good right now."

"Understood," Anari replied. "I feel the same."

"Are we safe?" Ursula asked.

"So far, nobody has made a hostile act," Kit offered. "Hopefully breakfast shortly and everyone's still friendly."

The Engineer appeared alone at that moment from around a corner, following the stream.

"I was alerted that you were all up early," she said as she bowed. "Shall we break our fast?"

They ended up following the woman to a communal kitchen not all that different from *Nubia*'s wardroom, save that Vahid wasn't in charge and the rolls were pedestrian at best.

She'd heard Nasrin and the other Mazhin call such things *gumbo brown* as a measure of bland sameness, both in food as in life. Lacking color.

Lacking emotion? The locals had all struck her initially for their calmness, but the civilization was ancient. Had it settled into some sort of senescence, having *withdrawn* from the wider galaxy?

Except that the Engineer seemed brighter today. More alive, perhaps?

More relaxed, at least, and lacking that edge of formality that had added a brittleness to things yesterday? That felt right.

The food was fresh fruit, a mild orangish cheese of some sort, and rolls. Nourishing, but not exciting. Even the butter was a strange yellow color, instead of the blue that marked a Khet export.

Good enough, but she supposed that she was a bit spoiled.

Fresh, cold water, instead of tea or coffee.

Nourishing, and little else. What did that say about the Yarikh as a people?

"How badly have we caused your world to stutter in surprise?" Ursula asked at one point, causing the Engineer to stutter herself, physically.

Anari knew that Ursula hadn't asked an innocent question, for all the woman liked to pretend to be a simple sailor.

"We did not know that other Humans existed beyond our world," the woman said after a long pause, no doubt formulating the right phrase.

And, Anari noted, she spoke accented Yarikh this morning.

Had she yesterday? Anari hadn't thought so, though the two tongues weren't all that far apart, having listened to the one man translate yesterday.

Had she learned it all overnight?

What other secrets did the Yarikh hide?

Kit leaned in and studied the woman closer.

"Are you going to toss us out on our asses, send us home with a letter for Uly, or come with us?" he asked her, point blank.

Anari didn't bother sanding any rough edges off that as she repeated it, even using his tones.

The Engineer twitched again, possibly unprepared for a less diplomatic approach. A more direct one.

However, Kit had nailed things exactly. There were only three options, assuming that they would be allowed to leave. Then there was a fourth she didn't bother mentioning.

"We are an old culture," the Engineer began, only to fall short when Kit laughed, so he must be picking up the language as well.

How soon until they could all speak as equals? Soon, if Kit was already on track.

"Ancient," the woman continued. "Selene Praxis deposited her ship roughly five thousand years ago. She was among the last to return to Traiffe, and we have had almost no connection with the outer galaxy since then."

Anari nodded, catching emotional tones that the Scholar and her translator hadn't had yesterday.

"It is not our intention to disrupt things any more than necessary," Anari told her. "Appreciating that we have already done so. What produces the best outcome for the least chaos?"

She liked the way the woman blinked at her, as if surprised at such precise language.

Moss School. And a diplomat representing the Corsac Fox himself. Those standards were both high.

"Would your Corsac Fox welcome an emissary?" the Engineer asked.

"Absolutely," Anari replied, with nods from Kit and Ursula. "That was why we came. Each species he has met has been invited to do so. A few have taken greater steps, and bound themselves to him personally, but we do not demand such things of the Yarikh, though that is also welcome if you so choose."

"We live lives of quiet deliberation," the woman said. "Introspective, as you might guess from a civilization as old as ours. At the same time, our curiosity has been piqued by your arrival. Without Kit, you would have been seen off. But discovering that there are other Humans out there has caused a minor ripple to jolt us, and Nomiki Marinos tasks us with answers."

"You, specifically?" Kit asked when translated.

"Myself, yes," she nodded. "If welcome."

"Absolutely," he said, turning to Anari for help.

She studied the woman, and the subtle interactions there. Not quite Uly and Dan, but she could see the attraction, though she wasn't sure the older woman reciprocated.

At the same time, they were Human, and Dan was the only Human female anywhere in any sort of range, so Kit might have been expecting to have to find himself an alien wife at some point, like Uly had.

What did the future hold for all of them?

FORTY-TWO

Uly hadn't come in by the normal route along his new Silk Road, so he didn't have a chance to stop and greet *Tanis Dragon* or *Wardog Charlie* in passing. Conductor DJ Gross had always taken his responsibilities seriously and diplomatically, once he knew who Uly was, so those had been pleasant breaks. *Wardog Charlie* was *Wardog Charlie.*

There was a new road being born. One that connected Saari to Daicia to any of several spots on the far side of the Ononguli interior, once word got out that it was safe.

And it would be safe for travelers. Uly was pretty certain that he had impressed those details on the folks at Daicia.

He could always go back and *reinforce* the lesson.

But he was over Rayzian today. Resting at the outer marker with *Tiikeri* on a close flank, *Nubia* protecting the smaller ship rather than the other way around.

Challenges had gone out and replies sent. He knew he was late arriving, but he had a pretty good reason. Several, in fact.

"Uly, *Fire Diamond* on channel five," Haydar announced. "Lukyan."

"I'll take it in my office," Uly decided. "What's the lag?"

"About two seconds, but we're cleared to head inward, so it will slowly decrease over the next several hours. Unless you were in a hurry."

"Absolutely not," Uly said as he rose. "You and Drew work with Eskil and his crew to get us in and settled. I'm presuming we'll take a shuttle to the surface, once Anna initiates the larger process that our arrival triggers."

"Indubitably," Haydar chuckled.

Uly got to his desk and settled, pausing for a quick breath before he brought the line live and waited.

Lukyan looked more relaxed than Uly remembered seeing him at any point in the last several years. Hopefully, that was a good sign.

"Welcome, Uly," Lukyan said. "I'm guessing you went and socially conquered yet another species on the way here?"

He was smiling, but he had been there to watch the Khet, the Ononguli, and the Isann come around.

"They are the Samuur, Lukyan," Uly replied. "They arrived at Bastion after you left."

Uly proceeded to walk him through the first meeting, the three missions, Saari, and the present.

"Wait wait wait," Lukyan broke in at one point. "Daicia?"

"Facing Tharn and Rebosk on the Ononguli border," Uly nodded. "Right at the edge of Sector Twenty-One."

"And you just dropped a battalion of your Samuur friends on the place as station security?" Lukyan confirmed with a whistle.

"While reminding them that I was coming directly to Rayzian to talk to Anna and tell her everything," Uly completed the thought. "And that failure to behave would make me a permanent enemy."

Lukyan blanched almost orange at that, but Uly supposed that the man understood the depth and power of such a threat.

"But you're here now?" Lukyan confirmed.

"For the moment," Uly replied. "Obviously, some major events to take care of. And some updates for Anna and the Horde that might change a few equations."

"What about that other ship?" he asked. "The one you sent looking for the folks that built *Nubia*?"

"It will be months until I hear anything, I'm presuming." Uly shrugged. "I'm hoping good news, but I have no way of even guessing if they will succeed, let alone what they might find. As Dan reminds me, I can only be in one place at a time, so I have to rely on competent people. Fortunately, I have Sterling to replace Maks as Governor for now. And Anari to send as an emissary. My hope is that the Bondarenko and the Sobol clans see fit to get deeper involved at this point, because I can use the help."

"I haven't spoken to Maks much, but you need to chat with him as soon as possible for what he's been up to," Lukyan offered cryptically. "Past that, welcome to Rayzian. I'm making arrangements to head to the palace, so if you wanted to swing by and pick me up, that saves me a trip."

"Shouldn't be a problem, Lukyan," Uly smiled. "Assuming Anna hasn't changed her mind."

"She has not told me, if she has," he said. "Chat with you in a bit once the schedule is nailed down."

And he was gone, just as quickly as that. But it was Lukyan. He'd said what he needed, and not had problems, so Uly was smiling when he emerged from his office and caught Dan's eye.

She ushered him back in, so they ended up across the desk.

"How quickly do we tell Anna that you have other wives who might have precedence?" she asked.

"Lukyan didn't have any new surprises, so I'm hoping we can arrange a day to land and settle," Uly replied. "Then a few days of meetings and negotiations, based on whatever trouble Rabiu and Ethir have gotten themselves up to without adult supervision. We'll take Anna aside early on and I'll let you explain, since this one isn't my fault."

He was grinning. She smiled.

"That will be the easy part," she said. "I'm wondering if the Paramount will have identified a few candidates for the Combat Team and the Congress by the time we get back."

"Probably," Uly nodded. "They move quickly when they set their minds to a thing. And it's not like they have a particularly pacific culture."

She laughed.

Warriors, but in the sense of athletes competing for prizes, rather than pirates or conquering armies. Individual champions, but everyone observing honor and rules.

"Now I just need to recruit people," Uly sighed. "I was telling Lukyan that, but I suppose that you'll need to make the case to Anna."

"And Maks's Mom when I finally get a chance to meet her and her sister," Dan replied. "But you have Anna's support, so I think it will all work out."

"I'm counting on it," he said. "We could easily have just gone off and lived the rest of our lives without worrying about the *Auga*, but they must be stopped. And nobody else is really willing to put in the effort. Even the Ononguli are too flighty to settle in and grind the *Auga* back like they've done to the Horde, so it's on us."

"We have friends," she reminded him. "And we'll have more when this is done."

He nodded.

He'd need them.

FORTY-THREE

Anna had taken to having dinner weekly at Lyra's house. They were old friends, however little she'd seen the women over the last decade or so, and it had worked out. Voldomir had initially been hesitant to remain at the table after dinner, but making one of those nights a triple date had sealed his participation in their little conspiracy.

Her and Lukyan, growing comfortable around each other. Maks and Chervonya getting serious but doing it slowly. Lyra and Voldomir, because Anna hadn't initially appreciated how much business acumen the man had, until both Maks and Lukyan had explained it to her.

Tonight, though, she and Lyra were alone with Lyra's sister. The Corsac Fox had just arrived in orbit, and Uly would be down on the surface in the morning.

The galaxy was about to change.

The Bondarenko, represented by Lyra and her sister Zoryana. Voldomir had put a pasta dish in the oven, set the timer, and grabbed a jacket to go have an evening at the corner pub. At least that had been his story as he walked out the door, leaving the three of them to talk.

"Should Halyna be here?" Zoryana asked as they sat around the table.

Anna noted that the woman appeared calm, but it was a slightly brittle thing. Sitting and conspiring with the *Vatazhko*, even though she'd begun the process more than a year ago.

"I've spoken with her," Anna replied. "And just had a chat with Lukyan *sub rosa*. Lukyan as himself, rather than as conductor of *Fire Diamond*. He had some interesting thoughts."

"What trouble is he about to unleash this time?" Lyra asked with a grin.

Lyra was the older sister. Still fighting trim in spite of being mostly a homebody. Zoryana had grown thicker with age, but they looked remarkably alike.

"He suggests that Uly needs staff," Anna told them both. "And that, being Uly, he's smart enough to understand that he can't do it all, and is hoping to recruit folks from the Horde who can help. Specifically, Bondarenko and Sobol, plus presumably Shevchenko, though that might be a bit more complicated."

"Once Maks and Chervonya make it official, it will be easier for you," Lyra noted.

Anna nodded. She'd done the same math, but those two were still sorting things out. Mostly because Anna absolutely knew that Maks would be moving his organization to Bastion as soon as everything with Uly was settled.

And probably permanently. Like Uly, he'd need to be in the center of the action, and that might be more in Sector Fourteen than Twenty-One. At least for a few more years while the *Auga* finished recovering from what Uly had done to them the last time. Times. Taeli and then Nyri.

And, at some point, Anna would retire as *Vatazhko*. It was a job for a younger person.

Or could she convince Chervonya to lean more into politics, thus anchoring Maks and his new bank closer to Rayzian?

Food for thought.

"I'm more interested in what the Bondarenko might do," Anna said, turning to the two women but mostly focusing on Lyra.

"Understanding all the assumptions about hard-horned punks and their specism, Maks's new bank and other corporate plans have defused a lot of tension with the major clan players," Lyra offered. "All quietly. Backroom deals, if you will, but a clan ownership stake has gotten their attention, mostly because they see you as another backer and want to remain in your good graces, Anna."

Anna nodded.

"Something else Lukyan mentioned," Anna continued. "Uly needs help. Personnel he can trust. People who can fill in for him in various places as deputies."

Lyra was giving her a bit of side-eye at this point.

"What did you have in mind?" her friend asked slowly and a bit defensively.

"Maks is no longer available to go where Uly needs him," Anna said. "He's building a new thing, and I want him to focus as much energy on that as he can because I can see where it will start paying off in another few years. And the Horde won't understand how important it will be until that day when they'll be happy he did it. I was hoping that I could entice you and Voldomir to become more involved."

"How much more?" Lyra pressed slowly.

"Zoryana will become Uly's mother-in-law, and thus more or less directly tied to Uly," Anna nodded. "Chervonya and Maks both did necessary things for me at Bastion, helping Uly build up his new base. Sterling Huff is doing it now, but he's younger than Halyna, for all Uly relies on the man. I'd like to send you to Bastion as my personal representative, Lyra."

She turned to the other sister.

"And if you and Anton would like to take up a more permanent residence there to be close to your daughter, that would help as well," she said. "I'd like to see about establishing a colony of Ononguli out there. Partly as insurance against a future where the *Auga* keep pushing us back and partly to make sure that Uly keeps facing this way, when the Khet and others might draw him other directions."

"How soon until the war comes?" Lyra asked.

"It's already overdue," Anna replied. "Probably would have started by now, save that Uly poked them pretty hard in the third eye twice and they haven't recovered yet. Two more years is the median estimate at present among my advisors."

"What can Uly accomplish in that time?" Zoryana asked astutely.

"He can continue building up the Ononguli," Lyra said. "And his base, but that is far away and will move slower, save that it likely draws in the distant Khet. Especially when my son gets there and sets himself up in direct competition to those fish-boys. I assume that's one thing you'd like kept tamped down, Anna?"

"I need the Khet trading with us," Anna confirmed. "And looking this way, so that they see the benefit in pushing the *Auga* back here, rather than maybe trying to do little things on the borders they have in Sector Fifteen. And I need whoever else Uly finds in Fourteen, because he'll be able to convince them to come. Look at the Isann and his brand new allies, the Samuur. Lukyan tells me that Uly basically recruited them in a week, then went to their capital and borrowed their flagship, pausing to crush some secret pirate base Haydar Ramezani found on the way here. Tomorrow, it becomes official, and a lot of wheels will be turning at the same time."

"As long as I can count on you to protect us from some of the Bondarenko elders, I can talk to Voldomir," Lyra said. "He's probably up for an adventure, especially if Maks is likely to move permanently to Bastion. Or is it permanent?"

"I see Maks going back and forth a great deal," Anna admitted. "Building at Bastion, but also putting down asphalt and way stations on Uly's gravel road. Plus whatever new road Uly threatens to build to the Samuur homeworld, wherever it is."

"Plus Chervonya," Zoryana noted sharply. "You'll need her running interference in all directions as well, won't you?"

"I will," Anna said. "And that's pretty solid, though not fully official. It will happen at some point, I think. Then hopefully she and Maks will be fabulously rich, well-connected, and in a decade I can fully retire, but that's our secret."

"We have enough," Zoryana laughed. "And I'll talk to Anton. We'd discussed at least visiting regularly, but doing something bigger is probably useful. What about the planet?"

"Surveyed and taking investors as well as homesteaders," Anna said. "Not as good as Rayzian, but I'm certain there are places on the surface where we could create Ononguli cities that felt like home. Perhaps that can be part of your mission?"

"I'll see to it," Zoryana nodded.

They both turned to Lyra.

"Of course I'm in, Anna," Lyra grinned. "Let's see what kind of trouble Uly and Dan have brought us this time."

Anna nodded. Some of the things she'd heard from Lukyan had greatly disturbed her, but she needed to talk to Dan before she said anything.

Trouble was brewing.

FORTY-FOUR

Looking around as he exited the small transport craft, Eskil was glad that he had spent time aboard *Nubia*, both at Saari and on the flight here. He was better prepared for a crowd of Ononguli waiting for them as he emerged from the tunnel and into the lounge.

It also helped that he walked next to Uly, with the Emro Elder close at hand to offer commentary, tidbits, and suggestions while Dan and her Combat Team maintained a perimeter.

Eskil had only met a few aliens before Uly had come to Saari. Rare Zuath merchants, mostly tinkers based on what he had learned about the wider galaxy.

That, and Saari was in a deep pocket with no real neighbors for more than fifty light-years in any direction. Only in his lifetime had ships gotten fast enough to span that in a reasonable time.

Now, look how far he had come.

Ononguli reminded him of mountain goats. He didn't even think prey animals in his head, because Suka Kuri had explained how high-strung their culture was. And how mindlessly violent it could be.

Not dishonorable. Well, frequently dishonorable, but as pirates. Thieves.

Brigands.

He wholly supported Uly's mission to destroy such anti-social behavior.

Today, he was walking on an alien homeworld. Not even a small colony close enough to Saari for some trade, but the cultural center of the entire Ononguli Sphere, as Uly and Dan had described it. A rough ball of worlds several hundred light-years across, almost solely inhabited by a single species.

It would be as if the Samuur had begun expanding a thousand years ago, because there was that much space they hadn't filled yet.

Eskil wasn't sure what would happen with Uly in command of that wide range. Certainly, more aliens would come. Would mix.

A year ago, Eskil would have been opposed to such a thing. Horrified. Then he discovered that many of the aliens he knew were people. Nice people. Honorable.

And they understood sports. He looked forward to what competitions the Ononguli might offer, though Uly had warned him that they were more of a persistence hunter species like Humans. Samuur were explosively fast over a short distance. They did not pursue prey on foot for over one hundred kilometers.

Humans and Ononguli apparently relished the idea.

They were not, however, particularly good wrestlers. Not like him.

He supposed that it might come down to archery and fencing, were they to create a multi-species octathalon that was fair to everyone.

Tomorrow's problem. Two Ononguli emerged from the wider crowd. Male and female, though seeing women who were the smaller gender still knocked Eskil a bit off-center.

The fellow traveler named Chayka embraced the male Ononguli.

Maks Sobol. Former temporary Governor of Bastion before Sterling Huff. A man Uly trusted with the most dangerous tasks. That trust that Eskil yearned to earn with Uly.

The woman would thus be Chervonya Borisov. Mated with Maks Sobol, perhaps. Or promised. Also treated with great dignity that extended to hugs.

The Samuur didn't hug, but Eskil had been warned ahead of time, and managed to embrace the two Ononguli at least well enough from the smiles on all faces that Eskil could see.

It was good.

And he survived falling into line with the group, headed in, and boarding a ground transport that carried him into a low, wide city in the distance. The terrain was flat.

He could do this.

FORTY-FIVE

Dan had whispered in Chervonya's ear that she needed to meet with Anna immediately in private, so she wasn't surprised when Harald Parzi motioned her out of the reception at the palace as soon as they got there, then into a side corridor. He gestured her into a room, then closed the door, looking like he was intending to guard it against all comers.

Harald might be older, and a bit of a dork at times, but Dan didn't doubt his seriousness.

Anna was alone in a small room that felt like a tiny library. Bookshelves on both sides. Two chairs and a holographic fireplace.

Anna gestured her to the chair and they sat.

"How much trouble am I in?" Anna asked immediately.

Dan nodded and grimaced.

"First off, it was my idea, not Uly's," she replied.

Anna laughed.

"As if that makes it any less dangerous."

Dan had to agree.

"As to the what," Dan continued, "I could say that I stole the idea from you, except that I already had most of it in place, at least in my head, and this was just the next, logical step."

"What have you done?" Anna turned serious.

"We call it the Congress of Wives," Dan replied simply. Not defensively. Not aggressively. Calmly, even though it might upend everything and make the woman an enemy of some sort.

"Plural?" Anna asked, ears straight out sideways now, like tracking radars.

"Most of the Combat Team," Dan noted. "Each married to Uly and providing him a stable, solid core of advisors, all of whom have met my standards for commitment and lethality, and are thus qualified to speak for their own species when such a thing is necessary."

Anna fell silent, her mouth fallen open.

Silence stretched, pregnant with some emotion that hopefully didn't turn out too bad.

Dan watched the anger take root in those eyes. Then swell up. Then fade.

"Well, that's one way to completely disrupt the galaxy," Anna finally said.

"Originally, Suka Kuri basically ordered me to collect at least one woman of every species that we dealt with on that level," Dan nodded. "I took it several more steps after that, but I think she saw something like this as a possibility from the start. And I sprung it on Uly, rather than the other way around. He's still getting used to looking at them as more than my team."

"Because they're also his team now," Anna nodded back. "Ingenious, if nothing else. Does it work?"

"So far," Dan replied. "Helps that I've known some of these women for many years. Nasrin is still concerned about what the Mazhin Convocation says when they finally hear about it. I specifically got the idea from them, where each of the matriarchs of their respective clans gather as the senior parliament of their dispersed government to decide important things. Here, we're extending it beyond just one species."

"You said most?" Anna asked. "Who have you left out?"

"Anari Supasei," Dan said. "She and Sterling Huff might turn into something serious at some point, and I intend to support both of them in it."

"That means that Uly already has an Ononguli wife?" Anna asked. "Uhm...?"

"Katya Zehlennko," Dan replied.

"And nobody has told the Zehlennko about this?" Anna asked, perhaps smiling just the tiniest amount.

"It happened after you left," Dan said. "We're the first ship that has made that run, to the best of my knowledge, so no, it has not become public knowledge. I wanted to talk to you, here, now, so that you were prepared if this pissed you off to the point that you didn't move forward with the marriage contract. I haven't even gotten the full details from Rabiu and Ethir, other than they both signed off on something."

Again, silence.

"If it was anybody but Uly," Anna mused quietly.

Dan nodded.

"I wouldn't have considered it, no," Dan agreed. "But he intends to build something that will outlive him by all the centuries necessary to make sure that the *Auga* are not a threat to the galaxy. This binds those species that want to join him. And provides them a guaranteed voice in the major decisions."

"Because there will be a woman of their species able to speak," Anna completed the thought. "And I know it works with the Mazhin, because you've sent several more Mazhin trade colony ships into Ononguli space, where I've hosted them and spoke with them personally. They are all matriarchal?"

"At the clan level, yes, at least according to my two groups," Dan replied. "Ships might have a conductor that is male, but there is usually a female making executive decisions behind him. They will see the Congress of Wives as a template they understand. And Nasrin is more than qualified to argue with those women when she sees them."

"What does this mean for Halyna?" Anna asked, pivoting.

"She will need to learn Tai Chi," Dan smiled. "And Sunflower Fist. And Terrible Gaff. And a few others. I'm just sorry that the Ononguli don't really have something similar that can be contributed to the training curriculum I'm building."

"I feel like maybe we should invent one," Anna chuckled. "There must be something. I've just never encountered it. Nor have any of the people advising me."

"So you are at least okay with me stealing a bit of your thunder?" Dan asked.

"Anybody but you, and I would not be," Anna answered. "And Uly. But you two are attempting something that has never been done before, and have recruited a lot of folks to your side. As Lukyan likes to remind me, Uly gets shit done. And he'd *still* pick Uly's side over mine, if we got crossways."

Dan noted the way Anna's voice changed.

"Are you and Lukyan finally getting serious?" she asked.

"After I scared the hell out of him, yes," Anna grinned. "He was stepping back, thinking he'd offended me, so I had to step into that space and not let him get away."

"Good, you shouldn't," Dan told her. "If you weren't keeping him, I was all set to start recruiting potential girlfriends for him. Same with Maks. Is Chervonya still there?"

"There have been double and triple dates since we got home," Anna offered.

"Triple?" Dan was intrigued.

"Lyra and Voldomir Sobol," Anna nodded.

"Maks's mom," Dan realized. "Dangerous woman."

"I hadn't realized that until very recently," Anna admitted. "I remembered her from when we were kids in the last war, both before and after Maks was born. She's a supremely sneaky person. That's why I've asked her to contact you and Uly directly. To represent me at Bastion. And provide Halyna with people she knows. Zoryana and Anton, Halyna's parents, will also go."

"Considering what we did to Maks, what are the limits with Lyra?" Dan asked. "Maks has talked about his mom and I want to meet her, but if she's out there, Uly might want to engage her in a formal manner."

"She'd be good at it," Anna confirmed. "And Voldomir will be good when Maks gets going."

"What's Maks done?" Dan asked, suddenly wary.

She remembered that young punk First Officer on *Compass Rose*. That *Tuesday*. And what he'd grown into with *Treta Envoy*. Then *Governor Maks*.

"He intends to become an Ononguli Trade Factor, possibly homeported out of Bastion, but I might need him here more initially, because he's talking about founding import/export banks and buying or establishing shipyards that Uly will need when the war comes."

"A Trade Factor?" Dan was astonished.

However, it was Maks. She'd seen his potential.

"He blames Rabiu and the Khet," Anna grinned. "And has recruited Rabiu and Ethir. Plus Lukyan. And the Bondarenko. Plus the Ononguli Horde itself, represented by their *Vatazhko*. Uly is the one partner he hasn't nailed down yet, but I'm not concerned there."

"Nor would I be," Dan managed, past a tongue dry with possibilities. "So we're all still likely to turn into a clan at some point?"

"It's already grown beyond what I think I could stop," Anna admitted wryly. "At least without causing so much trouble that the Horde itself might be broken into pieces and not recoverable before the *Auga* launch their next war."

"They haven't started yet, have they?" Dan pressed.

"No, but Uly and Maks might provoke them, when news gets out."

"Do we need another raid like Nyri?" Dan asked, watching Anna grow still and serious.

"We might," she answered after a long pause. "Hell of a wedding present, if you want to be so rude, but that's the sort of thing that gets horns engaged. And you have a much more dangerous vessel this time."

"Let's set up some meetings to go tactical and strategic," Dan offered. "The political is messy, but will resolve itself. I'd prefer keeping the *Auga* off-balance for as long as possible, at least until we're ready to invade them."

"INVADE?" Anna gasped.

"They recognize nothing but power, *Vatazhko*," Dan pronounced. "Let us show them power then."

FORTY-SIX

Suka Kuri made it a point to stay close to Eskil. He wasn't overwhelmed by all the strangers and aliens around him, but it still came close to overtopping his bucket every once in a while. A few words from her usually helped reframe things in a form that he was able to quickly internalize.

They found themselves standing somewhat alone on a long, stone patio, facing the northern sun as it climbed the sky.

"Endless Plains?" Eskil asked her, sipping at a bland juice selected for safety purposes. Blair Mitchell was here on the ground, so she had his medical expertise handy. Suka Kuri preferred not needing it.

"So they see it, yes," she nodded to Eskil's question. "Riders on mounts, pursuing vast herds of meat animals as those migrated between various climates and seasons. The weather can be intense with few mountain ranges to interrupt things, but there are enough forests here and there to help. Thus, they worship the Endless Plains."

"And the tall woman was introduced as *Vatazhko*," he continued. "The Lord of the Endless Plains?"

"Anna Shevchenko," Suka Kuri replied. "Head of the council

representing the various major clans of the Ononguli. Smart woman. Friendly to our mission both politically and personally.”

“How will she react to new neighbors on her frontier?” he asked. “Will she reach out and claim Daicia, or allow it to become a Samuur place?”

“I think that depends on you, Eskil,” she told him. “She will listen to your reasoning, if you chose to speak for the Paramount. Or you can send home for a diplomat.”

“No, that was included in my charges,” he shook his head. “To represent him and the rest of the species when Uly met with the Ononguli Horde. I would like to see that place as some sort of stellar lighthouse that draws the Samuur in this direction, but I fear we might not immediately pounce on the opportunities available, and thus allow the Ononguli to win by default.”

Suka Kuri nodded sagely. After enough time around them, she had come to appreciate that the Samuur frequently saw things in terms of athletic competition, which was a vast improvement over war.

Then she had an idea so terribly wicked that she couldn’t help but cackle.

He turned his entire upper body to watch her, perhaps a bit nervously, because she knew he saw her as a giant Samuur woman.

“Sports,” she imposed on his mind.

Eskil nodded.

“Competition between a group of folks,” she said. “Or multiple groups. Shaped by rules and expectations of fair play.”

Again, he nodded.

“What Samuur sports might we deploy to explain your kind to the Ononguli and others?” she asked, watching his eyes widen, then narrow.

“I had a similar thought earlier,” he replied. “Humans and Ononguli are persistence predators, so possessed of great endurance, but generally lacking speed and the mass to usually make effective wrestlers. Fencing and perhaps archery might be places where competition could be made fair, were we to invent an octathalon."

Suka Kuri nodded and smiled. Eskil really was a remarkable example of his kind. She could appreciate why they would make him Commander of their flagship. Possibly Paramount in another decade or two, depending on his desires.

And he already saw the various advantages that each species might bring to the table.

"Why not a team sport?" she asked. "Each individual participating in one facet of your proposed octathalon against a scoring structure. Or perhaps a full team sport that requires representatives of three or more species?"

"Would the Ononguli find such a thing meaningful?" he asked smartly.

"As long as it involved riding an animal, or running around a lot on a flat pitch, I believe so," she offered. "What sports does your kind indulge in?"

"Sprinting, wrestling, fencing, archery, staves," he ticked them off with one hand. "Leaping for height or distance. And throwing a javelin for distance and accuracy. Octathalon. We do not normally run for great distances. Or lift tremendous weights. Those might be things that others could contribute."

"Or we could invent a team sport that required groups chasing a ball," she said. "Tell me about staves."

She was familiar with fencing, archery, and javelins. All ancient hunting tools adapted to modern sports competition.

"Two competitors in a circular arena," he began. "Pads and helmets. Fighting is done with a Samuur-length wooden staff, unadorned. Points for contacts until one competitor is defeated. Injuries are generally bruises, with occasional concussion, though those are more common among new students."

"Are you a staff fighter?" she asked, intrigued.

She and Dan had inquired originally about unarmed forms,

possibly missing hints that the Samuur used weapons stylistically instead.

"I can," he shrugged. "All of us learn as part of our training, but I was never more than middling, as my interests focused on warships and command."

She nodded. That might be the person Dan would need later. And Uly.

A Samuur Octathalon athlete babe.

She noted Maks wandering close and nodded him to join them.

"Maks, this is Eskil," she introduced them again in a less formal mode. "Eskil, my friend Maks."

They nodded to one another.

"I know where Daicia is, sir," Maks began. "In my mission of fostering trade, how straight were the lines that might connect Saari, Daicia, and Rayzian?"

Suka Kuri watched Eskil turn a bit wary, but not terribly so. And they were all allies of the Corsac Fox. Daicia had shown the man what that meant.

"From Rayzian to Daicia, it is roughly forty degrees left of true," Eskil offered.

Suka Kuri smiled inside. Closer to thirty-eight, but near enough for polite conversation.

"Ah," Maks responded. "So roughly parallel to the road one might take to Bastion via Krilic? I ask because a new species means new trade, and I'm trying to get a running start on all the other merchants around here to see how I might serve your needs."

Eskil glanced up at her for confirmation, so Suka Kuri nodded.

"It is my understanding that our current rate of technology lags somewhat," Eskil offered.

Maks nodded as if he'd seen scans of *Tiikeri* and drawn the same conclusion.

"Given the location possibly roughly midway, would your elders welcome a modern shipyard to construct and repair vessels?" Maks asked. "It solves many of my geographical problems while assisting your economic development."

Even Suka Kuri was a little shocked at that, but she had to remember that Maks wasn't entirely Ononguli these days. He was more in Uly's mold than anything, he and Lukyan.

"I think it might be beneficial," Eskil replied. "We had expected the need to acquire such ships, possibly secondhand or worse, and then work from there."

"I don't have time for that," Maks stated flatly, one hand emphatically chopping air. "Not with new allies of the Corsac Fox. You and I will speak again later, and in much greater detail, so I can calculate what you will need and how we can get it for you."

Then he surprised them both by bowing, smiling, and walking away.

"What just happened?" Eskil asked quietly.

"You are an ally of the Corsac Fox, Eskil," she reminded him. "You have far more friends out there than you are aware of. And Maks will be an important one."

"I see," he said.

And she thought that he did.

The Samuur had come to Bastion to challenge Uly's right to build on their frontier, but it had been a sporting thing. Fair competition. Rules.

Uly had captured their minds and drawn them into his orbit, because he was Uly.

Now, they could be part of something much greater, to everyone's benefit.

Suka Kuri simply smiled that she'd been alive in the modern era to see it happen.

FORTY-SEVEN

Uly wandered through the crowd, being lionized by various folks. Harald Parzi had appeared at one point to say hello and gossip. Maks and Lukyan and Chervonya all circulated, mostly making meaningless small talk given the crowd.

Ethir appeared first, like a magic trick in the swirl of people. And smiling in that way that would make smart people put a hand on their wallet.

Uly steered him off into a space where they could pretend to have a bit of privacy.

"Haven't seen Dan to tell her, so you get to be first," Ethir chirped.

"She's disrupting Anna's day," Uly replied.

"Oh?"

Uly gave him a whispered barebones explanation, to which Ethir whistled.

"Okay, not sure we can top that," he muttered. "But we're turning Maks into a Trade Factor. Legal Department and Combat Team have an ownership share. So do you. Couple of other big players, and potentially huge upside profits once he opens a Class-B share pool to common investors."

Uly had spent enough time around Ethir and Rabiu to follow most of that explanation. Money. Power, as an outgrowth, but a lot of money involved if Ethir thought so.

What good was money, though, in and of itself?

"What does Maks do with it?" he asked.

"Charter a merchant bank and build shipyards," Ethir grinned wickedly. "Planning to develop a fleet for you when you need it to stomp those *Auga* punks. Most of what everyone is sailing today might be junior varsity, if we can reverse engineer some of *Nubia*'s gear."

"Talk to Sadeq about that," Uly replied. "He might be able to."

Nods.

It was nice, being surrounded by competence. Folks who could estimate where he was headed and what he would need, then take it onto their own shoulders to make it happen first.

New fleets? Shipyards? Trade? All the things that the Spinward Reaches would need to help the Ononguli and others resist the *Auga*. Plus, knowing Maks, it would draw in the Khet deeply, helping forge that thing Uly saw in his dreams.

"What other high points do you need me to approve?" Uly asked.

"Dan should be happy with the contract," he replied. "Niggling points, but we got most of what we wanted from Anna's people and the fiddly bits weren't that onerous. I've even met the bride, briefly, and I think you'll like her."

Good. He'd seen pictures of the woman, but that was it. And wasn't going to see her here, at a reception for Anna's government, because he and Dan had to sign the final contract before things moved forward.

Assuming Anna didn't pack him right back up onto *Nubia* and send him off for what he and Dan had done.

Then he saw the two women emerge from a corridor. Must have been meeting and Dan telling her.

Uly studied body language. Dan and Anna were both mostly satisfied, so he let go a bit of a quiet sigh. At least it didn't look like a major squabble was about to erupt.

You never knew, when playing in this league.

They approached. Folks seemed to sense the two women coming, because everyone drew back a shade, opening a circle around him and Ethir. Lukyan and Rabiu appeared out of the crowd, but didn't step close. Ethir and Rabiu shared a secret nod.

Uly studied Anna. She didn't give much away, but nodded.

"I've updated her," Dan murmured, so Anna knew that some of the other women about the room were more than bodyguards these days.

"I suppose I should give up trying to outguess you," Anna said as she stepped close. "But Dan and Suka Kuri take all the blame?"

"I found out last," Uly grinned. "After she got the Combat Team to approve."

Anna seemed mollified at that.

"And what changes with you, Uly?" Anna asked.

"Hopefully nothing, Anna," he replied. "We become much closer allies. I bring in the Spinward Reaches. You bring in the Sphere. Other friends contribute to building a thing that eventually stops the *Auga*. Honestly, that's my main goal."

"What about other Humans?" she asked carefully.

"If the Yarikh really are, then I'm recruiting them as well," he said. "At present, I don't foresee heading to *Danumash* or *Batyr* to recruit. At least not until I have an enormous fleet backing me that I can convince those folks to listen instead of shooting first. We Humans are not always the most rational people. I am a bad example of the rest."

She looked like she wanted to challenge him on that, but glanced at Dan and nodded instead.

He could tell her how either *Danumash* or *Batyr* would react to that sort of thing. Hell, an invasion fleet of aliens might convince them to make common cause, Humans against the rest of the galaxy.

That was literally the last thing he needed, even as useful as mobs of dangerous sailors might be when it came time to go at the *Auga* directly. He needed them willing to fight the *Auga* first.

"As to the rest," he continued, "that's up to you. If we're still on good footing, then Ethir tells me that we can sign and move forward quickly. Obviously, I need to talk to Maks, given the rumors I'm hearing. And you need to meet with Eskil Haldur, since he's a closer neighbor than I am."

"All of that can wait until later," Anna said. "Today, let us celebrate that you have come to Rayzian and brought friends. It strikes me as a beginning of something and we should acknowledge it thus."

Then she surprised him by hooking elbows and drawing him towards a cluster of folks back in a corner.

"Plus," she murmured, "I want you to talk directly to a few folks, because the fire-breathers will still be a problem tomorrow and I'd like you to work your charm on Teke and Pasternak. I think Stefaniya Baran will be more willing to support you openly these days, but that's because you aren't some upstart punk."

"I'm not?" he teased. "I have two warships, a station, and a single planet, Anna."

"And you have a dream, Uly," she corrected him. "Look at what you've already accomplished."

He supposed so. And she was right. Time to lock horns with some of the hard-headed elements of the Council, if he was about to become a major ally to the Bondarenko and the Sobol.

And the Shevchenko.

And, he grinned, someone would need to tell the Zehlennko that they had joined as well.

He was about to step ankle deep into the mire around here.

At least he had brought friends.

FORTY-EIGHT

Sitting in her front room, Chervonya had survived the day. And various people subtly asking when she and Maks would be getting serious. It helped that Uly and Anna were both distracted, the one because it was now common knowledge that he would be marrying into the Bondarenko and the other because she and Lukyan had taken to occasionally holding hands in public, though he still looked like a man ready to run for his life at any loud sound.

It was one of the ways she'd measured the fork in the road separating Lukyan Chayka from Maks Sobol.

At least so far. A rap on the door brought it all back. Hopefully, no emergency suddenly cropped up and required her to deal with it tonight.

Just about the only thing she could think of would be the *Auga* suddenly arriving or Uly suddenly departing.

She rose from the couch and opened the door warily.

Fortunately, it was only Maks. Only Maks?

It was Maks, and he was smiling. Hopefully, no emergencies.

"You still interested in company?" he asked, standing on the threshold instead of entering as she stepped back.

"Some," she admitted. "Maybe not a lot, but I'm glad to see you."

He nodded and followed her as she sat on the couch, taking the far end where there was space between them.

Did she want that? Maybe tonight. And Maks understood at a nonverbal level.

She smiled at him. He grinned back.

"I spoke with Anna this afternoon," he offered. "Also Dan, Uly, Lukyan, Suka Kuri, and Eskil Haldur, but each individually."

"Everyone on board?" she asked.

Anna had practically dragged her into the conspiracy of Maks's new bank as soon as he'd left her office, back on *Fire Diamond*. Since then, he had used her as a sounding board many times, adapting Khet and Human ideas of commerce into something that would make sense to the Ononguli. To the unruly Horde.

"So far," he replied. "Helps that Uly's people have already blessed it, so I've got a running start on that end of things. And Anna will support me at this end. I do, however, have one major issue that I feel needs to be resolved, now that Uly is here and the storm winds are beginning to pick up."

Storm winds. That howl off the Endless Plains warning you to get to cover while you were still dry. If you could.

It wasn't always possible.

Chervonya studied Maks, unconsciously flashing back to first meeting him. To Anna describing him as half-Human. To where he'd moved over the last few years.

Any resemblance was entirely accidental, because he hardly even looked the same, having grown more confident and something.

"Oh?" she prompted.

"You," he said, catching her by surprise. "I need to ask you some hard questions. You don't have to answer them tonight, but you will need to answer them at some point, because things are about to run."

She nodded. Stampede in the offing, if only metaphorical.

At least she hoped so.

"I'm going to have to spend a lot of time away from Rayzian," he explained patiently. "Partly at Bastion, establishing things, but many of those things start to happen now and will take time setting roots. Partly, I need to talk to Uly's latest new allies and see what Saari needs. What will make the Samuur formidable. How to permanently make them our allies as well."

"Our?" she asked, eyes narrowing.

"I am still Ononguli," he nodded seriously. "The Horde is still my home, though I am trying to expand it to include others."

"To build that thing Uly needs," she said.

"More than Uly, but yes, that thing," he said, pausing for a breath. "It means that I have to be elsewhere, while Anna has to be here, because that is her duty. And you are her niece and potentially her heir, if you desired it. Has she assigned you any specific duties beyond being her advisor and occasional ambassador?"

"She has not," Chervonya replied. "What do you know?"

"Nothing," he shook his head. "I would like to know if you would be interested in coming with me. With making what we have more serious, however serious you are comfortable with. With you traveling with me aboard some vessel as we spend time at Z'Gosza, Bastion, Taeli, Isann, Saari, and anywhere else that I need to go, as I build up the thing that eventually lets me retire somewhere and live in a big palace. I can't have the palace today, because I have too much to do. But I need to see about a ship. If you wish to join me, I'll need something big and impressive, so you have your own space, even as we have our shared space. If not, I can buy something small and fast and maybe not much more than *Scavenger Angel*."

Chervonya's breath caught. They'd talked in vague terms, but never personal. Never discussed living together on a ship as a couple. Or more.

She wanted more, but hadn't been entirely sure about Maks, since he had become the favorite son of so many people for what he'd done. Random strangers on the street publicly knew him as *Governor Maks.* Various mothers were scheming to introduce him to their daughters.

"How much more serious?" she asked pointedly.

"As serious as you're willing to go," he replied, grinning slyly. "I'm just a punk pirate trying to get rich here. You're the one with dangerous political connections."

Then he was smiling. She laughed. At the same time, there was a kernel of truth to it.

"How big a ship?" she asked.

"That depends on what Anna lets me buy." His grin got bigger. "War coming and all that, so it needs to be a warship. And fast. And big enough that I can decorate it with the sort of silly opulence that will make those Khet jealous when I entertain them for dinner."

"You'll never hire Vahid away," she teased.

"No, but I absolutely intend to find a chef willing to go work in Vahid's kitchen for a while, learning all those recipes," he agreed. "Uly has established a pattern here, and I intent to take advantage of it."

"Never return to Rayzian for long?" she asked.

That was her fear. That she'd have to choose between what he was offering versus what Anna had. Money OR power?

"When I can afford it, palaces at both," he turned serious. "And a yacht to travel between them. What would make Chervonya Borisov say yes?"

She gasped in spite of herself. After all this time, Maks was one of the few men she knew who could surprise her.

What would make her say yes? Beyond the fact that Maks was asking, and she'd pretty much already said yes to herself yesterday.

"It will need to be a large, pretty ship," she grinned. "So various Borisov and Shevchenko kin can travel in style. And whoever else."

"I'd considered buying *Treta Envoy,* but it's not fast enough for my needs," he described, still calm and sober. "Nor armed to the level

I demand, because the road is still dangerous and Uly will need help stomping on pirates. *Nubia* would be a pattern, but Uly's not ready for that."

"You might be the first person he would trust with something like that," she countered.

Governor Maks. Even to random kits on the street.

He fell silent, eyes locked on something over her left shoulder, probably ten thousand light-years away.

"He might," Maks mused. "And Anna might let me hire Lukyan away for something like that, because she'll know I'll keep circling him to Rayzian. Let me talk to Uly and see if he finds that acceptable. I had intended to build Interceptors initially. Fast and tough so we could swarm *Auga* Strikers. Maybe we simply need to ram them with our horns. But that's tomorrow. I could build you something that will make you say yes?"

"You already have, Maks," she said, holding out a hand he took. "The rest is merely adventures, and I would love to share them with you."

She pulled him close and kissed him. Neither of them were innocents, but it had an innocent delicacy that she savored. Maks was shaping his life in ways to make her happy, instead of demanding she adjust to his.

An alien concept, but that was what she loved about him.

And maybe, just maybe, the future of the Ononguli Sphere itself.

FORTY-NINE

Uly had on his best uniform, as Omid had personally cleaned and pressed it. Haircut, shave, shower, presentable, like this was an inspection.

And, he supposed, it was.

Dan was on one side. Suka Kuri on the other. The Combat Team dressed to storm a station, minus only the guns. Haydar to stand at his side. Sterling should have been here, but he had to be at Bastion.

Too much to do. Too many places to be. Never enough friends.

Maks and Chervonya held hands off to one side of the large room. Lukyan close by and a little jittery, but Uly understood why. Lyra and Voldomir Sobol had been introduced. Zoryana and Anton Bondarenko as well. He could see where Maks got it.

Various others, including the entire Council, with Harald glowering mightily whenever one of the fire-breathers muttered. Harald wasn't taking any shit from anyone today, and had made that abundantly clear early.

The room itself was open and airy. Something for receptions, with tables along one wall holding gifts wrapped in tissue. Food trays near the back wall, where catering staff could keep them filled or fill plates. Coffee bar on the third wall.

The room was by invitation only. Roughly one hundred people, half his and half Anna's.

Major players. Even the Zehlennko were only represented by Katya, though Uly would have a long, quiet conversation with them in a week or so. They would need that long to emotionally recover, being one of the smallest, poorest clans as Anna might measure things.

Suddenly thrust into some sort of alliance with Bondarenko and Sobol and Shevchenko because one of their daughters had been a pirate.

That brought a smile to his face. Reformed pirate. Mostly. Serious badass willing to bash horns with any of the Ononguli men getting out of line. Just like the rest of the Congress.

There were tables scattered about, but nobody sat at the moment. Uly and Dan circulated as Warlord and Chief of Staff, while the Combat Team and Legal Department went to work charming Ononguli politicians. And potential allies.

He needed everyone in this room, regardless of the height they might look down their noses at a Human. Or Samuur. Or Isann. Or Khet. Or any of the rest.

Nobody got to look down their noses at Emro, because Yanouk was looking feisty today and Suka Kuri was approaching this like it was the most important event of her already long and illustrious lifetime.

Uly hoped not, but kept his opinions to himself.

Exemplar of the Arts. Moss School. And occasionally Sabre.

Living Legend, and nobody was allowed to challenge her on those grounds.

Shadows at the door caught his eye, and Uly turned to see Anna escort Halyna into the room.

He flashed back to Dan's joke about a traditional Ononguli

wedding, where you met over breakfast, married right before lunch, and rode off into the sunset while everyone else celebrated over dinner.

Worse, Anna had agreed. The sun was barely an hour over the horizon. The air outside still had a damp crispness that wanted to be fog, but wasn't quite cool enough today. Give it two weeks.

She was a shadow, then she stepped into the room and Uly got a chance to see her in the flesh.

Long black hair, pulled back into a simple braid, as befit the ancient riders they still saw in themselves, looking in the mirror. Healthy red skin and sharp eyes.

Uly knew that she had chosen to go traditional, so all the colors were natural dyes derived from plants, rather than industrial things.

Old fashioned, though he'd been told that it was a political statement by the Bondarenko, rather than personal, as Halyna had trained and sailed for a a time right out of school. Possibly following in Maks' footsteps, but not nearly as far.

Opera cape to her waist, a dark gray he knew was derived from acorns, lined in a soft orange from hawthorn leaf. Good riding pants in a tannish-gray from nettle leaves, tucked into brown riding calf boots. Tunic a soft yellow from bog myrtle, belted in the same brown leather as her boots.

Uly smiled at her. He'd known enough Ononguli now to appreciate how attractive the young woman was.

Young? He felt old, but she wasn't really that much younger.

Still, she smiled back a bit hesitantly as Anna drew her deeper into the room and the crowd.

Conversations fell silent and Anna walked Halyna right up to the edge of the sudden circle that had bubbled around him.

Uly bowed to the woman. At the end of the day, this was a political treaty made flesh. She might have been given a choice, from what Anna had assured him, but Halyna Bondarenko was about to both sever herself from the Horde and be drawn far deeper into Sphere politics than she probably ever imagined.

"You look lovely," he told her.

"Thank you," she replied.

And she did. Prominent cheekbones on an inverted triangle face. Skin a hint lighter than scarlet. Delicate ears pointed straight sideways and perfectly symmetric. Black eyeballs. Glowing eyes.

Medium height and size for an Ononguli woman meant that he saw her as slender and a bit small. Taller than Ciah, weighing roughly the same.

One might think delicate, but he saw an iron fierceness in her eyes that gave lie to such a thought. This one had been raised a warrior and a scholar, and had it in her to become something much more.

And Maks had quietly hinted that none of the Ononguli men she'd ever dated had lasted long, simply unable to keep up with her brains and ambition.

It wasn't about to get much bigger than this.

"Ulysses Fortier, of Gralbo in *Batyr*," he offered formally, nodding again and following the traditional Ononguli script for such things.

"Halyna Bondarenko, of Rayzian in the Sphere," she replied.

She had a lovely voice. A throaty alto that carried well, even if the room was still utterly silent.

Over her shoulder, Uly could see Harald turn and scowl at a couple of potential troublemakers, utterly cowing them into submission because nobody wanted to be beaten up by an old, skinny Ononguli man.

Nobody gave Harald enough credit for what he'd done as a young man. Or maybe they'd forgotten.

Uly knew.

Uly stepped forward, separating from Dan and Suka Kuri.

Halyna moved away from Anna. They were almost close enough to dance.

"I come seeking your hand in marriage," Uly continued formally. "In binding our two clans and houses into closer partnership against the rest of the Horde and the galaxy."

Close enough to the traditional phrase, adding only the last bit. Because this was going to be so much more than just *The Horde*.

She studied him for a moment, seeking something, then held out her hand for him to take.

Around the room, a quiet sigh multiplied by dozens of mouths and possibly echoing clear to the *Auga* Imperial Palace on *Ajorn*.

"I give my hand that we might be married and joined as one," she replied, completing the formula.

He squeezed it just enough to convey something, watching her eyes but nothing changed.

Committed. Against whatever might come.

Uly turned to Anna next. Traditionally, the Best Man would announce it, but everyone presumed that the words would be better from an Ononguli than a Mazhin.

"My friends, there will be a wedding," Anna called to the group. "Come, let us gather and feast!"

Uly led Halyna to the largest table, seating her then taking up the chair on her left, where she reflected his dominant right hand and he became her shield arm. A traditional Ononguli thing that supposedly dated back to before starflight, if you wanted to believe the old sages.

Uly accepted it at face value.

They were committed.

All of them.

FIFTY

Dan was here today as Chief of Staff, rather than First Wife, so she had dressed in her best uniform and largely stayed off to one side. Once Anna handed Halyna off, Dan joined the *Vatazhko* in getting people moving to the food trays as they were uncovered.

The Ononguli didn't do long engagements. Not even when politics were involved. She wondered if this might jar Maks and Lukyan loose from whatever had frozen them emotionally, but Dan also understood that both men saw themselves as marrying way above their normal station.

Even the Horde could get a little weird about that.

Still, it was good. She got food, then moved to a second table, away from Uly and Halyna. Haydar would be over there, and could fill her in on everything she missed.

Harald sat beside her with a wry grin conveying all manner of impish evil. But she'd also seen him turn on the charm. And whatever the opposite of charm was when dealing with Bakhtiar Teke and Nihal Pasternak. Both were at this table, and minding their tongues, wonder of wonders.

Dan wondered what threats Anna had piled on beyond Harald's.

Food was simple fare. Meats sliced and sauced, with vegetables and flatbreads on the side. Traditional stuff, rather than some of the more elaborate things like Vahid might have come up with if challenged.

Uly and Anna, working to draw in the old-school thinkers. Traditionalists, like the two across from her.

Bakhtiar Teke locked eyes with her when they were both mostly done eating.

"What happens next?" he asked in a tone just short of demanding.

And just short of getting the sharp edge of someone's tongue. Dan had other allies at the table besides Harald.

"Next week or next season?" she asked back, challenging the old fart to step himself up, rather than making snide commentary from the back of the room.

Specism wasn't that far from the racism she'd grown up with. And dealt with until she met Uly.

Teke flinched a bit under her tone, but held firm.

"Next season," he offered, modulating himself to sound less like a pissy squirrel.

"Anna suggested we go blow up an *Auga* base somewhere," Dan smiled. "Take *Nubia* and a fleet of Horde raiders and blast the crap out of some punk somewhere."

Dan left it at that, watching Teke and Pasternak glance at each other in sudden surprise.

"Where?" Teke asked after a moment.

"I'm not from around here," Dan reminded him. "Where might you go, if you wanted to poke someone in their third eye?"

Lots of sudden buzzing around her as folks turned to neighbors and indulged in daydreams.

Dan nodded to Harald and finished off her bread. He smiled

knowingly, but he was also Anna's closest ally on the Council and had known her and Uly the longest, save for Lukyan and Maks.

"Nyri would be too obvious," Teke mused, eyes unfocused.

"And supposedly reinforced against another raid like that," Dan said. "I've given some thought to hitting someplace deeper. An *Auga* world, rather than one they've taken from the Ononguli over the centuries. Maybe something over in Sector Fifteen, where we can kick them in the shins extra hard where the Khet and Zuath get to watch."

More buzz. More excitement building, because most of these men were juvenile delinquents that didn't always grow up.

"How would you hit something that far away?" Pasternak asked now.

Slightly younger than Teke. Less bulky. Less mouthy, but only because he spoke with greater precision, according to Anna and Harald.

"Hire a fast cargo transport to haul food," Dan suggested. "Maybe a couple of them. Stage them midway somewhere, possibly like Taeli, so a squadron can quickly resupply and then race inward before anyone can get rich selling the *Auga* military intelligence."

She knew it had to happen, even though the Ononguli forbade it and denied indulging. Always under the table. Always subtle and untraceable.

If she thought that the *Auga* could possibly react fast enough, she wouldn't say anything here, but even then, the imperial overlords would have to reinforce more than a dozen places along that frontier to even try to stop her. And those ships would have to come from somewhere else.

The Ononguli around her grumbled sourly at the thought of spies in their midst. Dan wondered how much traditionalist specism would have to be overcome to actually help the *Auga*. Probably more than before, since Adrian Sobol had been sentenced to thirty years at hard labor.

Not that he didn't deserve it, being the putz he was, but that also broke with old traditions that saw *Auga* and Ononguli prisoners traded home pretty regularly.

Would she be willing to rescue the punk? Doubtful. Him and his ground forces commander, Ruvim Boyko, were at the very top of Uly's shit list. Even as much as Uly still hated Thorley Eldridge.

Some insults would never be forgiven.

"How official is this?" Teke asked, turning cagey on her.

"Anna wasn't sure that the Council would approve something like a deep raid," Dan lied smoothly to the two men. "Maybe you should get your folks on board and propose it to her instead? A wedding present? Uly would be willing. We've always been about hurting the *Auga* and helping the Horde. This entire alliance is so that Uly will be there when the Sphere needs him. When you need him."

Rude. Low blow, even, but it wasn't like they didn't deserve it. Uly could spend the rest of his life living in Sector Fourteen as Warlord, building up a nation there. But the *Auga* would come eventually. Perhaps centuries from now, having ended the Ononguli Sphere, just as they had absorbed and digested other neighbors that had been in their way.

"How soon do you need to know?" Teke asked.

"We're here for at least two weeks, meeting and setting things up," Dan replied. "After that, I don't know. You have that long to convince Anna and Uly otherwise."

She left it at that and tried not to smile as those two put their horns together and started scheming.

Anna had said that they'd talk themselves into it, if they thought it was their own idea.

Dan was happy to let them, because the *Auga* needed occasional deep raids to keep them off-balance. The Horde tended to be chaos, until the moment *Auga* ships arrived, then everyone swarmed.

They didn't understand how to create a strategic plan. Or maybe Ononguli culture was simply too fractious and individualistic to actually stick to one.

They needed Uly, just as much as he needed them.

She'd bring them to the battlefield to fight. Just watch.

FIFTY-ONE

Eskil had expected to be a minor participant, largely off to one side and ignored in the face of the much larger events going on. Thus, being seated next to the *Vatazhko* of the Ononguli herself was a surprise. Especially when Suka Kuri grinned at him with unspoken foreknowledge.

Uly, on the far side of Shevchenko, was concentrating on the bride, so Eskil was somewhat on his own when the *Vatazhko* turned and got serious.

Still, he had demanded this. And won his place on the platform enough times to earn it.

He watched the woman.

Tall, but not as tall as a Samuur woman. Just as intense. Just as *present*.

Just as dangerous, if not more.

"Daicia," she began somewhere in the middle, then watched him.

Eskil was here as Ambassador, as well as First Commander. Because he had demanded it.

Time to earn those points anew.

"Uly suggested a free port, given proximity to recognized

Ononguli borders," Eskil replied. "As such, it provides a direct link back to Saari, however long that trip is. Roughly two-thirds of the way to Bastion, but there are other places Haydar Ramezani suggested forward outposts could be established."

He watched her absorb that.

"Would the Samuur give way, if I demanded it remain Ononguli?" she asked slowly.

Eskil considered his words carefully.

"Probably," he replied. "But doing so breaks the connection back and necessitates a Samuur outpost somewhere between to draw a new border between us."

He left it at that. *Tiikeri* might be the flagship of the fleet, but he knew that it only ranked somewhere near the bottom of that class for the Ononguli. He'd seen the scans.

And there were at least two full *classes* of warships larger than that, here in orbit with *Nubia*, a half-step smaller than *Nubia* and a half-step larger.

Nothing that even a fleet of Samuur ships could deny.

Today.

Maks Sobol did offer a future where that was not the absolute case. And Maks was said to be one of the most honorable men Eskil might ever meet.

Still, the border was either friendly, or it wasn't. Uly and Suka Kuri had warned him about this woman. He caught her appraisal.

"Should we jointly hire the Zuath to administer it for us?" she asked.

It took him a moment to parse that, understand it, and place it.

A most interesting conundrum.

Eskil smiled and looked around until he found Chief Aibek Sulaymanov at a different table. Another of Uly's new allies. Newest, even, except that the Samuur had shown up and challenged everyone to a competition of honor.

Sulaymanov looked up and asked a question with furless cheeks and dark eyebrows.

Eskil smiled and nodded, so the Isann man rose and walked over.

"My friend?" Sulaymanov asked as he knelt between them.

Eskil turned to the *Vatazhko*.

"Perhaps we could jointly hire the Isann to administer Daicia for us?" Eskil countered. "It draws more allies into trade along that corridor, when they might singly face Bastion from the rear otherwise and largely ignore most of Ononguli space on their long flank."

She blinked, surprised.

Eskil grinned. Whiskers, ears, **and** chin.

He turned to Sulaymanov and watched that man quickly absorb the implications.

"Technically, we lack any sort of treaties with either Samuur or Ononguli directly," Sulaymanov offered. "That might make us a useful neutral third party to arbitrate, but I will point out that much of that region is claimed on paper by the Corsac Fox, with whom we are all three properly allied."

Eskil really liked the Isann, both Aibek and the people themselves. He had only gotten parts of their great national poem orally, because it was in a strange written tongue.

Explorers, instead of athletes, but both driven forward by a **demand** to excellence.

And Daicia would be deep in the darkness for them. They would see that as the same sorts of challenge Eskil did.

The *Vatazhko* studied the Isann.

"But you might not be opposed to such a proposal?" she asked.

"The Chief of Chiefs is not present himself, but did delegate me to make certain decisions in his stead," Sulaymanov nodded. "Those things that protect and support Uly. I believe that this might qualify."

It was Eskil's turn to nod. Uly had captured the Isann's minds first, though Eskil could see the Samuur doing the same soon enough.

The woman turned back to him. Eskil held her gaze.

"It is a start," she conceded. "I will delegate ambassadors to work out the details, but I think that will serve all of us the best."

Eskil nodded.

The Samuur had accidentally wandered into galactic politics at a dangerous level, but they had found Uly first, and that would likely mean everything.

Because it would be done with honor.

FIFTY-TWO

Suka Kuri approved. She had possibly tossed Eskil to the wolves, at least metaphorically, but she could see it working well as he, Anna, and Aibek quickly negotiated some deal, even as Dan and Harald were working some magic on the boneheads of the Council across the way.

She had placed herself directly across the round table from Halyna, watching that one absorb it all. From her own studies, Suka Kuri knew that the Bondarenko weren't traditionally all that close to the Shevchenko, but Anna and Lyra went back a generation on a personal level. And Maks and Lukyan had been in the right place on that legendary *Tuesday*, yet another of those wondrous coincidences that occasionally had her questioning if there really were gods out there, however black their sense of humor might be.

Still, Uly had luck and charm. It had gathered him unlikely friends and continued to do so as more fell under his spell, so it was just as well that he wasn't the sort of egomaniacal psychopath that would use such power for evil.

It would be her chore to establish the Moss and Sabre Schools of Bastion such that future generations held to that ideal, rather than falling into monstrosity later, when Uly and Dan were gone. To see that Starfare upheld the highest ideals as well, instead of turning into a school for piracy.

To save the future itself.

Halyna made eye contact as someone touched Uly's shoulder with some conversation. Three meters separated them, but Suka Kuri's eyes and ears were still probably better than many of the Ononguli in here.

She could see the nerves in there, having watched so many of Dan's women go through similar emotional arcs, so Suka Kuri nodded and smiled.

"You will be among friends and sisters," she told the youngster quietly, watching those words land like the first fluffy snowflakes of a winter storm. "They will challenge your mind and body in ways that Uly would never do."

She could say that, having spoken with all of the Combat Team —all of the Congress—directly and individually once they were all Wives. Uly had moved even more slowly than she had anticipated with everyone except Dan, but those two had shared a quiet love for years, unable to express it until pushed into a corner and forced to acknowledge such things.

Halyna would grow into her role at the pace she felt most comfortable.

"What will we build at Bastion?" Halyna asked, showing even greater intellect than Suka Kuri had expected.

Already understanding that she would be part of that thing, and seeking to understand what it would be.

And could be.

"All people gathered," Suka Kuri answered. "All worlds. All species. All equal under one justice and one law. That is Uly's promise to eternity."

Those words rocked the youngster, but Suka Kuri had been at this for lifetimes and knew how to split diamonds.

"What will the Horde think?" Halyna asked.

Suka Kuri saw Uly turn back, silent and listening as the other fellow moved on.

"The Horde will be of two minds," Suka Kuri prophesied in her terrible, oracular role for the history books. "One will see the future and seek to embody it. The other will cling stubbornly to the past, unable to comprehend a galaxy where they don't fail."

Halyna gasped. Uly grimaced. Anna Shevchenko glowered from where she was listening, but kept her peace.

"You, Halyna Bondarenko, must guide the Ononguli into that future," she continued. "Even the ones who would rather live pure lives in the ashes of their worlds after the *Auga* come. Because the *Auga* will come, if allowed. The Horde cannot stop them, even united in a way that only your legends ever speak of. The Ononguli must evolve into a new form. A new polity. A new civilization itself, because the current one is not enough."

Diamonds were among the hardest substances naturally occurring. Pure carbon aligned into a pattern of unclouded, ultimate strength.

It required utter precision to shape them.

"Not enough?" Halyna asked, an angry rise in her eyes never making it to her tongue.

"No," Suka Kuri pronounced. "If you cannot ally with the rest of the galaxy, they will eventually ally without you, and plan to fight over your conquered worlds when it is their turn to face the *Auga* directly. And you cannot do it alone. But you do not have to, because others are already offering to help the Ononguli in their time of need. Look around you at all the alien faces you see, if you had any doubts what could be assembled. And this is only the beginning. The *Vatazhko* understands. You must understand as well, if you are to save your people."

She left it at that. Rude, old women should also know when to let the children absorb their lessons and internalize for themselves.

Anna nodded, a ghost of movement that finally saw where Suka Kuri was taking things. Other heads as well out of the corners of her eyes, but she already knew that most were Anna's allies.

Uly's face was already neutral and friendly by the time Halyna turned to look at him. To study him with perhaps a new understanding of things than she'd had when she woke up this morning.

They held the tableaux, then finally nodded to one another.

Suka Kuri wanted to blow out a heavy sigh, but kept it internal. Halyna Bondarenko was literally one of the most important cornerstones of the future Uly needed to build.

If he got her fully on his side, he could beat the *Auga*. Suka Kuri understood that. He would bring in others to help. Khet, Isann, even Samuur.

But it all started with the Ononguli. Those fractious, juvenile delinquent pirates who could be terrible warriors, but tended to be horrible soldiers. Emotion over deliberation.

Uly and Dan brought that. If Halyna could get her people to listen. To understand. To expand their parochialism into something wider, they could hold the line.

Suka Kuri thought that she had moved the woman far enough.

For today.

FIFTY-THREE

Uly studied the woman from up close. He could see the emotional breaks Suka Kuri had just forced in Halyna's mind. He presumed that she had a greater purpose and would explain it to him later, but right now, his future wife was having some crisis of conscience or confidence.

He held out a hand for her to take. Felt her grip it. Offered his strength.

No words, because any felt like they might be wrong. She seemed to grasp that, because they sat in perfect silence for a few moments. Even the table conversation dropped to nothing around them.

"Can you win?" she asked quietly, something that might have been missed had there been any sound nearby.

"I intend to try," he promised her. "I do not believe the *Auga* as a people are evil, but the *Auga Empire* is. It must be thwarted. Pushed back. Possibly destroyed, but at a minimum forced to undergo the same drastic level of change as we will demand of the Ononguli Sphere, if we are to make the rest of the galaxy safe from them. That is my mission."

"And the others?" she pressed.

It might sound like a political conversation, but it also touched on the personal. Until this week, this woman had been expecting to be his only wife. Now she was one of eight. And not First, though not last in anything but current sequence. And he could see where there would be others later.

How many? He couldn't begin to guess, because that was Dan's job.

"The others have already volunteered to help," he told her. "I have offered time and again to let them head home, but all tell me that this is their home now. Thogin. Emro. Khet. Ononguli. Human. Others. Thus, we must build a thing. A place where they are welcome and welcoming. Where all are, because all are equal. One people."

He watched her absorb that. Anna had said that she ran quiet, but contained a vast intellect. It was part of the reason she had short-listed the young woman initially. And Anna had worked down from thousands of possible candidates to weed them out for any reason that gave her pause, so Uly assumed Halyna Bondarenko was the best candidate Anna could find.

Which said an amazing amount.

"And my role?" she asked.

"The Corsac Fox will need to speak to the Ononguli Sphere," he said. "The Sphere will need to be represented at the highest level of government. One will need to speak for them."

"And that is not Zehlennko?" she pressed.

"It is not," he said. "Katya has been with us from early on, a member of Adrian Sobol's crew who changed sides and broke out of prison with me. She is part of Dan's Team, as you will be. She became part of the larger group because most of them will be as well. Possibly all, save for Anari, but each woman will make that decision with Dan, and inform me later however much I need to know."

He saw that rock her back a little, but understood. Lukyan and especially Maks were more like Humans these days than Ononguli.

Adrian was, in his own dumb, terrible way, almost the archetype against which the average Ononguli male measured himself.

At least until yesterday.

Something landed in her mind, because she leaned out to look at Anna across him.

"You told me, but I didn't believe," Halyna muttered.

"You couldn't have understood until today," Anna replied with a touch of mirth. "You'd have accused me of fanciful bullshit, and, I seem to recall, did at one point."

"And I was wrong," Halyna nodded, then turned back to study his face.

He waited.

"Will the Horde come?" she asked, seemingly leaping over several chasms and fences to arrive at a new understanding.

"You will set an example, but you will not be alone in doing so," he said, turning now to Anna. "Will she?"

On an Ononguli, a blush made them turn a crimson verging on black. It still looked really cute on the *Vatazhko*.

"She will not," Anna said. "And Chervonya and Maks will also be there. If there were more Humans, it would be even better. Will there be?"

"I have an even-dozen men that have no prospects of a Human wife at present," Uly told both women, leaning back a bit. "Some probably would be interested, though all will likely be stationed at Bastion or aboard *Nubia* for the time being."

"What about Rayzian?" Halyna asked.

"I hope that the Bondarenko will step up and assist me," he said. "And the Sobol and others. The Zehlennko, for instance. People I can trust to work for the greater good across all species."

She nodded.

"My parents and aunt and uncle will be traveling to Bastion," she replied.

"And I welcome them and whoever else desires to visit or settle," he said. "Before I go, I hope your clan elders will be willing to step up formally and ally themselves directly to Anna so I can do what needs doing before I return home."

"What comes next?" Halyna asked, catching his tone.

Uly turned to Anna to explain.

"A suggestion that Uly lead another great raid into *Auga* space," Anna said quietly, looking around to nail everyone at the table. "Keep that quiet for now, because I see Dan already twisting minds to have them suggest such a thing to me shortly. *Nubia* will lead it. Others will assist."

Halyna nodded.

"As last time, a statement even the Horde can understand," she murmured.

"The Traditionalists," he corrected her slightly. "Many already support what I'm trying to do, and Bondarenko will gain more allies as people have to decide between this future and the comfortable past that is already failing."

"Bondarenko will send ships?" she asked.

"I haven't asked, and there are no Bondarenko on the Council at present to speak for them, save Anna," he replied. "Perhaps you could convince them?"

"Yes," she said. "I can see where this needs to go. It will be hard, but you think it can be done."

"I do," he agreed. "Otherwise, I'd have stayed at Z'Gosza or someplace over there and built up that corner to take the *Auga* in a flank, the next time they decided to go at the Sphere. This way, perhaps we can all fall on them at once and force them back. Force them to behave. Force them to change."

"Just as we must change?" she asked, a glimmer of humor in her eyes.

"We need to grow up, Halyna," Anna spoke first. "That is the challenge Uly places before the Horde. And he is correct to do so."

She nodded. Uly did as well. That largely summed it up.

Hopefully, he could pull it off.

If not, there was always the depths of Sector Fourteen to retreat to, building up something that might challenge the *Auga* after the Sphere was gone.

Maybe he'd need to go recruit his own hordes of insane Humans at that point.

Gods help the galaxy if it came to that.

FIFTY-FOUR

Dan was surprised that she didn't feel any tug of resentment or jealousy to see Uly kiss Halyna as Anna finished the ceremony. Already, she had adopted the woman into her tribe, it seemed, and found joy.

Looking around, the others were the same way. A new sister to induct into the Congress. To introduce to the galaxy. The Combat Team, against all comers, and bring your *entire* army if you decide to try.

That put a smile on her face. Others shared it as well.

Uly turned in place with Halyna on his arm, to polite clapping in some corners and raucous cheering and whistling in others. And not all of those were Bondarenko cousins.

A lot of Ononguli supported Uly. Probably the prospect of finally winning a war. Dan couldn't promise that, but the more enthusiasm she was able to generate today, the easier things would be tomorrow.

Quickly, Anna led the two to the door and outside, where a pair of saddled zeonx waited. As was traditional, the two would ride off and camp overnight on the Endless Plains, though there wouldn't be any orkac to herd or rope.

Traditional. Old school, from when the Ononguli rode the Endless Plains and followed their herds of orkac everywhere. One more piece to bind a few more minds to Uly's mission, by fully embracing what it meant to be part of those Endless Plains.

They rode off, discreetly surrounded by guards who would protect the newly wedded couple from a safe distance, then get them home tomorrow.

Dan turned to Anna.

"It's done," the *Vatazhko* breathed a sigh of relief as she stepped close.

"Harald would have challenged someone to a duel if they'd mouthed off," Dan reminded her.

"So would a lot of other folks," Anna agreed. "It was still a fear, right up until the end."

"I think I have Bakhtiar Teke and Nihal Pasternak largely recruited," Dan said, leading the woman to the sidebar for something to drink. "Bakhtiar, if anything, might be beating your door down tomorrow with plans. I got that impression from the two as they slipped out the side door when we were done."

Anna nodded and moved to the bar to grab a glass. Dan did the same.

The party itself would wind slowly down over the next several hours, but it was largely a celebration for the Bondarenko and Sobol folks to enjoy. Others had been arriving all morning, and were now winding themselves up, even as Dan led the woman to a different side door and Nasrin waved them through.

Up a flight of stairs, then down a long corridor, she found the players she wanted in a big space with a table on one side and various chairs, sofas, and bookcases elsewhere.

The Congress was there, deployed more as the Combat Team though, as Nasrin followed her in. The Legal Department as well.

Maks, Chervonya, and Lukyan. Harald. Lyra and Voldomir. Zoryana and Anton.

Trouble. Dan smiled.

Anna more or less threw herself into a couch, surprising the hell out of Maks, who was already seated there. Chervonya laughed and put him in the middle. Dan pulled up a chair. Folks began to gather around, including Oleh Bondarenko.

The formal Clan Chief was a heavyset man. Perhaps mid-sixties. Supposedly from the accounting wing of the clan instead of the piracy wing, whatever that meant.

He looked a bit nervous to be here, for all it had begun with his active approval when approached by Anna initially, having gotten down to a half-dozen candidates.

Dan smiled to put him at ease.

Then she turned to Maks. If she'd expected him to blush at all, that was old Maks. New Maks simply nodded and waited for her to speak.

"I've been deep in planning and general conversation with most of the major players," Dan told the group. "It got us this far, but everyone understands that we are only halfway. Uly is celebrating a well-deserved night off with a most interesting woman, but expects us to get things done while he's gone. What else needs doing, while all of us are in one room?"

Maks stirred. She'd expected that.

He turned to Oleh. Also about par.

"I need two accountants and a pirate captain," Maks announced, practically glaring at the man.

Bondarenko contained his shudder, mostly.

"For?" he asked, instead of the first words that made it to his tongue.

"Uly needs someone to be his personal representative to the Horde," Maks replied. "That person must be a high-ranking Bondarenko. Maybe you, but likely whoever is a generation younger and on track to challenge for your spot in another decade, because this is a job for someone with a lot of energy.”

Dan liked the way Oleh flinched under that tone. But he held back from his initial outburst. Then Lyra stepped around a few bodies.

“Nazariy might be a good candidate,” she told the man in a tone brooking no nonsense.

“My son?” Oleh asked, surprised.

“It earns him the job later,” Lyra stated. “And lets the rest of us know if he can handle it before you decide to retire.”

“What about Kira?” he pressed, horns down in challenge.

“She’d be another good one for that side,” Lyra agreed. “And that suggests Alla on the warrior side, if you can convince her.”

“I can convince her,” Anna reminded everyone. “Oleh, what do you think? It will be your ass on the line.”

He flinched again under that tone, but the Bondarenko had been one of the smaller clans until recently. Not flashy. Not rich.

Accidentally well-placed when Anna and Maks connected, and that had made all the difference as far as Dan could see.

Give the man credit, he sat and reviewed his notes in his head for a long pause before nodding.

“What do you think they will be doing?” he asked Maks.

“If Nazariy can be Uly’s Ambassador to the Horde here and presuming that he answers to Halyna, then I need someone like Kira to represent the Corporation when I’m not present. And, *Chornovil* being a dual-class, public joint stock company, that person will be on the Board of Directors. Possibly the Chair or Vice, depending, since someone here will need to be, at least initially. I’ll still hold a sole majority voting bloc to control things as I see fit.”

Dan liked the way Oleh blinked three times. Slowly, like a man recovering from a concussion. She’d had a few.

“It is the Khet way,” Dan saved him. “Maks and Lukyan learned much about business from your neighbors and new allies.”

And the various members of the Legal Department around the room had all contributed, Haydar and Piruz going deep into things Rabiu and Ethir had done.

"And Alla?" Oleh finally asked.

Maks smiled cruelly.

"Uly's going to go crack heads together," he said. "The Bondarenko better be sending a conductor capable of standing with him."

He paused and turned back to Anna and Lyra.

"I presume she's any good?" he asked.

Anna laughed. Lyra beamed.

"At one point, I considered introducing you to her formally," Lyra said. "If I could have ever gotten you home long enough. But you did far better for yourself without my help."

Dan laughed as both Maks and Chervonya blushed in tandem. And he had done well. With a little help from Anna and a few folks like her.

"She commands *Even Odds* now, last I remember?" Lyra turned to Oleh and got a nod.

"She'll need something more impressive," Lukyan spoke up from behind Anna. "*Even Odds* is no bigger than *Compass Rose*."

Dan glanced up and caught his nod. *Compass Rose* could be dangerous, but you needed a good conductor and crew. Even then, it was nothing more than an extra-large Ultra-Bomber, scaled up just enough to make the emotional transition from larger Seeker-class to smallest Interceptor.

"How good is she?" Anna asked Oleh pointedly.

"As a commander? First rate," he replied. "As a politician, she's unlikely to knock Nazariy out of the running for my job unless he fucks something up. Maul instead of shiv, if you will. She gets the job done ugly, most of the time. Last I checked, she was working the border between Imperial Sectors Eight and Nine, slipping in to raid commercial shipping in such a way that establishing jurisdiction to chase her tended to drive the bureaucrats nuts."

"Is she Uly's wing commander?" Maks asked ruthlessly. "Can she take orders from a Human and execute them without arguing? She's worthless to me and Uly if I have to bash horns with her to get anything done."

Dan was impressed, listening to the man talk. He sounded like he had promoted himself into another lieutenancy of Uly. Perhaps Sterling's peer, if you wanted to view it that way. At the same time, *Governor* Maks, so not that outrageous.

Possibly her own peer in certain things, at least in a few years. Could she step back from running things constantly? Did she want to?

It would be good enough that folks she could trust would be there to step in. Things were going to keep growing, and finding competent bodies to slot into new roles was literally the bane of her and Uly's existence today.

Oleh opened his mouth to snarl something, then remembered where he was. Who he was talking to and sitting with.

"I think so," he finally admitted. "Someone will have to ask her point-blank, but I wouldn't immediately rule her out."

Maks turned to his mom and his *Vatazhko*.

"I can handle that," he said. "I'll need a fast courier, plus Chervonya and Kira to go with me, but we can be gone quickly and either drag her back or have her rendezvous somewhere."

"Here, if you decide to keep her," Anna said, surprising Dan. "I have a ship we can finally dig out of mothballs and get reconditioned to fly. Pain in the ass, much of the time, because it is a pure warship with almost no comfortable spots for travel, but also a first rate asskicker."

"Who?" Lukyan asked from behind her.

"*Blue Widow*," she grinned.

Maks and Oleh whistled. Harald jolted in surprise. The name didn't mean anything to Dan, but their responses were good.

Lukyan merely nodded. That was enough for Dan.

"Light Striker," he explained. "Except upgunned. Not a Forward Striker because as she noted, not really designed for long sailing in comfort, unless you strip the crew way down. Otherwise, you need a lot of resupply. Heavy beast, though. Four dual 8dm turrets, two and two. Not enough to go at a Devastator one-on-one, but any other Striker out there will have a handful of live eels biting them. Warrior's warship."

"Excellent," Maks said. "You get it sorted out. I'll go see if cousin Alla is who I need in this role. Kira should be fine for what I need, based on what Mom has told me. Dan, what else do you need from us?"

She dropped back into the present from her various plans and studied Maks.

"The rest of a small fleet," she acknowledged. "Interceptors ready to do damage. Maybe some Light Strikers that can sail a long ways, understanding that this *Blue Widow* will set pace. Then I need two or more fast transports I can load up with food and resupply, staged outward so the fleet can get a running start and never have to drop back below a jog before we hit someone."

"Should *Tiikeri* accompany that force?" Eskil asked from the back of the group. "I would gladly wade into battle at your side, but the ship might be the weakest one present, and most at risk in such a battle."

"Think like an escort," Dan replied. "Like you and *Virta* did at Daicia. *Nubia* has a lot of firepower, and Ononguli raiders will be aggressive in attacking, so someone able to hold close flanks and corners will probably be more important. Later, we'll find you better ships."

"I'm working on that, Dan," Maks said, drawing a nod from

Anna, so those two were up to something. "Not today, but next year."

"Next year," she acknowledged. "Eskil, that sufficient for honor?"

"Better than sufficient, Dan," he grinned. "Excellent."

"In that case, I think maybe we should split up here," Dan said. "Return to the party perhaps, or get on with our next tasks, so that Uly is already in motion when he's ready for his next steps. Let me or Anna know what you need and we'll get it handled."

Nods. Smiles. Hungry ones, but smiles.

The core of that thing Uly was building, capable of operating without him in the room, because Maks and others already knew to step up.

This might work.

FIFTY-FIVE

Halyna had ridden for the better part of two hours next to Uly. Comfortable for her, but she could tell he'd never been in a saddle before. At least an Ononguli version. Still he handled himself well and did things as she showed him. Reins, bridle, stirrups, balance.

He would hurt later, but they weren't going far or hard to their destination.

And she could see outriders keeping pace in every direction, the *Vatazhko* having laid down the law that Uly be protected from anything and anyone.

Their goal was a yurt slowly getting closer as they switched back from a canter to a walk that would let their mounts cool. One of a cluster, in a pseudo trail camp designed for folks that largely lived in the city.

Not primitive, but low-key and low to the ground. Sort of.

A stable off to one side. A manager's office next to it with a shower and restroom building on the back. Small restaurant, but each yurt was equipped for isolation and she knew they would be able to take care of themselves.

Uly glanced over and gestured her to lead as they entered the courtyard. Halyna directed the beast to a rail and dismounted, tying the reins in place for now then turning to Uly.

He was slower getting to the ground. Moving with care, but she didn't detect any grimace of pain as he did. Merely moving with precision at a new task.

She understood that concept in her bones.

Standing, he was taller than her, though no broader than most Ononguli. Slender for a Human, she understood. She went ahead and tied off his reins, then nodded to the yurt farthest from the office, directly across. Someone would come take care of the mounts, but everything had been fully organized by the *Vatazhko* already, so the two of them didn't have much to do except get settled.

Uly stepped next to her and offered an elbow, so she took it and led him to the flap.

Entering, it was as she remembered from previous camping trips, though normally she would only stop here for one night each direction before spending as much as a week sleeping rough.

One should never underestimate hot showers.

Round interior of leather stitched together from several orkac hides. Hangings for decoration. Slatted wood floors underfoot with rugs. Bed on the left. Fire pit in the center with a flue above it. Kitchen opposite.

The illusion of primitive living, for city dwellers.

She followed Uly around as he inspected things, touching and asking questions about purpose or design as he seemed to be absorbing more Ononguli culture.

"I'm full already," he said finally. "Maybe some tea?"

Halyna nodded and located the correct jars. He took a smell of several and selected one that was already her favorite, so she filled two sachets and set water to boiling on an electric kettle, because she really didn't feel like starting a fire just yet.

Later, it would probably be necessary, but it could wait.

He moved to a chair and watched her without questions. She got the water boiled and both mugs steeped before setting a timer and joining him.

"What would a traditional first night be like?" he asked. "I've only ever heard the others talk in exceptionally vague terms that really didn't answer."

Halyna watched his face. Curiosity. That seemed to be the most common element with Uly. A desire to learn new things.

She already appreciated that about him.

"We would make dinner," she said. "Traditionally, I would make you a dinner, that is. Then we sit like this and talk, before retiring to bed later and consummating things."

He nodded.

"Is that what you want?" he asked.

Halyna studied his eyes. Weirdly white and unglowing, but they seemed to be the most expressive part of the face.

"As opposed to?" she countered.

"This was a political union," he reminded her. "A treaty marriage. I've not heard any reason to doubt your commitment, but I also am not Ononguli, and want to make sure that anything we do is something you want, rather than something forced upon you by expectations of a bunch of old farts who aren't here."

"Are you not interested?" she countered, feeling a touch of resentment.

"On the contrary, you are a most beautiful woman," he said, taking her breath away with his raw honesty. "Desirable. To date, however, I have only taken such a step with half of the women in Dan's Congress, for all that they are legally married to the Corsac Fox. Not all of them were emotionally prepared yet. They might get there. They might not. What would bring you joy in this situation?"

Halyna had to stop and pick her jaw up from where it had fallen on the floor. To find a way to reboot her brain, because she'd honestly been expecting a bull in rut.

What she was looking at was a partner, offering her a partnership of equals. She kept seeing him as an Ononguli male, when she needed to remember that Maks Sobol and Lukyan Chayka were more like Humans. Or at least more like Uly, according to the *Vatazhko*.

He sat and watched her like a hunter in a blind. At least she felt like prey.

No, she felt like he had just stripped her bare and left her standing naked.

Then he held out a hand, as he had done before. Humans, she had been told, tended to be more tactile than Ononguli. They even hugged regularly.

She took that hand and held it. He gave just enough squeeze to convey strength of purpose.

What did she want?

She'd had expectations, but Uly had just shattered all of them by offering her whatever depth of relationship she wanted out of him.

And Halyna could see why the Corsac Fox was so easily able to gather up so many disparate alien nations into a single, coherent unity.

She couldn't think of anyone she'd known with such calm charisma. It was like sitting next to a statue carved in a pale brown marble, when she'd been expecting...

What?

And he'd asked her a question.

What would bring her joy?

Halyna began to compare Uly to all the men she'd known. No, boys.

Yes, that was it.

Boys.

Uly represented a calm maturity that she found astounding when she knew how old he was. Most men took decades to get there. If ever.

Where would Uly be in those decades?

"You already do," she finally replied, tasting the honesty of it as it came out of her mouth.

Uly nodded, further endearing him.

"How can I do better?"

She had to pick her jaw up again. Halyna was nervous that it might become a habit, to have him surprise her in such good ways.

"I'd like a first kiss," she decided.

He rose and moved to kneel next to her, taking both of her hands now and moving slower than she expected.

It was a delicate kiss. She wasn't sure what she was expecting, but it put a smile on her face, so she held him close and extended it. Hands came up around her shoulders and she could feel his warmth.

Halyna couldn't help but compare him to other men she'd kissed. Again, mostly bulls in china shops, while Uly approached her like delicate glass, though that was a careful reserve as he looked for her boundaries rather than fear of her or her fragility.

Strangers, met in the morning, married at noon, and riding into the Endless Plains in the evening.

As the dumbass traditionalists preferred to do it.

He broke the kiss first, but didn't move back far. Enough to study her eyes.

And smile.

She shared it.

The tea timer went off and he turned to look, then started to pull back.

Halyna caught him and pulled him close again.

"It can wait," she said, then rose, drawing him up as well.

He watched her. She smiled, then took his hand and drew him towards the bed.

They could warm the tea up later, if they felt like getting out of the warmth.

She wanted to learn more about this dangerously interesting man.

PART EIGHT
SECTOR FOURTEEN

FIFTY-SIX

Maks had met Kira in passing a few times, but never really spoken with her all that much until recently.

Until it became clear that the Bondarenko and the Sobol would be moving into deeper waters in the future.

Helped that he was driving things.

Kira was the deadliest accountant he'd ever met. Piruz had hung that moniker on her after one of their meetings, and it stuck in his head this morning as she joined them in the launch lounge.

"I'm not sure you need me," Kira groused at him and Chervonya. "The *Vatazhko* can order her."

"Sure," Maks replied. "But I want her joyful enthusiasm at doing the task, rather than grudging acceptance. It will make all the difference in the world, when we get to the sharp end of things."

Kira shrugged. Maks rose and pulled Chervonya up.

"We're here," he said. "Let's get in motion."

The tunnel deposited them in the airlock of a larger courier than he really needed, but one Anna had assigned him.

Fast and ambassadorial, whatever that entailed. He didn't work for her directly on this one, other than everyone answered to Anna at the end of the day.

At least for now.

The crew was small and professional. One Chief Stewardess with decades of seriousness in her eyes. Maks smiled at her.

"Where do you need me, so I'm out of your way while we get going?" he asked her, catching the surprise in her eyes.

Most folks probably issued orders.

Maks preferred honey to vinegar.

"Your gear is aboard," she said when she recovered. "If you'll follow me to the lounge, I'll let the pilot know."

Maks nodded and fell in. Easier.

Interior was done in wealthy bordering on decadent. Gold and silver highlights on walls painted that faded golden-green that the grass got as the heat of summer first took hold, after the spring rains made it all emerald.

He sat and accepted coffee. Chervonya was next to him. Kira was across the table in a cozy booth. The Stewardess left them with two more junior folks and disappeared.

Wasn't too long and they were lifting off, then blasting to orbit.

"What's likely to happen?" Kira asked open-endedly.

"You, me, or Alla?" he asked back.

"Yes," she smiled.

"Hopefully, you manage things while I try to make us rich," he replied. "Alla decides that working with the Corsac Fox isn't an insult to her honor and goes in with both horns. Eventually, the Ononguli Horde grows up and helps Uly win the first of many wars intended to break the power of the *Auga*."

"You don't dream small," she shook her head.

"That is small," he growled, watching her horns come up. "Uly functionally wants to overthrow the *Auga Empire* as a thing and have something nicer replace it. I'm going to help. If you come to work for me long term, you will, too. Sector Fourteen turns into a place, instead of a blank spot on the map. The Sphere maybe recovers a few worlds we lost, but I expect that nobody wants to claim worlds that are already inhabited by other species. At least not immediately. Again, growing up means working as part of a multi-species team, so the Sphere might have to be more than just Ononguli. That, or you have to watch ambitious youngsters pick up and move to Bastion or someplace in Uly's realm. I'd rather they didn't, because a century from now we'll all be gone, and those kids will inherit every decision we make today. For good or ill."

He watched her blink in surprise at that one. Then lick her lips and nod.

Mom had said that she was probably the most open toward what he was attempting to accomplish here. Hopefully, Mom was correct.

Maks could always ask Dad to reach out to more of the Sobol side. That was also a threat to hang over their horns if they pushed back on him.

"Where do I need to focus first?" she finally asked.

Maks smiled.

"I have a lot of files for you to read," he said. "Bastion, both as it is today and where I want it to go. Isann and Saari, as places that need to turn into more important places. Daicia, apparently, because Anna is going to make it a tradeport with Uly's allies in charge. Rayzian you know, but I need to build up certain infrastructure here and at Z'Gosza, over in Sector Fifteen. Eventually, you'll have a wide variety of folks on the Board of Directors, but we have to build the thing first, then recruit money to back us at planetary budget scales. That's coming."

She nodded, perhaps taken a bit aback.

Maks smiled at her.

She'd grow into it. Or she wouldn't, and he needed to know that now, just like he needed to know how her sister was going to turn out.

FIFTY-SEVEN

Sterling was at dinner when the intercom chirped.

"Governor, we got company," it said. "*Niemi* at the outer marker, requesting lane assignment and headed in with good news, according to the report. Be here in half an hour."

"I'll be along," Sterling replied.

Maybe he finished his food a little faster than normal, but that was the promise of seeing Anari again, after so long. He'd found that he really missed her. Missed her wit and brains. Missed her calm confidence.

Folks in the control room cleared everything, so he was down at the airlock when they docked, holding himself perfectly still by force of will and waiting.

It beeped itself open and Anari emerged first, a look of seriousness on her face that kept him from stepping up and giving her a hug.

Governor Huff today, apparently.

Kit came through next, with Gulnaz a step behind, all of them smiling like they had a secret to share.

He waited as patiently as he could, then gasped when she emerged last from the airlock, escorted by Commander Nyman.

Sterling bowed to the woman. Middle-aged. Darker skin than anybody he knew besides Dan. Better shape than most of the young Human women he'd ever ogled. Hair gray with dark streaks. Wrinkles where she smiled.

"Sterling, may I present Melpomeni Michelakos, Engineer to the Court of Traiffe?" Anari spoke. "Melpomeni, Governor Sterling Huff, Commander of the warship *Batyr* on semi-detached duty."

Sterling nodded and shared the woman's smile.

"Greetings and welcome, in the name of the Corsac Fox," he said automatically, a speech he gave every time strangers came to trade or learn about this new thing.

"Thank you, Governor," the woman replied in a bright, cheerful voice.

They'd really done it. They'd really found a lost tribe of Humans, hidden back in the darkness of Sector Fourteen.

"I am given to understand that your cartographic skills located Traiffe, eventually?" she continued.

"Anari translated the *Karaŋgılıkka*," he deflected. "I helped her with some bits to locate *Nubia*, then worked with others to translate out various mapping systems to create something up to date today. It was a team effort."

The woman nodded and smiled like she didn't believe him.

He turned to smile up at Anari.

"Successful, I take it?" he asked.

She grinned.

"Extremely," she replied.

"I'm just sorry Uly and Vahid aren't here," he told the group. "I will let people know that a celebration is in order, but just the first one. There will be more when *Nubia* returns. Or did you need to immediately chase off after Uly? What orders should I be giving?"

After all, they'd been gone for some time, presumably stopping at Isann at least once, possibly twice.

And finding the Yarikh at Traiffe. Not the place he would have guessed from his maps, but successful, nonetheless.

"I've been filling Melpomeni in with some details about *Danumash* and *Batyr*," Anari explained. "But really, you folks don't talk much about your origins."

Sterling nodded, then shrugged.

"Mostly embarrassment, I think," he offered, noting that they were speaking in Yarikh now as a group. Even Kit seemed to be following along.

Must have been one hell of an adventure.

"I just had dinner, but coffee sounds good," he decided. "Shall we relocate to the wardroom and get you fed? Or at least something to drink?"

Anari took his hand and smiled.

"That sounds excellent."

Sterling was glad to have her home.

Whatever mystery she'd brought him this time.

FIFTY-EIGHT

Anari beamed as she listened to Sterling talk. He and the others honestly were reticent to discuss *Danumash* in any detail, so she'd had to prompt him deeper with questions as the others listened.

For all of them, history generally seemed to begin on the day Uly and Dan brought Kolya, Emil, and Gennady aboard *King Hewitt II*.

Melpomeni, however, had been deeply surprised that there were any Humans out there. Then more surprised at how far away they were.

And she had the impression that the Yarikh had selected Traiffe as their final home, but had come from somewhere else. And not anywhere near the far edges of Sector Seventeen where Uly and Dan had originated.

Where?

She would ask Suka Kuri. Perhaps new details would jar old stories loose.

"Seven Crowns, Sterling?" Melpomeni interrupted, drawing Anari's attention.

"That's correct, ma'am," he replied. "Seven worlds that formed up into a larger political entity called *Danumash*. *Batyr* is rimward from us—*them*—and the two nations have generally been at war for centuries at this point, though neither have been particularly aggressive about it.”

“But the region itself is relatively small?” she pressed.

“Combined, a rough sphere about three hundred light-years across,” he explained. “*Batyr* is more compact. From what I now understand of galactic geography, there is a fairly wide gap of uninhabitable systems coreward from both. Rather like Sector Fourteen in many ways, but without even primitive civilizations that might be elevated to modern technology. I am not certain how we got the technology, though I am given to understand from Dan that her ship fairly regularly traded with a few places that were alien. At the time, I was a young midshipman training on a civilian vessel under military contract, and didn’t really learn about aliens other than our prisoners until we were captured by *Iron Wasp*’s Ononguli crew and imprisoned with the others.”

Anari nodded. As with everything on Traiffe, she would form this into oral poems that she could transmit to Yanouk and Suka Kuri later, so the Humans would become more widely known.

Probably not the locations, but it was likely only a matter of time until someone went over and looked. Or recruited.

At least the Human worlds were far too far away for the *Auga* to get involved.

Yet.

“Interesting,” Melpomeni observed.

“And you?” Sterling asked Melpomeni. “*Invincible* was parked there for five thousand years before we located it?”

“Indeed, Sterling,” she replied. “Anari has given me many of the details, but I am still looking forward to speaking with Drew when I meet him, as that is an amazing feat of navigation on his part.”

“Drew’s the best,” Sterling nodded.

Anari had to agree. And she’d known a variety of pilots in imperial service before she’d been rescued.

"Now, I have a question," Sterling continued, both sides having gone over their various updates over the last few hours. "Should you be headed to Rayzian to talk to Uly and Dan? Or do I need to charter a vessel to make that run as quickly as possible? I'm not certain when they are due back here, because they had to swing by Saari first and talk to the Paramount. Then on to the *Vatazhko* and those meetings tend to spiral up and outward, especially as you'll have all the major players in one location for the wedding."

Anari watched Melpomeni ponder that topic. They'd discussed it on the flight to Isann and then home, but not drawn any conclusions. Melpomeni seemed torn between moving quickly to some end and merely waiting here instead of Traiffe for events to catch up with her.

In that, the Yarikh woman suddenly felt much more like Suka Kuri, who was far older.

Wasn't she?

"Melpomeni, if I can ask a potentially rude question, how old are you?" Anari said.

The two men flinched. Ursula nodded. Melpomeni's mouth pulled to one side and there was a twinkle in her eyes.

"Observant," Melpomeni noted. "As one would expect of Moss School. Or Sabre, as you are both."

Anari shrugged but didn't let the woman off the hook. It suddenly felt important in ways that it hadn't before.

"The Schools teach us to think," Anari replied. "To do that, one must observe. Only then can you learn."

Melpomeni nodded again.

"Older than one might expect," she said, turning to smile at Kit as she did.

Anari knew that he was a little smitten by the woman. And somewhat intimidated.

"And?" Anari pressed, verging over onto rude, but it felt necessary.

"One hundred and sixty-seven years old, as the *Auga* Imperial calendar measures such things," she offered with a wry grin.

"How is that possible?" Sterling asked. "Or has your technology advanced so far that you have mastered genetic engineering to that degree?"

Kit had turned almost alabaster, sitting perfectly still. Anari felt sorry for him.

She looked Human. Might not be, given the response of the two men at the table with her.

"When we withdrew, Sterling, we set out to forge a perfect society," Melpomeni said. "Our technology was already in advance of your current status on the day when Selene Praxis parked her ship. It has advanced significantly since then."

"Are you a threat to the galaxy, having emerged from your slumbers, Elder?" Sterling asked, dropping into that formal tone he used when Suka Kuri occasionally got serious.

Melpomeni seemed a bit surprised by Sterling's sudden change, but she wasn't thinking of him as Governor Huff. Merely a young man barely an adult.

Physically, she might be correct. Emotionally and mentally, she would be utterly far off the mark.

Governor Huff. Commander Huff, who Uly relied on as a warrior.

"We are not," Melpomeni offered after a moment of silence. "Usually, we chase off intruders, as we would have done without Kit here. Your people are, as far as we can tell, a lost tribe of Yarikh. Or us a lost tribe of Humans. We cannot be certain, and wished to discover that truth for ourselves."

Sterling had gone cold and formal. Anari leaned in.

"The only way to do that might be to travel to Gralbo, in *Batyr*," she noted. "I doubt that *Danumash* would welcome you, as they tend to be insular in their blood aristocracy. The Party might be more amenable. I doubt that Uly knows, and he was the only true officer in the original crew, with Dan and the others mostly enlisted technical specialists or extremely junior as Sterling was."

"And thus, I needed to come here, at least," Melpomeni concluded. "I will need to meet Uly and take his measure, because the *Auga* concern us. It is likely, from what you tell us, that they will be at least another thousand years reaching Traiffe, but what will be their power when they do?"

"Conservatively advanced only slowly on a technological scale, Elder," Sterling replied. "What they *will* have will be vast armadas of warships that can be brought to bear. Unless you possess super-weapons capable of driving them entirely out of your system, they will seek to subdue you. As they do everyone. And will not be denied without vast and terrible casualties in the process."

Anari didn't like the gleam in the woman's eye. It suggested that **Engineer** Melpomeni Michelakos might have already done that math. Or worse, that she knew how to build such a weapon.

What had the Yarikh turned themselves into, with five thousand years of privacy to think?

Sterling turned to Ursula and caught that woman entirely off-guard.

"Can I ask you to haul everyone to Rayzian?" he asked. "Or at least Krilic on the closest border, because they might be headed back this way and I'd hate to have you chase them all the way there and back. I can send messages to Saari in the meantime, updating the Paramount. Already, the first nervous trader had made the run here, swapping mostly art and cultural artifacts for technology, though I might have vastly overvalued his cargo."

"Overvalued?" Ursula was confused.

"Uly went there and made them allies, as you and I both expected," Sterling told her, smiling. "They came here, uncertain of what to expect. I offered value in trade, in order to draw more traders in their wake. And I have begun identifying Khet and Ononguli ships that I might trust enough to eventually give coordinates, but we need to prevent another Isann situation."

"Situation?" Melpomeni asked.

Anari let Sterling explain the two raids in better detail, as he'd been involved directly both times.

"So you protect the Samuur from others?" Melpomeni asked.

"The honorable path," he replied, making Ursula gasp, but *Koski* had been assigned here as a guard while Uly was gone, though Matti was off patrolling nearby systems at the moment.

Obviously, he and Sterling had gotten close emotionally.

"Yes," Melpomeni answered. "I need to travel to Uly. Ursula, may we impose on your hospitality for a bit longer?"

"It would be my pleasure, Melpomeni," Ursula nodded.

Anari did as well.

Things had just gotten surprisingly complex. Moreso than Melpomeni had let on earlier, but she was Human and had finally met Sterling Huff.

What would she think of Uly?

FIFTY-NINE

Kit was back in his bunk on *Niemi*, curtain pulled shut and night light on so he could meditate. The Samuur around him usually didn't snore, so he could sit and think deep thoughts.

Or dissolve into entropy. Same thing, today.

Shit.

And he knew enough mechanical engineering to understand the biological side in theory.

What was she?

Human? Maybe? At some point in their distant past. Say, five thousand years ago when Selene returned home.

Today?

Alien, in Human shape. No other way to describe it.

Utterly stunning in appearance. Intellectual. Charming. Friendly. And even knew some amazingly dirty jokes, once he learned enough conversational Yarikh to understand them.

But one hundred and sixty-seven years old?

Born about the same time as his great-great-great-grandsire, give or take. Maybe a couple more, depending.

And that suggested that the Scholar was even older, though nobody had known to ask.

Two hundred? More?

What were the limits of Human genetics, if you had time, patience, and technology on your side?

And at what point did you stop being Human?

Then somebody pulled open the curtain and let the main room light in, blinding him for a long moment as he blinked and squinted.

And offered a few choice profanities.

Melpomeni answered with a few of her own.

Kit had a top bunk. They were at eyeball level. Everyone else in the room was either hiding in their own bunks or had snuck out when she came in, because she appeared to be alone.

He let his scowl settle in.

"This is probably not the correct place to talk," she offered. "I asked Ursula for an office. Come."

Wasn't a question. Kit didn't figure he had any way out of it, so he slid out and dropped to the deck, grabbing his shoes and slipping them on as he hooked his messenger bag.

He was taller than she was. She smiled up at him and then set off at a pace he had to stretch his legs to keep up with.

Office. Impersonal. Desk. Two chairs. Comm line. Workstation to log into. Gray.

She started to take the spot behind the desk, then practically shoved him over there instead and settled in the one farthest from the door.

"There wasn't an easy way to explain it," she began.

Kit shrugged. She wasn't wrong there.

"And it might not have come up, save that I had a Moss School Seeker on my hands and my people didn't appreciate how sharp Anari Supasei really is."

"Most folks don't," Kit agreed. "Size throws them off. Suka Kuri is even worse, because she's smarter and more experienced."

"More like me," Melpomeni said.

"Probably."

"I'm still Human, Kit," she continued.

He had his doubts. Didn't express them at the moment. Just stared at her.

"Okay, granted, we have immensely different lifespans," she concurred. "And are no longer subject to a variety of diseases and infirmities."

"And I'd be willing to bet you a three-ducat coin that the engineering work is done at a molecular and genetic level, rather than as a treatment," he countered. "Thus, while we share a similar biomorphology and possibly similar-enough chemistry, we're technically not the same species as one defines such things."

From the look on her face, she probably hadn't been expecting him to know those words in Yarikh. Probably forgot that he was also an engineer. Just not in her league, obviously.

Long pause. Probably looking for the right words. The least offensive ones.

Like it would matter at this point.

"No, you're probably right, Kit," she said quietly. "You are what we call Baseline Human, because all our scans of you reflected the species we were before."

He didn't ask *Before What?* because he **really** didn't want to dwell on what that implied about what she was now.

She nodded after a moment.

"And yes, there is a lot of difference now, but all of it under the hood, if you will," she continued. "Externally, we look alike."

"We do," he agreed compactly. "Of course, erect biped with bilateral symmetry seems to be a fairly standard design. But for skin color and a few minor things, you aren't that different from the Isann or a couple of others I've met or at least heard about."

"It is," she agreed. "And I'm sorry I couldn't tell you. Didn't tell you. I didn't think anyone would ever figure it out. Not to the degree that Anari did."

"Smart woman," Kit agreed back. "Uly has a lot of them around him."

"Which makes it all the more interesting, given yours and Sterling's stories about what a terribly sexist place *Danumash* is. How insular and racist. Uly seems to have come from a more egalitarian place, but even then you've mentioned Dan and Thorley Eldridge."

She paused there.

"And I admit I wasn't emotionally prepared to be ogled by a youngster," she grinned sideways. "Yarikh culture is one of reserve. Of intellectual pursuits, rather than necessarily physical, if you will. We have our sports, both individual as well as team, but something I pointed out to Nomiki comes back to me now."

"What's that?" he asked, willing to play the straight man here. For now. Maybe.

"We have grown stodgy," Melpomeni said earnestly. "Dull and predictable. We have lost the fire of youth and excitement that marked us in the distant past. The sense of adventure. Most of my peers would probably balk terribly at being sent out into the wider galaxy on such a mission as mine. Nomiki sent me because I recognized how much we might have lost, simply because you held up a mirror to our entire culture."

"Me?" He was surprised. He was just an engineer. A mechanic.

"You looked at me and Nomiki both with a hint of lust in your eyes, though you never once said or did anything untoward," she explained. "Merely ogled, as it were. I don't want to suggest how long it has been since someone *ogled* me."

"You need to get out more," he said automatically, then SLAMMED his mouth shut and blushed.

"Obviously," she grinned at him. "That's what I'm doing. However, I've frightened you off."

Him?

Kit let backbrain chew on that for a second as he blinked to catch up.

Yeah, probably.

I mean, one hundred and sixty-seven years old. Looked a hot, well-preserved fifty, and his dad had mentioned more than once that at a certain age a woman knew what she wanted, how to ask for it, and might cook you breakfast in the morning if you listened to her.

But this?

She was watching him. Probably out-thinking him, because he had a pretty good idea how smart the woman was. Like, dangerously smart. Maybe Dan smart. Possibly Suka Kuri smart.

Uly would still chew her up and spit her out, but that was Uly.

"So, what are you saying?" he asked, damning himself ahead of time.

"I'm trying to remember how to not be stodgy, Kit," she said quietly. "To be ogled by a young man who sees the body and lusts after it. I'm hoping you still will."

Would he? Well, probably. It had been kinda natural, watching her bottom as they traipsed corridors to get here. Nice bottom.

Alien woman. Just think of her as an Ononguli without the horns. Or a tall, skinny Isann.

Furless Samuur? Weird thought.

"Maybe," he offered. "Not really sure what to think. Obviously, certain things are off the table."

"Agreed," she said, turning serious. "I will likely outlive you, even with the headstart I have. And remain in reasonably good shape until the very end. However, that is distantly in the future, and there are many things that require my attention today. I'm hoping I haven't chased you entirely off or offended you with the truth."

Kit considered it. Was he offended? No, she had had a really good reason to omit certain details. Finding a lost tribe of Humans had sure messed up their year. Or longer.

And he was back to not likely ever having kids, unless Uly snuck home or he adopted some from somewhere. For which he'd need a spouse of some sort.

Maybe. Shit.

She was watching. Maybe listening to his thought bubbles, from the look in her eyes.

And it wasn't like he hadn't already done the math on women-folk. Lots of Khet and Ononguli around. And Melpomeni was alien, too. Just closer in overall shape to Human.

Or something.

"Where does that leave us?" he asked her.

"Hopefully, somewhere where you are comfortable around me," she replied.

"Trying to get there," he said. "No promises."

"I understand, Kit," she said. "It's a bit overwhelming to process, I would presume. We'll talk again."

Then she got up and walked out, leaving him sitting there stewing.

Shit. Now what?

SIXTY

Chervonya was still getting used to this new Maks. To the man who had gone from quiet and a little goofy to a hard-nosed business tycoon.

Looking back, she could trace his evolution along the various steps, but at no point had she apparently stopped to calculate where it was leading. Even this far. Let alone what might be ahead.

They were in their cabin. He'd offered her space for this trip, but she'd moved in with him. Better to keep a close watch on the man. And remind him why he kept her around.

She was sitting on the bed reading. He was nearby in a chair, writing something on a small handheld, cursing occasionally and editing.

Knowing Maks, more business plans. Apparently, he'd acquired an entire basic legal library from Rabiu and Piruz, and was in the process of modifying everything for what he wanted Bastion Commercial Law to turn *into*.

And Ononguli, eventually, but he didn't plan to tell them until it was too late to stop him.

Maks could be sneaky. Obviously, he'd learned it from Lukyan, now that she knew both of them that much better. Nobody ever appreciated Chayka's guile. Except Anna.

Maks looked up at her, eyes still about a thousand light-years away, then he zeroed in and smiled.

"What?" she asked.

"Sterling and Anari," he replied, catching her off-guard. Again. Maks.

"Huh?"

"Inheritance," he explained. "Ononguli keep everything in the clan. Khet keep it all in the corporate entity. Both assume certain rights of blood relations because both are single-species edifices."

"And you're changing that," she completed the thought.

"Have to," he said. "Got Human men who won't have Human wives, depending. Got folks who will meet strangers and form families that have no direct blood relationship. Uly needs laws that recognize family by shape and commitment, rather than closest blood relative. That knife cuts both ways, so I have to basically reinvent Probate Court again. Helps that Uly already did that once, with the Khet, to set up their original Admiralty Court. Makes them amenable to what's coming."

"What's coming?" Chervonya asked, feeling just a hint of chill.

Maks wasn't the awkward First Officer on a small pirate vessel anymore. Or even Governor Maks.

He'd transcended again.

She paled as she considered that arc and extended it to where he might yet go.

"Dan," he said with a nod. "The Conclave and the Congress. A place where the Mazhin and the Ononguli meet on even terms with the Khet and the Isann. That means a general messiness, because I'm trying to outguess both her and Uly, and you can imagine how difficult that is."

"Where are you going?" she asked, putting the book down for now because things were getting serious.

"The Mazhin, the original ten of them, formed themselves into a small clan born of necessity," he told her. "From what I have since learned, they came off six different ships originally, captured at various times because *Danumash* doesn't believe in open commerce and prefers slave trading piracy instead. Haydar was in charge, until they elected Uly. More recently, they added all the kids off *Ahmadi*, about half of which decided to stay later and joined. Still run by Uly, with Nasrin stepping in as Matriarch, because the rest of the Mazhin can be dipshits about that sort of thing."

Chervonya nodded to prompt him.

"At some point, entirely new clans will come into existence at Bastion," Maks proclaimed. "Not even necessarily related by anything but choice. An even mixture of marriage and corporate acquisition, at least to the way Khet think."

She must have made a sound, because he smiled at her confusion.

"Think of a civil registry like we do with singular marriage," he said. "Except extended to a larger group. Like a floating partnership, but with more of a corporate management scheme in various layers. Folks who decide to belong to a familial group and want to make it legally formal. Clans, as the Horde would see it. Except representing everyone. Think of the Combat Team, if you added some men in, which is kind of what happens when Sterling and Anari get formal. He's absolutely part of Uly's clan, and so is she. I need laws in place that protect inheritance that way."

She blinked. Blinked again.

All the pieces had been right there, all along. Why had she never seen it assembled?

Because the Ononguli were Ononguli, and didn't generally like outsiders. Even open-minded ones like her, who did.

Culturally isolated, because it had always been the Horde against the galaxy.

Until it wasn't.

"Fortier Clan?" she asked, extrapolating outwards.

"The Congress of Wives," he replied evenly. "And all of their kids, when they start having them. *However* they start having them. Bondarenko is off to one side, connected, but Fortier becomes the thing at the core of Bastion."

"What does that mean for us?" she asked tentatively, suddenly seeing a much vaster arena than even five minutes ago.

"I'd like to add a Sobol/Borisov Clan at some point," he replied quietly. "If I could convince you that I'm both serious and not crazy."

She gasped. They'd danced around it, but only danced.

And she'd give him the former, while the latter might be a bit more objectionable.

But it was a good crazy.

"Sobol/Borisov?" she asked with a grin.

"At least until we come up with a better term," he said, nodding. .

"What about *Chornovil*?" she countered. "Black Ox, which is already the name of your new corporate entity."

"Clan *Chornovil*?" he asked, obviously intrigued. "I hadn't gone that direction, but it works for a variety of reasons. But you haven't answered. Would you do me the honor of considering formally binding yourself to me and to *Chornovil*?"

Chervonya smiled.

"I would love nothing more, Maks," she replied.

Because he was in the process of inventing the future.

For all of them.

SIXTY-ONE

Maks had put on his best military uniform, and left the rank insignia off his collar. Technically, he was only allowed the solid circle in rose gold of a conductor, but in his mind he had already moved up to the rayed sun of Rayzian in black. A clan leader.

Clan *Chornovil*. The Black Ox.

But because he was dealing entirely with internal Horde matters, it wasn't appropriate yet.

Maybe when he saw Anna next and informed her.

Let her argue with him then. He'd blame Lukyan for everything. Man had taught him most of it along the way. The Legal Department had just added technical polish.

Today, they had finally tracked down *Even Odds* at a supply station where Alla Bondarenko was storing stolen goods she'd taken from the *Auga Empire*. Resupply, so he was ahead of schedule locating her. And she'd stayed put after getting orders from Anna not to leave.

The same orders where Anna had appointed him Ambassador.

Even Alla would have to listen to that. She might still be pissy, which was why he'd brought her sister. And Anna's niece.

Serious firepower against need.

Station folks had fallen all over themselves offering whatever he needed, but this was a frontier place out *beyond* the boonies. Out where Krilic might look modern and sophisticated.

Didn't even have a name. Just a number. Wasn't even a station, so much as a big freighter that got parked in various places until *Auga* patrols sniffed around and chased them off.

Maks walked into the conference room with the two women behind him, both dressed as civilians.

Alla was standing near a coffee robot, scowling disdainfully at him. And her sister.

Maks ignored her to walk by and fix himself some coffee. Not a word as she watched. His two sidekicks had been warned, so they were also silent. Again, all Lukyan's fault.

His coffee done, he sat and watched. Alla was busy being tough, but he could already see the edges of concern working their way loose as nobody spoke.

Lukyan was a devious shit when he wanted to be. Maks would blame him for this, too.

Chervonya got coffee and sat. Maks sipped. Kira worked. Alla stewed.

Then Kira joined him at the table and they all watched Alla.

Five minutes, not a word spoken.

She was getting nervous. Maks smiled. He would outwait the woman, come hell or high water.

Took her a bit to understand that.

Long table. Him at the top. Chervonya on his right, about midway. Kira on his left right next to him. Lots of space for Alla, still standing there.

Kira was the older sister, about a decade Maks's senior. Alla was a shade younger than him. Same build, but Kira had a few extra kilos because she sat at a desk and Alla boarded *Auga* ships with guns in hand.

He waited. Finally, she sat. Already, her grumbliness had tapered off to concern. Maybe curiosity.

Alla studied her sister first. Then Chervonya, but she might not know her on sight.

Then him.

"I'm not going to outstubborn you, am I?" she asked.

"Oh, you could," Maks replied. "At some point, I'd get tired of your bullshit games and head back to Rayzian and tell Anna Shevchenko to find me someone else."

Blonk. Kind of a blink with a good bonk thrown in. The horns bounced back when the whole skull recoiled a little.

"What does the *Vatazhko* want with me?" Alla asked.

"Bondarenko needs a conductor," he said. "My mom suggested you. I've already recruited Kira and Nazariy for non-combat tasks. You interested in working outside the Horde?"

"Outside?"

Good, he'd surprised her. Uly and Halyna wasn't all that widely known yet. Especially this far out on a frontier.

"The Corsac Fox is going to put together a raid," he said. "Another one like Nyri, only bigger. And likely to piss the *Auga* off enough that a general war results."

"And you think *Even Odds* should be involved in something like that?" she scoffed.

"Nope," he smiled, slowly spalling fragments off her horns.

"What, then?"

"Anna suggested digging *Blue Widow* out of storage and sending it," he replied. "She needs a conductor. Uly needs a commander who can take charge of an entire wing and follow orders from a Human."

"Why?" she demanded. "And why me? What's going on?"

Maks turned to Chervonya.

"You get her up to the big part," he said. "Then Kira can add all the Bondarenko elements as needed."

Chervonya nodded.

"As of a week ago, the Corsac Fox is married to Halyna Bondarenko," she said simply. "Maks' sfirst cousin. The *Vatazhko* officiated the wedding."

"Who are you?" Alla asked, careful mixed with nervous.

"Chervonya Borisov," she replied. "The *Vatazhko*'s niece. Maks's fiancée. Your cousin by marriage at some point. Anna Shevchenko decided to ally the Corsac Fox to the Bondarenko and the Sobol by marriage. Oleh approved and attended. Clan politics intruded on everything, so you were suggested to help Uly with his raid. If you want in."

Maks liked the way she slipped that in there at the end. Like a shiv.

Alla turned to her sister.

"Is this real?"

"Utterly," Kira said. "Chervonya, let's start her at the beginning, assuming that she's not been following along like the rest of us."

Maks listened as the two woman walked the third one through his last couple of years in an abbreviated form. It sounded so much more impressive when you left off all the parts where he'd been making shit up as he went and hoping it worked. He almost sounded like he knew what he was doing, Tuesdays notwithstanding.

Alla locked hard on him when Kira was done. Pure shock, which was the best way to deal with his hard-headed cousin.

"*Blue Widow*?" she asked.

Maks nodded.

"Uly's new flagship is big," he said. "I've heard folks suggest that it might be tough enough to take on *Storm Crow*, horn to horn."

More blonks.

"That means we're going after something major?" Alla finally asked.

"Yes," Maks told her. "He wants to do something enormous and ugly to the *Auga*. Given that the region you've been operating in is close to where he'd like to hit them, I was hoping you had some suggestions about places big enough to matter and soft enough to make a huge splash. Things like underdefended regional capitals or some such."

He leaned back and watched her process all that. It was a lot.

Merely the future of the Ononguli Sphere. And the species.

Pocket change, but only when measured against what Uly and Maks had planned for everyone else.

"What has to happen with me?" Alla asked.

"If you're in, and you can take orders from Uly without giving him or me any grief, I'll send Kira home with you while I take the courier ahead quickly to get things ready for everyone. Your crew will transfer over, with additional folks added and hopefully partly trained on the ship by the time you arrive. Then load up, train in motion, and go hit someone as part of a fleet of Ononguli and their allies."

"Allies?" Alla asked.

"Human, Khet, Mazhin, Emro, Isann, Thogin off the top of my head," he replied. "Plus at least one Samuur warship that will be accompanying."

"The cats?" she asked.

"Our new neighbors to the northwest," he corrected her. "Everyone helping the Horde. And you have to be happy to work with all of them, or you can stay here, because it would be better for you to refuse now than to have me tell the *Vatazhko* that she needs to fire you later. Because all of Bondarenko will be on the hook at that point for any fuckups you personally cause. Am I clear?"

She wanted to growl at him. He could see it in her eyes. At the same time, she'd just been promoted to a really senior spot in the clan. A personal representative on the pirate side, when the accountants were in charge according to Mom.

The Big Time.

How badly did she want it?

His smile was cruel.

"It's worth it, Alla," Kira said in the stretching silence. "There will be many more opportunities later as a result of what we do here."

The sisters locked eyes, but not horns.

"Okay, cousin," Alla turned back to look at him. "I'm in."

Maks nodded.

Next step complete.

SIXTY-TWO

Ursula had an updated map. Or an entire extra volume of data from the one Sterling had provided before, on the way to Traiffe. As a ship Commander, she had a really good understanding of how good Huff was as a cartographer.

Better than anyone at Saari, for a start. *Anyone.*

Today, her guests were aft, doing whatever they did when they weren't needed here on the bridge. The ship was deep in warp, with Iikka supervising while Niina was aft. They had resupplied, taken a half day to handle some maintenance, and gone like hell for a new destination.

Iikka's ears rotating back got her attention. She turned hers in his direction.

"What do we expect at Krilic?" he asked quietly.

They hadn't had a lot of time without their guests handy.

"An Ononguli watchstation," she replied. "According to notes, a small squadron of warships also available to run messages and hunt down pirates that get bothersome. A vastly different reception than we got at Bastion, but we come as credentialed ambassadors this time, so I expect them to sniff at us a few times, then settle down and behave. We will also be on our best behavior."

He nodded, whiskers fidgety as he worked.

"Speak," she ordered the back of his head.

"Wondering how big the galaxy really is," he offered over his shoulder, eyes still on his controls. "We knew a few Zuath and Ugotha. Records show rare Ononguli traders. Now we are in the middle of things."

"And on friendly terms with several of the more powerful players," she reminded him. "Matti has done much to impress Sterling, thus he was willing to help us and keep us involved in the larger affairs that the Paramount might have chosen to avoid."

"We can't, can we?"

"We cannot, Iikka," she agreed. "The galaxy is rising. After talking to Melpomeni more, I understand that it has not gotten even to where it was when her people were travelers, but might yet in our lifetime. Thus, we need to make sure that Uly has the tools he needs. That includes the Samuur. I'm just sorry that we weren't able to visit Saari on this next leg, but we needed to be to Krilic as quickly as possible."

He nodded, relenting. It was there in the set of his shoulders. And his ears.

Ursula just wished that she felt the same.

A beep distracted her. Ursula opened the comm line to Gulnaz's quarters.

"How can I be of assistance, elder?" she asked with a grin.

"Don't make me come up there and show off that I'm in better shape than you are," Gulnaz laughed.

Ursula joined her. The Isann woman had started out quiet, but that was a cultural reserve around strangers. Gulnaz had slowly loosened up.

And was in better shape than just about everybody on the ship except Anari.

"Threat acknowledged, old woman," Ursula chuckled. Then she looked around and noted the time and energy on the bridge. "Perhaps tea?"

"I was actually calling to ask the same," Gulnaz replied. "Should I meet you in your office, or aft in the wardroom?"

"Iikka, you have the bridge," Ursula announced. "Try not to hit anything in warp. Gulnaz, I'll swing by and get you."

"Looking forward to it," the Isann woman replied, cutting the line.

Iikka grumbled under his breath, letting his whiskers carry most of the load. Ursula just grinned and headed to chat with the Isann ambassador, wondering what had come up today.

SIXTY-THREE

Gulnaz had seen and done much in her time, though space travel was new. Still a touch novel, but becoming old hat by now. And the Isann men wouldn't be able to keep it a male-dominated art much longer.

Not with Dan and the others having opinions.

She rose when the door chimed and stepped out to walk with Ursula.

Isann tended to be short, compared to Humans and Ononguli. Samuur large, especially women. Especially Ursula, who was only shorter than Anari of anyone on the vessel.

Still, she moved with quiet grace for her size, the inheritance of a hunter species that had frequently been arboreal in the distant past.

They got tea and settled, off in a corner where other sailors made it a point not to get too close.

"What trouble are you about to cause today, Gul?" Ursula asked.

Gulnaz grinned.

"I wanted to talk to you without Anari, Kit, or Melpomeni around," she replied. "Up until now, most conversations have revolved around those three. Or at least Uly and the Yarikh. There are other things that need to be quietly organized outside of the big things.”

“Such as?” Ursula watched her. Still grinning, but sober.

“The Isann and the Samuur are both newly risen to galactic travel,” Gulnaz reminded her. “Two generations, give or take, though in both cases we have old memories of the sky.”

Ursula nodded.

“We found Uly the dumbest way possible,” Gulnaz chuckled. “At least you showed up and challenged Sterling to a duel. We could have gotten annihilated for the stupidity of the men involved. But we are now both allies of the Corsac Fox. And part of that larger thing he is building in the Spinward Reaches.”

“Will the Yarikh remain involved?” Ursula asked.

“I think so,” Gulnaz speculated. “At least to a certain degree. I am certain that Melpomeni has many secrets she will keep from Uly. If she can. Advanced technology doesn’t just occur in one segment, so the Yarikh likely have all manner of advancements they could offer.”

“But won’t?”

“That is my estimate,” Gulnaz nodded. “And we will both trade with Bastion, while eventually extending that to other places. I want to make sure that the Isann and the Samuur start trading directly as soon as possible. That we become allies and friends separate from the Corsac Fox, because both of us are small and weak, compared to our many neighbors. There is a great deal of improvement available, leaping over whole generations of technology in the process and hopefully moving directly to the present.”

“*Sailing into Darkness*, Gul?” Ursula asked, grinning.

“Exactly that,” Gulnaz agreed. “Isann ships will happily carry trade to Saari, once they know the coordinates and have an introduction.”

“Because things have moved so fast that we haven’t had time to do it right,” Ursula noted.

“Isann is no better,” Gulnaz laughed. “We grabbed a Corsac Fox by the tail and have been holding on for dear life. And Uly has spoken of having too much to do and not enough time or people. Your arrival with three ships, I'm given to understand, was something of a godsend, because it let him do three things at once. We need to figure out how to do more to help Uly, because he will help protect us. Plus, you need to speak with your Paramount at some point about the Congress of Wives."

"Will Kalev not do that already?" Ursula countered.

"He is a man, and might not grasp some of the details as clearly," Gulnaz offered delicately. "Samuur society is less gender-separated than Isann, but what I have seen suggests that the warriors at Saari might not understand Dan because they will be focusing on Uly."

She watched the woman's eyes narrow. Hunter vision, locking on prey.

Gulnaz almost expected a little butt wiggle as the woman got ready to pounce.

"What will the Paramount miss?" she asked.

Gulnaz nodded.

"Dan is building up a council of civilian advisors," Gulnaz reminded the Samuur woman. "All of them are women trained in close combat, and thus young, competent, smart, and dangerous. The Ononguli woman that their *Vatazhko* offered will require a great deal of training, I presume, in order to fit in. The Samuur will need to locate a woman who can be offered up as tribute or sacrifice or treaty. However you might qualify such a thing. Those women will form the inner core that advises Uly on how things should be."

"Including your former student Zamira?" Ursula asked.

"She was already First Rank," Gulnaz smiled. "On her way to becoming my peer at some point, because she has the desire to learn such things. And to learn much more from Dan and the others, when exposed to completely new combat forms. In her case, it was a sacrifice that takes her away from her people, but not really, because she and Uly have already drawn so many Isann merchants and migrants to Bastion and presumably other places that Matti has been scouting while we were gone. It might be a sacrifice for Zamira, but it also opened up any number of interesting new doors for the woman that she never imagined possible."

"And Uly represents the same to the Samuur?" Ursula asked, recognition dawning.

"He does," Gulnaz agreed. "The Paramount will see the need to ally via marriage, but he might not see the more important criteria in his own, male parochialism."

"You are a most sneaky woman, Gul," Ursula grinned.

"We had to be," Gulnaz grinned back. "The men think they run things on Isann because we let them. Usually. Uly and Dan will strip away those blinders, and make Isann culture more open. Samuur already is, but still needs to approach things boldly. That was what I wanted to make sure you grasped. The others will have ideas, but most of them will play major, important roles in things, while I suspect that you and I will be relegated some to the side. Not immediately in the center of things, but able to observe and influence. Thus, we must be prepared."

Ursula paused, then nodded.

Gulnaz nodded back. She'd done the important thing, which was making sure that nothing got lost during the excitement of locating and recruiting the Yarikh.

It was certainly a momentous occurrence, but she doubted that those people would welcome many Isann traders. If anything, they were likely to only maintain a singular contact with Uly and Sterling at Bastion. Everyone else needed to be prepared to help one another while that was happening.

SIXTY-FOUR

Lukyan carried a sippy cup of coffee into Anna's office, mostly because after this many years, he had a hard time drinking from a mug. Too many times when gravity went sideways and you had to have a sealed bulb if you didn't want to wear it. Or breathe it.

Compass Rose had been a fantastic ship to make a living in, but it had still broken down too often. Being on the ground today didn't mitigate things all that much either. The first time that hail had fallen outside while he watched, it had been all Lukyan could do to not immediately haul his ass back to space.

Anna watched him enter and settle. She was still easy on the eyes. No. Utterly, stunningly beautiful, but he didn't say that too often. Even when they were alone. Just watched.

Today, she was seeing something in his horns, because she closed the tablet she'd been reading and set it off to one side.

Lukyan nodded. Sipped, looking for courage. Remembered who he was talking to.

"I need to go with Uly," he said simply. "*Fire Diamond* has to be there."

"Why?" she asked.

Not a challenge. An inquiry.

"The Samuur," he said, watching her eyes cross in confusion. "*Tiikeri* needs me."

"Why?" she asked again, a hiccup like a broken record.

"Because *Nubia* can kick ass and take names with the best of them," Lukyan reminded her. "*Blue Widow* is a sledgehammer that nobody enjoys sailing in for longer than a month because it's so damned cramped. But it is deadly for that month. Everyone else you send will be just as dangerous. *Tiikeri* stands out because they are not up to modern standards. I'm afraid that they'll get lost in the chaos of battle and get destroyed when we need them as allies. Uly's good, but nobody I've ever met is as good at holding an entire battlefield in his head as Sterling Huff, and he's not here."

"So you aren't trying to escape me?" she grinned.

Lukyan couldn't help but roll his eyes at the woman.

"If you were just another sailor, I'd shanghai you and drag you along," he said.

"If I thought I could get away with it, I'd stow away," she sighed. "But I have to be here."

"Yes," he agreed, sobering. "And I have to be there to protect *Tiikeri*. Uly, too, but *Tiikeri*. Mostly because I don't trust some of the yahoos you are sending."

"You expect a double-cross?" she perked right up, horns dropping forward.

"Nothing like that," he replied. "At least, I don't think so. This is more that nobody else would automatically shift over and cover their asses while they are covering Uly's. I've spent a lot of time around Haldur. Man's all in on honor. He'll be Uly's shield arm in ways that no other Ononguli conductor would probably ever consider. Problem is, nobody will protect him, and he's likely to be throwing himself headlong into battle. The *Auga* are going to be panicking when we hit them. And it will be total chaos. You need Eskil Haldur alive and safe on the far side of this, because he's your link back to the

Samuur who suddenly are our neighbor in a place all our maps show mostly blank."

"You know the worst part?" she asked, nodding some. "It's that you're right, and none of my other advisors spoke up."

"Most of them only finally see Uly because he's Bondarenko now," Lukyan replied evenly.

He left off the dumbasses who had quietly refused to take part in such a raid, merely because an alien was leading it. Not that he couldn't have written down a list of forty names ahead of time.

And gotten thirty-seven of them correct.

"You will stay safe while protecting them," she said quietly, giving him permission as a woman instead of a *Vatazhko*.

She could do that. They would be getting more serious at some point. More formal.

More something.

Him. Second son of the Chayka, and all that crap. Who'd have predicted this?

"I intend to stay close enough to Uly to wave at him out a port-hole," Lukyan replied.

He'd proven himself in twenty years on the Khet theater. And at Nyri, when *Fire Diamond* had been there for Uly and Sterling.

But they shared a nod.

It was a dangerous life. And he could have stayed home and nobody would have said a damned thing.

Except that he knew Uly would need him there, watching everybody's back.

He could do that for his friend.

SIXTY-FIVE

Uly reveled in being able to assign a few general tasks, define an outcome, then get the hell out of the way as folks figured out how to make it happen.

Two nights of honeymoon on Rayzian had seen mountains moved. Ships gathered up and assigned tasks. Refurbished. Crews moved around. Training started. Freighters acquired, loaded, assigned, and departed.

It had been a whirlwind two weeks after that.

From there, in motion, at the head of a convoy of warships headed out in a long corridor, each ship just to one side or trailing enough that they didn't step on one another.

Two cargo ships had already been dispatched, along with Maks to buy supplies when they got there. Or send local merchants scrambling for enough food to feed a mob that was coming up behind him.

Days like this, Uly missed Sterling the most. Lukyan was good. And had quietly explained his late addition to the fleet. But Sterling was the core of the Starfare School.

Uly could teach command the best, but Huff was the finest tactician Uly had ever met, including the ones who had taught him in school.

But, as more than one had mentioned, quantity of firepower had a quality of its own. A few Light Strikers in the fleet. *Nubia. Blue Widow.* And a lot of Interceptors, from *Fire Diamond* down to *Tiikeri* in overall lethality.

Not that *Tiikeri* wasn't dangerous. Still, Uly couldn't wait for the day when Maks built a newly designed class of Heavy Interceptor for Eskil. Or maybe it was a long-sailing Light Striker. Far more comfortable than *Blue Widow*, because it needed to range widely.

And more than capable of taking care of itself when it got there, because large stretches of Sector Fourteen were still unmapped wilderness, at least culturally.

He looked over to where Halyna sat between Nasrin and Dan, with Suka Kuri and Katya outside that, forming a frame that had already adopted Halyna and considered her a sister.

Dan smiled warmly. Nasrin did as well. Halyna was growing comfortable enough to express opinions in general conversation, rather than pulling him or Dan off to one side for a quiet word.

If nothing else, he had more people—more beautiful women at that—working at his side. Hopefully, Anari was growing into herself as much as Yanouk and Yeong-Suk were. He'd given her the hardest task, but it also gave her the greatest opportunity to spend time with Sterling.

They needed that. Needed their space and time to understand what they wanted. And how to get there.

Today, the fleet was en route to something big enough that he wasn't sure how long he'd be able to stay at Bastion, off in the darkness. Everyone knew that the *Auga* had been building up for their next major incursion into Ononguli Space.

That next bite of the Sphere, flattening off one side and claiming worlds that would be abandoned when all the Ononguli living there left rather than serve. The *Auga* didn't mind, and let them go, because empty worlds were more easily occupied as you cleansed them. Or let them cleanse themselves.

Just another kind of evil. One that needed to end.

Part of him, deep inside where nobody but Dan ever encountered it, wondered if the *Auga* would be just as willing to abandon a world if the Ononguli managed to claim it, either by arms or as part of some future peace treaty signed.

The *Auga* believed in such documents, and even largely honored them, but mostly because they tended to win each war, take more territory, then spend a generation absorbing and adjusting.

The Ononguli had only ever lost.

Uly had opinions on the subject.

Yaqub was flying today.

"Pilot, what's our current ETA?" Uly asked.

"Eleven hours to arrival at Krilic, Vanguard," Yaqub replied. "I'll be going off duty for a rest period in three hours. Drew will come back on about two hours before arrival, and I'll be an hour after that."

Uly nodded.

He wouldn't say he was looking forward to seeing Conductor Gross again, but everyone respected the man. And DJ would have a dangerous job after this, because the *Auga* were likely to lash out blindly in their rage.

Most of this squadron would be backtracking to Krilic and nearby worlds after the raid, expressly to hold this corner of the frontier. Uly would send them, and DJ would take over as their commander.

Thus, the station call to warn him that *Tanis Dragon* needed to be prepared. *Wardog Charlie* probably always was, but that was the nature of Conductor Avhust Holub.

The war was about to start again. This time, Uly intended to launch the first attack.

And say hello to some old friends in the process.

SIXTY-SIX

Maks was growing fond of the little courier Anna had assigned to him, *Yosyp Kyrylenko*, named for a hero of the Kyrylenko clan from a previous century and a famed rider.

He did not, however, mention that he'd already tasked a design studio back home with making him something faster and a bit more elegant and comfortable. A personal yacht, at least until he figured out how to make something big that was also deadly and fast.

Presumably based on *Nubia*, at least as much as they'd be able to reverse engineer it.

He was staying mostly on the ship. The station at Krilic wasn't all that nice a place to spend his nights. That, and his arrival had caused an earthquake to spasm through the system. Helped, though, that Uly was the cause of it. The locals had a firm and deep appreciation of Uly, given that merchant traffic in scanner range was double what it had been when he'd last come through here in *Scavenger Angel*.

Lots of people in the process of getting rich, now that they'd had a few years to get over being pirates. Maks had originally intended to make them even wealthier by building a trade depot and warehouse cluster here, but he'd already upgraded his plans to add a second at Daicia and a third somewhere midway between the two.

More trade flowing into Sector Fourteen and all the folks over there that needed Ononguli tech and could swap for raw materials and whatever else.

All that dark space needed to be filled in with people. Folks who had a vested interest in not belonging to the *Auga Empire* one of these days. And Ononguli tended to be a little too hard-headed for their own good on the topic, but money would move them.

And competition from Uly and his friends.

Maks was in his cabin. Chervonya was off meeting with some locals in Anna's name, because she was even more dangerous that way than he was.

A comm cheeped. He answered.

"Talk," Maks said.

"It's Faisal," the man said from the bridge, where he was technically only the pilot, but Maks had left him alone to act as Conductor as well. "Company just came out of warp, asking for news of the Corsac Fox. Samuur ship, but *Tanis Dragon* is slow getting their horns wrapped around that."

"Who?" Maks asked.

"Identify as *Niemi*, out of Bastion," Faisal replied. "They're broadcasting wide, so I figured it was worth waking you up."

"Send them a signal and identify me as Ambassador Maks, formerly Governor Maks," he said. "DJ will probably want to listen in, which is fine. If they want to meet in person, arrange it to happen here, then start a fire under various asses cleaning and cooking for major players. Uly's not that far behind us, but not prepared for something coming directly from Sterling. Questions?"

"Stand by," Faisal said. "*Tanis Dragon* just asked you to intervene, so I'm routing things. Three-second lag coming up. I'll drop out of the video but listen. They'll come up shortly."

The screen went gray, then blinked and took on an odd, reddish tinge that he recognized as being an artifact of Samuur equipment. He'd spoken with Eskil Haldur enough times.

Samuur conductor. Female, from scale. Several others on the edges of the screen that weren't very clear.

"This is Ambassador Maks Sobol," he announced, waiting for them to catch up with the light-speed wave. "Representing the *Vatazhko* and the Corsac Fox."

He sat and counted heartbeats. The Samuur woman nodded, clicked something, and the screen showed her whole bridge. Not as nice as *Tiikeri*, but designed by the same people.

Anari Supasei was there, standing to one side. An Isann woman. Kit Simonson.

And...

Oh. Shit.

They really did it.

A Human woman. Almost as dark-skinned as Dan. Older, with gray ringlets. Utterly stunning beauty, even with only Dan as a true comparison.

And a wry smile that spoke volumes.

Anari stepped up next to the Conductor.

"I'll be translating," she said. "Mostly because Spacer is a second tongue to my two friends. Hi, Maks. It's Anari. I'm so glad to see you here, because obviously we have news. First question, where is Uly and how quickly can we catch up with him?"

Maks nodded, pulling his horns in because she would only give him the bare bones explanation when she heard. And picking his jaw up off the deck where it had fallen.

"Uly should be about eighteen hours out," he replied. "There is a full Ononguli warfleet arriving here for a brief overlay, then routing on. Uly is in command of that fleet. You did it."

"We did," she emphasized. "Sterling's maps. Kit's logic. Commander Nyman here. Elder Gulnaz. Maks, it is my pleasure to introduce you to an ambassador from the Yarikh. Engineer

Melpomeni Michelakos, this is Maks that you've heard us talk about so much."

He listened to a quick byplay of a language that was alien, but fluid. Almost tonal, in contrast to the more guttural Common Spacer the *Auga* used.

"It is her pleasure to make your acquaintance, Maks," Anari said. "We didn't recognize your ship when challenged by *Tanis Dragon* and *Wardog Charlie*. If Uly is coming here, that solves our problem of having to chase him down to talk. Permission to join the moorage?"

Maks supposed that he'd already promoted himself to whatever role was capable of giving DJ Gross orders, but only because the man had decided to let him. Nobody told *Tanis Dragon* what to do but Anna, generally.

And he spoke for her at the moment. At least until Uly arrived.

"Permission granted," he nodded. "We've already started to prepare for dinner here, so have Commander Nyman bring along some of her crew, too. Then we'll all head over to *Nubia* tomorrow and do it all over again."

She cut the line from her end. Faisal appeared immediately.

"I've let *Tanis Dragon* know," he said. "And everyone else. More Samuur?"

"And more Humans, Faisal," Maks said. "The folks that built *Nubia* originally."

"Huh. Be interesting to see what they're like. Looking forward to that."

"Me, too," Maks agreed.

And what it meant to the rest of Sector Fourteen.

And maybe the rest of the galaxy.

SIXTY-SEVEN

Dan had seen *Niemi* in harbor when they arrived. Heard the tale. Gasped with Uly, Haydar, and all the rest when Melpomeni Michelakos appeared, standing next to Maks and Anari.

She was still vibrating with barely suppressed energy as she waited outside the airlock.

"Breathe," Nasrin muttered from behind her.

Dan tried. The woman could be her aunt in appearance.

It had been many years since she'd been around anyone with skin as dark brown as hers. Even Uly was far lighter, to say nothing of the former *Danumash* sailors, who always tended to remind her of albinos.

The airlock beeped and opened. Kit was through first, walking right up and smiling up at her. Then he slipped to one side without a word.

Anari came through next, hunched as always, but able to stand up in the mud room. They used this one for that reason. She moved to one side, with Suka Kuri stepping up next to her. Gulnaz and Maks.

Then Melpomeni Michelakos entered.

Dan couldn't help another gasp.

The woman nodded sagely.

"I'm told you speak old Yarikh?" she asked.

"I do," Dan replied, reveling in the sound of that voice. "I'm Commander Sheridan Chastain, Chief of Staff to the Corsac Fox."

"It is my greatest pleasure to finally meet you in the flesh, Dan," Melpomeni smiled. "Anari and Kit have told me so much about you and Uly. And everyone else."

"They are all waiting aft to meet you," Dan said. "This is my Combat Team who are also members of the Congress of Wives."

Quickly, she went around the circle one by one. Nasrin. Yanouk. Ciah. Zamira. Yeong-Suk. Katya. They circled back around to Suka Kuri.

"Exemplar," Melpomeni bowed deeply to the woman. "Anari speaks most highly of you."

"And I am an old woman who has seen many things," Suka Kuri replied. "But there do not appear to be stories of the Yarikh that do you justice."

"We successfully hid for a long time," Melpomeni agreed. "Kit drew us out. His friends made it a welcome voyage for me."

"I look forward to learning your tales," Suka Kuri replied.

Perhaps no greater greeting among Moss and Sabre schools. To sit and learn from one another as equals.

"Come," Dan said. "This way."

The gymnasium was her goal, because so many folks wanted to be involved. Even Maks had snuck aboard, along with Ursula Nyman and several of her people.

A mob.

Uly stood at the center when they got there, ringed closest by all the other Humans. Kolya, happily leaving Engineering to deal with people. Solomon, Emil, and Gennady from security. Del, Quinton, and Drew from the bridge. Uly was just sorry that Marlowe, Cleve, and Leon from Engineering were on *Batyr*, but presumably they had had their chance at Bastion.

Blair stepped up with a portable scanner and smiled as he gave the woman a once-over, then whistled.

"You must be Blair Mitchel the xenobiology expert," Melpomeni grinned.

"That's me," he nodded. "And you are healthy enough for me. I'd mostly worried about any bugs and things that might be able to jump across, but you are in excellent health."

"Indeed," she agreed.

Dan had read a summary that Anari had transmitted as soon as they arrived, so she and Uly were generally prepared for the woman, but hadn't shared most of the details with the others.

Trust Blair to pick up on it anyway. And to keep his mouth shut.

"Vanguard Ulysses Fortier, this is Engineer Melpomeni Michelakos of the Yarikh," Anari introduced them. "Melpomeni, the Corsac Fox."

Uly shook her hand and studied the woman closely, still polite and friendly, but ever-so-reserved about it. Dan supposed that most folks might not know him well enough to see, not counting Nasrin, who was also wound a notch tighter than normal.

Nobody was armed, but the entire Combat Team was within two long strides right now. And an entire Ononguli war squadron parked around them, including two Samuur vessels.

Many of those conductors had joined them. Maks's idea. Lukyan and Eskil and Ursula stood off to one side watching. Gulnaz near Zamira.

"Technically, you should probably speak more with Dan," Uly offered. "Looking at you, you are closer related to her than me. That was what caused us to send Anari and Kit, once we understood what *Nubia* was and who Selene Praxis had been, in her day. I'm merely in charge here. Dan commanded the rescue."

Melpomeni turned and Dan felt the weight of her judgment.

And those many decades that most of the people in the room didn't understand.

Dan wasn't any more sure that Melpomeni Michelakos was Human than Anari, Blair's medical opinion notwithstanding.

"Welcome, cousin," Dan offered, stepping up and shaking her hand, though it turned into a hug quickly.

Poor Kit. And maybe not. Anari thought that they had resolved some elements, but not all. Not the important ones.

Were the Yarikh really still Human after all this time?

And which of them was the Lost Tribe?

"It is good to know that there are other Humans, other Yarikh, out there, Dan," the woman muttered in her ear before they stepped back.

"How much history have you gotten?" Dan asked her.

"As much as Anari, Kit, and Sterling have been able to provide," she replied. "It answered some questions while posing others. You and Uly might need to come to Traiffe to answer more. And to see some things for yourselves."

"And I would like that, Melpomeni," Dan said. "However, we are on a mission right now, and timing is utterly critical, for all the obvious reasons."

"Because Uly is about to start a war," Melpomeni agreed. "Maks covered that part. If you would allow it, I would travel with you for a time. *Nubia—Invincible* in her time—was a powerful vessel, and I have seen the current state of technology to know that I am relatively safe here, even without Sterling."

Dan nodded at that. Obviously, Anari, Gulnaz, and Ursula had told the woman a lot, which spoke well of their opinion.

Dan turned to Ursula.

"What are your orders at this point?" she asked delicately.

"Eventually, I'm supposed to return to Saari and brief the Paramount," Ursula grinned. "At the moment, Sterling ordered me to track you and Uly down with a new Ambassador."

"Can we stretch that to join us on this mission?" Dan asked.

"I thought you'd never ask," Ursula laughed.

Dan turned to Eskil and caught his nod as well. He tended to see himself as a minor player, not understanding that Uly intended to build up Saari as a regional capital and trade center. Maks had sent along a few notes suggesting that he also had ideas.

Dangerous ones.

She turned to Uly and grinned. He matched it, then expanded his charisma to the entire chamber, so more than fifty people fell silent to watch history being made.

"My friends, Vahid and his staff are lurking nearby with dinner," Uly said. "Let us break bread as friends and prepare to embrace the future that comes."

He immediately started into the next chamber, where tables and food were prepared for a major party, because Maks had gotten the locals ready to refill everyone's larder here, saving the freighters from being mined until the next stop.

She could hardly wait.

SIXTY-EIGHT

Suka Kuri had placed herself between Alla Bondarenko and Melpomeni Michelakos, mostly by grabbing both and dragging them to the table with her.

What was the point of being a respected elder if you couldn't throw your weight around occasionally? And the two were the people least integrated with the greater whole around them. Even Eskil and Ursula had spent enough time around Uly and his people to largely fit in.

Alla walked like the odd duck out. Melpomeni walked on eggshells. Suka Kuri waved everyone else off, with Dan ending up on Melpomeni's far side and Halyna Bondarenko-Fortier next to Alla. Comforting presences, both of them.

Suka Kuri had questions. She started with the Yarikh woman.

"You are an Exemplar of Moss," Melpomeni moved first. "But supposedly only because it was easier on the knees than Sabre."

"Just so," Suka Kuri confirmed, understanding that Anari had felt comfortable going fairly deep with this woman. "And you would have chased them off, but for Kit?"

"We retired from the galaxy," Melpomeni agreed in turn. "Only the arrival of a Human we could not account for was capable of jarring us out of our languor. It has turned into something of an adventure."

"Uly's good at that," she chuckled. "I'm still catching up from when I was captured by pirates the third time. And that's been years at this point."

"Will he save the galaxy, Exemplar?"

"He has that singular power," Suka Kuri replied. "Others have facets. Only Uly has the whole. If it can be done, he is likely the cause. What place will the Yarikh take in that greater whole?"

She watched the woman nod. Alla had leaned forward enough to listen, but hadn't spoken yet. Watching and learning, because her own cousin had changed everything.

"My people seek to discover what the *Auga* imply," Melpomeni said.

"On the one hand, a universal law," Suka Kuri explained. "A form of peace, enforced by superior force. On the obverse, it is a peace that see the *Auga* as singularly dominant, with all other species relegated to a second or even third tier of relevance. Subjects of an empire run by and for the *Auga* themselves. Uly seeks to build a place where all species are guaranteed equality under the law. Thus, the Congress of Wives manifests that. He is young, and has decades to accomplish such a thing. Dan has the wisdom to build political structures that will retain a certain conservatism of purpose after they are both gone, thus holding perhaps long enough to push the grandchildren problem out as far as possible."

"Grandchildren?" Melpomeni asked.

"The first generation sweats and bleeds for a dream," Suka Kuri explained, turning to include Alla Bondarenko in her story. And wondering if this stranger had ever borne children. "They build a thing. Their children inherit some level of poverty and discipline from their parents as they grow up. In the time of the grandchildren, the stories of sacrifice have lost their motivating power, and at some point a generation is born to opulence that turns into depravity. Usually, such empires follow arcs that eventually collapse. With sufficient math, one can even predict them. It comes down to how the grandchildren are raised. Uly hopes that they will be socialized with the good things, while inoculated against the bad."

"And your goal?" Melpomeni asked.

Suka Kuri let the woman have her evasion for now. Grand affairs were afoot, after all.

"Moss and Sabre will be used to transmit Uly's dream wide and evenly," she continued. "Starfare will hopefully make it possible to build a thing capable of thwarting the *Auga*, while not eventually replacing them with whatever species ends up dominating at a later date."

She paused there, watching both women. Halyna had come around rather quickly to assisting. Alla would need more time, but wasn't immediately balking at anything.

Suka Kuri focused on the Yarikh Ambassador.

"What will *you* do?" she asked ambiguously. Smiling.

Melpomeni matched it, noting the subtle byplay of words for the trap they were.

"*Auga* dominance worries us," she said. "Even out at perhaps a millennium from now. The *Auga* will continue to grow stronger, according to Sterling, thus ensuring a threat unless and until they are stopped."

"Which of three options will you choose?" Suka Kuri mousetrapped her again.

Melpomeni let her amusement show.

"Three?" she lied innocently enough. If you weren't paying attention.

Alla probably missed it. Halyna probably didn't.

"One, you simply retreat to your world and decide to do nothing at all," Suka Kuri listed. "The *Auga* might collapse of their own inertia by then, obviating you of the need to act at all."

She paused for a nod.

"Two, you see what Uly and Dan will have built when they are gone, and perhaps step in at that point, mindful of the risk of unleashing advanced technology on an unsuspecting galaxy."

Alla did gasp at that, so she was paying attention. And Suka Kuri knew the Ononguli woman was smart, from talking to Maks and Halyna. Undisciplined, perhaps, as a result of a decade of piracy.

"And three?" Melpomeni finally asked, foot firmly wedged in the trap where she could see it.

"Three, you seek to shape the thing now, while it is still fluid," Suka Kuri stated. "Perhaps establish a polity strong enough to push the *Auga* back today, thus letting all the battles be fought far from your shores, as it were. Allied to the Corsac Fox and in a position to tweak things over a much wider time horizon than most people."

Melpomeni nodded.

"It is an interesting conundrum," she offered. "I was sent to investigate, but Nomiki Marinos, the Scholar of Traiffe, will make that decision."

Suka Kuri let the woman wriggle off her hook. For now. She turned to Alla instead, as if nothing had just happened.

"How have you been adjusting?" she asked blandly, causing Alla to blink again.

"Well," the woman said. "Obviously, a new galaxy is in the process of being born, and Bondarenko has chosen to charge in with both horns."

Suka Kuri loved that visualization. It was so evocative. And appropriate for them.

"Maks will be a good ally," she offered, reminding the woman that Maks and his dangerous mother Lyra had brought her in. "You should make sure to cultivate him over the longer arc. Especially as a war might be unstoppable at this point."

As in, *Blue Widow* was not a fun ship to fly, except when you got to blow things up. Everyone agreed on that point. Maks would be building bigger and better soon, from what Suka Kuri had heard. And would favor the Bondarenko, assuming they didn't piss him off. Anna would, as well, once she was formally connected. And the Corsac Fox.

Alla nodded with understanding that she was in water deeper than she was used to, but Suka Kuri didn't think that it was too deep for her to swim.

Merely more dangerous than before.

Like almost every day in this new place she had come to.

"Uly has many allies," Melpomeni spoke up, causing Suka Kuri to turn again.

"He has a rare combination of intellect, charisma, and composure," Suka Kuri replied. "He assumes that any stranger is a potential friend and works to make things better. Only his enemies suffer, and even then, they mostly have an opportunity to redeem themselves if they wish."

She pointed.

"Chief Aibek Sulaymanov there was part of the pirate raid on Bastion that might have ended far worse than it did," she pointed. "And the Isann quickly came to understand and appreciate Uly's unnecessary mercy shown to total strangers. Later, Uly found the thing that inspired an entire species when he recovered *Nubia* from the Black Moon. There will be many others as he goes."

Hint: *If you are not careful, you might find yourself on the wrong side of history.*

Melpomeni nodded. Conversation tapered off and people began to eat and think.

Suka Kuri had much to meditate on. This stranger would have more.

SIXTY-NINE

Uly was in his office. Dan and Melpomeni sat across from him. Anari knelt between them in her self-appointed role as translator, though Uly had a sense that the Yarikh woman was picking up Common Spacer impossibly quickly.

He didn't mention that aloud, though.

"Obviously, I am unable to visit you on Traiffe at present," Uly began, even as the other three settled. "The war between the Ononguli and the *Auga* will turn quite hot with what we are about to do, and Anna relies on me to be ready to assist her. Similarly, Dan is needed here, because she is my other half in just about everything, and most of the reason I am able to do as much as this. The Congress are her hands more than they are mine."

He left it at that. Not a *no*, but *not today*, instead.

"How quickly will you explore Sector Fourteen in the necessary depth?" the woman asked through Anari instead of directly.

"When I can spare ships or commission merchants," he said. "Each new friend I make often leads to others. The Isann led us to the Yarikh. Others found the Samuur. I am sure that there are many more, but most likely they are individual worlds just barely into space at this point. Possibly even more primitive, but few of those will be able to help us later, save by being more places where merchants can make a profit and bring folks up to modern standards as they wish."

He waited. Dan hovered. Anari was calm. Melpomeni nodded.

"We can add some places to Sterling's map," she finally offered. "Previous folks who would not take no for an answer, and were thus destroyed. Places our astronomers have been able to identify things that a younger civilization might have wanted to visit themselves."

"But not yours," he noted.

"Not ours," she said. "At least not yesterday. Suka Kuri has trained Anari exceptionally well, and I have now met the Exemplar to understand what both are capable of."

He waited patiently. She grinned when she realized.

"Kit, in his own way, forced us to change," she said. "Not to grow up, but to perhaps wake up from a long slumber into entropy. Some of the Yarikh will come out from their hives, though I think most will not."

Uly agreed. Anari had reported as much, as had Gulnaz and Ursula in their own quiet ways.

"What will you do with the power that *Nubia* grants you?" she asked abruptly.

It took Uly a moment to grasp the implications, then he nodded.

"Push the *Auga* back today," he said. "Strike them a blow resounding enough to make them understand that the rest of the galaxy has not been asked if they wish to join the *Auga Empire*. That perhaps they could ask, instead. Or could settle for what they have today. My many advisors warn me that the *Auga* cannot stop expanding, much like a shark that must keep swimming or it will drown. I do not have to destroy the Empire, but I must force it to change from what it is today. And each day, they will grow a little stronger, drawing on thousands of worlds, even at the slow pace they advance. Thus, I must exercise perhaps greater alacrity than is my preference, but I must also let the rest of the galaxy know that someone resists.

That will inspire others to stand up as well. The *Auga* are bullies, pure and simple. They only understand force, so I must speak to them in that language. Later, I hope that they discover other tongues."

He watched her absorb that and turn to Dan next.

"What will the Congress do, when you are gone?" Melpomeni asked.

Dan nodded, as if she'd already gamed this out with her women.

"Advise whoever comes next," she said. "Our child, or an adoptee. Or perhaps Uly will stand down at some point and we will create an elected position similar to the Chief Secretary of the Party, who is different from the President of *Batyr*. Bastion needs a governor. Each world that we settle needs one, just as each that joins us tends to have such an executive who sends a representative. Chief of Chiefs Usupov of the Isann, or Aarne Kallio, Paramount of the Samuur. Scholar Marinos of Traiffe. Those will form a joint body that is a lower house, representing every world. Each species will also have a voice. Those are the Congress, and will have the greater power. History suggests a strong, stable model, based on both *Batyr* and the Mazhin Convocation. Let us have that assembled into the greater whole and you will have your answer."

Uly watched Melpomeni fall silent.

"Anari and Suka Kuri both warned me that you two were dangerous individually," she finally admitted with a wry grin. "And that the combination could move civilizations. I did not necessarily believe them."

She and Anari shared something in Yarikh but too quietly to grasp.

Possibly *I told you so* from the looks on their faces.

Uly leaned forward and Melpomeni's eyes locked on his.

"I would like your eventual help," he said simply. "Right now, you can witness what it means to stand up to the *Auga* and force them to awaken to the evil they do, but I do not believe that you can tilt the balance of this battle. Nor can I. Later, you will take what you learn here and return home, hopefully with an ambassador of mine who can speak for me in your halls while I am forced to be elsewhere. Or you can bring the right people to Bastion, Saari, or Rayzian to speak with me. I ask you to have an open mind about what I'm trying to accomplish, and why. If you can help me, that would be even better, because it gives us a better chance to save the Ononguli as they exist today. And protect the Khet worlds in Sector Fifteen, because they might be next. Eventually, everyone needs to be able to protect themselves from the *Auga*."

"And from you?" she asked sharply.

"And from me, if I turn into the thing I despise most in the galaxy, yes," he agreed. "That's a problem a century from now, I think. For those who come after me. Your people will remember me, though, so I'm hoping that you can tell them."

She turned to Anari where the Emro woman met her gaze calmly. Maturely, in ways that Uly found to be a most pleasant surprise. Even when he'd known she had it in her when he sent her.

"We cannot change things immediately, no," Melpomeni finally announced. "But I think that Nomiki will see a way to aid you."

"That's all I ask," Uly told her with a nod.

Because he had a war to start shortly.

The only question was how quickly the *Auga* would finally waken to the threat he posed.

And what they decided to do about it.

SEVENTY

Lukyan loved *Fire Diamond*, but had begun to wonder what Maks might build for him as a replacement. An upgrade. Uly would always be sailing into trouble, at least until he was so important that he and Sterling needed to change places.

Every king eventually must retire to his capital and rule his realm.

Still, *Fire Diamond* was perfect for what he had to do today. Uly had assigned him command of the escorts at the center. *Fire Diamond*, *Tiikeri*, and *Niemi*. Not to charge madly into battle, but merely to sail just ahead of *Nubia*, where they could fire their smaller wavebolts defensively.

Starfare, as Sterling had envisioned it, where the Interceptors were a team, a single entity protecting each other as well as the Strikers behind them. Almost an alien concept to an Ononguli force, which tended to be 'every ship for itself.'

Lukyan nodded to himself and studied the backs of heads around him.

"Dmytro, what's the countdown?" he asked.

Slava was flying today, but Dmytro occasionally forgot that he was 2IC around here. Best to remind him.

"Three minutes. We're coming out a little high and wide," Dmytro replied. "Uly is dropping us on the corner instead of where we can threaten the station itself."

"No," Slava interrupted. "We're not attacking the station, except as a fleet getting their undivided attention. You people keep thinking like pirates raiding a system. This is Uly."

Lukyan grinned and turned to the newest member of his command team.

"Oh?" he asked.

Slava blushed a little. Hunched his shoulders in.

"Gonna drop in here so we can blow shit up," he said. "Uly wants us doing that because he doesn't trust the two wings to not get out of hand."

Lukyan nodded. That really did describe things, even with Conductor Kuzmenko on *Vortex* handling one side and Alla Bondarenko in *Blue Widow* on the other.

Nutcracker, but only if it worked. If it didn't, Uly still intended to make a signature statement here.

As he should, since the last time he was in Zhoralong, he and Dan and Sterling stole *Wren* from the *Auga*. Really, the start of the Corsac Fox legend, when you got down to it. Sure, he'd survived *King Hewitt II*, *Iron Wasp*, and an *Auga* jail at Vynchen first, but Zhoralong was when Uly started fighting back.

And today, he was going to top it.

With a lot of help from a lot of friends.

"Uly's doing the punching," Oskar reminded them. "We're protecting the Samuur if somebody big happens to be in port when we drop. We expecting leaks?"

"Uly assumes them," Lukyan said. "But also thinks that the folks leaking might not have gotten the intelligence where it needed to go in time to matter. Still, *Nubia* is tough, and they won't be expecting a trio guarding his forward flank. You make sure nobody gets us, okay?"

"Not a problem there," Dmytro laughed. "Pretty sure the *Auga* are done trading prisoners home for a while. Likely, you're looking at doing your full sentence for piracy, then being dumped on a planet somewhere and told to work or starve."

"They'll remember *Fire Diamond* from Nyri," Slava pointed out. "Not sure any of us actually ever get out of an *Auga* prison."

Lukyan nodded. General piracy was one thing. This, right here, was the war everyone had been expecting. Instead of waiting for the *Auga* to attack and the Horde to swarm, Uly was going on the offensive.

"Stand by to drop," Slava called.

"Oh, shit," Oskar said as his scanners came live.

Lukyan had to agree.

Well, shit.

SEVENTY-ONE

Eskil had studied Uly's old records of Zhoralong, years out of date at present, but the Thogin, Ethir Ewin, had assured him that very little ever changed in places like this. Ethir and Waltin had called it a county motor pool, quiet and sleepy.

Obviously, they had been exceptionally wrong. Or unlucky.

Or some dishonorable Ononguli had indeed sold the *Auga* information about an impending attack.

"Aava, stand by for defensive fire," he reminded her. "Assume anything small we need to engage at our outer boundary to weaken wavebolts for *Nubia*."

She looked back over her shoulder so he could specifically see her roll her eyes at him. He grinned. And he should go teach his grandmother to suck eggs, too, he supposed.

Aava Lehtonen wasn't one to worry him. Eskil turned to Hemmo Lindholm, his First Officer. The calm, quiet one that High Command had chosen to balance Eskil's aggressive nature. They made a good team.

"Hard scan them anyway," he ordered. "*Nubia* might miss something. As might *Fire Diamond*."

Hemmo nodded and began typing.

Next to Hemmo, Saku Korhonen was also working things. Saku was the Research Officer. If Hemmo hadn't been so good, he'd be handling scanners, but that freed Saku up to think about what he saw. And the implications.

They had a few minutes before all hell broke loose over there. But only those minutes. Then, it would get ugly.

"One Devastator, according to *Auga* Scale Rankings," Hemmo called. "Three Strikers of descending sizes, from something just smaller than *Nubia* to something about the same size as *Blue Widow*. Roughly a dozen Interceptors of various sizes and presumably design options. Enemy fleet was somewhat scattered, but is already beginning to coalesce into an onion-style formation, with the Strikers moving to the mid-tier and the Interceptors forward."

"Does anybody range at present?" Eskil asked.

"Negative on 12dm weapons," Saku called. "Oh, hey, that's silly. That middle Striker appears to be a carrier of some sort. They've just launched a pair of tiny vessels that appear to be all engine and a pair of wavebolt tubes. Sloop-scale, but I'm guessing fast attack craft. Presume a swarm coming?"

"Warn *Fire Diamond*," Eskil ordered. "Lukyan may need to start pounding those first, so we'll be engaging smaller things as they get closer. Ask him if we should close up tighter on the flanks and leave openings between the wings."

Eskil studied the mess. Most of the ships on his screen had more power. Presumably bigger weapons, or at least more modern ones.

Still, Uly had asked him and Ursula to protect his flagship. To guard him in battle. Against that mob, even *Tiikeri* was out-classed, but it often came down to spirit at that point, where the smaller cat that wouldn't quit faced a larger that perhaps wasn't as committed.

Today might be a good day to die, but he was taking a lot of them with him if he did.

"Aava," he said, pausing to get her attention. "That transport, the monster on the station's tip, that is where *Wren* was in our records?"

She nodded.

"Hit it with a wavebolt right now," he ordered. "Let them know we mean business."

SEVENTY-TWO

Uly grimaced as he studied the readout.

Indeed, someone had warned Zhoralong that he was coming. Had either omitted the size of his force, or the *Auga* assumed that their ships were more capable than his.

He was back to that day when *Marshall Castillon* ambushed a *Danumash* convoy, wounding *King Hewitt II* before chasing off some of the surviving destroyers and hounding after them.

"Haydar, how tough is that monster?" he asked.

One *Auga* Devastator. Bigger than *Nubia* by volume, but not necessarily even as powerful.

"Standard design," Haydar replied. "Three turrets with 12dm wavebolts in triples, so nine tubes. Same as us, but we have larger bores and thus greater range. Oh, and *Tiikeri* just opened fire on the motor pool station."

"Del, keep a hard scan going," Uly ordered. "Yaqub, 2s and 6s on the ships docked to the station. Assume folks on the station itself, like when we found Yeong-Suk and her people, so only hit the ships. And scatter your fire. I want all of them damaged and in need of repair, instead of killing one or two."

He nodded as they opened fire, then dialed his screen back to show the wider battle. *Vortex* on his left. *Blue Widow* on his right. If that Devastator could charge any one group, they could overwhelm, but *Auga* naval tactics were generally conservative that way. Waddle up with an irresistible force and bash on someone until they broke. *Nubia* might not break, one-on-one, but he also couldn't take on everything. Especially not if there were hornets flying around.

Still, Starfare School was specifically about taking the logic of Sabre and translating it up from something larger than a snubfighter. And Dan had spoken about how those lessons had helped her see the entire battlefield as a dojo floor.

Four drunks in the middle, surrounded by three of his people. Like a chop-socky movie.

He opened a command line that included Lukyan, *Vortex*, and Alla on *Blue Widow*. Everyone else he needed was on the bridge with him right now: Dan and her people. Haydar and his.

"*Blue Widow*, this is *Nubia*," he said calmly. "Fortune smiles on us today, since you are on a wing with that Light Striker. Your four dual 8dm have a higher rate of fire to offset his greater range and damage. Use that by letting him get past you some, then threatening to turn his flank. That forces the Devastator to either engage you or me, but not both. *Vortex*, keep your Heavy entertained, but understand that he matches you for barrels and beats you for range so hang back and stay somewhat defensive for now. *Nubia* has the surprise element that I expect to exploit once they come after me. *Vortex* only has to keep them honest, not win. Hold steady and force them to stay with you. Questions?"

Sterling would no doubt have already seen some edge he could slam a shim or shiv into, but that was Sterling. And Uly needed him at Bastion, at least until he could find another to act as Governor there. And built something that Sterling could command fleets from.

"Haydar, how's the motorpool?" he asked.

Uly didn't need to follow every detail. Merely understand the implications.

"Technically, if you wanted to put a salvo of 15dm bolts in, you could succeed in your mission and leave now," Haydar offered. "Since we need to deal with our other friends, I presume that your escorts will need a few more minutes. And your defensive gunners."

"Absolutely," Uly said. "Let them start to close. I want to surprise them badly. Yaqub, give me the marker where the 15s come into range."

A line appeared on his screen. Closing slowly, because the *Auga* fleet wasn't moving quickly yet, though they might be racing madly in their minds.

It would not be fast enough to keep him from bashing all the larger ships docked in storage, though it would prevent him from bombarding the station afterwards, which had been his original plan.

Still, let them come. He had proof he could offer to Anna that she had at least one spy in her Court, since not that many people knew their destination far enough ahead to impact on today.

He simply needed to survive this battle.

And win it.

SEVENTY-THREE

Alla had spent the better part of her adult life away from home, mostly being a pirate. Preying on the *Auga* and the Zuath. Living a life away from the politics and stupidity of Rayzian and the clan.

To this day, she still wasn't sure how Lyra Bondarenko had known who she was, but she'd have to meet the woman to ask her, since Maks either didn't know or wouldn't say.

It was good enough that she'd somehow been promoted inside Bondarenko to something that could slam horns with a great many ships. So, of course, they'd drawn an *Auga* warfleet today.

And Fortier had to be insane, except that so many people believed in him.

Alla had no choice but to do the same. It was that, or her and the ladies were all back aboard *Even Odds* in a month, assuming they survived. Not necessarily the worst outcome, but damnit, someone had waved a brass ring under her nose. Hopefully, they weren't about to attach it.

"Kati," she said, turning to her First Officer on scanners. "How bad it is?"

"Two dual 12dm turrets," Kati said. "Fore and aft. Useful broadsiding us as he sails by. We letting him?"

"No," Alla decided. "Corsac Fox wants a corner pushed in. I presume because he's got those massive wavebolts. Ofeliya, stand by to put all of your 8dm bolts into that Striker at once. Full broadside, and throw in both 4dm bolts just to give him something else to worry about. Hell, throw in the 2dm as well. He might get confused and shoot the wrong one. Then reload everything and keep up a sustained fire. Don't figure anything gets through, but he has to waste a lot of time and effort stopping us. Tell our Interceptors to fire their light stuff defensively, and anything they have heavier than a four into the target on the first salvo as well. Then protect this wing when the *Auga* decide to shoot back."

Alla drew a breath and turned to Raissa, who was piloting today. All of *Even Odds* crew had been female. Women she'd had around for years. Most of the recruits added for *Blue Widow* had been female, too, and the only males were currently manning guns and damage repair.

"Raissa, slide me long to starboard," Alla ordered. "Keep an eye on the Devastator, and flare away if he starts to turn at us, but I want our Striker to have to decide if he wants to go after us or *Nubia*. I expect the Devastator to sail forward, but if we can peel off some escorts to chase us, the Corsac Fox is supposedly a tactical genius. Let him save our asses. Or we'll turn fully away and withdraw enough that we can jump to warp. Everybody fears the *Blue Widow*. Let's remind them why, ladies."

Alla leaned back now and watched. A wall of wavebolts raced downrange, all fired practically at once. And her escorts had been paying attention, because they added their own fire as it went by. Everyone was suddenly shooting at each other.

Normally, heavier bores meant the difference, because a ship could back away and snipe at you from range. The *Auga* folks would have liked to do that, but the Corsac Fox had brought them out in three groups, widely separated and threatening to envelop the *Auga*.

Why anybody would want to do that, she had no idea, but she had her orders. And the *Vatazhko* had approved her being here, so she needed to make it look good.

Especially if she wanted to ever be important people inside the clan.

"Reloading all tubes," Ofeliya called. "Neutron Omnipulsar teams, fire at maximum range, regardless. Better to burn things out today. Defensive teams, work together with each other to identify things getting by the escorts. These are not people we know, and I have no idea whose asses they'll leave hanging."

Alla nodded.

"Raissa, back down your speed a notch," she ordered. "And nose up and away just a skosh. Draw him with us, because it looks like his bow is going to come around to keep broadside. Let the Devastator swap places with him."

"Up and away, aye," Raissa replied. "Is that one Interceptor getting frisky?"

Alla looked at the board. Maybe. She located the channel she wanted.

"*Gamma Dreams*, this is *Blue Widow*," Alla said, pretending like she was a squadron commander instead of merely the biggest goat in the fight. "Target Six needs to be dissuaded from closing. Give him everything you have. We'll follow up in a second with heavier stuff."

She cut the line and turned to Ofeliya long enough to get a nod.

"Turrets, rotate to engage Target Six with one salvo only," Ofeliya said. "Then back to the big girl. Time for a serious dance battle here."

Alla laughed. Not exactly how she'd describe it, but good enough for now. This was only the fringe of the action, as that Devastator kept sailing along like a small planet, while one whole flank of ships slowed down to engage *Blue Widow*. A gap was opening in their formation.

Maybe this Corsac Fox knew what he was doing, after all.

SEVENTY-FOUR

Uly watched things unfold.

Fire Diamond held the point of a small triangle, with *Tiikeri* on his port flank and *Niemi* to starboard. *Nubia* really formed the fourth point of a diamond, as close as everyone was sailing, but the Samuur took their sailing skills more seriously than most of the people he'd ever known. And he'd known Lukyan for years at this point, so he could trust everyone involved.

All three had turned away from blasting the motor pool and proceeded to engage every inbound wavebolt like starving hounds on a fresh bone.

It wouldn't be enough, but he already knew that.

"Drew, *Blue Widow* is succeeding," he said. "I want us to slide into the gap she's creating. Ignore the carrier that's staying back, except to make sure that someone shoots every one of those snub-fighters with something. Even wounded, they stop being a threat. Haydar, what do ships that small usually carry, anyway?"

"My scans suggest each has two 1dm launchers in an underslung mount," Haydar replied. "Single-shot, without reloads. Painful if they get close and launch, which is their usual tactic. Less so here, with so many Interceptors already standing to defensive chores. Next time, you might want to include a force of defensive Seekers."

"Remind me to talk to Maks," Uly replied. "Not sure I see the value in such a thing, unless the *Auga* get serious about it. Here, they are a nuisance rather than a game-breaking threat. But make sure the Neutron Omnipulsar teams shoot at them, too."

"Already on that, Uly," Haydar said.

"Uly, we're just about to get into range of the 12s to that Heavy Striker facing *Vortex*," Yaqub replied. "This is where I'd start firing back with my own 12s to support them."

"Understood," Uly said. "I want the first salvo into that Striker, ignoring the Devastator for the moment, even though we're in range to hit him. Let's overload that flank, because 15s will require a lot more effort to stop."

"Massed broadside standing by," Yaqub replied happily a moment later.

Massed, indeed. *Nubia* had the same nine launchers as that Devastator. Three triple turrets, with two forward and one aft, elevated so it could engage most targets if you weren't aimed directly at someone.

There was a reason why big ships tended to sail in parallel lines to one another, with the smaller ones in between fighting their own local duels while the titans slugged it out.

Today, he had surprise. At least at some level. Best to make the most of it.

"All batteries fire, reload, then shift to the Devastator for your second round," Uly ordered. "Pour fire into them with the 15s, holding the 6s and 2s defensive for now to help *Fire Diamond*."

They'd only ever done this in training. Nine monstrous bolts went out in a single pulse, tighter grouped than even *Marshall Castillon* or *Vanguard Lesauvage* could have done on their best days.

"Oh, that's panic," Haydar chuckled a moment later. "They're calling for help from anyone in the clear, just in case. Or they forgot to encode it."

"Or you have already cracked their local code?" Uly asked innocently, grinning at the man.

Tentacles grinned back at him.

"No comment," Haydar laughed.

Uly nodded. Haydar had said more than once that he had *forgotten* more about signals encryption than the *Auga* had ever *learned*.

"Everybody else just cut loose on that Striker," Yaqub called. "He's not going to get them all."

"I didn't expect him to," Uly said. "Haydar, order everyone on that flank to put their next shot into the Devastator while he's leaning forward to protect his escort. I want him off balance."

"Sir, can I swing the bow around a little on the gyroscopes?" Drew asked. "Make him think we're about to charge him, screaming obscenities and waving a sword?"

"Go ahead," Uly said. "Yaqub, have the rear turret stay on that side instead of circling. Aim at somebody over there until Drew shifts back. Drew, you are shifting back?"

Drew laughed that particular laugh that told you he was in the zone. Inside somebody's head and pushing buttons. Being rude.

"I thought so," Uly acknowledged. "Maintain fire priorities. Make sure nobody gets to Eskil or Ursula. Lukyan is less valuable than they are, and he knows it."

Brutal arithmetic, but necessary. He needed the Samuur. Needed these two crews to be able to tell all the others what was out there, because all of the little *Auga* Interceptors present were larger than *Tiikeri*, which was the grand flagship of the Samuur fleet right now.

"I've got a hit on the Heavy Striker," Yaqub called. "And *Blue Widow* managed to nail the light one on her corner. Haydar, what are they saying?"

"Stand by," Haydar replied. "Too many voices screaming at each other to make any sense. Drew, you are not helping."

Drew laughed again. Uly laughed. This wasn't a team he was facing. It was a collection of ships thrown together and expecting an *Auga* Admiral to issue orders on every little detail, instead of offering broad ideals and letting their conductors and crews work it out.

"Defensive teams, somebody's going after *Tiikeri*," Haydar suddenly called. "Engage and protect. Now!"

Uly nodded and watched as things started to get ugly.

SEVENTY-FIVE

Eskil had steeled his soul for battle. Written his death poem and prepared to die gloriously in battle, if circumstances demanded it.

At the same time, *Fire Diamond* and *Nubia* had been an umbrella against all the rain of wavebolts in the skies around them.

"Warning," Hemmo announced in that calm voice he used in battle. "Enemy Striker on our starboard flank appears to be going for a soft kill."

Coded language. No Samuur vessel had any business in this battle, fighting with more modern vessels. Eskil couldn't wait until his technology matched his will. Then, they would have a different conversation.

"Us or Ursula?" he asked, already shifting his screens around to a trio of inbound bolts.

"Target *Tiikeri*," Hemmo replied simply.

"Aava, rotate everything to engage," Eskil said. "Alert *Fire Diamond*, but they are currently holding the point against that Devastator, and *Nubia* is more important."

In his mind, they were fists, coming right at him. Not light speed, but exceptionally fast nonetheless. Twin 5dms forward. Twin 3s aft. Two Omnipulsars instead of *Niemi*'s one.

Against 12dm bolts that caused his scanners to simply redline and shrug at him when attempting to calculate the power involved.

Just like any other day in this new future.

He would die fighting. It was the only honorable solution.

"Engaging," Aava called, her voice only hinting at stress.

One 5 raced out at each of the first two 12s. Both 3s at the third.

Impact. Degradation. Insufficient, but he didn't need to hear Hemmo or Saku tell him that.

Physics was physics.

They were going to die today, and that was that. Pity he couldn't have done more damage to his foe first.

Then his screen beeped and a wall of wavebolts arose over his head on the screen.

Nubia, ignoring everyone else to protect him. Foolish move on Uly's part, because it opened him up to the rest of the *Auga*.

But a small part of his mind acknowledged that only a fool didn't appreciate friends.

"Status?" he asked.

"Bolts all disrupted," Saku replied. "They'll hit, but barely."

Eskil nodded.

"Aava, give him both 5dm bolts in return," Eskil ordered. "We have taken his punch. Honor demands that he take ours."

She looked over at him for one madwoman moment, then nodded and returned to her screens.

Two bolts went downrange. Uly had already hammered that ship, catching him off guard when he'd been busy attempting to pummel *Vortex*. And largely winning.

"Status?" he asked.

"*Nubia* just put three huge bolts in behind ours," Hemmo replied. "It appears that the Commander over there has to decide which to engage, and is placing his emphasis on the larger bolts. We may actually score hits."

Eskil nodded.

Let him take *Tiikeri*'s punch.

Honor demanded it.

SEVENTY-SIX

Alla watched the battle unfold. And nearby peed herself when *Nubia* let loose with 14.7dm bolts. Nine of them at once. At one target.

Thankfully, somebody else.

Still, she'd been a pirate for enough years to smell blood in the water.

"Ofeliya, bring us around," she ordered. "Tell the escorts to prepare to charge that asshole that's been bothering us. He's looking the wrong way."

"Damned right he is," Kati added. "Message from their flagship, decoded by *Nubia*. Orders to mass fire on *Nubia* and its escorts, ignoring us and *Vortex*."

"Raissa, burn out every tube," Alla ordered. "Fire as fast as you can reload, ignoring salvos for speed. And a one-ducat prize to the team that gets the most shots off from now until the end."

One ducat. One coin that didn't even buy you a beer, but she imagined that it would be welded to a bulkhead somewhere by the winning team as a taunt to the others.

Anything to take advantage of the sudden lull that was about to appear.

Except that the Light Striker facing her wasn't shifting their fire. Did they not hear the order?

Alla couldn't imagine an *Auga* conductor ignoring such a command. Had she hurt them worse than she'd thought before?

They were still pouring 12s in her direction. And their admiral was expecting help?

"Raissa, shift to defensive fire on incoming bolts," Alla twisted her thinking around. "Put a turret on that carrier and start forcing him to flee, because he doesn't have the firepower to hold us off. Ofeliya, bring our bow back around to chase that carrier down. Let the striker chase us, and stop him cold. Turrets facing aft keep firing, offensive if you don't have a target. Defensively if you do. Kati, let *Nubia* know what we're doing, and shift the escorts around on our rear flank. We might just win this battle when nobody is looking."

SEVENTY-SEVEN

Uly watched the ships. Haydar had done something so he saw where bows were pointed, so Uly could react as fast as they acted.

Pity that Sterling wasn't here, because that might have already meant the difference.

"Uly, the *Auga* flagship just raised the red flag and pointed them at us," Haydar announced. "Not everyone is acknowledging, however. Oh, and I think *Blue Widow* is about to live up to her name on that flank. I'm sensing a breakdown in communications over there."

Red flag. Old Mazhin language. Pirates not seeking prisoners. Merely killing everyone on board before stealing their ship.

Before his clan had reformed themselves after being on the other end of that blade.

Uly paused instead of acting. Judged what Haydar was seeing.

The Heavy Striker on his left was wounded and faltering. Possibly about to flee. The Light on his right was also damaged, and sailing ahead, except that *Blue Widow* came about as he watched, turning to go after that carrier in the rear, it seemed. That Striker began to turn, like it was chasing *Blue Widow*.

As he watched, Uly could see the *Auga* formation starting to disintegrate. Damaged escorts. Damaged Strikers.

The Devastator was mostly intact, having only taken blows from terminally damaged 15s so far.

Still, he thought he heard Sterling's voice in his ear, whispering.

"*Vortex*, this is *Nubia*," Uly called calmly. "Ignore your primary target entirely. Have your escorts close up and hold your wall. Turn inward and accelerate on the Devastator, firing everything you have at him. Drew, come about and give me a sideslip that keeps our rear turret tracking. Everything into the Devastator. Now. Heavy, light. Hell, the Neutron Omnipulsars if they don't have anything better to do. I want him psychologically overwhelmed. *Fire Diamond*, you are my defense."

"Roger that, Uly," Lukyan replied.

Risky, but the battle was shifting. And two strikers were making tactical mistakes. Bad ones. One had engines barely putting out any power. The other had just come about to chase after *Blue Widow*, opening an entire forward corner.

"Uly, I'm detecting panic building," Haydar announced. "On all channels."

"Drew, bow down ten degrees," Uly called sharply. "All ships currently engaged, shift down as well. I want us diving under them."

Because it gave them a moment to look up and see nothing but stars overhead, while terrible monsters were clawing at your toes.

Panic. Infect them with fear. Drive them. Harry them. He could practically hear Sterling's words.

"Maintain fire rate," Uly reminded Yaqub. And everybody else. "Drew, are they rolling to stay with us?"

Drew actually turned to look back for a long enough moment that Uly saw recognition in his eyes.

"No, they are NOT!" he called with a terrible laugh. "Going hard."

"*Fire Diamond, Tiikeri, Niemi*, rotate up and over us as we dive.

Vortex, stay higher on your engagement plane. *Blue Widow*, a random shot this direction might break them right now."

Sterling would have seen it already. It had taken Uly a bit longer.

So many battles tended to be fought on a general plane of engagement, because all the turrets tended to stick up from the main hull.

Instead of down.

Nubia getting under that Devastator, however little, meant that maybe *Auga* turrets couldn't depress enough to lock scanners on him.

"Warning!" Haydar called. "Blue shift imminent. Red shift to follow."

The *Auga* admiral had finally seen his mistake. And was ordering his ships to accelerate out of the box Uly had erected around his mind.

Nowhere else, but that was sufficient.

The man was running. Hard. Anything to get away from being overwhelmed as wavebolts continued to be fired at each other.

The Devastator's enormous engines began to push, with his escorts already pulling away and headed exactly the wrong direction to protect their flagship.

The Heavy on his left was turning away, but hardly moving. Across the way, *Blue Widow* had caught that carrier by surprise, to judge from the snubfighters madly going into turnover. Trying to stop. To turn around. To get back and protect their mothership, because the Devastator was outrunning them.

Chaos.

"Yaqub, put a turret on the carrier and give them a salvo. Rear turret to hit *Vortex*'s dance partner. Other forward to chase the rest. I don't care if they score hits, I want them herded up and away."

"That Heavy's in trouble," Haydar said. "He's asking his admiral for permission to surrender."

Uly had to stop and look at Haydar's laughing tentacles to make sense of that statement.

Surrender?

It wasn't like he could do anything with such a ship.

Could he?

"Yaqub, ignore the Heavy," Uly decided in a flash. "Put your fire into the Light and the flagship."

He leaned back and watched as the Heavy stopped firing anything bigger than a 4, and that defensively as folks charged by, chasing the others.

"Drew, let them escape," Uly called. "All of them. They're broken. The sooner they jump to warp, the better."

"Figured," Drew replied. "All ships, dial back your power and let some space develop."

Uly watched Drew send a course correction to everyone, no doubt calculated on the fly and perfect.

Drew was like that. Especially today.

Suddenly, Uly's screens blipped.

The Devastator had run. The Light Striker disappeared a moment later.

"Haydar, what are the snubfighters doing?" Uly asked as the carrier vanished off his screen as well.

"Fleeing in the direction of that station, way over yonder," Haydar said.

"Order them to run," Uly said. "Tell them we'll destroy all of them if even one turns back to engage us. Then do that."

He didn't need to slaughter them. *Blue Widow* had already taken out half by herself, and the others had generally fired their tiny wave-bolts to protect the Devastator when things got hectic there at the end.

They likely had nothing more than a short-range Omnipulsar. If that.

Not a threat.

He would still make an example of them if they demanded it.

"What's that Heavy doing?" Uly asked.

"Pretending he's invisible," Haydar replied. "They suffered some sort of power failure that they are attempting to repair. Currently, their Variable Pulse Spatial Generator is off-line and they are expecting you to slaughter them."

And if this was a purely Ononguli operation, they probably would have.

He had to represent something else. Something bigger. Better, even.

"Order them to abandon ship," Uly said. "They can make their way over to the motor pool station and we'll leave them alone. How long do you suppose their admiral on the Devastator will be gone, if he has to find all of his ships, then decide if he wants to come back for more?"

"Uly, I'm not sure he will," Lukyan said on the main channel. "They all went different directions, so probably a day or two to even sort themselves out. Maybe another few to repair what they can and see if they want to charge in or slip over to that station. Those folks are too far away to bother us, and probably too big to immolate, unless you wanted to spend a week working at it."

Uly turned to Dan. Smiled at her. She nodded.

"That is completely insane," she said calmly.

Nasrin nodded, too. Halyna was lost. Ciah grinned, but the *Troublesome Warrior Child* was like that.

"And risky," he agreed. "However."

"However," she agreed back.

Drew perked right up again.

"Time for crazy?" Drew asked.

"Haydar, have they agreed to abandon?" Uly asked. "If so, tell them we're claiming the ship. If anything happens to it, I'll hunt them all down and make sure there are no survivors at all. Maybe in this entire system. Tell them that. Then remind them that I'm letting them live if they don't vex me otherwise."

Haydar acknowledged with a tentacle, busy talking on a different channel.

"There they go," Del called. "I'm picking up escape pods and individual sailors in suits, riding on thrusters. Most of them are headed to the motor pool, but a few are aimed at the station."

"Can they make it that far?"

"Those are the escape pods," Del said. "Probably the officers, which is a dumb thing, but it makes our lives easier, since the enlisted won't have any supervisors for a while."

Uly agreed with that.

Haydar turned back.

"If you are willing to trust an *Auga* Captain," he said simply.

"Dan, you're on."

SEVENTY-EIGHT

Dan had risen immediately. Everyone but Halyna had understood and stood up like a dance troupe. Halyna had taken a moment to understand, but she'd only been with them for three weeks at this point.

Barely a student moving past her white belt. Still the representative of the entire Sphere in ways that Katya had gladly surrendered.

They were aft quickly, but Solomon was already supervising Emil and Gennady at the Team Armory when they arrived.

"Boarding teams either saw it coming or were that fast at responding to the order," Solomon said with a grin as he stood to one side. "I have them lining up in the flight bay now."

Dan smiled.

"Well done," she acknowledged.

She'd had the pick of over one thousand Khet troopers after Lacium. And had kept about two hundred. Then added about two hundred Ononguli. And a hundred others.

And refined that down to one hundred and fifty of the deadliest first line assault troops she'd ever known, going back to when she used to do this for a living in the old days.

Yes, they were chomping at the bit as soon as someone mentioned a ship to capture.

She looked over and saw Ciah and Yeong-Suk helping Halyna with a boarding vest. Heavy armor over the chest. Field suit with some plating and toughness over the rest. Good enough for most actions. Especially as Nasrin had her Omnibow and a bandoleer of Painspheres.

Dan looked around once, but her women had all done this enough times, both in training and in combat, that it was second nature. Automatic.

Deadly.

"You hold the fort," she said to Solomon.

"Already in place, sir," he nodded.

She remembered when he'd been short and scrawny. Now he had a hand in height over her and at least half-again her mass, all of it muscle. And he was the Security Officer for the Corsac Fox, so he'd gotten to pick from the troopers she'd washed out, keeping two hundred of them as his own armed sailors, with most of the rest turning into general crew.

Because you needed cooks, maintenance, fire fighters, and barbers just as much as you needed killers. And it helped if the barber could throw on armor when you needed reinforcements.

Uly was well served.

"Let's go," she told folks, setting a brisk pace to the flight deck and noting that her killers, while occasional goofballs off duty, were lined up today like a razor had scored the deck.

She paused in the middle of the mob and turned completely in place to capture everyone.

"Uly wants us to steal him an *Auga* warship," she reminded them. "It is supposedly abandoned, so shoot first and ask questions later. Stun weapons primarily, but do not be afraid to drop a hammer on someone at the slightest provocation. Let's board."

Her mob pivoted like a chorus line. No missed turns. Perfect rhythm. Dead run.

"Nasrin?"

"Ninety-three seconds to boarding complete," she replied. "Missed the record by five seconds."

"We'll do better next week," she replied, following everyone in and settling in her spot.

Four shuttles, equipped with fold-down seats for exactly this reason, plus folks could stand and hold on for short runs like this.

She had a ship to capture.

SEVENTY-NINE

Halyna had learned the start of the various close combat drills that Dan and Nasrin insisted on. She wasn't there yet, but they told her she was making excellent progress. That, and daily training with pistol, rifle, and sword.

Because diplomacy had a different meaning with the Corsac Fox. And she'd come to know Uly and Dan well enough to understand what that entailed now.

She still wasn't sure she was ready for something like this.

They docked with the *Auga* ship. Clanked loudly as magnets engaged and crew members did whatever they did in the airlocks to override things.

Not a situation she'd ever given a lot of thought to, but these men and women approached it with all the professional dedication of thieves stealing a zeonx from someone's barn with watch geese sleeping nearby.

Watching Dan and the others, she drew her pistol, confirmed that the safety was on, and held it down at her side as everyone rose and turned to the main hatch.

"Scout-Four to Command," a woman's voice came over the line. "I have a situation on Deck Three, Frame Seven."

"Go ahead," Dan replied on the line.

"Three locals demanding to surrender personally, sir," the woman said. "One male *Auga* officer. One male *Auga* crew member. One female Emro crew member. Unarmed. Non-threatening. Currently facing my team and two others, all a little twitchy."

"Scout-One, you hold our landing," Dan ordered. "Strike-One, reinforce Scout-One. Team-One, prepare to rotate to where Scout-Four is. Team-Four, extend your engagement flank to meet us half-way, prepared for ambush. Team-Two and Team-Three, continue on to secure your targets."

Then Dan was moving. Halyna wasn't as tall, so she had to stretch her legs to keep up. Ciah was Dan's other local unit commander, the four teams having two members each of the force.

Would they break it down nine ways at some point? Ten, after the Samuur added a wife?

Nothing the *Vatazhko* had told her had prepared Halyna for something like this. Of course, she hadn't really believed Shevchenko that much, either.

And that had been a mistake, because the *Vatazhko*, if anything, had undersold the reality.

Auga corridors. Halyna had been in the piracy business briefly. Long enough to understand that she didn't enjoy it as much as some folks, and with the family connections and resources to go into the business side of things instead.

Probably why she had been the first pick candidate of the Bondarenko.

Troopers jogged ahead. Secured intersections with lethal calmness. Dan had point. Ciah held the rear with Scout-One.

Halyna kept her mouth shut and tried to absorb as much of this as she could.

Live fire training. The best kind. If you survived.

Eventually, they connected with Team-Four elements, then moved at a jog to where Scout-Four had three prisoners.

Halyna must have muttered something, because Dan glanced over inquisitively.

"That's a conductor's uniform," Halyna explained, studying the man standing with both hands over his head and his third eye lidded half-mast.

They had some level of mental powers, though she was certain that most of it was luridly overemphasized to make other species nervous.

In person, they looked like short, exceptionally broad Humans. Rumor had it that they had genetically modified their entire species at some point in the distant past, aiming for intelligence and physical perfection of beauty.

She could see that they had succeeded.

The other *Auga* was older. Less impressive than the Conductor. Less everything. Uniform of a high-ranking enlisted crew. Maybe a personal aide?

The Emro woman was certainly tall. Big, in the ways of that kind. Not as fit or daunting as Yanouk or Anari. Especially not when Yanouk moved up as Dan approached.

Dan glanced at Halyna again, as if prompting her to speak. She'd recognized the uniform, after all. And was part of the Congress.

Halyna nodded and stepped up, standing between Dan and Yanouk, both taller and deadlier.

"The Corsac Fox ordered you to abandon ship and not look back, under pain of mass immolation," she said, pitching her voice into those clipped tones that educated *Auga* affected.

At least in the entertainment videos they exported galaxy wide.

"And I have so ordered my crew," the man replied with a crisp nod.

She was taller. He weighed more. And had a calmness about him that didn't fit the situation she'd been expecting.

What had she been expecting?

"Then why haven't you left?" Halyna demanded tartly.

"Because I will be executed as a failure," he explained calmly. "The Emperor does not suffer such losses as this casually. Better I spend my time in an Ononguli prison than dead, even if it makes me a coward. These two refused to abandon me, so their deaths would be on my soul, and I wasn't prepared to pay that price either when I faced my creator."

Oh, joy. A religious fanatic of some sort.

The Ononguli didn't have gods. They had the Endless Plains. And maybe stories of ancient heroes that had been accidentally deified. Or maybe people you invoked in a moment of stress.

Sometimes that was better than screaming a random profanity at the universe.

Sometimes.

"You expect us to take you three prisoner?" she challenged them, cognizant of Dan's icemace in one hand and Yanouk holding a squad-level cannon on the other side.

"I *demand* it," the *Auga* nodded up at her.

"Has the rest of your crew departed, or do we need to switch tactics and begin killing them indiscriminately?"

The Emro woman grimaced enough that Yanouk's barrel suddenly centered on her face.

Not there. Blink. There.

Everyone froze.

"They have all obeyed my orders," he said. "Except these two dunderheads."

Halyna caught herself short of laughing as she saw the façade crack about the man's personality.

He cared that these two aides refused to abandon him, but was too crusty to admit it.

It was one thing to consign your soul to hell. Something else to drag your friends down with you.

"And I am supposed to accept that?" Halyna demanded, pushing a little more, feeding him back those vids.

"My sword and sidearm are stashed just around the corner behind us," he said. "I presumed that I would get shot before I could offer them and my ransom to your Corsac Fox."

Halyna glanced at Dan.

"Scout-One, MOVE!" Dan ordered sharply.

Bodies swarmed around them on both sides of the wide corridor.

Deadly silent, though.

"Confirmed," the woman from the radio called a few seconds later. "Weapons belt as described. Three packs that might be bombs and might be personal gear."

The *Auga* scowled immensely at that and actually turned around.

"I have given my ransom," he snarled angrily in that direction. "They insisted on packing clothing and personal items for detention."

"Scout-One, open the largest pack," Halyna ordered, playing an intuition.

"Uniforms. One tablet. Female personal grooming and monthly kit. Spare socks."

The *Auga* turned back to her and nodded, still glowering but not hostile.

A man proven right, after someone had challenged his honor.

And Halyna had the key to his personality.

She'd spent enough time around the new Samuur allies. Mostly Eskil Haldur.

Honor. Above all things.

"I will accept your ransom, Conductor," Halyna stated. "On your honor, all things forward from today."

He nodded again, sharply, like a man who had *finally* gotten through to someone who could understand.

"As it should be."

"What is your name, anyway?" she asked.

"Conductor Urs Edvin Székely," he replied. "Commander: *Serene Naddoddur*. My personal aide: Jochen Leo Dohman. His assistant: Taki Izun."

The older *Auga*. The Emro woman.

Halyna looked around, but Dan refused to rescue her. On-the-job training day.

"Team-Four, I need a watch detail for three prisoners," she announced, pretty sure she had the language right. Or that they could figure it out.

"Scout-Four, in motion," Dan finally said something. "Team-One, secure Engineering. Team-Four, we'll accompany you to the bridge."

Halyna holstered her pistol and nodded to Székely. If he was a threat, she'd let Dan and Yanouk take him down. Or the rest of Team-Four, currently surging around them.

So far, so good.

EIGHTY

Sadeq had gone ahead and picked himself for the task, because they'd made him Chief Engineer.

Or rather, Kolya had won the coin toss again. That Human had the most amazing luck. Assistant Engineer. But that meant that Sadeq was in command today.

So he had joined the team headed over to see if this *Auga* beast could be repaired quickly, or needed to be boomed as a statement.

Of what, he had no idea. Not his job. He fixed shit. And lost coin tosses with Humans.

Auga ship. Uglier than *Danumash*, which was a pretty impressive bar to clear. Runts, but they had Emro crew, so things were scaled to them. Barely.

Wide and big. Should be airy. What idiot had selected that particular shade of mustard-puke yellow to paint corridors? And who had lost that coin toss?

Sadeq didn't do guns. He did wrenches and impact hammers. Had a variety. And several assistants at hand with backpacks full of heavy gear, because some fool had put him in command.

Let others carry shit around.

Standard *Auga* Engineering blastlock. Airlock designed to hold, even when EVERYTHING back here went up at once. Blow the front of the ship off and let it tumble away.

Currently open. He was back to stealing *Iron Wasp* with Uly and Dan, all those years ago.

He got through and looked around.

"Close that," he pointed.

Still, saved five minutes. Might matter later if he was about to blow up and Dan was forward.

Someone got to the controls and the vault doors began to beep loudly.

Sadeq moved to the command station. *Auga* ran things, but generally hired experts to actually run things. Like Engineering. One of the three consoles was currently his height. Two at Emro.

Must have been a pretty odd crew back here.

Nothing locked, so Sadeq started typing. Weapon damage, but mostly power and coolant failures. Probably lines pinched or circuit-breakers that hadn't been replaced on a proper schedule.

Shit does wear out. You know that, right?

But he was speaking ill of the dead. Or whatever you called the crew that was currently hiding out on the motor pool tree and hoping Uly didn't turn around and finish the job.

He ignored weapons. Electroshields. Life support was twitchy, but everyone was in suits, so he shut it down for most of the ship. Turned off lights in those places and overrode them, too, so anyone out there would call and ask, thereby discovering that they needed to move somewhere else if they wanted to breathe.

Not his problem, and the gungoons generally knew better than to wander off unsupervised.

"Engine team, I need an update in five minutes," he called over the secured line. "Warp team, two minutes and then an estimate on the repairs you need."

He sat and played with the controls while folks yelled at each other, wishing he could take his helmet off in here and taste the air. Probably could tell exactly what circuits had cooked by the taste.

But rules were rules. And Dan wasn't fooling around.

Plus, most of his boys and girls were Ononguli or Khet, so tentacles were technically cheating.

Might still be part of the reason he was CHIEF Engineer around here.

"Boss, we got a blockage on a coolant feed," someone called over the line. "Option A, we take it apart and weld in a new pipe. Probably six hours, depending. Option B, we cut it out, run some hose, and maybe get two days out of it before it melts or blows under pressure. B needs maybe thirty minutes at our end."

"Go for B," Sadeq replied. "Distance gets us to safety and we can repair it better while working on everything else. Uly's making a statement here, and he can't spray paint the outside of the main station this time."

"Roger that."

Sadeq nodded. Even mix of juvenile delinquents and nerds in his crew. And a lot of crossover.

"Dan, this is Sadeq," he called on the command line.

"Go ahead."

"Engines will take time, but we're an hour from warp, so I've got them working on that. Power should be better than eighty percent at that point. Not getting more without a long drydock spell."

"Good enough, Sadeq," she replied. "Grand Theft Starship is the goal here."

"Got you covered."

He cut the line and looked around. Assholes and elbows, which meant everyone was down in the bowels of something, fixing or inspecting. *Auga* built pretty standard stuff, from what he'd studied and learned over the years. Come up with a design, replicate it about a thousand times, then come up with the next one a generation later. Rinse. Repeat.

Dull, but effective. Well-built, but boring. And ugly paint jobs. He could only imagine what they tasted like. Omid would probably have his people sand it down to the bare metal and start cold.

Not that he'd mind. Boss. Supervisor. Chief Engineer. Even Omid couldn't order him to paint anywhere but his own quarters, if Uly ended up assigning him over here.

After all, he just knew it was going to come down to a coin toss with Kolya at some point.

EIGHTY-ONE

Uly looked around his bridge. Suka Kuri had moved to sit next to Melpomeni Michelakos, the two of them keeping up a running conversation at a low rumble.

"Dan, checking in from the Striker," Haydar's tentacles flagged him. "One hour to estimated departure. Enemy snubfighters have retreated to the main station. Main station is so flustered they're broadcasting a list of all the fines we're accumulating."

"Remind them that this is my second visit," Uly smiled. "Have them add it to my tab."

Haydar laughed. The two ladies looked up.

Uly locked eyes with the Yarikh woman.

"On the one hand, letting everyone surrender and survive sends a message," he told her. "Notwithstanding the three prisoners we'll sort out later. On the other hand, I need ships. Now, instead of later. Both sides have masses of Seekers and Interceptors, but *Auga* has a wide advantage in heavier vessels. Stealing and repairing this one extends my reach. My power. My ability to threaten them into behaving."

She nodded, but didn't offer anything. Not that he was expecting her to. He needed the Yarikh, but only if they intended to come out of their shells to help.

If they retreated, he would ignore them instead of wasting time and resources that could be used elsewhere.

Time seemed to be his most critical possession.

"Why show mercy though?" Melpomeni asked abruptly. "Why the risk?"

He paused.

Anyone visiting Traiffe had been warned to immediately leave, or blown up. Because they were serious about their privacy, and only Kit's presence had changed that.

"Cornered rats fight harder," he replied. "If they have nothing to live for, they will die fighting. If they are treated well and eventually sent home, most will have less inclination to be dead-enders."

She studied him with hooded, inscrutable eyes.

"It loosens the *Auga* hold on other worlds, too," he continued. "Eventually, parts of the *Auga Empire* might unravel of their own accord. I cannot defeat something that massive by force of simple arms. I need all the people of the galaxy to rise up and demand changes. Demand that the *Auga* behave in a different manner. More ethical."

"More ethical?" she asked.

"Everything they do is wrapped up in layers of legalisms," he described, remembering. "But those laws favor the *Auga* as a species to the detriment of everyone else. And the letter of the law is the single most important thing to them, without exceptions for circumstances beyond the control of someone. We would have been *processed*, and presumably thrown into cells with the crew of *Iron Wasp* for whatever sentence they faced. At no point was someone likely to treat us as rescued prisoners, because we were with the pirates. The law needs space for ethics, because the *Auga* and their morality are an evil perpetuated on the rest of us. *Auga*, then servants. I find that sort of thing unacceptable. The citizens of the empire who are not *Auga* vastly outnumber those who are. I am speaking to them today. Hopefully, they will listen."

"And if they do not?" she pressed.

"Then I probably spend the rest of my life trying to stop them," he said. "And the lives of a great many others who have rallied to my banner. The *Auga* must be stopped. Simple as that. I don't have all the answers. I don't have to. I have Dan and her Congress. Suka Kuri. The Legal Department. Moss and Sabre. The Ononguli Sphere and the Oligarchs of Z'Gosza. The Isann. The Samuur. Others. But it will not be enough. I need everyone. Everywhere. I need friends."

He ran out of words. It had been a stressful day. Week. Month. Year. Decade. Possibly lifetime, though he'd had a fabulous childhood, with loving parents and few wants when he got back that far.

Uly drew a breath and nodded, about to return to his screens when she spoke.

"You will have more friends," she said quietly. "I will convince Nomiki to send help when we get back."

"Thank you," he said simply.

That was all there was to say.

EIGHTY-TWO

Eskil had a private channel linked to Ursula and Lukyan, where they could talk without bothering others.

"*Tiikeri* and *Niemi* had no business being here," he told the Ononguli commander bluntly.

"Physically, you are correct," the man agreed. "We'll do something about that next time. Politically, you were utterly necessary. Both of you. I've heard the stories of how the Paramount sent you to Bastion to challenge for honor. And you've seen the outcomes from that, and all things subsequent. Uly needs you. The *Vatazhko* is beginning to understand that she needs you, and I'll reinforce that."

"And not expand your frontiers?" Ursula pressed.

"Can you think of something dumber than starting a two-front war?" Lukyan asked bluntly. "Especially when we'd have to piss off Uly to do it? No, all of our effort needs to be focused on the *Auga*. Pushing them back and holding that frontier. If anything, having an honorable neighbor on that front means that we might be pulling ships out of those border stations and asking you to patrol things for us."

Eskil couldn't help the way his ears went backwards. Or how his whiskers all flickered madly. Ursula was no better. Lukyan nodded, grinning in the manner of the Ononguli.

Samuur society was all about honor first. Warriors, but mostly because that was the toughest form of athletics in which to compete. And the Ononguli got that.

Uly got that. Presumably, the Isann and the Yarikh as well.

"We cannot engage your pirates," he told the man.

"Lot of Ononguli ships are going on the beach right now," Lukyan replied. "Crews swapped into warships instead. Part of our secret. But it also means that we might be able to sell you some old hulls really cheap. I own *Compass Rose* outright, and Anna might approve of such a thing. Plus I know Maks intends to shake things up. He's shared some of his private plans with me, and Saari plays a major part in them."

"Ononguli warships?" he asked.

"*Blue Widow* is too cramped for us," Lukyan said. "I can only imagine how much you would hate it after a week, being so much bigger. But you folks know how to build ships. You just need help building them bigger and better than you used to. Technology transfers get you there in a hurry. And you've got the planetary economy in place to do that. Uly's still coming up from nothing, with really only merchants, plus a few farmers willing to live on the ground below him and do things. More will come, but that takes time. Isann and Saari will be key factors."

"And you approve," Ursula noted.

It wasn't a question, at least to Eskil's ears.

"Absolutely," Lukyan confirmed. "I was there at Lacium on Day One. That infamous *Tuesday* when Uly arrived. Been there ever since, watching him work. It will be good for everyone. Even the *Auga* eventually, though they'll take some time coming to horns with that."

Eskil nodded.

The Paramount had tasked him with traveling to Rayzian with

Uly. Meeting their other neighbors and learning what threats the Samuur faced. Understanding this new Human neighbor that had convinced Kalev Karjalainen, Ursula Nyman, and Matti Lehtinen to suddenly turn completely around and join forces with a stranger.

Seeing what their entire future might hold.

"Now what?" Eskil asked.

"Plan calls for the fleet to back away," Lukyan said. "Got a captured ship, so we probably aren't going far initially. Then splitting, with most of them headed more or less directly to Krilic, to be parceled out along the near frontier for whatever silliness the *Auga* do in response. I was originally supposed to return to Rayzian to update Anna, but I think I'll forego that and stay with Uly, at least as far as Saari."

"You think that's our next step?" Ursula asked.

"Yes, because it covers a lot of things they need to know," the man nodded. "Then Uly goes to Bastion. I go to Rayzian, and the Samuur sort out their next steps. The war probably started today, but the *Auga* have been building up to it for years, occasionally thwarted by Uly. They might attack. They might recoil and rebuild. Anna's spies are going to have to earn their keep."

"Is Saari safe?" Eskil asked.

"You aren't," Lukyan replied evenly. "That's why you need updated ships. But the distance is great enough that you might be."

Eskil nodded. It made perfect sense. And this Ononguli was the future mate of their own Paramount, so he was speaking with her voice. Just as Eskil spoke for the Paramount until they got home.

He simply wasn't sure where he was headed after that.

Eskil did know that it would be war.

Honor demanded no less.

EIGHTY-THREE

Uly had retired to his cabin once the squadron limped away from Zhoralong. Damage had been fairly evenly spread among ships, but nobody had taken too much, beyond the Striker apparently named *Serene Naddoddur.*

Haydar and Dan had swapped places, with Uly convincing the Mazhin, willingly or not, to take command of the new vessel at least long enough to get the ship to safety.

Blackmail was such an ugly term...

Still, more crew to recruit and train. And a major warship to repair and impress into his service.

It seemed to be the story of his life. At least it had been a good one, so far.

The hatch chimed and he rose, smiling when it was Dan and kissing her as she entered.

"Any news you didn't want to tell everyone else?" he asked as they got settled, both on the couch and close enough to touch.

"Halyna thinks that Conductor Székely is more like the Samuur than anything," she replied. "Militant and bureaucratic, but honorable to a fault. She's dealing with him for now, but I got the impression that he'll refuse to be traded home, because he thinks they were already going to execute him as a failure and coward for losing, and now they'll tack traitor on. Says his two aides deserve better."

Uly nodded at that. His other wives had mentioned similar things when they got to the new rendezvous.

"What do we do about the Yarikh?" he asked, wondering where her thoughts had roamed on the topic.

"Send Melpomeni and an ambassador to Traiffe and see if they're serious about helping us," Dan replied. "I'd be the best choice, but that's impossible. Anari perhaps, but if we're going home for a while, I'd like to give her time with Sterling."

"What about Gulnaz?" he asked, watching her eyes light up.

"Yes," she agreed. "Those two built a quiet relationship, and Gulnaz has age and maturity, which the Yarikh venerate. And Anari speaks incredibly well of the woman."

"So does Zamira," Uly said. "Granted, her teacher, but Zamira has been willing to gossip about things more as she relaxes around me."

"Good," Dan replied. "All of them will get there. I just had the longest time to think about it."

He supposed that she did. Nasrin, Katya, and Yeong-Suk had been the most relaxed, but the latter two were almost as old as Dan, relative to lifespan. Mature, though the rest had it.

Still, a big step for some.

"Who gets the new ship?" he asked.

"I'm of several minds," she mused. "Anna has big warships already, so one more doesn't mean much, even though this was an Ononguli raid. The Samuur need things, but Lukyan sent me a private message about selling them old Ononguli ships initially, plus what Maks has planned. Personally, I think we need a new Governor at Bastion, and Sterling takes it, though I'm not sure who you promote to *Batyr*."

"I tend to agree," Uly said. "And I'm not sure about *Batyr*. But recruiting won't be an issue, so perhaps we take a lateral transfer from Isann or Saari. We know most of the players involved, and they will be answering to you and me."

"Have we bought enough time to be home for a while?" she asked. "Or do we need to look at acquiring a palace on Rayzian and staffing it, because we'll be spending too much time there?"

Uly paused to contemplate that.

Technically, he had such a palace on Z'Gosza, doubling as his embassy and staffed by folks Rabiu and Ethir had recruited and hired, an even mix of Ononguli and Khet. He probably needed to do the same at Rayzian, so a recruiter sent to visit the Khet for more bodies was probably in order.

Mixing peoples up and getting them to talk to one another. Breaking down old parochialisms and expanding trade. Capitalist in nature, but properly socialist in execution, because done for the greater good instead of the greatest profit for one person.

"That's probably an entire meeting we need to have," he replied. "With the Legal Department and the Congress. It can wait until we get to Saari. I suspect we'll be sending ships every which way from there, updating folks and establishing new trade routes."

"Yes, it can wait," she agreed. "You look exhausted."

"Am exhausted," he nodded. "Been running like hell for…years and need some down time, I think. Time at Bastion, where other folks can come to me, instead of me on the road all the time. Time to build up this thing we're doing, someplace other than on this ship."

"The Congress of Wives will be where we are," she noted.

"Agreed," he said. "But the Conclave of the Many Species needs a place to meet and do things. That's Bastion. On the planet itself, so we need to hire some architects and building crews to put a city down with all the necessary expansions designed in from the beginning. And the Governor needs them as advisors, so I need to be there establishing precedent and norms as we invent the laws that will govern us."

"None of it has to happen today," she said, rising and pulling him to his feet. "Let's you and I go to bed and snuggle for a while."

"I sleep better when you're here," Uly told her. "Good when I'm not sleeping alone, but best with you beside me."

"And I always will be," she told him, pulling him into a warm kiss. "Always."

Uly let her drag him back to the sleeping chamber. Shoes off, he slid into bed and sighed heavily. She wrapped herself around his back and he felt her breath on his ear.

He lay there trying to list all the things he needed to accomplish, but at some point, darkness claimed him and he slept. Warm and safe.

Because he had many friends. And many wives.

And Dan.

READ MORE

Be sure to read the rest of the Corsac Fox series!

https://www.knottedroadpress.com/product-category/science-fiction/corsac-fox/

ABOUT THE AUTHOR

Blaze Ward writes science fiction in the Alexandria Station universe (Jessica Keller, The Science Officer, Phil Kosnett, etc.) as well as several other science fiction universes, such as Corsac Fox, Operation Marrakesh, and more. In addition, he is the Editor and Publisher of *Boundary Shock Quarterly Magazine as well as Thrill Ride Magazine* . You can find out more at his website www.blazeward.com, as well as Patreon, bluesky, Facebook, Goodreads, and other places.

Blaze's works are available as ebooks, paper, and audio, and can be found at a variety of online vendors. His newsletter comes out regularly, and you can also follow his blog on his website. He really enjoys interacting with fans, and looks forward to any and all questions—even ones about his books!

Never miss a release!
If you'd like to be notified of new releases, sign up for my newsletter.

http://www.blazeward.com/newsletter/

Buy More!
Did you know that you can buy directly from the KRP website?

https://www.knottedroadpress.com/shop/

Connect with Blaze!

Web: www.blazeward.com
Boundary Shock Quarterly (BSQ):
https://www.boundaryshockquarterly.com/

ABOUT KNOTTED ROAD PRESS

Knotted Road Press publishes dynamic fiction set in exotic locations and unique non-fiction voices in genres such as autobiography, business, cookbooks, and how-to. Our authors cover a wide range of genres including science fiction, fantasy, mystery, literary, and poetry, appealing to all readers. We offer both DRM-free ebooks and print books for a global readership.

Knotted Road Press
www.KnottedRoadPress.com
www.KnottedRoadPress.com/Shop